Tales from The Lake

Volume 2

Crystal Lake Publishing
www.CrystalLakePub.com

Other Titles by Crystal Lake Publishing

Tales from The Lake Vol.1
Pretty Little Dead Girls: A Novel of Murder and Whimsy by Mercedes M. Yardley
Apocalyptic Montessa and Nuclear Lulu: A Tale of Atomic Love by Mercedes M. Yardley
Wind Chill by Patrick Rutigliano
Eidolon Avenue: The First Feast by Jonathan Winn
Flowers in a Dumpster by Mark Allan Gunnells
Nameless: The Darkness Comes by Mercedes M. Yardley
The Dark at the End of the Tunnel by Taylor Grant
Little Dead Red by Mercedes M. Yardley
Children of the Grave
The Outsiders
Fear the Reaper
For the Night is Dark
Through a Mirror, Darkly by Kevin Lucia
Things Slip Through by Kevin Lucia
Sleeper(s) by Paul Kane
Where You Live by Gary McMahon
Tricks, Mischief and Mayhem by Daniel I. Russell
Samurai and Other Stories by William Meikle
Stuck On You and Other Prime Cuts by Jasper Bark
Eden Underground by Alessanro Manzetti
Stuck On You by Jasper Bark
Horror 101: The Way Forward
Horror 201: The Silver Scream Vol.1
Horror 201: The Silver Scream Vol.2
Modern Mythmakers: 35 interviews with Horror and Science Fiction Writers and Filmmakers by Michael McCarty
Writers On Writing: An Author's Guide

Copyright Acknowledgements

"The God of Rain" by Tim Lebbon previously published in *Horror Literature Quarterly*, 2007.

"The First Header" by Edward Lee was originally published as a limited-edition chapbook by McGuire Press in the summer of 2009. It was actually an excerpt from the novel *HEADER 2*, published as a limited-edition hardcover by Camelot Book in May, 2010.

"Out of the Woods" copyright © 1996 by Ramsey Campbell. From *Ghosts and Grisly Things*. Reprinted by permission of the author.

Dallas Mayr's "Damned if you Do," Necro, 2004, David G. Barnett, ed., and then in the collection *Closing Time and Other Stories*.

"Bone Wary" by Jan Edwards First published—*A-Z Cities of Death*, 2013, Static Movement Publications.

Table of Contents

*In loving memory of Mairi Edwards
and Rocky Wood.*

For all you've done for others.

Foreword from the Editor/Publisher

In the words of the late Rocky Wood, if you came here to read about tranquil lakes, run to the nearest exit (referring to Rocky's *Tales from The Lake Vol.1* introduction).

Welcome to the second of what I'm certain will be many installments in the *Tales from The Lake* anthologies.

What follows are nineteen tales of mystery and suspense, horror and dread. Tales to share around the campfire or living room floor. It includes an array of international voices and locations.

This volume also includes the three winners from Crystal Lake Publishing's Tales from The Lake Horror Writing Competition:

3rd: Ripperscape by Vincenzo Bilof
2nd: Forever Dark by Jonathan Winn
1st: Descending by John Whalen

Before I leave you in the capable hands of these authors, I'd like to take a moment to remember Rocky Wood and Mairi Angus—two authors who in their own ways inspired many authors, myself included. I can proudly say that both would've enjoyed this book tremendously.

Dive on in . . .

Joe Mynhardt
Bloemfontein, South Africa
29 February 2016

Lago de los Perdidos

JIM GOFORTH

Moonlight **spread across** the unbroken surface of the lake, so damn perfectly it created a mirror image, its radiance splayed all out over the smooth waters.

The night was so still, so bereft of even the smallest gust of breeze or gentle wafts of wind through the surrounding trees, that the whole surface of the lake remained wholly flat, undisturbed and completely motionless. No tiny flickers of motion shifted eddies or miniscule waves along the lake surface, no swimming water creatures were in evidence, drifting up to break that flat reflective shimmer.

It could have been some bizarre wilderness ice skating rink or an extraordinarily large plane of glass out here among trees, such was the total lack of disturbance to its waters, and the proliferation of moonlight captured not just the reflection of the moon's own gleaming face, but all of those towering stationary trees encircling it.

This should have made for a picture of utter tranquillity, a beautiful panorama that most would find an appreciation for, but Booker Marsh considered himself incapable of no longer finding the beauty within anything.

Compelled by inexplicable reasons to be out here on this serene quiet night, far from the nearest port of civilization, he stumbled and shambled on wobbly legs. Down the gently sloping gradient of earth which would carry him right to the soft muddy edges of the still lake itself, he lurched. His shoes, partially sinking into sodden ground were splattered with wet flecks of mud and picked up fallen leaf debris and grass matter, so too the bottom of his trouser legs, but he paid that no mind.

Instead, he continued on his uneven, yet unerring path, towards that giant rough circle of water, spanned out like a black mirror bouncing back the benign gaze of the moon. Only then did he cease his movement, standing still right at the edge of the waters, his feet mired in a clog of murky sludge. With the moonlight spilling over his shoulders, his reflection looked more like a dark silhouette, a black cardboard cut-out of himself. When he dropped down onto his knees at the lake's edge, he saw himself in harrowing detail. A gaunt unshaven face populated by haunted eyes, underneath which black circles hung making him look like the recipient of a heavyweight boxer's double knockout blow.

He didn't see anything he hadn't seen in his bathroom mirror at home; there was the same defeated expression, the same desolation and brutally cold resignation, the air of a man who'd comprehensively given up and abdicated to downfall, and with the utter stillness of the lake, it showed in the very same clarity as any mirror.

Booker stared and stared into the depths, into his own reflection for what seemed to be an eternity, but nothing changed. Nothing altered or shifted, no revelations or answers swam up from below to break the still waters and materialise in front of him. He was on the verge of dashing his hand into the lake to destroy that terrible desolate face gazing back at him when another reflection appeared alongside it. Behind him. A pale woman with midnight waves of hair cascading down over slim shoulders, her eyes penetrating and dark.

"Lost somebody, too, have you?" she asked in a quiet but conversational tone.

"Everybody," Booker said simply, not even questioning the appearance of another soul, a stranger at his side next to this remote body of water. "Just . . . everybody."

"Tell me about it," she said, and Booker wasn't entirely sure whether she meant quite literally, or just in a simple colloquial sense—as if stating that she too, was well aware of the crushing feeling of losing everybody. So he told her about it.

"My wife . . . my family . . . my children. I've lost them all. And it is through my own doing. She left me, took away the kids, for good. I didn't see the signs, or at least if I did, I paid them no mind. I was too wrapped up in my own world, what I needed to be doing, what I *wanted* to be doing. I hated my stupid dead end mundane job, so I drank to be in a better place about it. Then I hit on the genius idea to win my way to freedom and financial success, so I did that. Fell in love with the idea that I could make enough money to drag us all out of a great big hole and make things right. Gambling what money I could and drinking the rest, marrying the two. I successfully managed to make a fucking vicious cycle out of it, by drinking the money I won or pouring it back in to double it, triple it, maximise it. That one big score, just that one; that was all I needed. What I was winning wasn't enough to take home, to worry about, not enough to consider any type of success, so I drank some, played double or nothing with the rest. Over and over and over again."

He paused briefly, still staring at his own visage in the water and hers, standing behind him. When she merely nodded once and didn't elect to add any words, he continued talking, the words spilling out like alphabet vomit.

"You ever hear that song by Cinderella? *'Don't Know What You've Got Until It's Gone'*? Well, that's me, that's the story of my life, the *summary* of my life right there. I was ignoring my kids, neglecting my duties, completely drifting through everything in a haze, desperate to be free of mediocrity and stress and goddamn everything! And I didn't even see what I was doing to myself, to us. To them. So, she up and left me. Took the kids away. Only then did I get smacked in the face by it and I tried to win them all back. Tried to show I could change, that I *had* changed. It was going to be different. Then finally, when all the restraining orders, and police involvement, and branding me a stalker failed to stop me trying to repair what I'd broken, Erica swore to me that she was going to take the lot of them far away, somewhere I would never ever be able to find them, no matter how hard I tried. And she was right. They're gone. I've looked and looked and searched this whole goddamn country over. I've looked every possible place, every . . . impossible . . . place. But they're all gone. I'll never see them again."

With that, he lapsed into forlorn hopeless silence, his voice cracking as he renewed his fervent staring at a reflection which never changed.

"And that's why you came to Lago de los Perdidos? You came here to end your search. Because of course, it isn't just known as the lake of the lost, it's the Final Swim. The Suicide Waters. Japan has Aokigahara, or the Sea of Trees, and we have the lake of the lost. Lost souls, lost hopes, lost lives. All come here."

"I didn't . . ." Booker hesitated, finally breaking his transfixed stare from his own countenance, turning around to stare in perplexity at her, oblivious to the wash of mud soaking through his pants legs. "I've never been here before, I don't even know where I am or what this place is. I just . . . came here. I came here . . . to think about things. I certainly didn't come here . . . to kill myself."

He faltered, finishing the originally adamant statement weakly, wilting under her searching gaze.

"Oh, really? Is that so?"

The woman stooped swiftly, one long slender arm reaching out and lifting up the hem of his hanging shirt, plucking the gun out of the waistband of his trousers. She held it up, highlighting it in the moon glow.

"This is pretty damning evidence that you did, but even more than that is the fact that you claim to have come here not of your own volition, instead obligated to travel here. That is proof that yes, you do belong here, Booker Marsh. Nobody ever comes out to Lago de los Perdidos just to think, or to have a family picnic or a secret lovers getaway. Nobody comes here to fish, or to swim, or to sunbake by the shores. They don't journey here to enjoy the scenery, to fornicate lakeside beneath the stars, or to whisper sweet nothings into the ears of their loved ones. They only ever come here for one purpose. There is no other reason to be here, and all those who have ever come here have come strictly for that reason."

Booker couldn't quite recall having introduced himself to her, but then again, maybe he had. After all, he couldn't remember why he'd been so fucking positive he had to be here, on the muddy shores of a lake he'd never heard of, much less visited before. There was a good chance he'd spaced out into a haze where a whole lot of things might have happened and he'd vagued his way through everything as if he was sleepwalking. *Why not?* It was perfectly feasible; he'd virtually done that with his marriage, his life, the lives of his children, and failed to realise until it crumbled around him, and left him kneeling in muddy debris while a complete stranger dissected his motivations more concisely than he could grasp.

Yes, the gun stashed in his belt was to turn on himself, though why he couldn't have just swallowed a dose of lead in his own home, or some dark lonely alley was a little beyond his comprehension at this point in time. What he hoped to discover in the depths of some expanse of water, he had no idea. Yet he'd been pulled here as surely as if some tether attached to him dragged him into the radius of it, pulled by whatever force suggested merely jamming the barrel of the pistol in his mouth and riding his brains on a bullet out the top of his skull wasn't significant enough.

"You are no exception to the rule, Booker Marsh. You came here with the same intention as all those who've come before you. Here, let me show you."

She moved up alongside him now, and stooped down next to him, directing her attention into the still Suicide Waters. Booker didn't quite follow, and for an illogical moment he thought she was about to throw herself in. Instead she placed a hand on his unshaven cheek and gently but firmly commanded his attention back to the reflective mirror of the water.

Temporarily he saw his gaunt haggard visage once more, then he was seeing different things. Scenes as though he were sitting back watching some form of film unfold.

A young woman, dishevelled and blonde in a short dress of indeterminable colour, rips and tears all through the fabric, her face a mass of lacerations and bloody contusions, was traipsing down the same slope towards the lake he himself had taken. In her arms she carried a small pile of house bricks with chain affixed to them. Calmly she sat herself down on the banks and proceeded to wrap the chains around her ankles, then shimmied on her backside right down to the very edge of the lake. When she was so close to the edge that she was fundamentally standing in water, she hoisted her armload of bricks, clinging to them tightly, and flung herself into the lake. Rather than a gradual slope into deeper water, there must have been a sudden drop into depths much closer to the edge than Booker would have anticipated. Weighted down by her bricks and her chained ankles, the young female dropped down into the waters and vanished from sight. She never reappeared.

In her place came another scenario, another vision of folks beside this very lake. This time a couple, possibly not too much older than the female bricks and chains wielder. They screamed at each other, furious and frantic words, spit flying in one another's faces, hair gusting around their heads as if they were in the centre of not just some argument storm, but a billowing windstorm, as well. Slaps were exchanged in the heat of the fiery exchange, the screaming and shouting escalating, before the man produced a thin knife, blade catching a spark of moonlight and briefly glinting in it. Then he stabbed the woman mid-scream, right in the throat, receiving a drenching torrent of blood in a shower all over his face. She slumped forward, collapsing and he caught her in his arms, then gently lowered her to the slippery mud-covered lakeside, before drawing the bloodied knife blade across his own throat. His figure tumbled in an awkward fall to recline in a bloodied repose of death alongside the slain woman.

A young boy, his face a miserable screwed up vision of despair, pedalled a bicycle at a rapid pace, racing through the woods, ducking under trees. He was on a different slope to this one, possibly situated around the other side, but it was unmistakably the same lake. Lago de los Perdidos. Only, the incline he came barrelling down at a breakneck speed, was far more angled than this side of the lake, a sharper and more abrupt one. One which pitched him straight down and way out into the water. The weight of his bicycle broke the lake's surface and hurled water up in a deluge before he came free of it, dropping with a splash of his own, independent of his machine.

Quite some distance from any particular side of the lake, the boy's head broke the surface and he spluttered, floundering somewhat. It became painfully evident that the kid could not swim, and didn't have the first idea where to begin. Yet, nor was he trying to, and nor did he cry out for help. His face was desolate and heart wrenching, with a grim expression of determination plastered upon it. The boy merely bobbed for a little while there in the ripples and eddies created by the bike crashing in, and then his head submerged. Unlike the previous girl, deliberately weighing herself down with heavy implements to nullify flotation, the small shape of the boy eventually did resurface. Motionless and still, drifting in a lazy float until the ripples all finally died away and the water resumed its completely still façade once again.

There were more, too, so many more. Some just pitifully sad and yet horrific in their own bleakness, while others were awash with brutal finality, grisly and gruesome with inundations of blood and a violence that kicked the breath right out of Booker, left him hopelessly terrified. They splashed blood against his eyeballs, thrust abhorrent scenes of self-harm and murder/suicides into his brain with the savagery of knife blades skewering him. They lanced his psyche, they scorched themselves into his memories with visceral horror in a relentless stream, seeming to speed up as the torment in each one escalated, building on the foundations of each preceding one until he thought his mind was about to crack like an eggshell dashed against a rock.

It was akin to being strapped into somebody else's nightmare, or forcibly injected into a horror movie, a series of self snuff films, made to endure the endless parade of misery, despair and ultimately death.

"No!" Booker screamed, yearning to force his voice into as loud a volume as he could muster, as if by puncturing the fabric of the night with a stentorian wail he could break whatever cursed conjuration this was, spilling grotesque and tragic scenes of death across the waters of the lake. "No, no, no! Make it stop! Make it stop now! I don't want to see any more. I want to live! Goddamn it, I want to live. *I want to fucking live!*"

Abruptly, the grisly torrent of images and people taking their lives in macabre and tragic ways dissipated, vanishing as if they'd never been rolling across the screen of the lake in lurid technicolour at all, supplanted by the all too familiar sight of still water and his shocked face staring back at him, the quiet woman's alongside it.

"I. Want. To. Fucking. Live," Booker reiterated, forcing the words out between gritted teeth, his jaw clenched so tight it felt like bone would break in his cranium.

"No you don't, Booker Marsh." His strange companion shook her head, a sad smile flitting across her lips. "You didn't come to Lago de los Perdidos to live. Which is fine, because nobody ever does. Nobody comes here expecting to walk away, or indeed, wanting to walk away. They come here to end it. Say their final goodbye. And, as I said, you are no exception. I didn't show you that to dissuade you from your plan, for nothing I do can alter that from happening. Those are just some of those who have come before you, that's just a little history of the place you've found yourself attached to."

"Attached to? No, no, there is nothing here I'm attached to. Thanks for the cold hard dose of reality lady, whoever you are and whatever the fuck you are doing out here, but listen.. That just reinforced my opinion that I'm a fool to consider taking my own life. I can pull myself out of this hole, I can start afresh. Things can never be so bad that thinking about taking a gun and blowing an exit wound in my head is a good idea. So, thanks for showing me the light—*however the fuck you did that*—but I'm good with things now. I will be walking out of here."

"That isn't how it works," she said, that sad smile now back on her face and firmly fixed in place, not a mere flicker of an expression, but an unyielding one, one which didn't look to be vacating any time soon. "You came here because you belong here. You didn't travel out here on a whim. You did so because you know and accept where your place is."

"No lady, not so. Whatever fancy trickery you just used now to screw with my head, actually just screwed my head on straight. Don't I have a choice? I'll tell you. Yes, I do have a choice and I choose to live, I choose to walk away with my head held high and to live."

"Of course you have a choice," she said softly. "There is always a choice. However, you have already made your choice and it is the last choice you are able to make. You chose to come to Lago de los Perdidos. That's the ultimate choice, and it is one which cannot be undone. All those who have gone down that path have remained here. They are all still here. Look around you, Booker Marsh. Look closely. At everything. What do you see?"

He'd come to the conclusion that this crazy woman was just some desperately lonely freak, who must have either followed him here, or perhaps had already been here, living nearby maybe. Either that or she was on the knife edge of suicide herself, and was fervently trying to keep him here in her presence, clinging on the thread of companionship he presented. Nonetheless, Booker humoured her by looking.

By her asking him to 'look around' at his surroundings, Booker made the assumption she was referring to the trees and things, the landscape and so forth. So, he gazed first at the trees, scrutinising them, for whatever mindless reason she wanted him to.

What he gazed upon turned his blood to ice water, blasted an explosion of shock and sheer dread throughout every fibre of his being.

Every single tree surrounding the spread of the lake, those on the far side and all of those circled out around behind him, were comprised not of wood, bark and leaves. Instead, their twisted gnarled trunks were constructed entirely of human bodies, knotted together in a hideous tapestry, a giant amalgamation of flesh with torsos, legs, and arms all intricately bound together to create the mass of the tree trunk. They spanned up even farther to compose stretching branches, whole bodies held impossibly in gruesome thrall out at irregular angles from the solid flesh trunk. Wide open, eternally reaching hands becoming twigs and smaller sticks growing off the ends of these branch entities. The skin of many of these ghastly tree components was so scarred and burned in places, evidently from whatever trauma suffered prior to their death, or during, that it actually resembled a hideous form of bark, making their tree-like resemblance even more uncanny. Still others were formed from collages of human bone, stark white femurs or fibulas, flesh stripped fingers, the curved blades of ribcages.

While many of these human choked tree creations were devoid of foliage, and stabbed stark spikes of branches and limbs—*human limbs and reaching extremities*—into the night sky, still others did feature their ghastly interpretation of leaves, and this came in the form of human hair.

The stillness of the night was no longer in occurrence, breezes were beginning to infiltrate, and as they did, blowing through these abhorrent trees of human flesh and bone, they buffeted the hair foliage around, spreading longer scalps out in billowy curtains whilst ruffling other shorter ones into freakish motion. Follicles captured by the gusting winds created an unearthly sound, not unlike that of leaves rustling in any ordinary tree caught amidst an upsurge in wind activity.

As Booker gaped in soundless horror, blinking, then blinking again, even temporarily squeezing his eyes as tight as he possibly could before snapping them open again to see if the visual atrocity remained, he found it wasn't just the trees which were not as they'd originally seemed. It was absolutely everything about and around the lake itself. Perverted, twisted, and morphed into something that must have been dredged from the deepest pits of the darkest nightmares.

The lake itself, now alive with churning currents, ripples and waves being generated by the increase in winds, starting to howl and whistle with a frenetic intensity around the vicinity, played host to images again as well, or were these terrible phantasmagorias actually part of the water, like the trees? They seemed to be. The choppy surfaces, the oscillating waves, they all appeared to be faces, spanning out all over the lake in its entirety, from shore to shore. So many faces complete with tragic eyes, filled with unimaginable suffering, all of them piercing into Booker's soul. And these waters of the lake, they weren't clear, nor did they generate the illusion of being blue, or here at night, even black. They ran red as though the body of water was completely composed of blood, the blood of all those whose faces merged in a miasma of grief and desolation. Faces in Lago de los Perdidos. The faces of the lost.

The muddy ground he knelt in wasn't merely sodden earth; it was as red with thick blood as the waters, coagulating around his saturated legs, seeping from the banks down into a merge with the lake, and faces stared at him from there, too. Bodies, side by side, or knotted inexorably around one another in bizarre entanglements one couldn't possibly hope to achieve in life, like some abnormally large mass grave, *were* the ground. The thin reedy grass lining the shores and marching back up the incline to the top of the embankment overlooking the lake was the human hair of many, waving and moving consistently in the bluster of the mounting winds. So too were the weeds, choking shallow sections of the lake near the bank.

Even those pale rounded rocks visible just under the surface of the water, and others partially submerged, looking as though they've been washed smooth by constant interaction with the water, were not rocks at all. They were human skulls, some adult sized, some horrifyingly tiny. Children's, even those of mere infants.

Blackened clouds, bruised and swollen, scudded across the skies, chasing the moon and the prior stillness of the night into first, retreat, and then complete surrender. Booker screamed himself ragged in equal measures horrified shock and complete disbelief. Though she hadn't touched him, bar that simple firm graze of her hand against his face to turn his attention to the visual horror soon to be exposed on the screen of the lake's waters, he was certain she must have done something to him. Perhaps she'd drugged him, hypnotised him. Somehow she'd insinuated her way into his mind with a hideous influence that led him to conjure up this panorama of impossibility.

"What have you done to me? What did you do to me? Did you drug me? *What have you done?*"

"I'm afraid there's nothing I can do to you, Booker Marsh. I can only show you the real face of Lago de los Perdidos, and this is it. This is what you see before you now. The rest, you have done yourself. You came here because you belong here, one with the rest of the lost. You know that."

"No, I don't!"

"If it is any consolation, and I'm sure it must be," she said, and predictably, that same sad smile adorned her pale features, swimming in her eyes as well with a forlorn resigned sympathy, an expression of the inevitable. "You will soon be with your family once more."

"What?" Booker stared at her with his eyes wide and wild, his hands curled into fists of shock at his sides so tightly that the nails sliced deep lacerations into his palms, leaking further blood out between fingers, to mingle with that of the ground and the waters. "That doesn't even make any sense! No fucking sense at all! My wife took herself and my kids away from me, somewhere where I would never find them. Ever. She's hiding somewhere and I won't ever be with them again because I can't find them, no matter how hard I try."

"She did, Booker Marsh, she did exactly that. She found somewhere where you wouldn't be able to find any of them. Until now."

"How do you . . . ? I don't understand . . . "

The woman didn't speak again, instead she repeated her gesture of putting a hand to his face and turning it back out towards the lake, as much as he had no desire to look that way. He had no desire to look anywhere at all; all around him was a grisly montage of death, of human suffering, misery knotted together in eternal bonds of hopelessness and finality in this terrible place where all who journeyed here, did so to die.

Nonetheless, Booker did shift his path of vision back out there, and once more the screen of images played, rolling on wretchedness over the skittering waves of faces. He recognised what was being depicted now as a closer view of a scene emerging in the barrage of torment which played out earlier, part of the mind numbing display of tragedies merging together once the images began to speed up and pound at his sight with jackhammer intensity.

It showed a nondescript car parked atop a cliff, not

unlike the highest point on the far side of the Final Swim. In comparison to much of the bloody horror, violence and gut-wrenching atrocity many of those ridden into suicide inflicted upon themselves in the previous visual headfuck, this scene was almost one of serenity and peaceful tranquillity. As if somebody merely travelled up to a nice vantage point overlooking the lake to drink in the view and enjoy the solitude.

Though of course, as Booker's abnormally adamant female companion here stated so firmly, nobody would ever come to Lago de los Perdidos for that purpose.

He hadn't witnessed the vehicle up this close before in the torrent of terror, and nor had he given it much consideration, merely filing that away with the rest of the terrible things, just another lost soul seeking the coup de grace on their meaningless existence in the presence of the Suicide Waters. This time though, there was more to see, more to take in. More horrific shock to shrink the power of rational thought down into nothingness.

Behind the wheel of the stationary automobile was Booker's own wife Erica, and strapped in by their seatbelts in the backseats, his children. The people he'd not seen since she vowed so comprehensively to keep their whereabouts from him eternally secret. Her expression was grim and resolute, and yet horribly melancholy, while those of the kids were just placid, filled with simple innocence and the lack of true acknowledgement of why they were where they were.

As if he were witnessing something happening right now, as if the terrified ragged pitch of his voice could even reach her, Booker screamed as the engine suddenly roared.

The car lurched into life and pitched forward, gaining speed as the accelerator was stamped on with a fierce determination, and as Booker's shrieks rose and echoed into the night in a hellish duet with the storming winds, the vehicle plunged over the edge of the cliff. It descended down into the waters. As the shockwave ripples of its impact eventually ebbed away, back to the perpetual stillness, nothing broke the waters. Nothing, and nobody surfaced.

Booker felt the last vestiges of his sanity draining, felt as though his mind was breaking up completely, and when the woman took him by the hand, still dripping rivulets of blood, lifting him up to his feet, he acquiesced with simple compliance. He followed her lead as she stepped on the bodies and faces of souls interred within the ground, wading out into the waters, pained faces swimming around their waists.

All around them the storm was a tempest of sheer ferocity and intensity, such that it blasted the fronds of human hair comprising the grass flat to the corpse ground, kicked up enormous waves of blood water and even bent the trees—*Humanitrees,* Booker giggled inanely inside his head, swirling down into a deep chasm of madness—literally in half.

Then one of those congested tangles of bodies, morphed and fashioned by whatever bizarre power shaped every inch of this lake and its freakish surroundings, one of those tree entities was buffeted by a surge of wind which whipped it right over into an arc that carried out right across the lake to where he and his silent companion stood, now up to their necks in water and bloody face shapes.

The branches swinging human finger twigs and

hairy leaf matter out towards him were those of his wife, the bodies of his children inextricably entwined with her body lower down the tree. They snagged him and plucked him up from the choppy frothing waters, and as the wind snapped the tree upwards again, Booker Marsh was taken with it, enveloped within it. Branches encircled him, trapped him and embraced him with inexorable force, clinging tight to him with twig fingers until his corpse, too, was one with them.

The blustering squalls of wind died away, the humanitrees stilled their motion, the woman immersed in blood waters slipped beneath the surface. The smooth flat plane of Lago de los Perdidos once more stretched from shore to shore, completely still beneath a moon in a sky no longer blackened by clouds.

Out of the Woods

RAMSEY CAMPBELL

The glass of Scotch gnashed its ice cubes as Thirsk set it down on his desk. "I don't care where it comes from, I just want the best price. Are you certain you won't have a drink?"

The visitor shook his head once while the rest of him stayed unmoved. "Not unless you have natural water."

"Been treated, I'm afraid. One of the many prices of civilisation. You won't object if I have another, will you? I don't work or see people this late as a rule."

When the other shook his head again, agitating his hair, which climbed the back of his neck and was entangled like a bristling brownish nest above his skull, Thirsk crossed to the mahogany cabinet to pour himself what he hoped might prove to be some peace of mind. While he served himself he peered at his visitor, little of whom was to be seen outside the heavy brown ankle-length overcoat except a wrinkled knotted face and gnarled hands, which ornamented the ends of the arms of the chair. Thirsk could think of no reason why any of this should bother him, but—together with the smell of the office, which was no longer quite or only that of new books—it did, so that he fed himself a harsh gulp of Scotch before marching around his desk to plant himself in his extravagant leather chair. It wasn't too late for him to declare that he didn't see salesmen without an appointment, but instead he heard himself demanding "So tell me why we should do business."

"For you to say, Mr Thirsk."

"No reason unless you're offering me a better deal than the bunch who printed all these books."

That was intended to make the other at least glance at the shelves which occupied most of the wall space, but his gaze didn't waver; he seemed not to have blinked since Thirsk had opened the door to his knock. "Do you know where they get their paper?" he said, more softly than ever.

"I already told you that's immaterial. All I know is it's better and cheaper than that recycled stuff."

"Perhaps your readers would care if they knew."

"I doubt it. They're children." The insinuating softness of the other's speech, together with the dark wistful depths of his eyes, seemed to represent an insubstantial adversary with which Thirsk had to struggle, and he raised his voice. "They won't care unless they're put up to it. If you ask me there's a movement not to let children be children any more, but plenty of them still want fairy tales or they wouldn't buy the books I publish."

The ice scraped the glass as he drained his Scotch and stood up, steadying himself with one hand on the desk. "Anyway, I'm not arguing with you. If you want to send me samples of your work and a breakdown of the costs then maybe we can talk."

His tone was meant to make it clear that would never happen, but the other remained seated, pointing at his own torso with one stiff hand. "This is for you to consider."

He wasn't pointing at himself but rather at a book which was propped like a rectangular stone in his lap. He must have been carrying it all the time, its binding camouflaged against his overcoat. He reared up from the chair as if the coat had stiffened and was raising him, and Thirsk couldn't help recoiling from the small gargoyle face immobile as a growth on a tree, the blackened slit of a mouth like a fissure in old bark. When the hands lowered the volume towards him he accepted it, but as soon as he felt the weight he said "You're joking."

"We seldom do that, Mr Thirsk."

"I couldn't afford this kind of production even if I wanted to. I publish fairy tales, I don't live in them. The public don't care if books fall to bits so long as they're cheap, and that goes double for children."

"Perhaps you should help them to care."

"Here, take your book back."

The other held up his hands, displaying knobbly palms. "It is our gift to you," he said in a voice which, soft as it was, seemed to penetrate every corner of the room.

"Then don't look so glum about it." As Thirsk planted the book on his desk he glimpsed a word embossed on the heavy wooden binding. "*Tapioca*, is that some kind of pudding cookbook?"

Whatever filled his visitor's eyes grew deeper. They

struck Thirsk as being altogether too large and dark, and for a moment he had the impression of gazing into the gloomy depths of something quite unlike a face. He strode to the door, more quickly than steadily, and threw it open.

The avenue of pines interspersed with rhododendrons stretched a hundred yards to the deserted road into town. For once the sight didn't appeal to him as peaceful. Surely it would when he'd rid himself of his visitor, who he was beginning to suspect was mad; a leaf and maybe other vegetation was tangled in his hair, and wasn't there a mossy tinge to his cracked cheeks? Thirsk stood aside as the other stalked out of the door, overcoat creaking. Too much to drink or not enough, he thought, because as the figure passed along the avenue, beneath clouds which were helping the twilight gather, it appeared to grow taller. A sound behind him—paper rustling—made him glance around the room. The next second he turned back to the avenue, which was as deserted as the road.

Had his visitor dodged into the bushes? They and the trees were as still as fossils. "Get off my property," Thirsk warned, and cleared his throat so as to shout, "or I'll call the police."

By now it was apparent to him that the man hadn't been a printer. Thirsk was tempted to hurl the book after him, except that might bring him back. As he stared at the avenue until the trees seemed to inch in unison towards him, he found he was unwilling to search the grounds when it was growing so rapidly dark. "Go back where you came from," he yelled, and slammed the door so hard the floorboards shook.

A chill had accompanied his visitor into the office,

and now it felt even colder. Had one of Thirsk's assistants left a window open in the warehouse? Thirsk hurried to the stout door in the back wall of the room. The door opened with an unexpected creak which lingered in his ears as he reached a hand into the dark. The fluorescent tubes stuttered into life, except for one which left the far end of the central aisle unlit. Though all the windows crammed into the space above the shelves were closed tight, the fifty-yard-long room was certainly colder than usual, and there was more of a smell of old paper than he remembered. In the morning he would have to fix the lights: not now, when at least two of the tubes were growing fitful, so that the flickering contents of the shelves kept resembling supine logs multicoloured with lichen, the spines of the dust jackets. He thumbed the light-switch, a block of plastic so cold it felt moist, and as the dark lurched forward, shut it in. For the first time ever he was wishing he could go home from work.

He was already home. The third door of the office led to the rest of his bungalow. When he opened the door, the cold was waiting for him. The heating hadn't failed; he had to snatch his hand away as soon as he touched the nearest radiator. He poured himself an even larger Scotch, and once he'd fired up his throat and his stomach, dumped himself in the chair behind the desk. The unwelcome visit had left him so on edge that all he could do was work.

The late afternoon mail had brought him an armful of packages which he hadn't had time to open. The topmost padded envelope proved to contain the typescript of a children's book by Huntley Dunkley, who sounded familiar. In his present mood, just the title—*The Smog Goblin and the Last Forest*—was enough to put him off. "Send your bloody propaganda somewhere it's wanted," he snarled, grabbing a copy of the Hamelin Books rejection letter. "Fit only for recycling," he pronounced, and scrawled that as a postscript.

Usually one of his assistants would see to the outgoing mail, but he couldn't stand the sight of the typescript a moment longer. Having clipped the letter to it, he stuffed it into a padded envelope and slung it on the desk next to his, and glared at the discarded packing as it tried to climb out of the waste-bin. Presumably the silence of the room emphasised its movements, though he could have imagined it wasn't alone in making a slow deliberate papery sound, an impression sufficiently persuasive that he glanced out of the window.

The light from the office lay on the strip of grass outside but fell short of the trees, which were embedded in a darkness that had sneaked up on him. He knuckled the switch for the security light. The fierce illumination caught hold of the trees and bushes, and he felt an irrational desire to see them shrink back from the blaze which he could summon at the touch of a finger. Instead they stepped almost imperceptibly forward as though urged by their shadows, a mass of secret blackness interrupted by the drive. Just now the bright bare gravel looked as though it was inviting someone or something to emerge onto it, and he turned away so furiously that he almost tripped over an object on the floor.

It was the discarded envelope, writhing slowly on the carpet and extending a torn brown strip of itself like the remains of a finger towards him. He closed one fist on it, squeezing its pulpy innards, and punched it into the bin before grinding it down with his heel. "That's enough," he shouted, not knowing what he was addressing until his gaze fell on the book his visitor had brought him. "Let's see what you are," he said through his teeth, and flung the book open, wood striking wood. Then he let out a gasp that would have been a word if he'd known how he was feeling.

The thick untrimmed pages weren't composed of paper; each was a single almost rectangular dead leaf. For a moment he thought words were printed on the uppermost, and then he saw the marks were scattered twigs, formed into patterns which he could imagine someone more susceptible than himself assuming to be words in a forgotten language. "If this is a joke," he yelled, ignoring how small his voice sounded in the empty room, "you can take it back," and hoisting the book off the desk, ran to the door.

As the cover banged shut like a coffin lid, the tilting of the book rearranged the twigs into a different pattern—into words he was able to read. He fumbled the door open and raised the volume in both hands. By the glare of the security light he saw the title wasn't *Tapioca* but *Tapiola*. What difference did one letter make? "Come and get it," he roared, hurling the book from him.

It struck the grass with a thud which seemed to crush his shout. The cover raised itself an inch and fell shut, and then the book was as still as the trees and their shadows. Beyond the unlit road, and around his property, the forest stretched for miles. The words he'd glimpsed were growing dearer, embedding themselves in his mind. **YOU TURNED AWAY ONE MESSENGER**. The night sky seemed to lean towards the patch of light which contained him and the book, as though the sky was the forehead of the blackness behind the mass of trees, in which he heard a sudden gust of wind. Its chill found him while he waited to see the trees move, and he was continuing to wait when it subsided. It might have been a huge icy breath.

"Not likely," he said in a voice which the darkness shrank almost to nothing. He backed away and closed the door. The breath of the night had smelled of decaying vegetation, and now the room did. He thought he saw a trace of his own breath in the air. Hugging himself and rubbing his upper arms, he went to his desk for a mouthful of Scotch. As the ice cubes clashed against his teeth, he almost bit through the glass. Beyond the window the lawn was bare. The book had gone, and there wasn't so much as a hint of a footmark on the grass.

"I bet you think that's clever. Let me introduce you to someone who's cleverer." He was speaking aloud so that his voice would keep him company, he realised, but he wouldn't have to feel alone for long. Without glancing away from the window he groped for the phone on his desk, detached the receiver from its housing and jabbed the talk button. He was already keying the number for the police as he brought the receiver to his face.

A sound came to find him. Though the earpiece was emitting it, it wasn't the dialling tone. It could have been a gale passing through a forest, but it seemed close to articulate. He clawed at the button to clear the line, and listened to the welcome silence; then he poked the talk button again, and again. The phone was dead.

And there was movement among the trees. High on the trunks, branches sprang up and waved at him, a series of them rapidly approaching the house. A branch of a tree at the edge of the grass drooped before gesturing triumphantly at him, and then a severed length of the telephone cable which they had all been supporting plummeted onto the grass.

"Having fun, are you?" Thirsk demanded, though his throat was so constricted he barely heard himself. "Time I joined in." He dropped the useless receiver on top of a pile of typescripts and dashed kitchenwards, switching on lights as he went. His bedroom lit up, the bathroom and toilet next to it, the large room in which he dined and watched television and listened to music, and finally the kitchen, where he lifted the largest and sharpest knife from the rack on the wall. Outside the window he saw an image of himself almost erased by the forest—an image which grew fainter, then was wiped out entirely as his breath appeared in front of him and condensed on the window.

He saw himself being engulfed by fog in the reflection of a room which had been invaded by trees. The glint of the knife looked feeble as a lantern lost in a forest. "I'm still here," he snarled. Driven by a defiance which he felt more than understood, he stormed back into his office.

He was still there, and for a while, since he couldn't call a taxi. He laid the knife within reach on the desk and drafted a letter to his printer. . . *looking forward to the Christmas consignment . . . any way you keep costs down is fine . . .* His words seemed insufficiently defiant until he scribbled *It's only paper, only pulp.* Of course he would never send such a letter, and he was about to tear off the page and bin it when he realised how like taking back a challenge that would seem. He drove the knife through the pad, pinning the letter to the desk like a declaration nailed to a door.

At first there was no apparent response. The only visible movement in the room was of his breath. It took him some minutes to be certain that the smell of decaying vegetation had intensified—that the source was in the room with him. Did the colours on the jackets of the new books resemble stains more than they should? His chair trundled backwards and collided with the wall as he reached the shelves, where he dug a finger into the top of the spine of the nearest book.

It came off the shelf at once—the spine did. The cheap glue had failed, exposing bunches of pages which looked aged or worse. His hand swung wildly, hooking another spine at random. That fell away, bearing a patch of its rotten jacket, and his finger poked deep into the pages, which were a solid lump of pulp. He dragged his finger out of it, dislodging both adjacent spines. Their undersides were crawling with insects. He staggered backwards just as sounds began in the warehouse: a ponderous creaking followed by a crash that shook the office.

"Leave my property alone," Thirsk screamed. He ripped the knife out of the pad and pounding across the office, hauled open the door to the warehouse. The bookcases that weren't attached to the walls had fallen together, forming an arched passage, in the darkness of which piles of books were strewn like jagged chunks of chopped timber. Not only books were in that darkness, and his hand clutched at the light switch before he knew he didn't want to see.

As soon as his hand found the switch, the block came away like a rotten fungus from the wall. The surviving fluorescents lit for an instant before failing in unison with a loud sharp glassy ping, and he glimpsed a shape stalking up the passage of the bookcases towards him. It resembled a totem, carved or rather shaped out of a tree, walking stiffly as a puppet, though it was considerably taller than any puppet had a right to be. It grew as it advanced on him, as if whatever feet it had were picking up or absorbing the books on which they trod. Its disproportionately large head was featureless and unstable as a mass of foliage, and its arms, which were reaching for him, were at least half the length of the warehouse. So much he distinguished before he threw the door in its face. Twisting the key, he wrenched it out of the lock and shied it across the room.

There was silence then, a silence like the quiet at the secret heart of a forest. He heard his pulse and his harsh unsteady breaths. Gripping the knife two-handed, he glared about. Half a dozen spines sagged away from books, spilling grubs, as the telephone let out a hollow exhalation and began to speak in the voice of the wind.

Thirsk shouted louder, drowning out its words. "In here too, are you? Not for long. This is my house, and one of us is leaving." But he wasn't sure why he was rushing to the front door—to eject an intruder, or to confront the source of all the intrusions?

The trees were out there, and the darkness behind

them. Neither appeared to have moved. "I know it's you," he yelled. "I know you're out there." He saw his shadow jerking towards the trees before he was aware of heading for them. As he reached the nearest he slashed at the trunk, slicing off bark. "You're my property and I can do what I like with you," he ranted. "If you don't like it try and stop me, you and your big friend."

He felt his feet leave the gravel for the plushy floor of fallen leaves and pine needles. He was well into the woods, hacking at every tree within reach, when all the lights of the house were extinguished. He whirled around, then discovered he was able to see by the faint glow of the sky, which no longer felt like a presence looming over him. "Is that the best you can do?" he cried, reeling deeper into the woods, no longer knowing or caring where he was. "That's for you, and so's that." When the trees around him began to creak he chopped more savagely at them, daring them to move towards him; when the mounded earth seemed to quiver underfoot he trampled on it, ignoring how the forest had begun to smell as if the earth was being dug up. He might have been miles into the lightless forest when the hand whose enormous fingers he'd just slashed raised itself with an explosive creak, soil and undergrowth and decaying vegetation spilling from its palm, and closed around him.

Winter's Dollhouse

RENA MASON

Early morning frost crunched with every step Kirsten took across Lake Champlain. Twice her body had swayed when a wave rolled under the ice, offsetting her balance, threatening to lurch her forward then onto her ass. Unease diminished the confidence she'd built up for her first dive beneath a solid layer of frozen water. The third time, she slowed and looked back at Thaddius.

"Don't stop." He motioned his hand for her to keep moving.

"It doesn't feel right."

"You've never been out on—"

A long, metallic groan sounded to the right.

"What was that?"

"Perfectly normal. It all is, except for loud cracks and pops. If you hear those, run."

"Great."

"Claude's shanty should be up there to the right of the bridge. See it yet?"

Kirsten faced forward then hastened her pace. "Light, quick steps, light, quick steps . . . " she whispered. Bright glare and lingering breath vapor made it difficult to focus. She squinted at the radiant, monochromatic landscape. A dark object stood out on the ice not far from the gray skeletal structure that went halfway across the sky then faded into the whiteness before it reached the other side.

The weighty dive bag pulled her shoulder down. *If the ice breaks, that side's going in first and sending me straight to the bottom.* She leaned left for counterbalance.

"I think I see his place." Kirsten shifted the gear to the middle of her back. The stiff dry suit made dull squeaks. *Just cold neoprene not cracks and pops.* A thermal dive skin and wool socks underneath the outer layer clung tight, everything constricting. Awkwardness on land always made submerging surreal—a fish out of water back in again—pure bliss. "I'm glad you're carrying the tanks," she shouted.

"Keep your voice down. People do live around the lake you know."

"Light, quick steps, light, quick steps . . . " *Dammit, if this site's safe then why all the precautions?* Thad insisted they walk ten feet apart with her in the lead. 'Don't talk too loud, walk fast and light,' he'd said. His Navy Seal training probably made him this way, intense and overly astute.

She'd done one wreck dive in the lake but never an ice dive. Thad had though, and she trusted him. They'd been dating off and on for the year after her scuba lessons with his company. He had all the certifications including dive master, ice, wreck, cave, and even rescue. One she hoped he'd never have to use, especially not today.

Kirsten stopped, gasped. "Oh my God!"

"What?"

She pointed to the left. "There."

"I'm too far back."

"It's a crack, Thad. And it's frickin' big."

"Even huge ones are normal. Can you see the lines? They're dark, like the lake water's visible through them."

"Not really. It's white inside. Looks filled in with snowpack."

"Then it's all right. Keep moving, stop talking, and listen."

"I don't think I can." As fast as her heart pounded, blood didn't seem to be flowing to her legs to get them moving.

"You want me to come up there and walk with you?"

"No! Stay back. I'll go." *Light, quick steps . . . now move!* Before he gets here and adds the weight of those steel tanks. Kirsten took a deep breath and held it, lifted a foot, stepped down and waited. The crack remained still.

Thad's crunching steps grew louder. Twenty feet ahead, a small, brown square stood out on the white. She exhaled, resumed her former pace. Her heart rate didn't slow until she reached the inferred safety of the shanty.

A frost-covered padlock hung from a latch and bolt.

"I've got it." Thad nudged her aside, brushed the ice off, and wiggled a key around, then opened the small door. "Go on in."

Kirsten hunched then stepped inside. "Wow, this

is bigger than I thought it would be." She lowered her shoulder and let the bag slump to the frozen-lake floor. A makeshift anchor pulley system, rigged to two pallets, nearly touched the ceiling, which was at least eight feet high. The contraption sat in front of a bathtub-sized hole opposite the entrance. Black water rippled inches below the white edges of the open rectangular area. A small recliner sat to the right, up and behind it, a shelf of . . . she rubbed melted frost from her eyes and looked again.

"Sweet place right?" Thad shut the door; the room darkened, lit only by the daylight glow reflecting from the ice.

"Um, what are those?"

"Old dolls."

"That's creepy as hell. Wha—"

"I told you about his kid, right?"

"No." Kirsten's eyes stayed fixed on the toys. Their empty, painted stares gazed back at her.

"About five years ago, Claude's wife came home from work and found their six-year-old in the backyard with a broken neck."

"That's horrible." Expressions of shock and fear shadowed the porcelain faces. Tingles rolled through Kirsten. She shook them off. "What happened?"

"Trampoline accident . . . I wish they'd ban the pieces of shit, unless you're trained."

"Where was Claude when—"

"There."

She tore away from the hypnotic stares of the replicate little girls and looked at Thad.

He lowered his voice. "Claude fell asleep in front of the TV, didn't wake up until he heard his wife screaming. Jen divorced him after it happened, moved out of state. He's been kind of messed up ever since."

Kirsten turned back to the china dolls. "I see that. So, these were his daughter's?"

"He told me she collected them. They bought her one every year for her birthday."

"But there's got to be at least ten dolls up there. You said she was six."

Thad shrugged. "Maybe he still buys 'em, Claude's always been a bit off, ever since we were kids. He's exactly the kind of guy who buys a big old boat and gets a permit to sink it just so we can dive it. You still want to, right?"

She nodded, her attention focused on the painted expressions.

"Then gear up over there but not too close to the hole. Dang it, I forgot to put up the dive flag, be right back."

"I don't think anyone's going to . . . " Kirsten turned toward the empty doorway then back to the dolls. "Come 'round." Their ceramic heads appeared to motion agreement.

She picked up the dive bag and stepped toward the hole. Soft clinking came from the shelf. Kirsten looked up, and the dolls seemed to have shifted and now faced the open water. The door closed, Thad walked toward her. "What are you doing?"

"Huh? Nothing . . . getting the gear ready."

He set the tanks down, took the bag from her hand, and unzipped it. "Come on." He readied and tested the gear. "What's up with your compass?"

"I think it broke and all the oil leaked out."

"Why didn't you say anything before?"

"I forgot about it."

"Remind me when we get back to the shop. I'll try and fix it, but I might have to order a new one. Not smart to forget before a dive."

"Sorry."

"We'll go off mine for this one. You can owe me." He winked.

After that, he inspected and purged the octopus twice. As her dive buddy it made sense since she doesn't always stay on top of her equipment like he does. If he ever ran out of air and needed to use her second regulator to breathe air from her tank, at least he'd know it worked. Thad can be a bit old school when it comes to his techniques and his gear. He sticks with all the ancient brands he trained on, which means she did too.

"Adjust your mask, then the weight belt, fins last. We'll do a walk-in entry. Follow the anchor line down."

"Is that what this rigged thing is?"

"Yep."

"You sure it's stable? Looks heavy. I'm surprised it hasn't fallen through the ice."

"Don't yank or pull on the rope too hard, and it'll be fine."

Kirsten secured a sheathed dive knife against her calf then stood up and clicked the vest. Thad released his hold on the tank. "Geez, that's heavy."

"You need the extra weight, the dry suit's more buoyant. And try not to skip breathe down there, especially on this dive." Thad disconnected an air hose, created a bubble layer between her insulated latex skin and dry suit, then reattached the tubing.

"I don't skip breathe."

"I'm the dive master, and you do, so don't."

"I'll pay more attention to it." *Wow, he's good.* On some of the certification dives, Kirsten had caught herself not breathing normally but couldn't help it. Everything below is so surreal, you get caught up, and as silly as it sounds, it's easy to forget to breathe.

She lowered her mask, spit onto the tempered glass, and smeared it around, then adjusted it onto her face. The tight layers of neoprene, the weight, small shack, and dark water in front of her all bore down—claustrophobia set in.

"'K, you ready?" He faced her, put a flashlight around her wrist, and signaled *okay* with his fingers.

"Yeah, but . . . " Kirsten glanced up at the dolls again. They stared at her with painted fear in their eyes.

"Let's do it." He put his mask and snorkel on the ice next to the open water. "Oh, and hey, I forgot to tell you this, but they say the best part of ice diving is the warmup sex after."

"Is that right? Who's *they*, exactly?"

Thad shrugged and grinned, indenting his dimples. An impish look of adorable innocence only he could pull off. She wanted him more than ever.

Kirsten inflated her vest with a big smile on her face, then put the regulator in her mouth and took in a breath. The mechanical sound of intake always reminded her of Darth Vader. She pressed the mask against her face with one hand, held the octopus and computer against her thigh with the other then stepped into darkness.

Cold bit into the exposed flesh around her mouth, the sensation of a hundred needles injecting her face with ice water all at once. She took in a deep breath, kicked twice, and floated to the far side of the hole. Thad stepped in then bobbed up. "Whoo! Hell yeah! I love the cold!" He shook his head like a wet dog then waved her over. "Turn your flashlight on. Everything's programmed into the computer."

Kirsten took the regulator out of her mouth and put the snorkel in to save air.

"Bottom depth right here is about 160ft. The boat's at 90 feet. Let's head out at 30 till we get there. What's your psi?"

"2400."

"Good. Stay close." He grabbed his mask and snorkel from topside and put them on. Then he made another okay signal, inserted his regulator, and deflated his BC. The black neoprene dome of his head sunk and disappeared into the water.

She thought about the dolls. *Don't look at them again.* She didn't and followed Thad down the line.

***

The flashlight shone on thousands of ice crystals in less than two meters of visibility, twinkling in an otherwise abysmal darkness like nighttime snow falling across the headlights of a moving car. Shadows encroached upon her peripheral vision, a swirling darkness that moved in and out of her clear line of sight. Kirsten wiggled the mask around for a better seal. It didn't work.

Icy cold and murky, layers of spandex and neoprene constricted everything, squeezing her head and face. She pinched the silicone over her nose and continued to equalize but found it difficult to differentiate temperature from pressure.

Thad grabbed her wrist, directed his flashlight next to her head not directly into her face, then signaled *okay*. She nodded. He shook his head *no*, then tapped two fingers against his mask pointing to his eyes. Kirsten looked at him. Thad squinted then tapped her mask. She understood he wanted her to close her eyes and calm down, so she did. She pulled in a deep breath, then let it out slowly. The robotic inhalation and burbling exhalation were drowned out by loud crunches, pops, and metallic cracks.

Her eyes opened wide and she sucked in a quick breath. Thad pointed to his ear, signaled *okay* again, then shined his flashlight up. Unsure what his signaling meant, Kirsten followed the beam and floating bubbles through a sea of dazzling, illuminated flakes.

Above, the ice glowed in grays like an encompassing thunderhead rolling and booming. Visible cracks sent a shudder through her. The ice shifted and rolled before her eyes. *Ah, that's what causes those weird sounds. It moves . . . duh. He's going to think you're an idiot.*

Kirsten loosened the hold she had on the anchor line, then closed her eyes again, took deep, calming breaths, then scissor-kicked once. She pinched her nose and forced a breath through her head—a Valsalva maneuver. Air moved slowly through her sinuses and then a lessening of pressure came. Thad rose, made another *okay*. This time she signaled back, *okay*. He pushed a button on his dive computer, pointed out to the darkness, and let go of the rope. Kirsten followed.

***

Constant, muted echoes of moving ice filled the void.

Varying pitches of different lengths vibrated through the water, amplifications of whining, twisting metal noises. She kept her focus on Thad's light and ignored the sensation of things moving in the blackness around them. It swam in her periphery, kept out of sight whenever she glanced sideways.

Thad stopped, inspected her once more, then nodded, and gave her a *thumbs down* to descend. Kirsten signaled *okay*. He took hold of her arm, then let a blast of air out of his BC, keeping his eyes on her, the dive computer, and equalizing between purges. She did the same, and together they sunk farther into the abyss.

He slowed and signaled to *level off*. They'd reached 90 feet. Shining the flashlights all around showed nothing in every direction. No bottom existed, no gray ice cover, only blackness. Thad looked at his computer screen, then reached for her pressure gage and pointed to her psi; it read 2000. He held his up, 2000. Thad tapped his regulator then tapped hers. Kirsten knew she'd been skip breathing but couldn't help it. On normal dives she'd always suck down at least 200psi more than him. He showed her his compass, signaled that he'd lead, she follow, then he moved away to the right and kicked, gliding through the water. With his flashlight up front, he reminded her of a comet hurtling in space. He even left a short light trace behind him in the darkness.

In under a minute, they reached a large white fishing boat, its hull partially submerged in the silt. The boat sat upright in pristine condition like it waited for something.

Thad put the palm of his hand in front of her face,

signaling her to *be still*, then dived head first toward the bottom. He waved his glove over it, and a vortex of particles rose. Thad looked up at her and she signaled *okay*. *Don't stir it up, I get it*. She'd have to keep an eye on the position of her fins.

A wave of calm moved through her after reaching the site, but Kirsten noticed she'd had to work harder and suck the air from the regulator. *Must be the cold combined with the depth. Don't skip breathe.*

They swam around the boat and shined their lights down inside. Thad showed her where he and Claude had written their names and date on the stern. She swam around to check out the bow. A dark blur moved past a port window. She maneuvered up, saw Thad's light near the stern, then dropped back down. He'd come over soon enough.

The glass had been removed from all the windows, so she put her flashlight inside and looked around. An open maw with jagged teeth came at her mask. She pushed away and watched a massive pike swim out of the hole. Kirsten put a hand over her chest, sucked in a deep breath and laughed to herself. She kicked up again and Thad's light had disappeared.

Kirsten scissor-kicked twice and hovered over the boat, shining the beam of her flashlight in all directions as she made her way toward the stern. Girlfriend or not, Thad had always been a strict professional when it came to being a dive master, and with this as her first ice dive, she knew he'd never joke around—not him. Her heart rate tried to increase in the cold.

Darkness closed in around the wreck, along with the stronger sense of something inside it watching her.

Any minute now, she expected to see Thad's light coming toward her. Time passed, and she couldn't remember taking a breath during the waiting span, so she sucked one in, and grabbed her pressure gauge, which read 1000psi. They'd have to head back soon.

She circled the boat three more times, reminding herself to breathe when she reached the bow, then stern. After the first pass with no sign of Thad, Kirsten felt her heart pounding underneath all the layers. The beats thumped in her ears and overpowered the underwater crunches and cracks. She knew better than to panic, but felt it coming on. *He's a dive master, knows what he's doing . . . maybe he's testing me. But why?*

At the bow on the third round, the air gauge read 800psi. She'd have to head back alone. Kirsten reached for the dive computer and held it under the beam of her flashlight. Nothing appeared on the screen. With stiff, icy fingers, she pushed the buttons— all of them, shook it, tapped the glass. The screen remained green-gray. The dive watch around her wrist also had an empty face. No compass. The threatening blackness around her moved closer.

Kirsten closed her eyes and drew a long, deep breath. *Stay calm. Remember safety rules.*

Her eyelids slid open. She grabbed her second regulator, and pressed the purge button, shining her beam of light on the bubbles. She followed them up. Escaping air tingled the nerves in her pores, and the bubble layer shifted across her chest. Kirsten kept a steady position and made a slow ascent. At 50 feet, she stopped and counted for at least 120 seconds knowing she had to decompress but not for exactly how long.

When the burbling slowed, her air gauge read 500psi. Kirsten sucked in another breath, kicked up, and collided into something. She looked up and screamed through her regulator. Bubbles swarmed her vision.

The space in front of her cleared, and Thad's blue, distorted face came into focus. His eyes wide open, mouth agape, a look of horror frozen upon his face. *What happened? Why isn't your regulator in?*

Kirsten fumbled over his BC and grabbed his gauge, 0psi. That can't be! She got hers. Just under 400psi, almost in the red zone. Darkness moved everywhere below, currents swirled around her calves. Time to go, but where? Thad's watch had a compass. It took all her concentration and too much air to undo the strap without dropping it. She checked her position and aligned herself toward the west. The needle spun 90 degrees, and she followed, continuing to face the west the compass showed. It rotated another 90 degrees to its original position.

Go now! Before it changes again.

She pushed Thad's body to the side and watched his blanched face recede into shadow.

The flashlight went out, and she closed her eyes to avoid seeing whatever Thad had seen. *What did he see?* Something horrible enough to disfigure his face, unhinging his jaw in an open scream . . . his face . . . so awful! In the absence of light, his gaping mouth and bulging eyes came at her through the darkness.

Stay calm. Close your eyes. She couldn't remember the last time she'd taken a breath. When Kirsten exhaled, she put her hand just over the back of her regulator and hoped she'd feel the bubbles. She did. And followed them up a little ways then stopped again and counted for another 120 seconds to avoid the bends. Movement brushed across her legs. *It's the nitrogen, the bubbles.* A tug on her fin, and she descended several inches. *No! Not down there!* Kirsten scissor-kicked as hard as she could and didn't stop.

Her head rammed a solid surface. An exhale of relief came when she saw the glowing gray ice sheet above her. She unsheathed the dive knife from its sleeve and thrust the blade up into the frozen crust. The tip went in and not much else. Even if all the steel penetrated the layer up to the hilt it wouldn't get through enough of the thickness to do anything. *Damn.*

Kirsten watched bubbles coalesce and dart across the ice toward a large crack. Scaling the underside, she followed their movement, then worked the blade into a branch of the fracture and wiggled it around, yielding no result. She placed both hands up against the ice and pushed then punched with all she had, turning her head to look down into the darkness for what exactly, Kirsten didn't quite know. Her gauge read 200psi, and with no memory of the last time she'd taken a breath, she did, then exhaled and watched the bubbles move up into the crack. Tears trickled down and mixed with the water that had already filled up a third of her mask. No sense purging it, the water felt warm on her face.

The only way out meant getting back to the hole, a near implausible task. Remembering Thad had led them west to the wreck, she looked at his compass and headed east using her gloved hands to grip then launch her body from icy projections, propelling along the undersurface of the frozen lake. Only several feet of ice lie between her and the light of day, freedom, air. Air

. . . Kirsten promised herself she wouldn't check the gauge again.

A shred of hope returned. She moved fast, gliding like a superhero, grab and push off, grab and push off, *quick light steps, quick light steps.* Her knees would occasionally bump the underside, or the fins would scrape now and then. The louder sounds of crunching and cracking occupied her thoughts. Anything to distract from the infinite black abyss just behind her, waiting to swallow her. Kirsten tried not to think of letting go and falling back. Muscles in her arms started to ache, along with her head and chest. She took in another breath. It tasted oily and felt thin. *Last bit from the tank probably, stay calm. You've got to be close.*

Kirsten gripped and glided faster, frenetically sucking the regulator, getting nothing. Her face stung, eyes bulged, then pain exploded through the top of her head.

She'd run into the edge of the fishing hole. Kirsten breached the surface and pulled the regulator from her mouth, gasping for air. When the stars cleared and through the lake water and condensation built up in her mask she saw the dolls. They stood around the opening and moved forward. Kirsten's eyes shifted back and forth between them, and they weren't dolls but something else. More real. She shook her head. *No!* It's lack of oxygen to the brain, not living toys. Kirsten blinked, gasped for more air. Her lungs burned and ached.

The pulley system stood tall apart from the dolls. *They'll be back on the shelf when I've got enough oxygen to my brain.* Kirsten shut her eyes, float-kicked to the pallets, reached for the line, and pulled up. A loud crack sounded. She looked up and saw the entire rigging coming down. One last gulp of air and for a second, the dolls reached out for her.

Kirsten's head squeezed, every part of her tingled and stung as she fell back into the blackness and let it swallow her. Too much time passed while the silt cloud she'd created when her body hit the bottom settled. Her flashlight must have fallen behind her and worked again, because she could see. Pinned, Kirsten only moved her eyes under the water in the mask. Her arms and hands drifted up at her sides but felt disembodied. Darkness closed in.

In the billows of settling silt, the dolls floated toward her. No, no, not living toys . . . .

Real little girls! All of them, dead.

Maybe Thad saw them too, and they scared him to death. Absolute horror was the look that had contorted and then froze onto his face.

Through the darkness and drifting haze, they moved nearer, their arms out in front of them as if flying. Tiny hands reaching out, they stopped over her. Pale faces with lost stares and white eyes, nothing like the painted expressions on porcelain. Everything else about them looked perfect—preserved—china dolls. Kirsten saw rope lines, maybe chains, tied around an ankle of every girl, the other end secured to a block.

Light shined from above making the children glow like angels. It grew brighter and continued to intensify. They all turned their heads and looked up. Kirsten could see the interior of the shanty through the ice and the gray skies past that.

***

A camper pulled up next to the wooden structure. A man got out of the cab and walked to the opposite end.

The man, Claude, pulled something out of the back and carried it into the shack. He laid it down on the ice then unrolled a small, limp body from the tarp it had been wrapped in. Claude removed a doll from under the little girl's arm then walked over and put it up on the shelf.

The God of Rain

TIM LEBBON

Francis was building a god in her local forest. She went there regularly after Gordon died, gathering materials, scouring the ground for sticks and leaves, roots and nuts, fruits and grass that she could combine into the thing she so wished to find. She was using a sapling as the backbone. Around this she had weaved the skeleton of her creation out of willow for the ribs and heavier, bark-stripped twigs for the limbs. Leaves were rolled together and stuffed within, held in the new cage of sticks to form the insides.

The head was an old rook's nest which Francis had fetched down from a tree. It had taken her a whole morning to climb, extract the nest from its twisted bindings and transfer it down, relatively whole and undamaged. She filled holes with moss, and stuffed its insides with a bracken brain.

But it was nowhere near complete. It stood in the forest, her statue, her creation, and every time she left she would imagine its mocking laughter rustling through the trees. She could almost hear its dry chuckle following her until she was out of the shadows and into the fading light of dusk once more.

She came to fear that it would never be complete. That her god would always be merely a collection of forest waste, and that one day it would be discovered and taken down by wandering teenagers, or those offended by its existence.

But then nature started to give it flesh.

***

She spoke to Gordon a lot more now that he was dead.

"Started off fine this morning," she said. "Clouds are coming in now, though. You'd have liked a day like today. 'Good for the roses,' you'd have said. Silly sod." She looked at him sitting in his familiar chair, his outline visible in dust motes drifting in the fading sunlight that slanted through the french doors. She thought she saw a smile on his face, but it could have been a shadow. She smiled back but nothing changed.

Francis sighed. Gordon had passed away seven weeks ago, and every morning she rose and bade him good morning, dressed and then left their bedroom. She never returned there until bed time, but she did enjoy speaking to him throughout the rest of the house. Sometimes she saw him there, sometimes not. Her favourite time—and the place where she most commonly saw her dead husband's ghost—was when she sat here drinking tea and looking out at their back garden. It would always be *their* garden, not hers alone. They had made it together, crafting it from the blank it had been when they moved in. It now contained a water feature, a dozen rose beds, beautiful borders, several trees and a stone bench that Francis had built on her own. Gordon had been delighted with that, but he had also scolded her for picking up the heavy slate slab that formed its seat on her own. 'I would have helped you,' he had said. 'We could have made it together'. Now that was the part of their garden she liked the least. One day, perhaps, she would take the bench down and hide it from view.

The trees upset her the most. They had planted them young, and now they had grown thicker trunks, larger branches and their reach increased year by year. They marked the passing of time, not as definitely as death but more insidiously. She hated to think of the trees that way, but sometimes her thoughts were dark.

In the forest she halted time by stripping twigs and using dead leaves in the construction of her god. It was only the sapling that was still alive, but when it was finished she would tap a copper nail into its trunk and kill it. When she finished—when it came to life—it would be frozen in time forever.

"I'm making a god in your own image," she whispered through the steam from her tea. Clouds obscured the sun, and Gordon's faint image faded away for the day.

***

She watched the skies. When it started to rain she shrugged on her raincoat, pulled on her boots and left the house. It was only a five minute walk to the fields across which lay the edge of the forest, and on the way she passed four people coming the other way. They nodded polite greetings and she returned them, but she saw their eyes, and she knew what they thought of her. Mad old woman who lives in the Old Vicarage. When it rains, she goes out into the forest and everyone else comes home. When it's warm, she closes all her windows and everyone else opens theirs. She did not care what they thought, and did not think that Gordon did either. But she would have to be careful.

She was the one doing all the work here.

Francis was so excited. Something was happening! As things moved on she started to view herself a little more objectively, and the woman who had built that thing in the forest was someone she was not too sure about anymore. She recognised her own handiwork— remembered each branch, each tied creeper, every twisted leaf—but she could not recognise where her mind had been back then. So much had changed.

She hurried on, climbing the gate into the forest with the grace of a woman half her age. A dog barked and she paused by the timber bridge across the stream. A young couple emerged from the trees to her left, laughing quietly and holding hands. They fell silent when they saw her, as though they had been sharing secrets, and she returned their restrained smiles.

"Not great weather for a walk in the woods," the man said after he crossed the bridge. The woman dug her elbow in his ribs.

"I quite like being alone in here," Francis said, and the young couple moved off towards the village. Their dog lolloped after them, all wet fur and mud.

Francis crossed the bridge and stood on the other side, eyes closed, face upturned. The rain hit her eyelids, flowing coolly down the back of her neck, and she welcomed it. It was giving life. She sighed and started walking. "I'm alone in here," she whispered to herself, confident in that knowledge. But she was also certain that she would not be alone for long.

She had hidden her sculpture in a small dip at the

heart of the forest. A huge wood ants' nest stood at the gully's lip, writhing and blurring in the rain as a million ants hauled things into their pile of pine needles. Francis knelt down and leaned in close, and a hundred ants reared up ready to fight. She often wondered what she was to them, and whether they saw more than trees and plants in the forest.

When she reached the god she gasped and fell to her knees.

It's filling, but that was not quite accurate. The god was manifesting out of the forest floor up in the form of rainwater. Already six inches deep, the water formed the shape of two bare feet and bony ankles. It was as if she had chosen exactly the right place to build.

She reached out, rain slapping down onto the back of her hand, but she dared not touch the water. If she broke its surface, perhaps it would spill out and filter away into the ground?

Rain splashed in its upper surface, casting ripples that overlapped and broke against the invisible confines of the growing body. The water was still completely clear, and she could see the stick bones, the veined leaf cartilage.

A thrill of fear passed through her. What had she done? She could not claim ownership of this emerging thing, and neither could she allow her ego to assume relevance. She was a grieving widow who had sought to avenge death with a semblance of new life. That the sticks and leaves were taking a shape she could not imagine had little to do with her.

Francis fell onto her rump and leaned back, hands splayed behind her. Her coat ruffled up and water soaked through her trousers, but she did not care. She looked up at the sky, the dark clouds promising a continuance of the downpour, and she started to laugh. "Keep coming!" she said. "Keep coming down!" Perhaps every raindrop that fell was the potential flesh of a god, but only the chosen few could retain that promise.

She sat there for an hour, and watched the shape grow by another couple of inches. It was filling faster than the rain was falling. Sucking up water from the ground, perhaps, like a newly-planted tree.

It was only as the forest began to grow dark that Francis knew she must leave. It was with some regret, but she glanced back several times and promised to return.

And besides, Gordon was waiting for her at home.

***

Francis went to the bathroom, stripped and bathed. She was shivering from the cold and it took her a long time to warm up. After her bath she wrapped up warm and walked around the house, then shielded her eyes against a window, peering out into the back garden and seeing the way raindrops bounced from the slate bench.

At last she went into the bedroom and back to Gordon. Sometimes she thought he'd shifted during the day, but she guessed it was merely tricks of the light. Each second that passed she was seeing him afresh. He lay in his bed, a shadow of what he used to be, and even the smell was not too bad. When he died and she decided to keep him for herself, she was terribly afraid of what that would entail. But in death Gordon had been as kind to her as he had in life.

"Goodnight, dear," she said, snuggling into bed beside him. She was careful not to touch because she did not like his coolness.

In the night she woke up and thought she heard Gordon breathing. But only once.

***

Next morning the sun was blazing, the birds were serenading the start of a fine day and Francis was annoyed. The rain had looked as though it was in for a long time, but the ground was already almost dry when she woke, and the skies were clear of cloud. It was going to be hot and muggy today, and as she prepared breakfast she debated whether she would even go into the forest at all.

She saw Gordon sitting in the garden. He was on the old wooden bench beneath the honeysuckle, a shape of shadow and suggestion that she could discern clearly. She debated taking her breakfast out and sitting beside him to eat, but she thought better of it. Perhaps his ghost was merely enjoying a day's sunshine. He seemed to appear to her like this when it was hot, as though ghosts were like plants and needed sunlight to survive. She was not looking forward to winter at all.

She ate her breakfast in the small dining room, enjoying the crunchy cereal and sliced fruit. She'd had fruit every morning since she and Gordon met, and so had he, right up until he died.

"To the village today," she said as she stood from the table. "Some nice bread and cheese for lunch, fresh tomatoes from the vine in the garden." As she walked into the kitchen she glanced into the living room, and Gordon's shade was in his usual chair. She could see the slope of his forehead and his delicate, piano player's fingers. He never had played the piano. He'd once told her that the potential was keeping him alive.

"Morning Gordon," she said, but the shade did not turn. Occasionally he smiled at her, but never in response to something she said. Now and then his expression became sadder.

She returned to the bedroom to dress. Gordon's body lay in their bed. She tried not to see the state of the sheets. As she left she looked back into the bedroom, glanced into the sitting room door, thought of the forest, and wondered where Gordon really was.

***

"Morning Francis," the shopkeeper said.

"Beryl."

"Lovely morning."

Francis nodded, frowning. Beryl had been her friend for a long time, but things had changed so much over the past few weeks.

"How's Gordon?"

"Do you have any fresh basil?"

Beryl moved from behind the counter and went to the rear of the shop. Francis watched her limping from arthritis and panting heavily by the time she returned with a bunch of basil.

"You're my friend," Beryl said.

Francis nodded. "And some fresh bread? That crusty loaf that Janine makes in the next village?"

Beryl nodded. "Today, yes, you're lucky. I'm worried about you, dear."

Francis smiled what she hoped was her sweetest smile and shook her head. "Nothing to worry about. Gordon's a bit under the weather."

"Jenny and Peter from the Old Mill said they saw you in the woods yesterday, in all that rain."

Francis stared at Beryl, not sure how to react or what to say. She tried not to think of the god growing around what she had made, but it was difficult, and she feared she gave it away with her eyes.

"You sure you're okay, Francis?" Beryl almost seemed ready to cry, her voice filled with hopeless desperation. Francis felt sorry for her.

She smiled. Nodded. "And some of that lovely Camembert?"

***

She wanted to have lunch before going out into the forest, but she was worried about evaporation. Gordon was in bed and nowhere to be seen, so she put her food away, locked the door and started walking.

It was more unsettling this time, because so many people had decided that the forest was a good place to be. Perhaps it was the weekend—there were several families with young children, and dogs scampering through the undergrowth. A few acknowledged Francis and she returned their smiles. But when a young woman said something to her she turned the other way and started walking. *I'll give it away*, she thought. *I'll try to say yes, what a lovely day, but instead I'll tell them there's a god growing around the body I made. And if I tell them about the god I'll tell them about Gordon, because . . .*

Because? She paused beside a fallen oak, listening to rude whispers as the woman and her family walked away from her.

Because . . . they were one and the same?

Shaken, she moved on. She waited until she was

sure no one was watching before she left the beaten track and started forcing her way through the ferns. She went a different way every time, keen not to leave too much of a path to where it was happening. And as with every time she came here on a day like today, she started to fear that it had vanished.

The ferns parted around her, and as she passed into the section of the forest dominated by pines, fine spider webs broke across her face.

She found the dip in the ground, skirted around the ants' nest and looked down. It was still there. She sighed in relief, then saw how much more complete it was and caught her breath again.

The invisible mould of the god was full to the hips. The clear water seemed to have its own currents, swirling and drifting across the flat surface and down through the contours of buttocks, thighs, knees and feet. Francis walked around the gully's slope until she saw the front of the shape, confirming that it was male. It seemed like a perfect sculpture. Perhaps her hands had twisted the twigs just so, her fingers kneading and pressing the leaves to the right consistency.

"You're almost here," she said.

The god did not move. Other than the shimmer of water it was motionless as a statue. A goldfinch landed on the sapling where it emerged from the watery stomach, dipping its beak and drinking, leaving only a tiny splash behind. It did not seem changed by the experience. Its head darted around, here, there, and when it set eyes on Francis it paused for a while.

She let out a held breath and the bird flew away.

I could touch it.

But though she sat there for six hours waiting for more rain, she never went any closer.

***

Francis did not really understand the change that was occurring in the forest. There had been no moment when she had thought to herself, *There, the model is finished.* As she left the shadow of trees and started back across the fields towards the village, she could not even recall why she had started building the god in the first place. It seemed that something had driven her, but she did not know what. Gordon lay in his death-bed and drifted through the house, but she never saw him beyond the confines of their garden, never felt him watching her as she worked. If she had sensed him in the forest she would have stopped at once, because her husband had been a religious man. He was not one to pay attention to unholy images.

Unlocking her front door, she glanced up and noted that heavy clouds were forming once again. A woman she knew walked by, looked in Francis's direction and rolled her eyes skyward. Francis smiled.

Inside was warm and stuffy, so she opened some windows and went about preparing lunch. The bread was crusty, the cheese soft and creamy, and with a handful of basil leaves and a glass of red wine she went outside to eat.

Gordon was sitting on the slate bench.

Francis paused on the footpath, unable to breathe. She had never seen him sitting there before. 'We could have made it together,' he had said. Now his echo was a vague shape made of sunbeams, dancing dust and a strengthening breeze. His face was hidden in shadow but Francis moved sideways, never taking her eyes from where his should be.

"I hope you're not sad," she said, and her face started to crumple. She put down her plate and glass before she dropped them, sat heavily onto the wooden bench beneath the honeysuckle and started sobbing. "I hope you're not scared, or upset. I hope you know where you're going." She cried, an old woman sounding like a baby, and as she leaned forward and watched her tears strike the dry pavement they were shadowed by raindrops. They touched the back of her head and neck, and for a moment they felt like a comforting hand.

At last she sat up and wiped her eyes. The sun had slipped behind the clouds, and Gordon was no longer visible.

"I'm here if you want me," Francis whispered. "Always here." She sat in the downpour, watching her bread grow soggy and her wine change colour as her glass overflowed.

***

It rained all night. The downpour was so heavy that it kept her awake, and several times when she adjusted her position in bed she touched Gordon, his cold flesh feeling wet. She thought about that thing in the forest, trying to picture the water level rising. Most of all, she tried to see its face.

Just before dawn she rose and dressed, leaving the light off so that she did not have to see her dead husband's corpse. She bid him good morning when she saw the ambiguous shade of his ghost sitting at their small breakfast table. He was cast there by the shifting shadow of a bamboo outside the kitchen window, its long leaves bombarded by rain, dawn's early light doing its best to push through the clouds.

"Time to go and see," she said. Forgoing her regular early morning cup of tea, she dressed in her raincoat and grabbed Gordon's old walking stick from the back porch. She'd never needed a stick herself, and she was not quite sure why she took it. But its weight felt good in her hand.

As she walked down her driveway and turned left towards the forest, she saw curtains twitching along the street. She ignored them and went on, tapping her way gently along the road. Water flowed through gutters and gurgled down drains, carrying leaves that should not have fallen for another ten weeks. She pulled up her hood. It muffled the noise around her and amplified her breathing. She realised she had not said goodbye to Gordon and almost turned around, but she was close to the path to the forest now, and could even see its smudge through the heavy rain.

The ground was boggy and muddy, but she did not mind. She wore boots, and she was so used to the path that she knew where the more solid parts would be. In the forest the ground was not so bad, sheltered as it was by the tree canopy, drained by the dozens of small streams that veined the woods. She crossed the footbridge and plunged into the undergrowth. She no longer needed to think about where she was going, because her god was drawing her in.

When she reached the gully at the centre of the forest, she found it hard to breathe. She was terrified at what she was about to see, and even more afraid that she would see nothing at all.

The shape was there, whole now, a statue made of

water from head to foot. The skeleton of branches, twigs and sapling fit it perfectly. It was motionless, other than a dozen raindrops splashing its surface each second.

Francis slipped and slid down into the gully, never taking her eyes from the thing she and the rain had made. She crawled around so that she could see its front, waiting for it to turn its head, expecting at any second to be fixed by its gaze and changed. And when she at last saw its face she let out a cry of grief, because no one can ever know their god.

***

She did not recall going to sleep or fainting. When she opened her eyes again the rain had stopped, the morning sun was blazing down and the water god had disappeared. The sapling that had been its spine was sheared off neatly at the ground, the break smooth and clean. There were no footprints in the mud, no trail of bent, snapped and tied sticks, nothing at all to show where it had gone.

The ground around where it had stood was totally dry, a precursor to the long, dry spell to come.

Francis made her way out of the woods, and she was met in the field between forest and village by her old friend Beryl. The woman was worried and upset, and Francis let herself be helped back home. "You'll catch your death," Beryl kept saying, and Francis wept for the vanished rains.

She told Beryl to stay in the back garden, went inside and made them both a cup of tea. She breezed quickly through the house, checking every room except the bedroom, and she could not find Gordon anywhere. His chair in the sitting room was empty, the impression of his body long gone.

Weeping silently, she took the two steaming cups into the garden.

Beryl was sitting on the slate bench. Francis paused for a while, then sat next to her friend. She looked around the garden at everything she and Gordon had planted and tended, and the thought of taking the bench apart seemed ridiculous. It would be like deconstructing that other thing she had made.

"What's that terrible smell?" Beryl said.

Francis ignored her. She took a sip of scalding tea. "I think I'll change the garden," she said. "Get rid of everything apart from this bench. Start again from the ground up." She sighed, closed her eyes and welcomed the sun on her face.

A Grand Perversion

BEN EADS

Over the backfire of Milton's truck, Lee heard a scream echo through the empty street. It punched him in the gut, his heart pounding like the pistons knocking under the truck's hood. The sound of a friend, a fellow Marine, in agony.

Speeding toward the barber shop, Lee leaned his head out the passenger side window. The memories were so fresh, the November night smelled like the Iraqi desert: agony, grit and despair.

Gears grinding, Milton yanked the stick shift down as Lee's hand crept to where his engagement ring had been before Iraq. Before he came back home.

Where everybody thinks I'm a fuckin' hero. If they only knew . . .

"You all right, Lee?" Milton asked, barely audible over the motor. "Your hands are shakin' again."

"Yeah . . . just exhausted, that's all. Can't sleep."

Keep lying to yourself.

"Peggy's been askin' about you. Don't mind her stayin' at my place until you . . . well, until you—"

"I don't want to talk about it now."

Milton sighed. "Fine by me. But, you ain't been the same since ya came back home. I ain't afraid to say it."

"And I'm not afraid to knock your damn teeth down your throat if we don't change the subject. Are we clear?"

"Yes, sir," Milton said, taking a sip of liquid courage from his flask. "Gary's hollering something fierce. It's serious, Lee, that's why he asked for you. Ever since he lost his daughter in that haymaker . . . and, damn, tried to save her and lost his arm, too."

"Just hope it's not those phantom pains from said arm."

Remember when you found Peter's leg for him back in Iraq? You could have saved him . . .

Lee could feel Milton's stare, and prayed he wouldn't ask . . .

"What if it is?"

"Eyes on the road!"

"Sorry," Milton said, swerving back into his lane.

They pulled over in front of the barber shop and Milton cut the engine. Another wail bounced like a bullet between Lee's ears. They got out, taking in the cold air. Lee pulled out his chill-pills the VA gave him for P.T.S.D from his pocket and dry swallowed a few.

"How long has he been like this?" Lee said, joining Milton by the front door. Through the glass, he watched as the sheriff and a handful of townsfolk restrained Gary in the barber's chair.

"I wouldn't come a' callin' this late if it weren't important. Look at him!"

"They just lost their daughter. Show some respect. He's a Marine, too."

"I'm just concerned is all. Didn't mean anythin' by it."

Lee's fingers massaged his dog tags. "Well, hell, let's see what we can do."

What you can do? Look at your track-record, bud!

Overworked men studied them as they entered. A glimmer of hope showed in Sheriff Gus' eyes as he acknowledged Lee.

"Let go!" Gary said. "Get yer hands off me!"

Sheriff Gus wiped the sweat from his brow. "Caught him stealin' gas from Grady's pumps. Keeps screamin' about having to burn his crops on account of something getting to them after they drained the lake by his house. None of this is makin' sense."

Lee pinched the wrinkled flesh between his eyes and squinted. "It's probably the phantom pains again."

"Nah. He's as full as a tick, 'bout to burst. Smell it on his breath. I'd lock him up, but after all he's been through, I can't hardly blame him."

Ignoring the sheriff, Lee moved closer to where Gary sat. He could smell the booze and sweat. Gary sat, his eyes shut against a pain Lee knew all too well.

"Gary? What's wrong?"

His sunken chest rose and fell in sharp hitches. Teeth ground away like furniture against a hardwood floor. "Ya'll wastin' ya' time here!"

"You have to tell me what's wrong. Is it the phantom pains again?" Lee said, studying the nub where Gary's arm used to be.

"God, yes!" he said, and spat on the floor. "But it's my crops that matter! We've lost everythin'. I told the fuckin' *E.P.A.* what my daddy told me," he chuckled, "but they didn't listen. Drained the damned lake anyway. And those things . . . *old* things . . . they came out."

He grabbed Lee's shirt, pulling him so close he could smell Gary's rotten gums.

"Let go of me, Gary. Don't make me—"

Gary let go of his shirt. "I'm sorry, but not as sorry as ya'll gonna be. My daddy was right. What come out—it's changing things. Everywhere! And if you don't let me go, we ain't got no chance. Ya' hear me?"

"I need you to breathe for me. Can you do that?" Lee placed his hands on Gary's shoulders.

"It doesn't matter, anyhow. We're already dead." Gary laughed and relaxed back into the barber's chair. "Hoss, we're all dead. And not just us. Bet on that one. Yes, sir!"

Lee approached the sheriff. "Did he take his meds today, Sheriff? The docs at the VA have him on them for a *damn* good reason."

The sheriff cleared his throat. Long, dirty nails scratched stubble on his chin. It reminded Lee of sandpaper. "Not my turn to watch him this week."

"Did you serve your country, Sheriff? Gary did. He's a Marine. A Marine! Is this how you're gonna treat him? Huh?"

Heads bowed, the small crowd parted like the Red Sea, reinforcing those that had Gary restrained.

Lee watched the sheriff shrink. Fingernails drew crescent moons on his palms.

Shrink you pudgy little fuck.

"You're right, Lee. I'm sorry as hell. I'm being a Grade A asshole. My apologies. So, what're we gonna do?"

Lee collected his thoughts. "It's either a fever, or it's alcohol poisoning. His skin's yellow and his eyes look like every capillary burst. Or . . . "

Just like Peter. Back in Iraq . . .

Gary slammed his fist on the armrest of the chair. Lee turned and when he saw that switchblade smile, a wince ran up his cheek toward his eye. "Here comes the fuckin' hero to save the fuckin' day!"

Lee backed away and turned to go outside, pulling the sheriff and Milton with him. "Look, we'll drive out and ask Darlene if he's taken his meds. If he hasn't, it's probably his damn arm again. What happened to it after the accident? Where'd he bury it?"

"The *hell* kind a' question is that? I may be the sheriff, but I don't have a crystal ball."

Milton bounced from one foot to the next. Lee thought he looked like a kid about to open his Christmas presents. "I know where! It's next to his daughter in the family cemetery behind the house."

"Good," Lee said.

"What's good?" Sheriff Gus said.

"On patrol back in Iraq, a boy, Peter was his name, stepped on an IED. Damn thing blew his leg off, and he's lucky that's all it did. I went to see him in the trauma center, before they sent him home. And you know what?"

You know what? You could have prevented it. How many more people will you lose before you realize . . .

Both stared at him, the look of men attempting to solve the world's hardest math problem.

"Lee?" The Sheriff said, and then snapped his fingers. "You okay?"

Take deep breaths. Just like the doctors said, filter the static in your head. Filter it.

"Sorry. Anyway, I asked him 'You going to be

okay?' and he says to me, 'I'll be fine if someone would scratch it. It's driving me nuts.'"

"What're you sayin'?" Milton removed his hat and rubbed his balding head with stubby little fingers.

"The doctor that amputated it said it was 'phantom pains.'"

"You shittin' me?" Sheriff Gus said.

"May God strike me down if I'm lying. Something to do with his nerve endings remembering. Anyhow, doc said he'd get over it after a couple a months. But the damnedest thing? Said it was the only way to shut Peter up was to rub it every now and then."

Tell 'em what it smelled like!

"You gonna go dig it up and do what? Scratch it?" Milton said.

"Look, I'm just covering all bases. My money's on him missing his meds. If he has taken them, well, we're gonna go find it and scratch it . . . with a rake or something. This time, we'll seal it up good so the ants and bugs can't get to it, like that doc wound up having to do. We'll look after him until he sobers up, too."

Lee pulled a cigarette from his pack and struck a match to it. "Well, you got a better plan, Sheriff?"

Sheriff Gus looked over his shoulder at the chaos inside, considering it. "Go with him, Milton."

"You serious?"

"Get! And don't come back 'til this is handled. You know what his family's been through. Go help the man!"

Lee got behind the wheel of Milton's truck. He watched Milton take one last glance at the mess inside the barber shop. He hopped in, and they pulled out of the parking lot, headed for Gary's farm.

Lee adjusted the rearview mirror and saw Gary run out of the barber shop, the sheriff close behind. "Dammit all."

"What?"

Lee sighed. "Gary's out the door. Sheriff's chasing him."

He floored the gas pedal.

"Just call her, Lee. She waited so long for you to come back home. She deserves it. We've been as thick as molasses pie since element'ry school. If you need someone to talk to, well, now's as good a time as any."

Lee balled his right hand into a fist. Milton shut up.

***

They sat in the truck staring at Gary's farmhouse. Fog drifted and caressed the somber house. Tall grass shivered in the moonlight, rattling against the hollow shells of rusted trucks perched on cinder blocks.

"You got a flashlight?" Lee said.

"Nah."

They got out and Milton grabbed the lantern from the bed of his truck.

"Got a match?" Lee said.

Milton lit the lantern.

"All right then. Let's get this over with," Lee said as they headed for the house. "Wait. We should let Darlene know we're here. I don't wanna get shot tonight."

"Fine, fine."

"Darlene! It's me, Lee."

Lee watched the windows for any sign of movement.

"I got Milton here with me."

Not even a light came on. The darkness inside made him squirm.

"We're here to *help*." A headache bore into his brain like a greedy termite. Lee massaged his temples and motioned for them to move.

Milton held the lantern with a shaky hand, the glowing hue a sporadic pendulum cutting black and orange across the grass. "What?"

"Give me the damn thing." Lee said, and jerked it from him to lead the way. "Let's find the arm."

"Wait!" Milton stopped and sniffed the air.

Lee turned to him and laughed at the expression on his face. "What now?"

"You don't smell that?"

"It's just the lake. It always—"

"Nah, it's worse. Jesus H! I think I'm gonna be sick."

"Shh! Did you hear that?"

Remember the funeral? It took you, Milton and the Sheriff to pry Darlene's arms from her daughter's tombstone. What if she's waiting for you?

"I heard somethin'," Milton said.

"Come on. Just be ready."

They cursed their way over brambles, edging closer to the graves. Tripping over the vines, the jagged spikes of their hungry thorns ripped through Lee's jeans, seeking sustenance.

From somewhere close, Lee could have sworn he heard someone sobbing. A child's sobbing.

Orange light brought the tombstones into view. Lee approached them as if they were ticking time bombs.

He brought the lantern to the last one. "There's his daughter's stone. My God. Elizabeth Harris. 2006-2015. He only got to see her one day, you know?"

"How's that?"

Lee pointed the lantern at Milton. His face was a roadmap of wrinkles and lines. "We signed up at the same time, same place. The day he saw her was the day he came home. The day the haymaker took her. He lost his arm trying to save her."

Tell him what you lost playing hero!

"My God . . . "

Lee stepped on something soft, his foot sinking. "Over here. Look. Ground is freshly disturbed. Only patch of dirt here like it."

Lee stabbed the earth with the blade of the shovel and began to dig, tossing the dirt off to the side.

After four good shovelfuls, he hunkered down with the lantern and brushed the dirt away, exposing an arm as fresh as the day it was amputated. Not one ant or worm had bothered it, as if it were tainted.

Lee touched the arm and felt the suppleness of the flesh. And for a moment, a faint pulse thumped against his finger like a tiny drum.

"What the hell?" Lee said.

"What's wrong?"

It's all in your head, Hoss. Just hold your wad, Marine.

Lee grabbed the arm and tried to pick it up.

"It's stuck. Damn thing won't even budge. Here, take the lantern."

He slid the tip of the shovel's blade underneath the dead appendage and gently forced it up. Holding the handle for leverage, he crouched down for a better view.

The orange from the lantern began to fade.

"Bring the lantern down. I can't see a damn thing."

Milton lowered the light.

"There. That's better. Now, let's—"

Tendrils grew from the arm, whipping and slithering like hungry snakes, and rooted into the ground. The lifeless hand clenched into a fist. Lee let go.

Lee felt his jaw go slack as he watched it dig its way back into the soft earth, the severed end sticking up toward the sky. Arteries flopped over the edge, hanging like wet noodles. A toad's face pushed its way out from the center of a bone, its eyes blinking in the light, the torn muscle and sinew sticking to its thick, amphibian flesh. Its face began to swell as its mouth opened. Rows of jagged teeth glistened in the moonlight like ivory.

"What in the? Here, let me—" Milton said as he reached down to touch it.

The creature burst from its home and enveloped Milton's head in one bite.

Every person you touch . . .

Milton dropped the lantern.

In the moonlight, Lee's eyes couldn't steal away from his lifelong friend as he struggled, hands trying to pry off something he couldn't make out. The toad gobbled the head and bit down on Milton's shoulders. A long, wet crunch filled his ears.

I'm drowning . . .

A shotgun boomed.

Entrails and fluids splattered the ground. The sloppy splat reminding him of rotten pumpkins hitting pavement. Milton's body fell.

Darlene motioned with the shotgun. "Put him out his misery. Damn things are everywhere! But Gary'll be home directly, so I'd sit a spell if I were you. 'Sides,

Elizabeth is comin', too." She pumped the shotgun, loading a fresh shell. "She misses you. Hasn't seen you since—"

SNAFU. Run!

Lee ran, the sound of shotgun fire chasing him. A sharp pang punched through his right arm, spinning him around. He fell to the ground and grabbed his forearm. Blood seeped through his fingers.

Just a flesh wound. Move, Marine. Move!

He surveyed the lay of the land, the obstacles. A tractor rumbled to life as another shotgun blast echoed. Holding his arm, he stood up.

Lee staggered as the ground shook.

He watched as a bright-green, fluorescent chaos exploded from the ground, shooting upward like a geyser, ripping the earth in two.

Lee's hands covered the top of his head as dirt and rocks rained down.

Freed, it towered over the farm. The oil-slick mushroom cap eclipsed the moon. Flailing tendrils swayed about while others wormed their way into its shaft like children's hands playing with and re-arranging the swirling contents like puzzle pieces. Lee could see cars, and trailers spinning inside. He recognized the small house churning around with the rest of the debris.

Not the Wilson's. Their son's only five.

The front door opened and the family fell out. A limb grabbed their little son David around the neck and squeezed. It tore his head off and sculpted it like clay until it became the top of a mail post—a barn and farm machinery spun inside, waiting to be reassembled into other perversions. A tornado of reality's contents; *terraforming.*

In a rhythmic pulse, it churned, growing until it filled the atmosphere above them, scarring the ground with dust storms.

"Isn't she gorgeous?" Darlene pointed up at the nightmare with her shotgun.

Lee saw the same look on her face as those who were shell-shocked after battle: vacant, empty.

"You see my Elizabeth in there? She's holding Mee-Ma's dolly. She's happy now, you hear? She's happy . . . my baby's happy." She began to cry.

Instinct allowed Lee a few backward steps. Tendrils rose from the ground and gouged their way through his ankles, sending him pin-wheeling downward. Flesh separated as they cinched, seeking bone.

Lee went for his pocket knife, but they slithered up his legs and wrapped around his hips. Bloody hands would undo a bond while four others took hold. Slick fingers fought to loosen their hold while a sandpaper wind scraped his face.

Red and blue grew brighter as the police car drove up into the yard—a sharp contrast to the neon-green illuminating everything below.

The rude grinding of exhausted gears grew closer.

Lee saw the driver's door open. Gary pulled himself out and leaned against the door. Under the otherworldly colors, his face was battered and bloody.

"Is that sheriff with you?" Darlene said as the nightmare in the sky continued to grow.

"No, baby, it's just me."

Darlene dropped the shotgun and ran up to him. They embraced.

Lee struggled with his unforgiving bindings. "Get this mess off me!"

Lee tested what leverage he had to break free. They wouldn't budge.

"Don't worry, I didn't hurt the sheriff too bad," Gary said. "Shouldn't have any problems. Made sure of that."

"I've been thinkin'—"

"Baby, we're burnin' it down and that's that."

"Can't we—"

"No! You *know* we can't."

A dust storm gathered beneath Lee, stealing his breath. Blankets of little razors nipped and tore his flesh, his clothes. Stars shot behind bleeding eyelids and then passed. He sucked in a lungful and choked it out, spitting dirt.

You've been here before . . .

Darlene pointed up. "That's your daughter." It began to spin faster, its contents coalescing, and there was Elizabeth, stroking her dolly's hair. "What would it be like if we—"

"We're not havin' this talk again."

Bending closer, Elizabeth danced around, her face came into view and the midnight-black eye sockets froze Lee. It reminded him of the doll he'd seen laying at the bottom of that ditch while on patrol back in Iraq. Cracked porcelain that spider-webbed all over.

And some of them weren't porcelain dolls, were they? Remember the one that was still warm, and how it cried?

"Let her go, baby. Let her be the way she was—"

"How she *was*? Gary, *she* was mangled, torn, trapped in the haymaker. She *was* in that little box we put in the ground where she couldn't breathe, and I couldn't hold her. Now it's all different. Can't ya' see?"

The thing eclipsing the moon and stars ripped her little body apart and put her back together again, in its own way.

"That ain't our daughter, baby."

Darlene grabbed her husband and held him. Gary stroked her sand-filled hair and said, "It's gonna be okay, baby. I love you."

"I love you, too," she managed through sobs, "but I don't know 'bout this. She needs me. She needs her mother!"

Darlene walked toward the growing aberration. "Elizabeth? It's momma, baby. Can you hear me?"

Lee watched as vines sprang from the ground and twisted around Darlene's legs.

"Darlene!" Gary said.

She writhed on the ground, reaching for the shotgun. "I won't let you take my baby!"

"Get this shit off me!" Lee said.

"Fuck it!" Gary said. "We're doin' this! Just hold on, Lee! I got a lot of gas. Shouldn't need much, but just in case. Damn . . . talk about a one-armed-paper-hanger with the crabs."

Gary pulled gasoline can after gasoline can out of the trunk of the car. As he began spilling the acrid contents into the earth, the beast changed direction, as if poisoned, and loosed the top half of a barn from its collection. It crashed to the ground and bounced, spinning above them. Farm tools fell and assaulted them. A lathe nicked Lee's leg, producing a horrendous howl.

"I can't get my knife! Give me something. A goddamn shovel," Lee said. "Anything!"

"Hang tight," Gary said and ran inside the house.

Lee watched Darlene's fingers clutching handfuls of dirt as she dragged herself toward the shotgun.

"Shit!" Lee managed to free his pocket knife and began to saw through those bastards. He tried to stand up, but two more shot up and cinched around his bone. He screamed.

Breathe. Breathing makes the pain go away. If anything, do it for Peggy.

Lee watched Gary come out of the house with matches in hand, but dropped them. He knelt down to pick them up. A series of vines speared his legs like pencils through paper. They held him like a vice. Another God-awful scream filled the night.

Lee cut himself loose and headed for Gary. Every step was full of fire. "Light the fucker! Now!"

From the corner of his eye, he saw Darlene grab the shotgun.

Two vines danced in front of him. He took a deep breath and feinted left, then made for the right. The tips pierced his legs. His vision blurred.

Don't you dare, Marine!

He wanted to just stop. Lie down.

Is this what your brothers, your sisters died for?

He took a breath.

Get that gas!

He cleared his head.

And burn that fucker down! Save them!

Lee grabbed the last can, feeling the vines turn and their spines sever his hamstrings, hollowing them out. Despite the pain, he snatched a gas can and threw it onto the dead sage brushes and searched for the matches.

The haymaker was so close Lee could smell its exhaust. Once again, the vines held him in place.

The storm of something older than the stars ebbed closer, its massive top full of body parts and machinery that it was molding into one, swaying to and fro in anticipation of the infinite meal.

It's eaten the Morrison's house . . .

"Light it!"

We just have to hurt it. But hurt it good.

"I lost the matches. Goddamned wind!" Gary said.

Lee heard a shotgun pump.

"I've got a Zippo." Lee said, and then he saw her. "She's got the shotgun!"

"Sugar," Gary said. "Can't let this spread." Gary brushed a tear from his eye. "Please, baby, it's our only chance. Put the shotgun down, okay?"

Darlene sighed and wiped away her own tears. Lee felt his waterworks turn on, too.

"She misses me too much. I can feel it," she said and pointed the barrel of the shotgun at them. "Ya'll can't stop me or her!"

"Baby, don't!"

Click.

Lee watched the shock on Darlene's face turn into a scowl.

She pumped the shotgun again.

Click. "Shit!"

She dropped it and ran toward the grand perversion that held her daughter.

"Stop!" Lee said, placing his hands on Gary's shoulders. "There's nothing we can do."

"I . . . I . . ."

Lee squeezed his shoulders. "Once a Marine, always a Marine, right?"

"I'm comin' baby!" She said, running. "I'm comin' for—"

They watched as two large, glowing limbs wrapped around her. They pulled her inside the massive, swaying trunk. She floated up to Elizabeth.

"What in the name of—" Gary managed.

"Don't look. Just close your eyes."

Easy for you to say.

Darlene held her arms open for Elizabeth. An umbilical cord burst from her stomach. It wrapped around what was left of Elizabeth's little neck and squeezed until blood shot out of her sockets, turning midnight black into crimson showers. Darlene's body twisted, and Lee could have sworn he heard the spinal cord break. Tiny hands placed an engine block inside Darlene's chest, the pistons thumping and firing to life. Exhaust escaped her mouth as she brought what was her daughter into her arms.

"Lee, stop! I can't watch anymore of this."

"Are you sure you're ready?"

Do it now, or you'll never have the chance. Now!

Gary's chin trembled. He nodded. "I'm ready."

Lee struck the Zippo.

Nothing. The wind had picked up again.

"Goddamnit, work!" Lee struck it, and again, the wind put it out. A wind that followed the whim of the *other*. He waited for another lull, and when it came, he tried the wheel once more.

A tiny flame came to life.

Lee flung the Zippo and it found its target. The cans ignited, flames raced toward the fields. They engulfed the monstrosity.

Lee's hope sank like a cinder block in a lake as he

watched the chaos devour the inferno. Spinning and weaving, the flames appeared in the fat green trunk of the maelstrom. Inside the older, *other* world. Orange tongues licked and spread upward to the cloud-like top and then dissipated.

It's getting closer.

Lee sat, hypnotized until the heat of the flames set in and the whir of the tractor's massive, metallic maw nipped at his flesh. He leaned forward . . .

No.

Giving himself a few more inches . . .

Not like this.

But the vines held him back . . .

You'll never see Peggy again. And she waited so long for you.

Lee felt the flames kiss and fondle his shirt. The haymaker's blades so very close.

Another lull came. A deafening silence sucked the wind from Lee's lungs.

Gary cleared his throat, choked back tears. "My daddy always said: 'Every species can smell its own extinction.'"

"What do you smell?"

"My home. My memories . . . My daughter . . . *burning.*"

Lee smelled something he hadn't since the desert: Despair. He felt something he hadn't felt since he set a government issued boot on foreign soil—a ravenous hatred others had for the blood of those who dared to step on the heated sand of Iraqi soil. But now this was *its* soil they were stepping on.

Its holy ground.

So this is what it all comes to? I'm so sorry, Peggy.

Lee put his hands together and closed his eyes. "The Lord is my shepherd; I shall not want . . . "

Whirling blades began to sink into Lee's back.

Gary reached out for him. Lee took his hand and squeezed.

Gary joined Lee. "He makes me lie down in green pastures—"

Bone Wary

JAN EDWARDS

Henry dabbed his finger tip into the dust trickling from the out-chute's lip and touched it delicately to his tongue. It had reached that ethereal softness of good velvet, yet still retained a certain gritty 'afterness.' It would make a pouring slip like nobody else knew how to make.

It is so close to perfection.

He glanced up into the gallery, where the hoppers were sited, and noted that some of the hoist ropes needed replacing. Restoring the mill had been a snip back when the Arts had money to burn. Henry Plant had created a Craft Worker's Cooperative with that one purpose in mind. Now that most of those arts foundations no longer existed, the cooperative's membership could rest in peace— and most of them had already done so.

A screech and the echo of running feet dragged him back to the now, and he swore, wiped his dusty hand on his apron and bellowed, "Don't run, child. If you fall in there you'll be turning up in one of my pots. Would you like that?"

Jan Edwards

Two faces appeared over the gallery rail, so challenging and so very insolent. Children had no respect for their elders these days, clambering over and into everything, everywhere. He opened his mouth to yell again. This time Miss Callam beat him to it.

The perfect Miss Callam.

She thought she was so good, merely because she'd won some teacher of the year thing, she'd got the council to bully him into this last event. Well, bribe him if he was honest. He was not stupid enough to turn away a treble fee. Right now he had to wonder if turning it down would have been so stupid after all.

Miss Callam had been a pain from the moment she'd stepped off the coach. Wanting this and wanting that. She didn't get what she wanted here. He chuckled quietly. It had done his heart good to be able to turn down most of her requests. The only thing he had wondered on seeing the perfect Miss Callam, after acknowledging she was passably pretty, was how that slim brunette, teetering on her heeled pumps that were so ridiculously impractical for a school trip—how anyone so ridiculously young—could be a Head Teacher.

He heard those shoes now, tip-tipping along the gangway long before he saw their wearer.

Miss Callam strode into view and set both of her bags down in order to fold her arms in the approved confrontational mien. Or, as Henry thought, her disapproving stance. She glared down at Henry with her chin tilted aggressively. It should have been a perfect 'looking down her nose' pose, except that from Henry's angle her sharp nose apparently pointed toward the rafters. He used his handkerchief to wipe away his smile with the layer of dust that coated his lips.

"Is there another problem Mr Plant?" she called to him. "I'm sure the boys meant no harm."

He watched her cautiously from the shadows of his hard hat. She could be a dangerous woman, in his not so humble opinion. So slim and delicate to look at, yet hard as iron; just like the bone china that he so loved. Pity she was such a strident sort. Though maybe that was a good thing in a school teacher, he thought. In his day, women teachers had all been harridans, or they'd not have lasted five minutes. He hid a smirk. Maybe these lads weren't so bad. He'd have been raising Cain with the best of them at their age. He still was in his own way.

"Keep those youngsters under control," he muttered. "One of 'em trips into that hopper and no emergency stop's going to keep 'em from being minced meat."

She flinched, just for a moment. "Please. Mr Plant. You will frighten them."

Deep frown lines creased her brows and wrinkled the corners of her mouth and eyes. Older than she first looks, Henry thought as she stepped between him and her charges. He smiled grimly. Did she think he could leap fifteen feet at a single bound? "They need frightening. Teach them to do what they're told."

"Well, we are just leaving, Mr Plant. Earlier than scheduled of course, as you were too busy to show us round."

She could not have been less sincere if she had tried, but Henry didn't care much. If anything he relished her reluctance to pander to niceties. "Not my problem. The City Council says I wasn't to. They said I needed some bloody certificate just to speak to kids. Meh. Why would I want to? They're the reason I'm shutting down school visits. I've no time for all that. Why put myself out? No bloody respect!"

"Something to be earned," she snapped.

"The money? Or the respect?" When he laughed the short sound was swallowed by wood beams, deadened in their sackcloth and dust. He was the first to admit that he was not sociable. Never had been. He liked himself that way. "I don't need either from the city elders," he added. "I just like being left alone."

"And you will be, Mr Plant. I can't envisage any other option open to you." She slipped her shoulder bag across her chest and signalled her open-mouthed pupils toward the stair furthest away from the hoppers and from Henry.

Henry could not help noticing how the strap divided and enhanced her meagre bosoms. He watched her totter along the gangway and clattered down the wood steps, hustling the boys toward the exit, and he noted how her retreating buttocks jiggled all the better for high dudgeon. He grinned. "Well. I might be old but I'm not bloody dead." He rubbed a dusty finger under his nose and sniffed loudly.

As she reached the doors she paused, glowering at him over that finely formed shoulder. "We shall be out of your way before 3 o'clock," she called to him. "Goodbye, Mr Plant."

He bowed low, sweeping off his hard hat and clasping it to his chest in a mocking civility. When he looked up she and her irksome charges were out of sight.

"Good bone structure," he told himself. "Fully formed, and not a sign of osteoarthritis." He sighed lightly.

She really is close to perfection.

Another half hour and both school bus and she would be gone. He regretted that much from today's madness.

She is so very close to perfection.

Accommodating school trips had always been the downside of gaining grants, but though that income had ended it would not be missed. When it meant having his yard free of screeching kids he'd happily do without grants and bursaries and all the other hand-outs he'd skimmed over these past years.

Henry swung himself up the rough-hewn stairs to check on the hoppers. He'd had brats hurling all manner of things into the mix resulting in whole bags of meal being discarded.

Henry hated waste.

Yet another ghastly child tripped along the gallery and leaned over the barrier rail to peer into the mill's teeth; despite all the warning signs. The temptation to boot the boy in his designer-jeaned rear end was considerable. Henry's fists clenched inside his pockets as he looked away and resisted.

After today, he would have virtually no visitors to fret about. Although his working museum was a short distance from the centre of Stoke-on-Trent, he didn't advertise. The few souls who did discover the mill usually arrived via the canal, and then mostly by accident. This was a quiet spot, some might even say desolate, but he liked it. Once there had been a lot of local mills like this one churning out the finest grade bone meal for Josiah Spode's finest grade bone china.

A perfect match.

"There was a man who knew all about perfection," he muttered. "And I'll bet he wasn't bothered about the neighbours."

In the early years Henry had dealt with carcasses as his predecessors had for centuries. Meat for pet food and gelatine steamed from the bones for the catering industry. But even if greedy feed manufacturers and their mad cows hadn't put a stop to that, the smell of rotten flesh, and subsequent burning had enraged incomers on housing estates across the valley. They had gathered a petition, and the local council insisted he use the less malodorous and, as it turned out, far more efficient full-body incinerator to clean off the flesh and calcinate the bones.

He still required the services of the mill however.

In TV shows the criminal forensic scientists may give the impression that bone is destroyed by fire. The truth is every crematorium pulls the remains of our deceased through a bone crusher because even their furnaces are not hot enough to reduce a body to dust. That was where the mill still had its uses. It pulverised bone to this silky powder just begging to be mixed with the kaolin and crushed stone and then churned into the butter-smooth slip essential to manufacture his precious ceramics.

Those hand crafted ceramics that emerged from Henry's studio and were sought by collectors the world over. He no longer needed to promote himself, now taking commissions for whatever artefacts the collectors wished to possess. Occasionally he would make homage, but never once had Henry manufactured copies or fakes. Each piece of finest bone china differed from any another—a true Henry Plant original. A different glaze; a different colour; an added handle or lid; a scattering of decoupage, each process applied with delicacy and precision.

Henry Plant Ceramics are close to pure perfection.

Henry wanted to be there in his studio now, plying his trade in the most perfect way he knew, except for having this damned trip to oversee.

He sidled to the window and rubbed a hole in the dust to peer down into the yard. Not long now. The teachers were rounding up the last of their charges and herding them toward the coach that waited in the gloom of a mid-winter's afternoon to carry of its noxious cargo of infants and their jaded handlers. His only regret in their going was that he could have used some of those fine straight limbs. He shook the thought away. That was foolish. One could not use the paying visitors for his craft. Apart from anything else they would be too easily missed.

His foot nudged something close to the barrier rail. A large, saggy bag, made from the palest, softest, leather. Henry bent to retrieve it. He glanced through the window and watched the school party clattering excitedly across his courtyard, their shrill chatter penetrating even here within his solid stone walls.

And then they were gone.

Perfect.

"End of an era," he muttered. Henry took the side stairs down to the ground floor, locked the mill-house doors carefully and trotted almost happily to his studio.

He paused in the threshold to revel in the quiet of that private space, before checking the contents of the slip churn and throwing a red switch on the wall behind it. It made that pre-start cough, like a maestro preparing to sing, before it roared into ear-numbing life, rattling jars on shelves and tools on racks in its enthusiasm.

Mixing a fresh batch was going to take a while, so he moved on to the next bench and inspected the rough form of a newly cast urn. Straight from the mould the urn was thick and grey with a flange of irregular flaps where slip had oozed and solidified between the mould's halves. He would need to turn it down to the right delicately before its first firing, thinning it to that elegant slenderness where the light could shine through. To a fineness where the fuzzy shadows of his fingers, when he held it, could be observed through the walls. Henry tutted. He would have to make a new mould if that one was leaking so badly. It was wrong to waste so much of the mix.

Waste is disrespectful.

He wandered into the kiln room to check the temperature gauges on the smallest of his three kilns. It had cooled now and that thrill of anticipation ran through him. Here came that moment of truth when all the stages of his care and passion came together.

The door was stiff to open, and he made a note to adjust the hinges. Cool, in relative terms, he still took a step back as the fetid air generated in the firing rolled out to greet him. It was several seconds before he could step forward and inspect his treasures. A triptych of graduated bowls, gleaming both iridescent and white, stood side by side in the grubby, tomb-like, space. These were the apex of his craft.

He stared at them for a longest moment, examining them. There was never a time when he didn't experience a febrile tremor, fearing, he would drop them, getting them from kiln to table. Or worse still that they would crack and shatter the moment he touched their flawless integrity.

Henry grabbed a heat mitt and lifted out the smallest of them, turning slowly so as not to risk it slipping from his grasp, and set it gently on the nearby work top; ears sensitive to the slightest hint of trouble caught tiny tinks and chinks of cooling china. He waited, willing it not to crack, nor even the fine white glaze to crackle.

It seems perfect.

Lowering himself so that his face was level with the work top he peered at it, turning it to examine every angle. His fingers, caressing the pot gently as he twisted it, bulged dark shadows through the translucent walls like fat, rolling clouds wafting across its far side. The bowl possessed the glowing sheen that came only from the finest and slenderest firing. So fine that the leaves and birds painted into the whiteness on the obverse side could be identified almost as clearly as those that he examined just inches from his nose.

It is so very close to perfection.

Lifting the second pot, from the womb he examined it with the same anxious care. Then the third.

His face crumpled in horror.

Right there, under the rim.

Imperfection.

Jan Edwards

Despite all the loving care he could muster a small bubble had erupted through the glaze and died leaving a tiny pockmark in its wake. It could have exploded and shattered its companions. Yet to Henry a blemish was worse. That white perfection spoiled for a few molecules of air, making the pot worthless. Not just to the commissioner of the work but to Henry himself. He had failed his art. A momentary lack of care had brought the process to a screaming halt right at the last instant.

He pondered on whether it could be passed over.

He hated waste—yet he hated imperfection far more.

Sighing regret Henry carefully wrapped the rejected piece in a length of ripped sheeting and, taking a few deep breaths, tapped it sharply with a hammer.

The muffled shape collapsed into itself.

For a moment he wondered if he should discard the whole triptych. No, he decided. Those two were in reprieve whilst he had enough slip from that batch to cast a replacement.

There will be no waste.

Henry gathered up the shattered remains in its cotton shroud and carried it into the walled garden that backed along the edge of the canal. At the far end of this very private space was a swathe of grass and an ornamental pool, artfully floodlit to highlight playful water fed by a natural spring.

With the small spade he had collected en route Henry cut out a small square of turf close to the pool and dug a pit just large enough for his bundle. He placed the broken bowl inside and backfilled before carefully tamping down the turf over the top. He stood up, gazing down at the disturbed path of grass for a moment, before reaching into his pocket for an earthenware marker and pushed it firmly into the centre.

He took a step back onto the path for a better view, at the few ceramic markers. Some quite new, but most already sporting some kind of moss or lichen. Henry didn't make mistakes often.

Imperfection is a waste.

But when imperfection did strike, Henry treated his object d'art with proper respect and a decent burial.

Now that the sun was gone his private garden was shrouded in rapidly cooling shadow, the cold seeped into his aging bones, tweaking at his pitted and worn joints. With a final glance at his latest memorial Henry hurried back to the warmth of his studio.

The phone was ringing as he entered. He frowned at its harsh double ring jangling at him like a reveille. He never liked the phone. On the other hand, of course, it did bring him trade. He just drew the line at hauling the intrusion round with him in mobile form.

"Hello. Henry Plant speaking."

"Henry. How are you my dear?" The slightly high pitched voice paused, but not for long. Abe Venker knew how to turn a penny and silent Transatlantic calls were not in the running. He knew Henry would respect that when he hated waste so much. "I have a request. Matching vases. The client says she wants something in a Loutrophoros style. Can you do it?"

"Athenian wedding vase? Is it for her own nuptials? Or her daughter's?"

"I doubt it's either. She's not exactly in her prime

and no kids to my knowledge. So let's go with a no on that one. Just between you and me, my dear? I don't think she knows what a Loutrophoros is. Just a name she's picked up somewhere and thinks it sounds good. The woman is a complete horror."

"Okay . . . So size? Colour?"

"Maybe around thirty inches tall? Don't ask me what that is in your metric. Colour? She was abominable vague. She said, and I'm quoting here Henry, 'Those women in all the floaty drapes, something between Moorcroft and Mucha. Oh . . . and it had to be bone china."

"Deco? Mucha? She means . . . "

"I know, what can I say? The woman does not have a clue. Just do your magic Henry. Like only you can."

"How can I, with a brief like that? It's monstrous! Making something so complex for a complete inadequate."

"Ah, but the price tag that goes with it is monstrous, darling. Says she'll pay five hundred thou per. And that's pounds, not dollars. You sure you're not interested?"

Henry pulled at his lip, mentally listing the pros and cons. Making any piece of that size was not easy. If it went wrong . . . The waste . . . On the other hand a cool million for two pots. It was tempting. "Do they need to match? I'd prefer to make a complimentary pair."

"I will leave that to you. She's paying for matching Loutrophori that she can brag about, because they have to be made by you. Go to town. It's your pitch."

"All right. I'll take the commission. On my terms. She gets the patterns I choose," Henry said. "And no time limit. No pestering for delivery."

"As it should be. Can't hurry a master craftsman." Abe chuckled quietly. "I'll call her in the morning. If you need any help with details Henry, my sweet old thing, you only have to call."

"No thanks Abe, I should be fine. I'll be in touch when they're ready for viewing." Henry replaced the receiver without waiting for Abe to 'reply,' certain that if the American dealer wanted to say more he'd ring back, which he didn't; mainly because Henry had flicked the telephone cable free of its socket. He did not want any more calls tonight. With a new commission of this size such distractions were not welcome. He didn't want to answer the phone, or doors, didn't want to have anyone disrupt his train of thought.

Henry had eaten an early supper and was piling plates into the sink, mulling over designs for his vases, when the doorbell chimed. He stood stock still in the chaos of his kitchen and waited for a second ring feeling sure he had not imagined it, but hoping he had. He was not expecting anyone, and he didn't get casual callers. Even the Jehovah's Witnesses had a job finding him.

He made his way to the front and peered cautiously through the spy hole.

Miss Callam. Henry stood back, shaking his head abruptly, and then took another peek. Yes, it was her. He could not help smiling. Fate could be so very kind now and then.

Perfection.

He was still smiling when he opened the door.

She seemed shocked at his expression and he supposed he couldn't blame her. His features didn't lend themselves to upward mobility and he knew it gave him more than a hint of rictus.

"Good evening Mr Plant." She smiled back at him. It was a warm and genuine smile, if a little strained. "I really am so sorry to bother you. It's just that I left something in the mill this afternoon. My bag." She paused, shrugging her shoulders. "I am sorry to be such a nuisance. I wouldn't bother you so late, but my iPhone and my house keys are in it and I can't do very much without them. I can't believe I was so stupid to leave it behind. Obviously I do need them both quite urgently, especially my house keys. I was just lucky that I had my car keys in my coat pocket."

She was babbling and a little breathless. *And perfectly charming*, he thought. He tilted his head as he stared straight into her face, his smile descended now into a quiet smirk. "So you need the bag now?" he asked.

"Please." She glanced behind her, nervous and agitated, almost gauche.

Different tune than she had before, he thought. Not so much of the supercilious 'miss teacher-ma'am all mighty' now. She was just a pretty young woman alone in the dark. She kept looking back toward her car on the far side of the locked gates. Henry didn't know if she was afraid of the darkness or gauging her escape route. Probably both, he imagined. "You can ask your friend to come in," he said.

"Friend? Oh. I'm on my own—On my way home, I mean—which is why I need my keys. My husband will be wondering where I am."

Those big eyes stretched wider than ever in her fear. And for a moment he was afraid also; afraid that she would run and his chance would be gone. He glanced down at her hands. No ring. Afraid enough to lie, it seemed. He liked her for that. It made her seem so much more human. So much more fragile. More perfect in her human frailty.

"Your bag's here. I found it up on the gallery," he said. "After you'd all gone." He dipped his head to hide a broader smile. Fate was being more than kind tonight. "Come through. I brought it down from the mill to keep it safe," he added. "Rats."

"Pardon?"

"In the milling-house. Plenty of rats. They love bone meal. Nice leather bag like that one would get shredded in no time. I thought to myself, that young lady's going to be back for that. And I put it somewhere really safe. Come. Come."

He beckoned her to follow him, out through the house into the studio, past the kiln rooms to the last of the line of interconnecting out buildings. "I left it in here," he said. "Most secure room I have, you see." He unlocked the heavy, steel lined doors to the incinerator room and ushered her inside. He picked up a handy length of iron piping as he followed her in.

***

Fresh spring water to mix his slip; never a drop from the tap, when there were so many chemicals to spoil the chemistry. He poured water from his garden pool into the newly scrubbed slip churn, added Kaolin and ground feldspar, and finally the bone meal. It was freshly ground and milled, still warm and slightly moist.

Perfection.

Closing the lid firmly to keep every waft of dust

within, he switched it on. By lunch time he'd have the moulds filled, and by tomorrow it would be in the kiln under first firing.

Whilst he waited he took down his note pad and began doodling some ideas for designs. Something with delicacy and strength to do her justice. He gazed at the rumbling churn and recalled the previous day's encounter. Tall and slender and elegant, she was so perfect. A lady that stylish needed something personal. The client wanted Mucha, but Henry could not resist leaning a little toward Lempicka.

It will be perfect—if such a meld is possible.

He had yet to consider the second Loutrophoros. When he filled commissions for pairs he avoided mirrored images, preferring to design pieces where each complimented rather than aped the other. Somebody would turn up to inspire him he had no doubt, but for now he was fixated on this one piece that would evoke the spirit of its partner when it came into being.

Days of frantic work, casting and fettling, bisque firing and glazing, painting and finally—it had come. The day when her piece would emerge.

The kiln was cold, and had been for six hours and more.

Inside it there could—should—stand a masterpiece.

Perfection is the ceramicist's art—or else unmitigated waste.

Henry stood at the kiln door, one hand resting lightly on the clasp, as he had stood a dozen times in the last hour, the tremor of anticipation had somehow warped into a tremble that set the kiln's padlock jingling in its hasp.

This one mattered. He always cared how his work emerged, but this one mattered half a million pounds' worth of matter.

He flicked the padlock to the floor and breathed out as he leaned back on the catch, hauling the fire proofed door open.

The vase sparked a gleaming shell pink and white, with subtle apricot and mauve highlights picking out the female form swirling across the curved surface.

It was habit that made him whip a cloth from his belt to pick it up by its twin handles though it wasn't needed. The ceramic had cooled to a bare blood heat and cooled faster still as the kiln room's dual air vents pulled tainted fumes into the open.

He turned to place it on the nearest worktop and lowered himself to take in his creation at eye level. He took an eye glass from his top pocket and screwed his brow and cheek into holding shape. Under its round gaze he first scanned every centimetre of the plain, unpainted side for the smallest notion of crazing or popping. If there were the slightest hint of either that iridescent surface would show up to Henry's practiced eye as sure as if it were neon signed.

It is perfection.

He blew out the breath he had not realised he was holding and turned it around to inspect the front, his eye glass almost touching the glass smooth china.

Perfection.

Henry stood slowly and stepped back to examine it with the scrutiny of an art critic's eye. This was destined for the New York scene and there were none more savage in their commentary should it be lacking in any smallest way. He could see no blemish, no fault.

He felt his heart pounding, faltering, labouring under the burden of his goal. He had reached his zenith.

There is no perfecting on this moment.

The female form striding around the front panel was as muted and pastel as the Mucha mirror art that his client had asked for. But his model was also straight backed and assertive. Much of the frippery that Alphonse Mucha had made famous had been strengthened; more akin to the rich drapery that Tamara de Lempicka had made her own with cloth and skin tones which glowed from the surface of the vessel like a freshly airbrushed Vogue cover girl.

The perfect Miss Callam was mutated into classical beauty.

The classical Miss Callam, turned to perfection.

The perfect Miss Callam, in classical pose, one arm languidly outstretched, gazing away into the urn's perfectly curved horizon. Her perfect head poised— ready to turn her perfect gaze on him. And those perfect red lips parting, ready to speak.

Photograph of You

MARK WEST

It started with the nightmare.

Cindy lay in the dull gloom of the bedroom, the curtains partly open to let in fresh air, watching spots of light track across the ceiling as cars drove by. She gently rubbed her belly to soothe whichever one of the twins cocooned in there was moving about. A bad case of acid reflux stopped her from sitting up and reading.

It was 3:10 when Steve began to whimper and she turned her head on her pillow to look at him. He was on his side, his back to her, left arm draped across his thigh. Cindy wanted to pat his back, but since it felt like too much effort, she didn't bother. Everything felt like too much effort now that she was almost seven months pregnant.

He whimpered again and his left arm jerked. She watched him for a minute before looking back at the ceiling.

"No," he muttered, his voice higher than usual, "that's not right."

"Steve," she said, "you're dreaming, wake up."

"But you shouldn't be here, that's not right."

Cindy sighed and wondered if she'd ever manage to fall asleep again.

Steve rolled onto his back, his left arm dropping onto her so that he backhanded her right breast.

"Ow," she hissed, grabbing his hand and thrusting it back towards him, "that hurt, you bastard."

"No," he said, his voice louder and sharper, "you mustn't do that."

"Steve—"

He sat upright in a quick, fluid movement that startled her. He rubbed the side of his head with his hands and muttered, "No, no, no." Cindy struggled to sit up and put a hand on the back of his neck. As she did, his hands dropped to his sides.

"Steve?"

As if her voice had startled him, he twisted to face her but it was clear from his expression he wasn't properly awake.

"You were having a bad dream," she said, as calmly as she could, "You're okay."

He nodded and muttered something, looking through her. She touched his cheek, which made him jump and woke him.

"Cindy?" He looked around, as if trying to work out where he was.

"Of course it's me, who else would it be?"

He started to say something, then blinked and rubbed his face. "I don't know," he said, "I must have been having a dream."

"What about?"

"I don't know, I couldn't tell."

"Was it about someone?"

He looked at her and shook his head briskly, twice,

the movement betraying the lie. "Can't remember," he said and lay back, pulling the duvet up to his waist. "Goodnight."

Within a few minutes he was breathing deeply and evenly. Cindy gently lowered herself down and went back to staring at the ceiling, sleep not coming to her for another hour or more.

***

Steve woke Cindy with a kiss the next morning, leaning over her—his hand clasping his tie to his chest—and saying, "Good morning, sleepy head."

She came awake slowly, her eyes refusing to focus properly. "What time is it?"

"A little after seven."

"Wow, I must have had two hours sleep."

"The babies again? Or the heart burn?"

"Both, plus your nightmare."

He frowned at her. "I didn't have a nightmare."

"You did, you were calling out and slapped my boob."

He laughed, touched them both gently and stood up. "I doubt it. I never have bad dreams."

Cindy struggled into a sitting position as Steve walked to his dresser and put his cuff-links in. "You did. Don't you remember?"

"Not at all," he said, his reflection looking at her. "What is there in my life to give me bad dreams?"

"You don't need—"

He turned, kissed her on the lips, said "Got to go" and walked downstairs.

***

Her mobile buzzed as Cindy was waiting for the kettle to boil. She put her travel-mug on the kitchen counter, delved into her bag for her phone, and looked at the display.

"Morning, Angie," she answered.

"Hey, how're you?"

"I'm fine, just waiting to make my coffee then I'll be off. Why, what's up?"

There was a pause. "Nothing, just checking."

Cindy took a deep breath, making it loud enough that Angie could hear. "I'm fine, honestly. I look like the side of a house, but I'm fine."

There was another pause and Cindy thought she heard Angie draw breath, as if she was going to say something. "Is everything okay, Angie?"

"Yep, no problem. I'll see you at work."

"Okay."

Frowning, Cindy closed the call. Her phone wallpaper was a selfie she'd taken on a beach in Devon, with her too close to the lens and Steve behind her, his eyes wide and his big grin partially hidden. Photographing him always made her smile.

She pressed the gallery button. They'd been to the common at the weekend and she'd left her camera at home, but had taken several photos with the phone— a good substitute but not in the same class as her Nikon. The first picture was Steve standing at the pond, throwing lumps of bread at ducks and swans that weren't interested at all. The next photo was another selfie, but it was unfocussed and she seemed to have at least three chins.

"Not the most flattering," she said.

The third picture was Steve walking towards her, a big smile on his face. He'd taken a call, standing well away from the trees to get a better signal and she'd walked on a little way. The last picture was him in the distance, his back mostly towards her, the phone pressed to his ear.

Cindy looked at the photo, looked up at the kettle as it clicked off, then back at the picture. A woman was standing right in front of him and they were clearly talking to each other. She was blonde, her curly hair blown by the wind, her eyes wide, her mouth a thin line. She was wearing black boots, a knee-length skirt and a black jacket she was hugging to herself.

Cindy didn't remember seeing a woman standing with Steve when she took the photo.

Who was she?

***

The traffic that morning was murderous. Cindy sat in a queue, locked inside her car, Chris Evans on the radio as she tried to zone everything out and keep her breathing steady.

As much as she couldn't get comfortable these days, with her due date less than three months away, she was thoroughly looking forward to the prospect of motherhood. Her nesting instinct had kicked in early, so although there were always pretty new blankets and soft toys to look at, she knew she had enough now— and if she didn't, her mum was topping up the collection every time she came around. Steve had re-decorated the back bedroom, the cots and furniture were set up and the Moses baskets waited patiently, though they would be moved straight into the main bedroom as soon as the babies were born.

Babies—even though it had been clear from very early on, the fact she was going to have twins never failed to amaze her and made the swollen feet, ankles, hands and belly worth it. Steve often told her he loved her, he applied the various stretchmark creams for her, he kissed her and hugged her and yet she still often felt down about him and them and life in general. Now, after seeing that one photograph—how had she not seen that woman when she took it?—she felt even worse.

Cindy and Steve had been together for less than a year and it was a whirlwind office romance—he had called it "lust at first sight," which thrilled her. She and her then partner, John, had almost reached the end of the road anyway, and so it wasn't difficult to take the final step. He moved out in a flurry of bitter tears, profanity and empty threats. Steve hadn't made the same commitment, though she didn't want to know about Fiona, his soon-to-be-ex partner. It was a combination of gossip and mild scandal at work, and her finding she was expecting that forced his hand. He was a salesman, used to living out of a suitcase and his flat was in a different part of the country, but he liked Gaffney. Cindy now had too much room and so he moved in.

She'd worried, initially, about how he'd react to the news of the pregnancy, as it wasn't planned, but he was overjoyed. Equally excited, they discussed the future, how they'd sort everything out, the kind of life they wanted to lead. He spent a lot of time away from home, building a "nest egg" as he called it, but promised he'd cut down on the insane hours once the babies were born.

As the days turned into weeks and months and her once slim figure bloomed, she noticed him pulling back slightly. He put it down to not wanting to hurt her, that he was worried about making love to her in her condition, regardless of the reports and pamphlets she showed him, proving that it was safe. Cindy would look at herself in the mirror, thrilled at how her body was developing but growing ever more worried that as she got larger, Steve's affection was diminishing. She talked it over with friends, who all assured her it was natural, that Steve probably *was* being careful, that he still loved her, that things would be all right.

But the paranoia had settled.

The traffic moved and she drove a few feet before braking.

Would he leave her? Why had he left his previous partner? Had he left the one before that, taken what he wanted and then moved on to the next one? Of course, this was completely ignoring the fact that she'd moved on from John—dear, sweet dependable John, he of the five-year relationship and four-year joint account—but the paranoia twisted and nagged and muttered and suggested.

If Steve easily left his previous partner for her, he could more than likely do it again. And if he left an attractive, intelligent woman for her—Cindy had never met Fiona, but mutual friends had—now that she weighed a lot more and looked like a blimp, why would he stay?

No, this was silly, she was making something out of nothing. The photograph was a glitch, it had to be, there was nobody else around at the time. Or was there? Had she perhaps been far enough away that with the sun and the angle of Steve's body, she'd been blocked from Cindy's vision? Had he been different with her afterwards? No, not according to the pictures of him feeding the ducks and that stupid selfie.

Mark West

Cindy took out her mobile and opened the gallery. She flicked along to the photograph of Steve and the woman and worked her way back. She smiled at his expression, grinning broadly as he came towards her and she touched his lips with the tip of her finger. The contact made the picture slightly bigger and she could now see something over his left shoulder. Could it be? She expanded the picture as much as she could and bit her lip.

The car ahead moved slightly. She didn't follow it until the car behind honked its horn. As she pulled on the handbrake again, she stared at the picture.

The woman, difficult to make out because the image was badly pixelated, was standing behind Steve, her left arm raised. Could she have been calling him back, or maybe saying goodbye?

The selfie held no surprises and she moved to the next, of Steve at the lip of the duck pond.

The car in front moved half a length as the local traffic news came onto the radio. It seemed she was stuck in a jam caused by a burst water main and wasn't likely to move any time soon.

"Marvellous," she said and went back to the image. She'd taken this one because she liked the way he was standin'—tall and solid with his bum looking good. Smiling, Cindy magnified the image and panned it slowly across the screen. Beyond the pond were the trees, unrecognisable at this magnification. She moved the image slower, straining her eyes, looking for something, for anything, though she didn't know what.

Nothing. She pulled the image back to normal and there was the woman, standing across the pond from Steve, her arm raised in greeting. Cindy felt her breath catch in her throat and one of the babies moved sluggishly. Instinctively, she cupped her left hand under her belly and slid it gently up over her bulge.

Had the woman always been there? Of course she must have been but why had Cindy not noticed her before? And if not this one, how about the others? Who was she? If Steve had arranged to meet a friend there, surely he'd have introduced them? Unless it wasn't just a friend . . .

"No," she scolded herself, "that's just crazy."

But was it? What did his ex-partner Fiona look like, had she ever actually seen a picture? Cindy thought she was blonde but that was only supposition, since she was and Steve had mentioned it was one of his things.

Without fully thinking through what she was doing, she dialled Steve's mobile. It rang out to voicemail. That wasn't unusual because if he was in a meeting, he wouldn't be disturbed—whilst he was with a client; he was smooth and professional and they were his only focus.

The traffic moved very slightly and one of the babies shifted position.

"Shit," she said and went back to the photo of Steve and the woman on the common. She shook her head, but it wasn't enough to shake the image free. "No," she said aloud, as if to definitely dispel the silly idea, "it can't be." Why would he arrange to meet his ex, on the common, in full view of his new—and pregnant— girlfriend? It wouldn't make any sense and, yet, it would make perfect sense—hide in plain sight. Steve hadn't fully committed until Cindy discovered she was pregnant but now that she was getting bigger, now that her body was changing, might he be having second thoughts?

He had a laptop in the spare room at home, which he used when he was surfing the net. Maybe he had pictures on there—she'd never thought to ask before. Hadn't wanted to ask, because there'd been no reason. Well now there was.

She tried him again on the mobile and, once more, it rang through to voicemail. Then she rang Angie.

"Hi, it's me, I'm still stuck in traffic and I've got heartburn like you wouldn't believe and if I don't pee soon, I'm going to explode."

Angie laughed. "If you're in the traffic in the centre of town, you're not going anywhere fast."

"I might cut off down one of the sidestreets and work from home today, what do you think?"

"I think that's a good idea." There was a pause. "You're okay, though, apart from the peeing and heartburn business?" There was something in her voice, a catch that hinted at concern for more, perhaps unsaid, issues.

"Yes, I'm fine, honestly. I'll see you tomorrow, but I'll be on email as soon as I get home."

"Okay, if you're certain. See you tomorrow."

Cindy rang off and even though she could see the junction with Evison Road, which would enable her to get back to the ring road and out of the centre, it took her twenty minutes to reach it and another thirty minutes before she got home. By then, she really did have a burning patch of heartburn and daren't walk to the house too quickly in case she wet herself.

*****

Steve had adapted the spare box-room at the top of the

stairs into an office. His desk was in front of the window. There were three book cases against the far wall and a chair. It was Spartan, but served a purpose.

Cindy opened his laptop and it whirred into life as she sat and hotched the chair forward until her belly gently touched the edge of the desk. She entered his password, which he'd told her a long time before and she'd never forgotten. Within moments, she was at his desktop. The wallpaper was a picture of her, in a bikini top and shorts, on the beach. The sun was behind the camera so she had a hand to her face, protecting her eyes from the glare.

"Happy days," she said and moved the mouse pointer over the 'My Pictures' link, then paused. This was a big step to be taking. Did she really want to do it? Would she want him looking through her pictures and files, even though there was nothing untoward in there (apart from a folder of images of Vin Diesel topless)?

"Too late now," she said and was just about to click the icon when movement in the garden caught her eye. She looked out of the window, but everything seemed as it should. The garden was long and thin, with a paved patio that extended about ten feet from the back of the house, then twenty or more feet of lawn before the line of conifers that marked their boundary. There was a scrawny oak tree against the neighbour to the left's fence, and her shed was behind that. Standing in the middle of the lawn was a football, probably from the kid next door on the right, which she'd have to throw back.

She looked back to the laptop and, again, movement caught her eye. She stood up and leaned forward, just able to see the edge of the patio. Nothing, apart from the football, seemed to be out of place.

Cindy pushed the chair away with the back of her knees and went through to the nursery, what had once been the guest room. It ran lengthwise down the house, from the top of the stairs to the main bedroom, and had a good view of the garden. Standing at the large window, bathed in sunlight, she still couldn't see anything untoward on the patio or lawn.

"You're going mad," she said, then took a picture of the garden with her mobile and went back into the spare room. She sat down, wheeled the chair forward, and looked at the photo she'd just taken.

The woman was standing in the middle of the lawn, just in front of the football, looking up at her. She was dressed as she had been on the common, but now her jacket was open and Cindy could see she was wearing a white blouse, the hem of her bra visible through the material. The sun caught her curly blonde hair and she was staring at Cindy with an expression somewhere between annoyance and hate.

Cindy almost dropped the phone as she scrambled to her feet to look out of the window. Nothing. She rushed through to the nursery but the garden was empty. She took another photo and the woman was there, a pace or so closer to the house. Cindy felt a tremor run through her, as if everything had tensed all at once and a burst of fire bloomed in her chest as heartburn flared. Saliva filled her mouth and she felt sick, putting her hand to her lips until she'd managed to swallow it all. There was nobody in the garden, nobody at all.

Cindy turned away and sat on the windowsill. None

of this could be real, she could see with her own two eyes that the garden was empty.

Without looking back, she walked as steadily as she could back into the spare room and sat at the desk. She tried to ring Steve again and the call went to voicemail.

"Where the hell are you, Steve? Ring me as soon as you get this, something bloody weird is going on."

Bloody weird—yes, that'd cover it. Was she going mad? There was only one way to find out.

She clicked on 'My Pictures.' It opened up to a directory filled with folders, all of them neatly labelled—'Cars,' 'Playboy,' 'album covers.' She scanned them quickly, some featuring her name or places they'd been. One, called 'Scans,' had as its icon the first scan picture they'd had, two little white shapes against a dark grey background. The image and memory of that afternoon in the hospital made her smile. Finally, she saw one called 'Fiona.'

Cindy took a deep breath and clicked it open. A new page full of folders appeared, a relationship safely ensconced in yellow boxes—'Crete,' 'Work do,' 'Christmas,' 'Park,' 'Bike ride,' and many more. Looking at the dates, some this year, some back two or three years, she was suddenly and unaccountably jealous of the time Fiona'd had with him. She clicked on one of the Christmas ones and inside were two dozen photos, featuring people she didn't know apart from the man who shared her bed. She clicked out of it, angry at herself for looking and angry at him for keeping the pictures. And angry at Fiona, too, who still had this hold on him.

Cindy rubbed her belly gently and bit her lip as the mouse hovered over a folder labelled 'Fi.' She opened it and the screen filled with images of the woman she'd seen—pretty and a bit older than Cindy, with white blonde curly hair, wide eyes, full lips and high cheekbones—from the common. And her garden.

Cindy screamed and rang Steve again, railing against the voicemail. "What the fucking hell is going on, Steve? Ring me as soon as you get this."

She slammed the mobile onto the desk, breathing heavily through gritted teeth. She rubbed her belly and felt a sharp pain in her right side. She ground her teeth and bent forward, rubbing the spot. The babies didn't seem to like the movement and kicked out. The heat in her chest flared.

"Oh God," she said and leaned back, her eyes closed, trying to control her breathing as the pain eased in her side and chest. When it had retreated enough to be tolerable, she got up and went into the nursery, taking three pictures of the empty garden that showed only the empty garden.

Her phone rang, startling her.

"Steve? Where the bloody hell are you?"

"What's wrong, are you okay? Are the babies?"

"We're fine, I'm just . . . " What was she? "I'm just fucked off because . . . "

"Fucked off? What do you mean, what's the matter?"

"Everything. I saw the photograph."

"What photograph?"

"Of you, at the common from the weekend."

"Of course you've seen it, you took it."

"I didn't see her at the time, though." There was a pause from the other end and Cindy could hear noise in the background, as if he was standing in the middle of a busy office. "Where are you?"

"I'm . . . " He took a deep breath. "I'm at the hospital."

Another spike of pain in her side but that—and his words—helped clear her mind of everything else. Here she was, hallucinating or whatever. She'd been doing and calling him everything under the sun for not returning her calls and he was at the hospital. "Are you okay? Are your mum and dad okay?"

"Yeah, I'm fine. And I assume Mum and Dad are."

She walked back into the spare room and sat at the desk. "So why are you there, who's hurt?"

"I don't know what to say," he said carefully.

"Steve, tell me." She turned the chair away from the photographs of Fiona and rubbed her belly absent-mindedly. "What's going on?"

"She rang me, yesterday."

She didn't need to ask and it appeared Steve wasn't going to volunteer a name. "I didn't think you still spoke."

"That, ah, might not have been the truth."

Her head felt as though someone had draped a cold flannel over it. "What?"

"Cin, it was five years, she was reeling and couldn't settle herself."

"Not our problem."

"I know," he said, slowly and with effort, "I realise that. But I felt bad, I took her calls, we talked."

"Did you fuck her?"

"What? No, of course not."

"Did you kiss her?"

"No, I can't believe you're—"

"Did you hug her?" The silence told her everything. "You bastard, I trusted you."

"Cin, you have to believe me, I didn't do anything. I'd stopped answering her calls, but she used another phone and got me by surprise. She wanted to meet up in town, said she had something to tell me. I told her we couldn't meet, that I was happy where I was."

"Liar," said Cindy, softly.

If he heard, he didn't respond. "She told me she could give me the world and, without thinking about it, I cut her dead."

"How?"

"I told her you'd already given me the world, in a way that she never could, because you were pregnant."

It wasn't what Cindy had been expecting to hear and his words stopped her abruptly. The thing that she'd worried about, had fretted over, the thing she thought would drive a wedge between them, was what had made him leave his ex. All of it, wasted worry.

"But that's good, isn't it?"

"No, because she didn't take it well, I shouldn't have told her. When we were together, we spent years going for tests, both of us and although I said it didn't matter it was her, she never believed me. She got angry. She called you names, said she hoped you lost the babies. I put the phone down."

"When was this?"

"Last night, that business call I went into the garden to take."

The nightmare, Cindy thought, before she started seeing Fiona in the pictures this morning. "So what happened?"

"She rang again this morning, when I was in the car, told me she was in the bath and had slit her wrists and taken a bottle of paracetamol. I went straight to her place and she wasn't lying. The ambulance got caught in traffic and she lost a lot of blood and that's why I'm at the hospital."

"So where is she now?"

"She's dead, Cindy."

There was a sense of movement from the hallway at the bottom of the stairs and Cindy looked up quickly but couldn't see anything.

"I have to go," she said and ended the call, quickly pressing the camera button. Pointing it down the stairs, she took a photo of the empty space and then pulled it up. Fiona was at the bottom, as if she'd stumbled onto the stairs. She wasn't wearing her jacket any longer and the right sleeve of her white blouse was caked to her arm and red.

"No," said Cindy, as pain speared her right side, "no no no."

She took another photo and Fiona was further up the stairs. Her expression was one of hatred now, her nostrils flared, her teeth gritted. One, two, three more photos and still she came, a couple of risers between each image. Cindy pushed her chair back and got to her feet. Fire flared in her chest and her breath felt hot in her throat. Another photo and Fiona was almost at the top of the stairs. The belly of her blouse was now red where her arm had brushed against it.

Another photo and she was at the top of the stairs. The colour had drained from her face and her eyes were dull and dead but still she came. Cindy, looking at an empty doorway, landing and staircase in real life, could only back up until the edge of the desk pressed into her thighs.

"Leave me alone," she yelled and held the mobile at chest height and took another photograph. Fiona was in the room now, coming at her on all fours. Cindy kept snapping photographs and Fiona kept coming, more colour draining from her face, more blood staining the arm of her blouse. She was leaving bloody handprints on the carpet. She came closer and reached out her arm.

The pain, when it ricocheted through her stomach, made Cindy scream and she dropped heavily to her knees, her mobile bouncing on the carpet and sliding away. She clutched her belly and drew her knees up as she felt something in her knickers. She hoped it was only pee but knew, from how heavy it felt, that it wasn't.

Cindy reached for the mobile, needing desperately to ring Steve or an ambulance. She grasped it, her fingers closing around the plastic case and pulled it towards her.

The last photo was on the screen.

Fiona's face filled it. There was a smile playing at her lips.

St. Thomas of El Paso

LISA MORTON

he **train whistle** blew, and the gunslinger was jolted out of another dream of the succubus.

He rubbed his eyes as he looked out the window. It was late in the morning, and the interior of the rocking wooden car was already heating up. How long had he slept? Had he missed a stop?

He pushed the panic down to focus on the dream. It was the third one he'd had since he'd started tracking the succubus, and it had been the most detailed and precise yet: He'd watched from an overhead angle as she entered a dusty, two-story bar, her beauty thrilling and yet cold, as perfection would be. Pale skin, raven hair, eyes so green they nearly glowed. Four men gambling with cards looked up, their money and hands forgotten; a traveler at the bar paused with drink still poised inches from his lips; the bartender, making notes in a ledger, spilled his bottle of ink and didn't notice. She walked to the center of the room, slowly, wallowing in her power over the half-dozen men. She stopped; the men began to drift toward her, chairs overturned, other actions pushed aside. They floated to her like dust motes in a ray of light. She waited, smiling. The first one—the traveler, a man dressed in a grimy business suit—was closest. She gestured at him, without effort . . . and he collapsed. Not fell, but almost deflated, his skin a sad, punctured flesh balloon. The other men didn't react, but simply continued to draw toward her until, one by one they, too, succumbed. Finally she stood alone, panting slightly, skin flushed, surveying the six withered carcasses at her feet with some satisfaction. She turned to go, and for an instant he saw the street beyond her, a sign on the other side of the muddy avenue . . .

Los Lunas Feed and General Store.

The gunslinger's head jerked up, adrenaline coursing through him. Was that where she was now? Or had they been past that stop while he'd slept, and he'd missed her?

He rose, turned, spotted a conductor at the far end of the car. Staggering slightly as the train rocked, he made his way to the man while tickets were checked. "Excuse me, sir," he said, his voice soft; the gunslinger wasn't much good at talking.

When the conductor turned to look at him, he added, "Is there a stop for Los Lunas?"

"You missed it two back."

Damn. He was ahead of her now.

"How far to the next station?"

The conductor went back to punching tickets. "San Diablo's about another fifteen minutes."

San Diablo. The gunslinger understood just enough Spanish to appreciate the irony of the town name. He'd get off there, let her come to him, and then he would end the life of the demon in a town called Saint Devil.

He returned to his seat. Soon he would be able to put Father Montaigne's fears at ease and redeem himself.

Soon it would be over and his life would finally begin again.

***

Thomas's life had ended five years ago, when Father Montaigne had thrown him out of the mission's orphanage.

Or perhaps it had really ended earlier . . . at the age of six, when he'd seen his mother shot to death. She'd been working in an El Paso saloon, where she'd told him she made their living by "being nice to the menfolk." Tommy didn't really understand why she had to go behind closed doors and make strange sounds to be nice, but he understood anger when he heard the man yelling at her in Spanish one day. He'd been outside tending to some of the patrons' horses, hoping to earn a penny, when he'd heard the shouts and ran into the bar. He saw his mother standing in a doorway, her face red in fury, and then the angry man pulled his gun and shot her. Tommy had screamed and run to her, kneeling helplessly by her convulsing body, her blood covering his hands and knees until she'd died. He barely noticed when there were more gunshots.

Lizzie, the nice lady who worked in the saloon with Mama, had pulled Tommy aside and held him as other men arrived and sorted things out. The angry man, whose name was Gonzalez, had shot two other men after he'd killed Tommy's mother; he'd been wounded, though, and the sheriff arrived to arrest him.

Three days later, Gonzalez had been sentenced to hang, and Tommy had been sent to the orphanage. He was allowed out long enough to watch Gonzalez die. After the killer had dropped through the trapdoor and his body had stopped jerking, Carmen—the saloon lady Tommy didn't like—had stepped up to him and told him Gonzalez had been his father.

Tommy—now Thomas—was taken to the Orphans Asylum run by the mission at the northern edge of El Paso. There were fourteen other orphans when he arrived, and two stern nuns who had apparently never been children themselves.

And then there was Father Montaigne.

Father Montaigne was the priest who ran the mission. He'd come from France nine years ago, still had an elegant accent, and was widely reckoned to be a learned and kindly man. He took a liking to the quiet, industrious new arrival, and began personally tutoring Thomas in the ways of the good Christian. He taught Thomas to read the Bible, to quote Scripture, to write sermons. Father Montaigne told Thomas that someday he could go to France—the most beautiful place on earth—and study to become a priest, too. If he worked hard and loved God, he could overcome his past and redeem himself as the son of a fallen woman and the outlaw who had shot her.

Then, at 15, Thomas had confessed to carnal thoughts . . . of Pedro, the handsome young handyman who made repairs around the mission.

The next day, Sister Mary Elizabeth had told him he was to leave the orphanage immediately.

The nun wouldn't reveal why, but Thomas knew: he'd been betrayed. By Father Montaigne, who he worshipped like a true father.

He wasn't given the usual job assignment or reference or train ticket; nothing but one extra suit of clothing and the vague suggestion that he try the local ranchers for employment. He never even saw Father Montaigne. He slept on the street that night. Two days later, he was hired to ride a cattle drive. He lied and told the foreman that he knew horses; the foreman laughed, saw through the ruse, and hired him anyway. He assigned Thomas to a middle-aged cowboy named Cyrus who'd been riding the local ranges for nearly twenty years. Cyrus taught him how to ride, shoot, and live. He told him not to sass the rancher's wife, showed him how to double up in the bunkhouse on cold nights, and gave Thomas an old set of spurs.

One night, when it was well below zero and Cyrus and Thomas lay huddled together under their threadbare blankets, Cyrus told Thomas about the "mutual solace" of the range rider. Their bodies entwined, and by morning Thomas knew he'd found his first true friend.

That'd been five years back. A year ago, Cyrus had been thrown from his horse during a storm and had broken his back. He'd died a month later. On his deathbed, he'd told Thomas to go out and find himself a wife, settle down, raise a family. Thomas had nodded, feeling the lie burning in his heart.

For one thing, he'd become good at his job. He'd discovered that he was a dead-eye shot, and had used the skill on occasion to win money. Maybe one day he would stop cowpunching, become a sheriff, discover again the respect only Cyrus had shown him . . .

. . . but in the meantime, he'd keep riding. Maybe he could outrace the memories of Cyrus.

***

Thoughts of Cyrus vied now with the dream of the succubus. The train started to slow as it pulled into the San Diablo station, but Thomas didn't hurry; he knew he had several minutes before the train chugged to a stop and allowed passengers (only him, probably) to disembark. He was thinking now of Father Montaigne; he wondered again if pursuing this quest made him even crazier than the man who'd suggested it.

He'd pondered that question a great deal over the last three days.

***

Only three days ago . . .

"There's somebody asking after you, Tom."

Thomas had just returned to the bunkhouse after two weeks driving a herd north to San Antonio. He blinked in surprise at the foreman, who continued on into the main ranch house.

Nobody ever asked for him. His world was the ranch, the herds, the trails, and the other cowboys. Then he spotted the tall, craggy figure near the bunkhouse doorway, and his blood froze.

Father Montaigne.

His immediate urge was to flee, hide, but then Montaigne had looked up, his thick eyebrows arched. Thomas knew he'd been seen. Too late.

He took a deep breath and walked forward, struggling to keep his eyes level, but when he reached the priest he still found himself staring at his scuffed boots. He said nothing, just waited.

Montaigne inspected him, then nodded. "Thomas. You've grown into a fine young man, as I always knew you would."

Thomas wanted to shout at him—"Lies!"—but instead he shuffled his feet and said, "How'd you find me out here?"

"Is there somewhere out of the sun where we can talk?"

Thomas didn't answer, but led him to the barn, empty for the moment.

Montaigne sighed as he lowered himself to a hay bale, and Thomas realized the man had aged twenty years in five. The rugged features Thomas had once loved had grown sallow and sharp; although he couldn't have been more than fifty, Montaigne's back was already bent, bony knobs outlined beneath his black coat.

Thomas remained standing as he waited for Montaigne to begin. The old man looked lost for a few seconds, then recovered himself.

"I've spent the last few days searching for you, Thomas, because I've . . . I've done something dreadful. Truly dreadful. I have sinned greatly, I have committed terrible acts . . . and only you can help."

A large spider scuttled across the floor. Thomas raised one booted toe and felt satisfaction as he ground it underfoot. He imagined its deadly venom seeping into the dirt, forever poisoning the soil.

"Have you ever heard the word 'succubus'?"

Raising his eyes, Thomas peered uncertainly at Montaigne; was this some sort of test? The word was unfamiliar, though, so Thomas shook his head.

"It's a female demon, a creature manifested from a man's lustful desires. Yes, I've lusted. All men share the sin of lust, but my sin took form. First, it appeared in my dreams every night, taunting and tormenting me. And God help me, I did nothing to turn it away. In fact, I welcomed it.

"This continued night after night, week after week, the demon impelling my lust so it could feed. It grew stronger, and when it was strong enough . . .

"It took on human form. Oh my God, my God, forgive me . . . "

Montaigne moaned, hanging his head in his hands.

Five years ago Thomas would have sought some way to comfort him, but now he merely felt shame. He glanced about nervously, assured himself they remained alone and unobserved, and waited for Montaigne to continue.

"It came to me," Montaigne finally said, head still lowered, "every night, a flesh-and-blood woman, and I . . . *mon dieu*, I lay with it, Thomas. Every night. It sapped me, until I am as you see me now. And when I'd finally decided that I must destroy it . . . it left me. It left me, and I fear I have now loosed something horrible upon the world.

"That was three nights ago."

"You're crazy," Thomas wanted to say. Montaigne had obviously gone mad, but Thomas couldn't walk away yet. He had to hear the end, so he kept silent and let Montaigne continue.

"It must be destroyed. This thing will control men through their desire; control, and then drain them. It could be draining whole towns. Last night a man came into the mission from Anthony, just north of here, and told us that two men had been found dead there yesterday from some sudden illness . . . but it was her, *mon fils*. I know it.

"I think she's heading north, probably on the Santa Fe. She'll be stopping at towns along the way, taking what she needs, sucking the life from her victims and moving on. She'll slay more at every stop. She'll become powerful beyond understanding . . .

"Unless we stop her. She's human right now, which means she can be killed, although church documents also suggest the recitation of the Angelic Salutation to permanently expel the demon from this world."

It dawned on Thomas just then what Montaigne was asking, and he actually gasped once in surprise. "You want *me* to go after this . . . thing?"

As Montaigne clutched desperately at Thomas's hand, Thomas was shocked by how weakened the priest's grasp was. "Don't you see, *mon fils*? You're perfect, because you won't be enthralled by the promise of female flesh." The priest struggled to his feet and placed his trembling fingers on Thomas's shoulders. "This is your chance to find true salvation, Thomas. If you kill this thing, I'll make sure you are accepted back into the graces of the church. You will be celebrated, like St. George and the dragon."

Thomas only vaguely recalled a St. George from his holy studies, but the idea of himself as a saint amused him, and he smiled. Montaigne took that as a sign of agreement, so he pressed Thomas's shoulders more tightly. "You'll do it? You'll go after the succubus for me, hunt it down and destroy it?"

A shrug was the most Thomas could manage. Montaigne threw his arms excitedly around the young man. "Thomas, *mon fils*, I am so very proud of you."

That was when Thomas knew he would go.

***

A day later he was on the Santa Fe heading north, with the mission's money in his pocket, his pistol on his hip, and a head full of confusion.

What was he really looking for? Did he believe any part of the Father's story?

All he really knew was that he had gold, and a mission that could only be called sacred. Thomas wanted something in his life to be sacred again; he'd been adrift since Cyrus had passed. Maybe it wasn't too late to follow his young dream of going to France, training for the priesthood, becoming a holy man who would serve both God and the people of his birth city.

That first day on the Santa Fe (his first time on any train), he'd let the swaying motion lull him to sleep, and he'd dreamt:

The succubus entered a small town saloon. She was blindingly beautiful, and somehow Thomas felt her connection to Father Montaigne. The men in the saloon were drawn to her like iron shavings to a magnet . . . the first one that reached her, died—

Thomas had awakened, startled.

He believed all of it.

He'd stepped from the train at the next stop, a station called Black's Bluff. It was like so many of the stops that had arisen around the new Atchison, Topeka and Santa Fe line—little more than a single-room depot, a saloon and hotel, a handful of stores. A single main street lined with gulches of odorous slop. Dust coating everything.

The town had been empty.

Thomas had wandered its streets for a day, but the town was simply dead. The saloon was boarded over; the shelves of the general store were barren. He supposed the town could have died a natural death, having never found the prosperity promised by the new railroad.

But when he'd spent the night in an abandoned assayer's office, he'd had terrible dreams, of shriveled corpses blowing away in the Texas prairie wind while watched by the distant silhouette of the succubus. He woke in the cold pre-dawn, shivering and clutching his gun, half-expecting the succubus to appear before him any second, to feel his life ebbing . . .

He was on the platform waiting when the train reappeared, his determination fresh.

***

The train stopped at the San Diablo station. The gunslinger stepped down.

As he'd guessed, he was alone. No other passengers got on or off.

The town was like Black's Bluff—a handful of flyblown wooden buildings—but at least he saw signs of life. He stepped into the saloon and was relieved to see three other men present: a bartender, cleaning glasses; a drunk, asleep at a table; and a boy, sullenly sweeping sawdust from the floor.

Thomas ordered a steak, whiskey, and a room. He knew she hadn't been here yet, that he might be two days ahead of her. But he knew somehow that she would stop here.

That evening, the saloon gained a dozen more customers—the usual assortment of cowboys in from riding the wastelands, ranchers looking for entertainment, local merchants anxious to be anywhere but home with their wives. Thomas was intrigued to see that this town had no saloon girls.

It would be easy pickings for her.

The next day passed in a swirl of boredom. Thomas cleaned his gun again. He went over the words of the Angelic Salutation, committing them to memory. He walked the single street of the town, looking for her.

But he didn't pray. His gun was better than any prayer.

The second night passed. The third day dawned.

The train arrived early, and Thomas missed it. The sole employee of the train station had looked up from his telegraph and told Thomas that he thought he'd seen a single passenger get off the train.

A woman.

Thomas ran back to the saloon, his heart beating double-time like a runaway horse's hooves on sandstone. He loosened the gun in its holster and wiped his sweating fingers on his worn pants. He burst through the bat-wing doors of the saloon—

And saw her.

She stood at the bar, facing away, surrounded by four men. Thomas saw the look on the bartender's face, an obsequious leer; although the other three had their backs to him, there was lust displayed plainly in their hip-cocked postures. She was laughing, a high, musical sound, one delicately gloved hand poised in the air. Her green velvet gown hugged her voluptuous curves perfectly, her hat balanced atop a mound of crimson hair.

Thomas drew his gun and pulled the hammer back,

but then he hesitated—red hair? In his dreams she'd been a brunette, with hair the hue of a crow's wing—

She heard the sound of his gun and turned. When Thomas saw her face, his hesitation vanished: Her features were Father Montaigne's, impossibly reshaped into beautiful feminine form. She looked at him inquisitively; the way her eyebrows arched reminded Thomas again of the priest.

He inhaled and pulled the trigger.

His aim, as always, was perfect. The bullet struck her in the chest, a scarlet flower instantly blossoming across the verdant fabric. She fell back against the bar while onlookers stood by, paralyzed in shock. Thomas strode forward resolutely, finding the voice that had so often eluded him in his life:

"Hail, Mother of God, Virgin Mary, full of grace, the Lord is with you. Blessed are you among women, and blessed is the fruit of your womb; for you gave birth to Christ, the Savior and Redeemer of our souls."

The Angelic Salutation completed, he stepped over to her, the gun held ready in case it was required again, but she was crumpled against the foot rest of the bar, blood spouting onto the rough wooden floor, and Thomas couldn't help but be reminded of his mother. He barely noticed as the men finally found their wits and wrested the gun from his grasp, then pulled away, shouting for the sheriff. Instead his eyes were welded to hers when she looked up at him and, red froth staining her lips, said:

"Those words sound like Papa."

She died.

In that instant Thomas saw how he'd been deceived, by his own dreams and by the sick guilt of a dangerous man, a man whose lust had conceived long ago. At least he wouldn't live long with the knowledge, because they'd hang him soon.

He hoped he'd at least see Montaigne again in Hell.

Forever Dark

JONATHAN WINN

The dead girl laughed. The staccato tumbled down the grassy slope of the gentle hill, the sound darting into the long blades choking the meadow below.

I saw the shade of the distant trees. Imagined the echo of her voice slipping between the saplings, this too soon winter having stolen their leaves, before ducking into the dark where the larger trunks stood, tall and green, the threat of the cold embraced and then ignored.

Beyond that lay the edge of a pond.

A pond?

My mind stopped, holding that thought. Behind me the road waited, the cars not quite still, their journey slow and frightening. But I wouldn't look at the road. I kept my back turned, the clouds gathering overhead.

She glanced at me, the dead girl, her eyes catching mine as she started down the hill where the yellow grass grew tall.

I wanted to go back to the road. Return to the car

and sit behind the wheel. Close the door. And my keys in hand . . .

My keys in hand?

I couldn't get beyond those four words, *"my keys in hand."* My head was sluggish and thick. And the pain, it squatted like a helmet tied too tight, the weight of it pushing down. Closing my eyes, I swallowed, the metallic taste of blood blanketing my throat as I gritted my teeth.

Taking a breath, I stopped. Untangled my thoughts.

On this hill lived horrible things. Dangerous things. And they walked, hand in hand, with the dead girl. Their steps careful as they tempted me with—

I couldn't remember. I didn't *want* to remember.

What I knew was that I stood on the slope. And there were others. Behind me. Strangers, quiet and still, waiting where the concrete crumbled to scatter in the dirt.

The dead girl had stopped. She watched me, lifting the mangled memory of her hand to beckon

Come.

Beyond her wrist, the flesh had been scraped. The tender underside weeping and raw, the skin peeled back. And her fingers dangled, the bones broken at the knuckles, the bright blue polish sparkling though the bloody nails hung, torn and cracked.

I looked away.

And, one step after another, I followed this familiar stranger with the sundress stained red. In the quickening shade of gathering clouds we walked, her thin blonde hair cleaved rudely where the skull had split, the brain beneath slashed and gashed and sobbing.

But her eyes, they tormented me. One blinking through a curtain of crimson, the other threatening to slip from its socket and swing against her cheek. Were she to move too fast—

I turned away, my stomach heaving, the rancid threat of puke flooding my mouth. I wanted to be on the road, in my car, the door closed, the window up. I wanted to sit, keys in hand.

But the road was too far, now. The cars still moving much too slow.

Long grass grazed my calves and brushed my knees. I didn't remember walking into the yellow of the tall grass. I'd been in the short green of the slope, at the top, there, far from where the trees stood, waiting.

This journey into the meadow, it was a stolen memory. I feared those missing moments. I swallowed, fighting the growing terror of something going horribly wrong.

Still, I walked behind the dead girl, the bloody white of her gaping skull slick and shining as she made her way to the water's edge.

Don't, I wanted to say. It isn't *there*, what you're looking for.

It was *never* there.

The others had drawn close.

I turned and watched a large woman escape into the tall grass, her steps slow and careful as she trudged through the shivering wave of yellow.

And over there, a smaller man. Was that her husband? He crouched, hiding beneath the shadow of the saplings. His hands resting on their slender trunks as he gazed skyward through the barren branches to the heavy clouds that rolled overhead.

Don't look at the clouds, I heard that silent voice saying. *They've eaten the sun.*

Don't look at the clouds.

At the top of the slope, a hapless woman waited as the metal maw of a yellow school bus hiccupped children onto the road. My eyes followed them as they walked, a cautious wave inching along the concrete to wander, muted and slow, down the short grass.

But there was something about this—

I looked away, not wanting to see the woman as she remained, alone, refusing the slope, her hand to her mouth

Trapped

No, that's not what I meant, the voice in my head insisted.

That word, that single word—*trapped*—was a key to some Pandora's Box where every mistake waited. Where every random thought ricocheted with the sharp ping of a rebellious bullet. Where every regret simmered. Every choice seethed. A box where every inescapable moment that led to this—here—now—still lived and breathed and raged, locked up tight,

My keys in hand.

No.

I should follow the dead girl. Yes, I should go to the pond

and not watch

I closed my eyes

you've seen this

My fingers pressed against my temples, desperate to quiet the constant ache throbbing in my head.

I turned away and there, surrounded by the tall grass, the large woman stood. The one with the flabby arms that jiggled when she walked and the mop of wispy curls dyed garish red and the cheap lipstick smeared along her cheek and down her chin.

See the missing teeth

She opened her mouth and I could see the gaping holes where the blood still ran. As if these nuggets of bone had been knocked out, pulled out, punched out. The red pooled in her bottom lip spilling in a slobbery stream as she tried to speak.

I had to move. My feet needed to take a step. Just one. One step.

My head turned as I heard the meadow rustle and snap. I saw the grass moving around the woman's swollen ankles. Watched as the long yellow blades stretched like fingers, searching for her, wrapping around her thick calves. And she waited, trapped, as they moved up her swollen knees to disappear beneath her faded skirt.

Then she lifted her arms, holding them akimbo, as the grass spread. The blades unfurling like a blanket winding 'round her hips and stretching over the girth of her stomach to nestle in her chest. A rippling wave that swallowed her breasts before inching up her neck to cover her chin.

Her hands pushed and pulled. Ripped away the hungry grass as her fists beat, slapped, smacked. Her fingers moving to her arms to scratch and dig and pull at the suffocating skin.

There'd been no time to scream. And when her mouth did open, her hands no longer pulling, her nails no longer scratching, her arms lifting

Surrendering, helpless in the air

more yellow had emerged, the blades coming from

her ears, eyes, nose. More grass darted from her mouth and whipped around her head, smothering her face. Every inch of her covered in a twisting, tying cloud of trembling gold.

I watched as her soul let go. Watched as she gave up. And the shudder of that last breath, I watched that, too. The flame of life flickering until she grew still, a husk of woven grass.

I had to get to the pond.

No

Forcing my feet, I took a step, and then another, drawing toward the trees. I had to sneak under and through the trees to where the dead girl with the broken skull and blood-stained sundress waited.

The old man stood in the gossamer shade of those barren branches.

I saw him as he gazed through arms of wood that punched the sky, his opaline eyes watching the clouds gather and swell. The dark above unfolding, the black growing deeper as the man's weathered fists and thin fingers clutched the stiff trunks of the saplings.

I turned my head. Those trees. I couldn't watch them, my eyes instead on the hill where the cars still moved too slow. The hapless woman still standing on the road. The children still waiting where the short grass was green, their arms at their sides, their eyes on the clouds.

There was a scream building. A living thing, hungry and stirring.

From deep in my stomach, it struggled to wake. From somewhere in my throat, it cocked its head. From my very being, it searched for its voice.

But it could not. I wouldn't let it.

My eyes squeezed shut, I pushed my hand against my mouth. Focused on the red worming 'round my teeth as I strangled silent the clamor in my mind and counted back

five, four, three, two

until the beast grew still. Its despair smothered by a terror too great for the simplicity of a scream.

My heart calm, I opened my eyes and saw the old man.

He fought, his knuckles beating the sapling as it gnawed. The bark cracking and creaking as it grabbed his other arm, the trunk chewing in great big, bloody bites. That bony fist moving much too slow, punching

two, three, four, five

as the tree pulled him closer, drew him in. Gulp by gulp, the elbow disappearing into the wood. The skinny bicep followed by the scrawny shoulder, the other hand pushing against the ravenous bark. The old man's helpless tears trapped in the lines on his face.

Get to the pond. Look away. Turn away.

Step by step, the water's edge came near, my thoughts refusing the memory of the old man, my focus now on the kneeling dead girl.

She turned. She saw me.

Drawing close, I noticed bits of bone nestled in the thick of her mauled scalp. And soft locks of blonde clinging to the peeling edges of torn skin and the bloated craters of festering wounds.

My stomach lurched.

I turned, my eyes catching the grass of the hill. Then the old man, the sapling having swallowed him, his reaching arms now barren branches waiting for the leaves of spring Then the children, silent and slow, creeping down the slope, their eyes no longer on the clouds.

The dead girl stood and reached, her twisted, splintered fingers cradling my chin, her touch smearing my cheek with warm crimson. Shredded skin dangled from her palm and stuck against my neck. Pulling close, her eyes, one secure, the other still slipping from its socket, met mine. She sighed, a vile cloud smelling of rotting and rancid things that scorched my throat with a fetid burn

I tried to turn my head. To the woman. The road. The children. The fluttering waves of grass. The dome of clouds overhead.

She stopped me.

Don't, she said, her lips not moving. *Don't look.*

I nodded, my head spinning.

Then, taking my hand in a fistful of shattered bone and butchered flesh, she led me to the water.

Wait

She stepped in.

Please

I glanced at the children. They had stopped, and the trees . . .

those trees—

The water crept up her shins, the hem of her sundress floating. She held her arms out.

Come, they said again.

Scraped raw and ripped from the bone, the skin had split, hanging from her elbows like sleeves, the gleaming muscle marred with sharp bits of gravel.

I winced at the sight of this, the pain in my head now a pounding thump that rattled my teeth.

But I had no choice. I couldn't look at the children

standing on the hill. Or the trees. I refused to watch the trees. So, my eyes closed, I faced the dark. And found fear. Fear that fed memory. Memory that gave way to nightmare. Nightmare that led to—

I opened my eyes.

The water was to her waist now. It was eating her— her flesh a bloody scum covering the pond. She paused, her hands toying with the discarded skin of her legs as it spread. Her fingers lifting the smaller bits that had been her toes as they bobbed within reach. Her eye found mine, the other having slid free and resting against her nose, her fingertips dipping in the pond as they melted to drip, drip, drip—

She lurched downward, the waves splashing, the water having eaten her legs. Her upper body listing, the liquid washing over her stomach as it ate that, too. The poor dead girl soon up to her neck, more ribbons of skin floating away. The pond taking her chin, her lips, her cheeks and eyes and forehead. And then, in one last swallow, crawling over the battered remains of her blonde skull and claiming her head.

Moving slow, I turned to the trees, and then remembered the old man. But I couldn't go to the grass.

I stepped back, my heel tempting the water's edge, my eyes on the children as they stood on the slope, the clouds above a blacker than black storm of churning, turning, twisting fear.

And the trees,

those trees

They were eating the children.

These tender innocents silent and still as the branches picked up their little bodies and popped off their tiny heads and ripped from them their arms and legs. The bark wet with blood as the quiet treats were shoved into the green of their leaves.

I stepped into the pond, shocked by the burn as it devoured the soles of my feet, my toes. The slender arch and the bone of my ankle. Another step and the water ate its twin. The same heat, the same burn. The skin from both soon gone.

My keys.

The water splashed my knees now, the pain so great it was beyond words. A slow slicing of skin from muscle. A shocking snap of bone splitting, the jagged bits ground by concrete and metal.

Had I tears, I would have wept. But the pain was too great for even that.

Haunted by the consequences of the mistake, the thought, the regret, the choice,

My keys in hand

I opened Pandora's Box.

Earlier that day, the sun had risen to climb the blue of the sky. Behind the wheel I'd sat, clutching the keys to a house that was no longer mine. And I'd run. A MISTAKE. Yes, I know. I THOUGHT I could escape. I did. That if I drove fast enough, the smoldering destruction of my life would be left behind. Forgotten.

The pond took another bite, the water rising, my thighs burning. My skin cast off and floating within reach. But I would not caress the floating flesh.

Why?

I couldn't remember, my thoughts impossible to catch.

But I'd been unable to escape my Armageddon, earlier that day. Or my guilt. The self-borne havoc of stupidity fed by arrogance had followed me to the road. My life eaten in big, bloody bites by debt, failure, REGRET.

I'd driven too fast, my hands gripping the steering wheel, my foot on the gas. My mind had been slow, my thoughts thick, as I'd made the CHOICE to look away from the road and glance at the trees.

The water was snaking over my hips, the gurgling splash blending with the grate of metal grinding and the bizarre, happy sound of shattering glass. The stench of the pond that chewed my flesh mingling with the acrid stink of tires squealing and brakes slamming, desperate and useless as they fought, unable to stop, unable to save.

I glanced at the road. Those cars, they moved now, once again alive. Still slow, yes, but faster.

The car in front of me swerving

the water to my waist now—

and turning sideways as I slammed into them. The large woman with her cap of garish curls, her heavy arms taken from the wheel

surrendering, useless in the air

as we crashed. Her husband next to her, his thin arms

barren branches waiting for the leaves of spring

reaching as they braced for impact.

And behind me, in my rear view mirror, the bus leaning as the brakes screeched, the hulking yellow tipping and holding

heavy and slow

in a too brief moment of hope before little bodies pitched from open windows to roll in tumbling heaps. Skulls smacking. Necks snapping. Hands reaching to save and stop as the bus flipped on its side, barreling forward. The high-pitched keen of metal scarring concrete merging with the sloppy chomp of tender flesh being gnawed and delicate bone being crunched as

the trees

on the slope enjoyed their feast.

I'd looked to the shade of those trees as the world moved slow and my car turned and spun. Metal buckling and bending, I'd held my breath, the smoke of the tires gripping the road stinging my eyes as I'd watched the dark of those strong, desolate trunks.

Their appetites had slowed, the trees, the children no longer silent and still. Their legs, tired and distracted, kicking as they were lifted higher and higher. And there on the slope, where the blades were short and the grass was green, the dead girl stood.

Again.

I should have come to the pond first.

No.

Yes.

I felt the water nibbling my ears and kissing my cheeks, knowing my eyes would soon follow, forever dark coming, the unknowable following that.

Above me the sky was red, the thick, heavy clouds lit by fire. They bent low, these clouds, smothering me, taking me. The road above alive with the morbid singsong of distant sirens as strangers drove past, curious, their hands to their mouths, their eyes on the dead girl from the pick-up truck. The one in the sundress stained red who had been the first to panic and slam her brakes. To swerve. To have metal meet concrete. To smash through the window and land and

skid, her body twisting, her blonde skull splitting with a smack, the blood pouring
always
The road slicked with red
again
Our cars, our brakes, our skids and swerves and shattered glass to follow.

Yes, I should have come to the pond first, I thought as the water washed over my eyes and crawled over my head, the heat squeezing like a helmet tied too tight, the weight of it pushing down.

I knew she'd be standing, waiting where the grass was green.

I'd always known.

I should have come to the pond.

A breath later, it was over.

The dead girl laughed.

Ripperscape

VINCENZO BILOF

Just because I'm telling the story doesn't mean I'm not dead, and just because I'm telling you there's a possibility I'm not dead, doesn't mean I am in fact dead. I'm trying to establish my credibility—I know how this whole storytelling thing works.

I wasn't expecting such a big turnout for the experiment. I didn't realize Jack the Ripper was a celebrity on the scale of a popular basketball player.

Spectators and media pundits crowded outside the lab, cameras flashing, voices raised. Mindless journalists and bloggers, idiots who saw an opportunity to advance their own careers by giving the audience at home a chance to experience the unveiling of a legend. The identity of Jack the Ripper.

I had to push my way through the crowd and flash my identification at too many guards, and I was annoyed by the time I found the colonel and the scientist.

I study serial killers and sexual deviancy, but as far as qualifications went, that was the extent of it; I've been a desk man for most of my career in the agency.

Vincenzo Bilof

The media circus was inside the lab, too, and I had to stand beside the colonel with my fingers balling into fists, my jaw clenching. Awkwardly waiting until he would acknowledge me while hundreds of people gabbed. I could have answered their questions about the Ripper, but I didn't want to talk to anyone. These people could twist information and create false impressions, establish false expectations. I hated crowds, and I spent most of my time at a desk or in libraries. Finally, the colonel walked me into a briefing room where I met the scientist for the first time and shook his hand.

I should remind you that most scientists have extraordinarily large egos. I knew he would take this opportunity to brag about his accomplishments and theories, even though he had ample opportunity to brag about them to the press, and had done so already.

"I hear you're a big fan of the Ripper's work," the scientist said with a smile in an attempt to massage my ego.

"From which victim did you swipe the DNA?" I asked.

He pushed his glasses up the bridge of his nose and looked at the colonel, as if to ask him why I was there. He wasn't expecting questions that could challenge the validity of his enterprise.

"From Mary Jane Kelly," the doctor said and folded his hands in front of him as if to suggest his words were backed by a higher authority.

I could not hide my disgust. The entire episode already troubled me. "Mary Jane Kelly may not be a Ripper victim," I said.

If he excused me from the venture, I would not

have been disappointed; this scientific foray had become a mockery, a carnival show for the masses. Instead, he ignored my comment and introduced me to the other members of my expedition into the hypothetical consciousness of a killer.

The scientist introduced me as a "Ripperologist," a term I thought silly and insulting. My work for the agency was very important; my research and insight helped aid the apprehension of several villains, yet my expertise was being reduced to nothing more than something of a hobbyist.

I can't remember their names because I pretended to acknowledge them by offering a polite wave. Who was going with me? A team of five celebrities and a female porn star. Seven people in all. I was surprised one of the celebrities was a female basketball player, but I had never heard of her.

The doctor explained the specifics, most of which you already know. Our criminal apprehension agencies have the technology to enter the consciousness of suspects with a tiny piece of DNA evidence; the idea originated from a bad horror film, according to the rumors. With a bit of DNA analyzed and graphed and fed into a machine, our detectives can enter the consciousness and memories of a suspect and discover their identity. Of course, our entertainment industry has also sent people inside the minds of dead celebrities, but most of those adventures aren't available for syndication, because they proved to be a bit too disturbing (the famous Michael Jackson debacle, if you can remember those headlines); most of the time, the entertainment industry has falsified our "sur-reality" experience.

Vincenzo Bilof

So here I was, doubts about the venture creeping in. I had work to do; deviants were prowling the streets and I could predict their next moves, their motivations, desires. A historic moment was being exploited, and I was part of it. These people understood nothing about the psychosis of a killer, and they could never appreciate the breakthrough.

Inside the briefing room, the colonel and the scientist explained obstacles and experiences we could anticipate from the technology; these celebrities had already been briefed, and some of my own research into the Saucy Jack phenomenon was provided. I wanted to pay attention. However, I was sitting next to the porn star, and I recalled some of the images and videos I had seen on the Internet. I was familiar with her body of work, if you can forgive the pun.

Her fingers drummed on the tabletop, her head resting in her hand. I blushed when her eyes found me looking at her curves, her thighs and hair. I tried to look away, but I looked back to see if she was still looking, and she was.

"Hey," she whispered, "do you think we'll see a lot of dead women? A lot of dead prostitutes?"

I shrugged and wanted to say that maybe the colonel and the scientist were attempting to inform us, and we should listen. It was difficult for me to look directly into her eyes, as it wasn't every day that a woman who upheld the standard of sexuality and beauty wanted to speak to me, wanted my opinion, my expertise. I didn't speak to women often, for I had work to do.

"He may have fantasized about murder and brutality," I said in an attempt to answer her question.

"Mary Kelly's murderer may not be our man, so we may be witness to more specific brutality-fantasies, maybe even thoughts of suicide and guilt."

"Oh, so you know a lot about the Ripper?" she asked.

"Well, yes. I have studied him, and other serial killers."

"You see a lot of pictures of dead people," she said, her leg kicking the air beneath the table. "You're probably used to this stuff. You should be the tour guide. Especially if these guys ripped me off and this isn't Jack the Ripper. Are you excited?"

I still couldn't look into her eyes. She didn't have a wedding band on her finger, and I began to wonder what her real name was, and I began to wonder, as I had before, whether or not sexual deviancy is a form of sociopathy. Ted Bundy once said—and I paraphrase—that our society's obsession with pornography can be blamed for desensitization. Could this woman hold another man in her arms and love him, adore him, want to build a family with him? So many sex workers were single mothers, and some of them had families—I knew this because pornography was another field of study I had a vested interest in—but what nightmares did she have? What was there to fear for a woman who did not feel compelled to fear her own body and its power over men? How could such a woman know love, or understand it? Of course she could love, but what version of love?

I glanced at the porn star again, and I wanted to know her real name. I wanted to know the extent of her emotional/sociopathic capacity. Certainly, I have an obsessive personality, and I could not let my questions go.

And there I was, forgetting I was about to meet the man I had spent so much time attempting to understand. I was going to meet Jack the Ripper, or in the very least, the man who savagely murdered Mary Kelly.

After the conference, the science team strapped us into our chairs and placed helmets on our heads. Electrodes were attached to our skin, and some other scientific gadgetry was involved. I began to worry if this little trip was going to feel like travelling on an airplane, because I hated planes. You're not listening to my story now to understand how the technology works, and I couldn't tell you how it works even if I tried.

But I don't think I felt anything, because I blinked my eyes, and everything changed. Like that, I was in Whitechapel.

***

Twisting, narrow streets. A maze of anonymous structures that stretched high above me, reaching whatever passed for clouds inside this murky universe. The buildings were like towers, and a sickly-yellow glow shone from hundreds of windows, perhaps from meek candles or lanterns.

I had to remind myself I was inside the mind of a killer, even if this might not, in fact, be the Ripper's mind.

There was nobody else on the street, and this wasn't the Whitechapel I had visited in my imagination, or on virtual tours. This was not what I expected, yet I knew I was there. I knew I was in some twisted version of my expectations. I was alone and the street was silent. I wore the same clothes I wore when I stuck my head into the machine, and the air was cold; I wanted a jacket. We should have been dressed fashionably for the occasion. How else would we fit in? Were we supposed to fit in?

The others would have probably chattered their heads off with speculation, oohs and aahs, pointing their fingers at this landmark or the next. Like a group of teenagers in a bad horror film, they would freak each other out with postulations.

The semantics of this exercise, my purpose, my destination—I didn't know these things as much as I wanted to. I like things to be very direct, to be very precise, and here nothing was. My mission was vague, and the people I had met—those who were supposed to be with me—where were they? I could barely remember their faces. The world revolves around me, as it must revolve around you, and I don't deny this fact. So many of us are in denial of this very fact. But here I was, in a place I did not understand, in a world in which I did not have control. I fully expected to know the streets of Whitechapel, as I had spent the previous days studying and memorizing every detail I could stuff into my carefully-ordered mind.

I walked along the cobblestone streets and I felt the gaze of a million windows, all of them tall and lean, thin slashes of light cut into the faces of buildings that were huddled too closely, crowded together, cramped. I wanted to peer into the alleys where the destitute huddled; the squalor and terror caused by shadow and filth, hunger and desperation. I had imagined myself in Whitechapel, and this was not the city I envisioned. This was not the city I wanted.

I walked upon an endless, silent road. I wondered who might be dwelling in those lighted rooms, if there were faces that looked upon me and wondered how I might scream.

Information. I would have to look for the others on this endless street, this street without a name. Loneliness was not unfamiliar to me, for solitude was embedded in my lifestyle, a matter of fashion and choice. But I was stranded in this nightmare rendition of a city.

I stepped into a doorway off the avenue, and though it was a doorway mirrored by the cobblestone-carpeted eternity, I ventured to guess. I took a risk, which was not in my nature, as my heartbeat's fluttering excitement reminded me.

At first, I was forced to contain my delight upon realizing I was no longer alone. I began to hope and wonder at the possibilities that had nagged me every night since I received the assignment; I would be the first to meet Jack the Ripper, the first to look into his eyes and know him.

My eyes wandered to every corner of the room and perceived an inn of old decorum, something that didn't seem to fit into the nineteenth century, something more medieval. Wood tables and chairs, a dead hearth, little decoration, a room more suitable for serving the impoverished patrons who would have wandered in and out from the dizzying street. It did not resemble the interior of a Whitechapel inn as I had imagined it.

Sitting in a rocking chair by the hearth was one of the celebrities, the basketball star, a woman of immense height and stature, long-limbed and powerful. She nodded in greeting, and my eyes wandered to the macabre display on the center table, though I hadn't seen it a moment earlier; strange how it escaped my searching eyes.

A carcass of rib cage and meat chunks ripped and torn haphazardly, pieces here and there. Two legs dangled over the edge of the table, but an arm was halfway across the room. The face was nothing more than a spaghetti-soaked skull with long locks of blonde hair spilling out of the scalp. Several chunks of bloody flesh had fallen to the floor in a chaotic pattern of violence.

I was not disturbed, nor was I queasy. This surprised me, for I did not have a penchant or desire to experience violence, nor did I relish in gory fantasies or partake in blood-spattered media. I was pleased with my self-control, but there was a part of me that couldn't help but be upset at the scenario. My frustration was evident.

"What is this?" I asked the basketball star.

"Mary Kelly," she said with a shrug.

"No it's not," I said. "It's all wrong. This isn't how her corpse looked. This is the porn star we brought with us."

"I know that," she said. "I figured I would practice until you got here."

"Have you seen him?" I asked, changing the subject. "Have you seen the others?"

"They're upstairs," she said and pointed to the ceiling. "Why did you take so long to get here?"

I didn't understand her question, but instead wanted to convince her to accompany me upstairs. The whole notion of "going up" was alarming to me; I had thought we were supposed to wander the maze of streets and perhaps experience the psychological meltdowns that led to murder. My disappointment in this scenario was growing. The real Mary Kelly had been murdered sloppily and hastily, betraying none of the methodical caution and intricacies of the other murders, so I had doubted she was connected to the Ripper mythos. I had no desire to delve into the mind of a second-rate murderer, a clumsy killer whose crime was one of confused passion that became a mock-up of butchery to confuse the detectives and throw them off the trail, make them think Jack was still on the prowl.

"Upstairs," I said, repeating her to make sure.

"Yeah. I can't believe you knew that wasn't Mary Kelly. You really are good."

She had no intention of getting up and accompanying me. Alone, my feet carried me up the creaking stairs, until the stairs themselves no longer creaked because they were made of more solid stuff; the steps took on the luster of broken concrete, and the wall along the banister was a chain-link fence. Beyond the fence: nothing. A rush of heat down the stairwell made me think I was ascending into a blast furnace.

At the top of the stairs I found myself in another city, a neighborhood filled with a red sky, the street replaced with an iron grate beneath which a thick red fluid sluiced, oozing into gutters and filling the street. The buildings themselves were metal obelisks, structures imagined in the nightmares of metallurgists and factory workers. These massive buildings stretched into the red sky, lording over us.

Us. People walked the street. People attired in modern clothing, not the clothing of 19th century Whitechapel.

Now I could feel my irritation rising. I had been duped somehow. I was being used as part of some game, another experiment at the expense of corporate television sponsors. I was a character in an unreality show, one of the more popular forms of entertainment to emerge since the Jennifer Lopez technology became mainstream.

An iron bridge connected both sides of the street, and beneath the bridge a large group of people had assembled. Among them were those who were supposed to accompany me into this nightmare, including the basketball star and the blonde porn star, who I assumed had been the "practice" Mary Kelly in the inn below.

I turned around to see if the stairs remained behind me. They did not.

While approaching the crowd, I noticed a tall, shadow-cloaked figure standing upon the bridge, both hands on the guardrail, shoulders hunched, a top hat sitting atop his head (I assumed it was a man, obviously). He wore a billowing cape, but his entire form was clad in shadow. There was not a single distinguishable feature, not a single speck of color or flesh that would mark him as a mortal man, yet I knew it to be a man. I knew, somehow, this man's gaze was everywhere and everything, as if he was the sponsor behind the nightmare, the shrewd businessman who concocted this enterprise. We were under this man's spell, and we served his pleasures, whatever they might be.

Vincenzo Bilof

The crowd beneath the bridge was gathered around several gurneys; upon each was the corpse of a recently-murdered woman, all of them, I noticed, resembling victims who had been included in the Ripper mythos. There were eight corpses, a number which I figured to be circumspect, since some of these murdered women were not commonly accepted as victims who met their fate at the hands of the same killer.

The scientist from the lab circulated among the corpses and pointed out how and why each could belong to the Ripper canon.

"Sexual deviancy and repression are common afflictions we have come to associate with male serial murderers, in general terms," he went on. He demonstrated his expertise to all those assembled. Bragging, of course.

I couldn't help but notice the blonde porn star's eyes lingering on me. I met her sky-blue eyes, and did not look away. A sly smile touched the corners of her red lips. She tossed hair over her shoulder. She moved with the crowd, seemingly attentive to the doctor's demonstration.

The shadowed figure watched us, a blood-red sky beyond him.

"And here is Mary Jane Kelly," the scientist pointed to the gory mess that had once been a woman. "Many theories suggest the killer was in a hurry, or he was occupied by a bout of rage that transcended rational thought. The killer was no stranger to such a gory scene, for the amount of mutilation should be enough to drive a rational or sensible person into the throes of illness. A copycat killer would not have to go to such great lengths to make anyone believe the Ripper was involved, because there was such a high degree of hysteria and mystique surrounding this killer, who was very likely a man. We have before us a model of insanity and delusion, a man held captive by his own desire, a man who sought to extinguish some part of the terror that captivated him, as if he stood in the presence of a visage that was a vile mockery of the man he wanted to be, a visage that compelled him to such ferocity, such mutilation. Mary Kelly's murder was the climactic moment for our killer, a moment that represented the point of no return, as he walked into the embrace of the terror and became that terror. He wanted desperately to stay away from the shadows that tormented him, the shadows that tempted him, and Mary Kelly's death signifies his surrender."

A round of applause from the crowd, but I did not participate.

When I was a young man obsessed with the Ripper legend, I had studied the murders at length and had come to a similar conclusion. This doctor was a hack, hardly original, having perhaps copied the idea from another prominent theorist. It was a romantic idea, having manifested from the idea that the Ripper was one man who could not be caught, an unstoppable force that represented certain death for the unfortunate women who haunted Whitechapel's avenues. He was their release, their redemption, their personal cataclysm.

I looked up to find the shadowed man upon the bridge had gone.

"He was their release, their redemption, their personal cataclysm," the scientist said and bowed as the applause descended, the noise of mutual satisfaction.

The buxom blonde porn star winked at me.

This could not be. My words. My theories. My beliefs. Stolen from me.

***

I fled the scientist's demonstration and ran into one of the nearby buildings, one of those iron monstrosities that extended beyond the ocean of blood and sky, of blood-sky and red ocean. The liquid beneath the ground was blood, I surmised. And it was everywhere, for there was no carpet, no floor besides the iron grate, wherever I went.

I had stepped into another inn, this one filled with the dusky and dirty tribe of Whitechapel residents who would have found succor in such drunken revelry. Women upon the laps of toothless men, mugs full to the brim with syrup-dark liquid. Laughter. Squeals. A disgusting place full of the disease of squalor and classlessness, of degeneracy, illiteracy, and poverty. I ran up the stairs without so much as a glance or a notice from any of the assembled, and found myself upon another street, one that resembled the last street in every way, save there was no crowd beneath the bridge, and the populace was nothing more than a spectral presence; the people had become casual shadows, flickering like light bulbs on the verge of suicide.

When the arm wrapped around my shoulders, I leapt, surprised. The basketball player had found me again.

"I'm very repressed," she told me. "I can't help myself, you know. All this repression. Will you participate in the contest?"

I didn't understand her nonsense, and when I didn't respond, she pointed to the middle of the street, beneath the bridge. The shadowed, flickering figures paused as the blonde porn star was lead into the street by four men, each of them dressed in the garb typically associated with the Ripper character: cloak and hat, boots, gloves. All black.

She was thrown to the iron-grated avenue, but she did not scream.

"Let us see who is the most repressed!"

The announcement came from a figure who stood atop the bridge, and from where I stood, I could see the colonel's face, the colonel who I had met inside the lab before beginning my out-of-body quest. He, too, was dressed in Ripper attire.

"The winner shall have the first glimpse of Jack the Ripper!" the colonel declared, his arms spread wide over the avenue.

One of the Ripper look-alikes in the avenue brandished a long knife, and the others followed suit.

"Shall we start with the womb?" one of them asked.

"We don't have to be precise. Murder is not precise."

"I disagree," the third said. "Strangulation is precise, and we may visit atrocities upon her flesh afterward, since it will be easier. While she struggles, it might be difficult to do what we want."

"Well, I'm going to start with the womb."

I could see their faces from where I stood, and all of them were men who numbered among our Ripper-contingent. The first man inserted his knife into the porn star's stomach and began making a circular incision while she screamed and writhed; he placed a gloved hand over her mouth while she kicked, and the other two men looked on, fascinated.

Beside me, the basketball player nodded, as if in agreement with the method being used to murder the woman.

The killer decided to sit astride her torso. "The bitch won't stop struggling!" he said, his calm demeanor melting into pure frustration.

He was cutting sloppily, without any of the precision the Ripper had demonstrated upon some of his victims (the Ripper, as we know, was likely a male, and it has always been accepted thusly) he removed the knife and slid it across her throat. Blood spurted and bubbled from her neck. He frantically began sawing away at the lower part of her stomach as if possessed by the knowledge that a terrible deadline loomed and he must finish his work. The woman was still alive, clutching at her throat while the man freed his hand from her mouth to dig his hands into her stomach.

"I thought we were going to rape her first," one of the men said.

"I thought so too," the other replied. "Disappointing, to say the least."

I removed myself from my comrade's embrace and ran down the street. I did not understand why this grotesque scene unnerved me, when looking upon corpses thus far had not proven to be upsetting. While I ran, I heard the applause of the flickering shadows amid the colonel's announcement.

"Are we not all repressed? Is our sense of personal horror nothing more than an extended nightmare sequence, something buried, something we do not want to acknowledge? Something that exists no matter how much we turn away from it? Do we not find out greatest horrors in nightmares . . . ?"

His words trailed me, dogged my heels.

I found myself in another place of ill-repute, a room stained in blood and dust. An inn filled with laughter, laughter that emanated from shadows that did not have faces. It was otherwise the same place I had come from, though I looked far too long upon those dark, wavering forms; I watched mouths open in those black heads, mouths bereft of teeth, tongues wagging as spittle or alcohol exited those open faces.

The horrid mouths of open shadows, shadows that flickered, immaterial things in an immaterial universe.

"I'm here," a woman said. Standing behind me was the blonde woman, who had been eviscerated in public view. She did not seem harmed in any way.

"Do you think Mary Kelly had blonde hair, or red?" she asked me.

I gestured for her to come closer. "What's happening?" I asked. I finally betrayed my confusion, my lack of understanding. It was still difficult to make eye contact with her; she had been the subject of many mid-morning, mid-afternoon, and late-evening fantasies. My fantasies.

"What do you mean?" she asked.

"I thought we were supposed to find Jack the Ripper," I said. "I thought we were going to identify him, but instead we're . . . in some kind of . . . nightmare."

I struggled with my words, but she did not struggle with hers. Her hand traced the line of my jaw, her fingertips gentle, her hair white gold.

"I think we're looking for him," she said. "It's kind of exciting, isn't it? The more horror we witness, the more we understand him. I think we should understand him. He wanted to be understood. I mean, if he was repressed, wouldn't he want that?"

Before I could answer her ridiculous question, the basketball player appeared from behind and spun her around.

The tall athletic woman shoved a knife into the porn star's stomach. The actress's mouth opened; she gasped, and her hands held the basketball player's fist, nearly embedded in the bleeding woman's abdomen. Blood spilled over their hands.

The basketball player winked at me, then knelt with the knife inside her victim's stomach. Blood dripped onto her face as if she were holding her head beneath a waterfall after a long day trekking through a desert. She moved her head to allow thick streams of blood to pour into her eyes, her forehead, into her hair.

"I'm not allowed to have fun," the basketball player said, her mouth full of blood. "You don't know what it's like to be famous. I'm working in my sleep. Oh my God. Oh my God, this tastes just like I thought it would. They didn't tell you. I know they didn't tell you. This is a playground. Oh wow. Such a nice place. You don't know where you are, whose mind you are inside. They don't tell you, but we know. They don't tell you, but oh God, the taste. Oh God, now I will be a good person. I know I will be a good person again."

I was supposed to understand something. Something kept from me, something I wasn't supposed to know. But I was the expert. I knew deviants and killers. I understood them better than I understood myself. Yes. I tried to think like them. Dream like them. But I had been betrayed. This was a mockery of truth. A mockery of the darkness which hides inside the hearts of killers before they take their first victim.

The porn star's hands gripped the basketball player's head, and her body shuddered as more blood was expelled.

Enough was enough.

"Get me out of here!" I shouted to nobody, though I hoped the scientist and the colonel in the lab saw me. They must have been watching the monitors. They must see this horror; at the very least, the content was too graphic for the television audience.

"I want out!" I continued to protest.

The crowd inside the bar laughed. Those shadow figures with rolling tongues and yellow, crooked teeth guffawed, all of them facing me. The blonde still bled onto the basketball player's face.

I fled up another flight of concrete steps, and on my way up I saw the blonde again. She was going downstairs.

"You can't go down there," I said, stopping her. "We have to get out. We have to leave."

"Why?" she asked. "I want to find Jack."

"There is no Jack," I said, though I don't know why. "They brought you here to hurt you, abuse you. This is some kind of experiment. We're not here to find Jack."

"Jack is here," she said. "The real Jack the Ripper."

"You don't get it," I said insistently. "If you go down those stairs, they're going to hurt you. I've seen it happen already. I . . . I know it sounds silly. Just come with me. Come with me and we'll find a way out of here. There has to be a way out."

Vincenzo Bilof

Heroics were never my strong suit, but I wanted to protect her from the horrors that had been visited upon her consciousness. Why didn't she know? I could only guess, but she took my hand willingly while I led her up the steps. The girl accepted my hand, and I realized no other woman had ever trusted me, never so willingly.

Instead of another blood-and-iron street, we walked into a familiar room, a room I could identify down to the most minute description. Five tall figures wearing Ripper attire stood in front of the bed, but I could smell the blood. I could smell the human waste.

But the color had been drained from the world. The blonde and I stood inside a famous black and white photograph.

The cramped room where Mary Kelly had been murdered.

On the bedside table, a lump of flesh. I thought of cold lasagna.

A photograph I have seen hundreds of times, but I could not see the corpse beyond the Rippers. I could not see the corpse of Mary Kelly. I realized I wanted to, more than anything. Perhaps more than identifying and meeting the man who murdered her, I wanted to be present in her room, to stand over her slaughtered body.

The Rippers turned around slowly. Each of them belonged to our group of dream-explorers.

"So much repression," one of them said.

"I think the rage became his nightmare," the basketball player's voice added.

And another: "He was not afraid of the blood. He reveled in it. He wanted it. He wanted it like he never wanted it before, because he didn't know how badly he wanted it until this moment with her, this last moment of her life."

"We're here for a reason," I said, backing up against the wall. "We've spent so many hours researching the killer, and we should be able to find him. That's what we're here for! That's what we were promised!"

"I just hope the audience at home is excited," one of them said.

"They'll have to edit what you said out of the episode," another man said.

The porn star was behind me.

"Give her to us," the basketball player said. "If she gives herself willingly, maybe we can help you find him."

"We don't assume he hated women. We don't assume he vowed revenge against them. We don't assume he could not have loved a woman, could not have had a family."

"It's possible he had children of his own . . . "

"Enough!" I shouted at them. "You can't have her. She has suffered enough."

But she pushed through me and gave herself to them.

"If I exist to please him, maybe he will be okay. Maybe he will reveal himself," she said.

The men did not respond. They picked her up and cradled her in their arms. One of the men in the center didn't have to hold her; he shoved a knife into her abdomen and began to carve. The man who held her head placed one hand around her throat and squeezed.

I had witnessed one atrocity after another, as if I

had been flipping through my scrapbook of murder scenes at home, taking a moment to simply absorb the imagery while sipping on a glass of wine and watching the History Channel. I was helpless—mesmerized, by this display of butchery.

She did not scream this time, but when they dug into her exposed abdomen, they removed pieces of intestine and flung them at me. They carved out another organ, an oblong, dark shape in our black and white nightmare, and flung it at the wall. Blood splashed my face, and the men laughed.

The woman's eyes had rolled to the top of her head. Only a moment ago I wanted to protect her, keep her safe from these men and whatever horrors awaited her.

And I could not protest. I was weak before these men and whatever terror they decided to visit upon my own flesh. But I knew that was not their intention.

"Why won't you join us?" one of them asked. "You're the expert, after all."

"You must understand him to know him," another said.

I shouted back at them. "I know him! I've studied him for years. Why can't you see this is madness? All madness!"

It was useless. They continued to laugh, to throw blood and viscera at the walls like children playing in a kiddie pool.

There must be a way back, a way to protest this exercise, a way out of the nightmare.

A dream that was a prison, or a sequence of dreams that had become a prison, a prison that had become a nightmare. I had studied theories and had become a theorist. I spent my life in these nightmares, and was supposed to know them, understand them. But I did not know. I did not understand. I wanted out. This had become a farce of the science I dedicated my life to. This was my work. This was my way of life. Reduced to a mockery.

I was not an expert and I should be an expert. An awkward man. An awkward presence that did not belong. But I was trapped. Maybe in front of thousands of people at home.

And I was no closer to discovering who Jack was. At least, so I thought.

When I turned to leave the room, the stairway had disappeared. I found myself in another room, a chamber composed of iron fencing and pulsating blood above and below. The room was red, the inside of a throbbing organ, a functioning membrane of human consciousness. Red everywhere. I was inside of a fence, a chamber made of iron and blood.

In the center of this chamber was a platform that served as a bridge, connected to both fence-walls. Upon it stood both the scientist and the colonel in their Ripper attire.

A voice from behind me said, "Why didn't we go inside the mind of the victim?"

There was an answer to this question, an answer I wanted to provide, or at least, an assumption. But that answer no longer made sense.

I turned around and found a Ripper-form, a shadow looming over me, towering, a hellish image as tall and powerful as those enigmatic buildings that populated the streets of this nightmarish city. I stood in awe of its majesty, looking up for a face that did not exist.

My voice failed me. There may have been words I wanted to say.

I could feel the presence at my back, and I could not look back again. I stood before the five Rippers, the repressed volunteers who had spent hundreds of thousands of dollars to participate while I was allowed to venture inside this demented place free of charge.

"Tell us how you feel," one of them said.

"There's no need for you to be a lone wolf," another said. "We're a team. We're all together. We have things in common, too."

"This man is broke as hell," a third chimed in. "He doesn't have anything in common with us."

"We should help him belong," the fourth said.

"There is nothing to fear from the crowd," the basketball player said, though I could not see her face.

The last voice came from behind me.

"Nothing to fear at all."

It was her voice, the porn star. I found the strength to turn around and meet her bright blue eyes because I knew it was her, and I had wanted to keep her safe. I wanted to be her hero; she would thank me and appreciate me for everything I did. This was something I didn't understand until I looked into her eyes. I didn't understand anything until that moment.

"Do you want to see his face?" she asked, her voice calm, gentle. Her voice had power enough to soothe a man and bring him from the edge of death. "I have seen him, and I can show you what he looks like."

"It's what I've always wanted," I said pathetically.

I didn't know I had lied to her.

Her hand was on my neck and she pulled me close. The sound of her delicate voice became a whisper.

"You have seen his face before. We have all seen his face before. And we will see his face again."

I shuddered and caught the glint of silver between her fingertips in my peripheral vision. When the point of the knife touched the contours of my face, I did not resist. A scream began to manifest from my throat, but again, it was caught. Stopped forever. I wrapped my arms around her waist and allowed her to reshape me in the likeness she thought best. She was hard at work, like a landscaper carving the perfect front lawn for all the neighborhood to see, a lawn that would be good enough for everyone to think it a normal place, a happy place, where normal people lived.

I remember what she said.

"My real name is Mary . . . "

I don't know if you can see my face on the screen now, but I hope you can hear my voice. You have waited this long to hear the results of my journey, to see the face of the man who murdered Mary Jane Kelly.

To begin, I recommend you shut down this recording. You cannot see my face, and I can feel the flickering shadows of Whitechapel closing in. If you listen closely, you can hear the applause of the city's people. Shut down this recording or the monitor, for you should not see my face. It is no longer mine.

Look for me tomorrow, and I will be there. Somewhere close.

Descending

JOHN WHALEN

Lichfield Psychiatric Hospital had its secrets. However, as was true with most institutions, the majority of those secrets were forgotten in the bowels of file cabinets and resigned to the recollections of select veteran employees. The elevator murder of 1974 was not typical in this regard. Indeed, it was known by every member of the Lichfield staff as the greatest of the hospital's mysteries. Though many explanations were proposed, none were able to fully discredit the event as something singular and tragic. Intrinsically, many believed the evil responsible to still be at large, waiting in the deep recesses of the elevator shaft.

James Miller had heard about the murder far too many times. It was beyond getting old at this point. The version he was told involved a particularly violent patient who had gotten loose and somehow managed to hide in the elevator shafts. Were there holes in the story? Of course. But it was the story he was told first, and the one he was told most. In fact, James heard it nearly every day from Henry the janitor on his path through the hospital to work.

"And when the doors opened that morning poor Mack's body was so slashed up that the blood *poured* out on the fifth floor. Could you imagine that," he laughed nervously, "all those crazies getting a load of that to start off their day?" Henry paused for approval, but James showed all the signs of a man in a hurry.

Frustrated that Henry was not getting the picture, James quickened his pace. "But it was *grisly*," Henry said with a sort of needing. "Just plain gruesome." He attempted a dramatized shivering noise, but was so short of breath from pushing his janitorial cart fast enough to keep up, that it came out an awkward exhale.

James inched toward the elevator door with every word the janitor spoke, and with every inch, Henry spoke louder and faster. "You couldn't get me to go in that elevator for the life of me. No sir, I take the stairs when I can. And when I've got my equipment, I go around to the main elevator near the lobby." Everyone talked about it from time to time, but Henry lived it. His attitude and ritualistic behavior in regard to the event revealed an apparent paranoid streak in the old man. James knew it well enough from his job as an orderly for the patients on the tenth floor.

"But Henry, that's half way through the entire hospital," James reminded him. "You walk that far out of your way because of something that happened 30 years ago?"

"See that's the thing! They never—"

"I know, I know. They never caught him. I'm sorry but I've heard it a million times. I get the tragic unsolved crime thing, but it's been so *long* since it happened."

"Jimmy, who's to say he didn't hide in the elevator shafts? It's a big hospital, and you know about the basement?"

"Yes, I know." James pressed the button repeatedly. "Listen, Henry, I like talking to you, man, but I really need to take a rain check. You're making me late again."

The doors opened.

"Alright, alright Jimmy . . . I— It just makes me nervous is all. I don't want to see that happen to a nice kid like you."

James laughed and shook his head as he entered the lift.

The doors closed.

Henry hung his head and resumed his duties, slapping the mop to the tiles with force.

***

James was not running late. Indeed, he wasn't even in a hurry. Which was why, when he noticed that someone had goofed around and pressed the buttons for the 2nd, 4th, 5th, 6th, and 10th floors, he didn't get off to take the other elevator. After all, if someone messed with this one, they might have messed with the other one, too. Better he ride this one until he got to his stop on the tenth.

The old machine shivered awake and started its ascent.

James pondered the absurdity of a dangerous mental patient living in elevator shafts for thirty years, feeding off rats and scraps of garbage. More laughable yet were the farfetched tales of satanic rituals in the basement: burnt out candles, chalk scribbles, and even eviscerated rats. The evidence of such rituals was supposedly discovered by the janitors years ago. So apparently, not only was this mental patient dangerous and homicidal, but he had been charged by Satan himself. Oh, and he must have gotten the inhuman strength he needed to pry open the doors from a radioactive spider.

James shook his head and smiled. How absurd the tall tale sounded when all the pieces were put together. No one knew what had really happened that day, and it was likely no one ever would.

James focused on his blurred reflection in the metallic sheen of the closed door. Despite all the chatting and gossiping that went on between the janitors, no one could argue the quality of their work; the pristine condition of the elevator was a testament to that. James could make out his hair enough to see the tuft that stuck up in the back. A cowlick he had from birth, he struggled with styling his hair every morning. His parents used to call him Alfalfa, after the character from *Our Gang* who was plagued by a comically dramatized tuft of hair that always sprung up at inopportune times. A classic from before his time, he'd admittedly only seen an episode or two. He licked his hand, looked closely at the crude reflection, and began patting it down into obscurity. The elevator slowed.

With no notice, James' reflection was replaced with a grimy brick wall; the elevator doors had opened prematurely. James, concentrating on his reflection, recoiled. Stepping back, he assessed the situation. The red glowing floor indicator read "5" and there was a sliver of open space toward the top of the elevator's opening. He might have been able to step out on the fifth floor if he happened to be the size of a mouse.

"Well, fuck *me*," James whispered.

Now he would be late. Stalled elevators were rarely fixed in seconds.

James stepped over to the buttons and pressed "Door Close" repeatedly. The doors closed halfway and sprung back open, mockingly. James let out a long sigh. There was no denying it now: He needed the help of a janitor or a maintenance worker. He began pressing the red "Emergency" button. The doors closed this time.

"Alright! There we go," he said in one excited breath as he backed away.

The elevator began its descent. His smile faded.

"Shit."

He rushed back over to the buttons and pressed "10" furiously. Nothing lit up.

The elevator must have reset. I'll probably have to start from the first floor again. He let out another long sigh, closed his eyes, and massaged his forehead.

A jolt brought him back. The floor indicator read "L."

Good, back in business.

Another jolt and the elevator descended farther.

"Oh, goddamn it!"

James pressed the "10" again, but to no avail. The red indicator read "B." B for basement, he guessed. James double-checked the floor numbers on the buttons to make sure there were no B1 or B2s like he'd seen on other elevators; B was the lowest floor. *Okay, fine. Let's be done with this now.*

But it didn't stop.

The machine's movements became jittery, strained. James held onto one of the courtesy rails to keep his balance. With each shake of the elevator car, his panic grew. His heartbeat was loud in his ears, his breathing heavy, and his thoughts racing. Could he fall down the elevator shaft like this? If so, could he really survive if he jumped at the last second? How long would it be before someone came to his rescue?

An eerie metallic sound resonated above: stretching cables. James pressed the "Emergency" button feverishly. He mumbled obscenities under his breath.

The glowing red indicator now read "—."

In an instant a sound like the rushing of wind was all around him. The tone of the stretching cables warped into a sound he'd heard in a Hendrix song. He could feel movement, but could not wrap his head around its direction, blind in the enclosed space of the elevator car. James was suddenly stricken with dizziness. His vision blurred and his legs became shaky. He held tighter to the courtesy rail.

All at once, his mind rationalized the sensation: He was *swinging*. Despite the narrow space of the elevator shaft, in no sense of the word was the swinging moderate. It felt like James was aboard a pendulum through a dark, impossible space he could not comprehend. He closed his eyes, but it did no good to soothe the feeling.

It's just vertigo, James rationalized. *It's normal to experience it in a time of fear.*

But the wind from within the elevator shaft continued. It was palpable through the brisk, chilly air that entered from the cracks of the doors.

But wind? *Now how was that possible?*

Yet defiantly it howled, making a wind instrument

of the elevator car. He felt it from corners he didn't even know had openings to the outside, and it did horrors to his sense of safety. It was as if he were alone on a precarious rope bridge above an endless dark chasm. James held tight and prayed. Like a child on his first roller coaster he was curious, yet desperate and helpless.

It felt like an hour before the swaying sensation subsided. He couldn't be sure of time, anymore. The wind tapered off, as well, but its recession brought with it a new development. He hadn't noticed it before: the weak humming noise that lingered in the background. His mind tried to discredit it as electrical or mechanical in nature, but there was no denying its strangeness. It sounded oddly *human*, like a chorus of thousands in the distance, wildly out of tune. In fact, he was certain it was far too distant to even be at the very bottom of the elevator shaft. He had just passed the basement level, so it should follow that the bottom wouldn't be far now. Yet as he continued to descend at a constant pace, the sound (or sounds) grew louder still. No longer a hum now, its cadence had some eerie repetition to it, like a chant of some sort. Try as he might, he could not distinguish any words.

It then occurred to James that something was very wrong with his spatial conception: the swinging, the continuous descent and the noises below what would be the bottom of the shaft. There should be no reason he hadn't yet landed safely at the bottom by now, emergency crews on their way to reboot the faulty machine and elevate him to safety. Even if the hospital had the largest basement conceivable, he should have reached the bottom minutes ago. Were there tunnels beneath? He had thought not. And even that theory became less likely as the continued descent haunted his sense of logic. He was running through explanations like wildfire, and was already afraid of what he would find beneath the used up cinders. The screen for the floor number glitched confusedly, as though it too could not comprehend where it was, where it was going, and what it should do.

And still the humming.

The din had become noticeably stronger now. It *was* human, and it sounded eager.

A young woman's shriek somewhere outside the car startled him from his thoughts. He froze in place, dumbstruck and curious. *God, has someone fallen in?* Was his descent into the bowels of the elevator shaft creating such havoc with the system that someone accidentally stepped through to nothingness? He pictured the poor woman losing her balance at the precipice and plummeting. His morbid curiosity even allowed him to see her at the bottom: her broken body landing with a dull thud, coating the walls with the red of her insides.

It wasn't long before there was another shout, a man's this time. The howl of pain, fear, or both, echoed cruelly, magnified by the acoustics of the elevator car. James backed away from the door. His heartbeat was strong in his ears. He shook uncontrollably. He had burned through the rest of his explanations and was left to read the ashes.

This was wrong. This was not natural and it was wrong.

An orchestra of agonized screams rushed from every direction, and the elevator shook noticeably in its wake. James instinctually clasped his palms over his ears and pressed down tightly. It cut the piercing nature of the sound, but its power still vibrated within him like an amplified bass drum. Hundreds, maybe thousands, cried out simultaneously, directionless, swarming. The sound clung to something primal within him, clung and reverberated deep within his viscera. Warm, acidic vomit welled up in the back of James' throat and he winced as he caught and swallowed it.

Something in the corner of his vision drew his attention away from the sound. He noticed some shift of light on the steel sheen of the far wall. Approaching, James noticed the anomaly fade and disappear. He cocked his head and looked closely at the wall, the drumbeat of his heart ever so loud in his head. A handprint appeared, foggy against the metallic surface.

Briskly stepping away, he saw more and more make their presence known against the cold shiny surface. His eyes darted around. Every reflective surface in the elevator car had handprints appearing and fading at rapid pace. Where one disappeared, two more replaced it, all to the backdrop of the horrible disembodied screams. On the wall to his left he noticed a large patch of fogged up surface, like a breath upon a window by winter. He watched in horror as the words *"Vae Victis"* were scribbled by some invisible force. James screamed and retreated to the middle of the elevator car, equidistant from the shifting surfaces.

With no warning, it all stopped. Nothing, not even a murmur remained. The handprints and words faded as abruptly as they had appeared. The only evidence of the strange event was the ringing in James' ears as they readjusted to the silence. The sound of his heavy breathing became noticeable again in increments. He let out a long exhale.

Something outside found this funny.

A deep roaring laugh echoed around the elevator, into the elevator car, and into his mind. It was outside and within simultaneously. It was surrounding him and inside the car with him. James looked to the manufactured cold glow of now functionless buttons, and the red floor indicator that zapped in its last spasms of electrical life. A sense of hopelessness gripped him like the bitter embrace of an iron maiden. This was insanity.

Still the laugh bellowed at him, harmonizing with distorted sounds of stretching cables.

An image jumped in front of his mind's eye. James pictured the elevator car dangling by tightening iron cords as an immense, endlessly powerful being toyed with him: a cat and its ball of yarn. Whatever was laughing had a vastness about it that made his pulse quicken and skin hot. It was cosmic and deep, and he its little organic plaything. Sweat pooled in his brows from the thoughts just behind them.

The polished metal doors shuddered loudly with the erratic spasms of something in its death-throes. James leapt to the back wall and huddled as far into the corner as he could get. The noise of the shaking doors was horrendous, deafening, powerful, and a reminder of the door's hollow fragility against whatever lay on the other side. James let out a whimper. He shook uncontrollably as warm urine trailed down his khakis.

As if to answer, the first trail of dark red blood

leaked steadily from the right side of the elevator door. It slid down silently and amassed in a steaming pool at the base.

James was a cornered animal. He found himself clamoring up the courtesy railing and trying to balance on it. Slamming the wall of the elevator car with the palm of his hand, he screamed, loud and desperate. The flow unyielding, the pool of blood grew. The off-center floor of the elevator, beaten by daily foot-traffic, led the stream of blood toward him. James shivered and felt himself grow lightheaded.

As he scrambled into the corner, he felt burning vomit well up in his esophagus again. This time he could not hold back: It leapt from his mouth with a sick splat on the floor in front of him. The brown of his eggs and grape juice of this morning's breakfast mingled with the blood that chased him.

But the flow behind the dam of the elevator door did not let up. He noticed a rhythm now, a sound familiar to him during the course of this ordeal: loud metal knocking in the pattern of a rapid heartbeat. Another stream slid from the top of the door, then another, and another, until every inch of the perimeter was shedding blood as if from some mortal arterial wound. The strength of the flow mimicked the heartbeat. It was as if an immense heart was forced against the other side of the doors, pumping its copious yield of blood through all the surrounding crevices.

Against the bending steel perimeter of the door, the blood splashed to the rhythm of the pulse, coating the walls in red splatter marks. The air became heavy and pregnant with the scents of salt and iron as the blood poured from the top of the door down in sheets. James flailed in his corner. He tried to pull his legs up onto the railing as he sat. The growing crimson pool reached him now. He was able to keep his balance on the railing for half a minute before he let one of his legs go and splash into the pool of red.

The searing revelation of his nerve endings caused him to howl; the encroaching blood was boiling hot.

James stood on the tips of his toes to avoid further contact. The puddle was warm on the soles of his shoes. Instinctually he reached up to grab hold of something to elevate himself with. Instead his fingernails scraped along the cold, unyielding metallic walls. James could feel the boiling red liquid enter the small crevices of his work shoes and winced. Tears welled up in his eyes. He fell into hysterics to the cacophonous beat of the elevator door's spasms.

"Oh god . . . not like this," he bellowed *"Please not like this!"*

The elevator door shuddered open slowly. Steaming hot blood hissed maliciously, spurting from the growing gap in the door like an arterial laceration. James recoiled. He protected his face as the blood scorched his hands and scalp, sending screaming neural signals from synapse to brain. Between his fingers he glimpsed horror itself: a boney, taloned hand crept between the doors, trying to pry them open. The fingers themselves were half the size of the door. As they pried, a glowing, viscous object resonated on the other side.

A preposterously large pupil peeked in at him from behind the narrow opening of the portal. He watched as it blinked huge sheets of spongy red flesh across its form.

His body had enough. James fell into a merciful temporal darkness that swept like a black cloth over his senses. He lost his balance, hunched against the wall, and slipped away into unconsciousness.

***

When James awoke there was no evidence of blood: no stains, no lingering scent of iron, nothing. Even the heaviness of the once steam-filled room vanished. The air was mockingly still. Only the itching pain of irritated red skin was left to remind him that his memory was to be trusted. But even the pain receded like the loosening grip of a hand from around a small animal held too tight. Held too tight by massive boney—

James knelt to the floor, haunted by the blurred images of what he saw before he blacked out: the blood, the steam, the claws, and the eye. He saw the eye again in his mind, how it squinted from behind the elevator doors as though it were a tiny peephole. He closed his eyes and prayed.

He was startled back into reality by the laugh he had heard earlier. Sadistically it echoed, as if to mock the futility of his prayers. James kept his eyes closed. He'd had enough, given in to what would be. Faced with this unknown realm, he had no understanding, no control, and certainly no hope. His eyes remained closed even after he heard the grating friction of the opening elevator doors.

It wasn't long before the fear of the unknown got the best of him. Reluctantly opening his eyes, James was startled by the sight with which he was met. Expecting a claw scraping at the elevator's interior for him, or the focused eye of his extra-dimensional watcher, he was surprised to find the grimy wall of the elevator shaft. In the center of the wall was an old-fashioned wooden door. It was beaten and worn, an antique. Chipped white paint flaked from its intricate design. It had a rusted old doorknob and a skeleton style keyhole, from which the glow of a faint light seemed to escape.

James sat a while pondering his next move. He was hesitant to leave his corner and approach the gateway. The closer he got, the more vulnerable he would be to the reach of whatever lay outside. When he stood, James' movements were jerky and strained. The sweat from his brow overflowed and burned his eyes. He wiped it away with his palm. Each shaky step he took toward the door was like walking through a thick jelly. He could feel the bones in his legs with each movement. Breathing quickly, and with a heartbeat quicker still, he inched toward the open door and the closed door. As James approached the precipice, he took a careful glance in each direction to ensure nothing was waiting to strike at him from the gap. When his shaking subsided slightly, he bent and spied into the keyhole at what lay beyond. Squinting, he batted his eyelashes to move them out of the way, and focused.

Through the keyhole, James saw himself looking through the keyhole of an old door, outside of an elevator door, from the far end of an elevator. His heart skipped a beat. Confused, he kept staring, hoping that some piece of the reality he once knew would give him an understanding of this infinite loop. But before he could put any real effort into wrapping his head around it, a black cloth barrier shrouded his view through the peephole. Eyes wide, James jumped back. He turned around quickly.

At the back of the elevator was a man in a black robe sitting in a wooden chair, his head shrouded in black cloth.

James went stiff with fear. The scream at the back of his throat was muted by his tightening chest and held in as he hastily contorted his body into the corner farthest away. The man in the chair squirmed and thrashed. Muffled noises of desperation came from beneath the black hood. The man appeared to be bound and gagged.

James let out the breath he had held tight in his chest. He moved from the corner and slowly approached the restrained man. As he got closer, he noticed something glimmering at the man's feet. Sensing the danger, James stepped forward and kicked the knife out of range. He walked over and knelt down to retrieve it. He couldn't help but notice the level of detail in its hilt, the ruby encrusted silver, the strange symbols and engravings. The blade itself was curved in a peculiar way, lending it the likeness of a talon.

Knife in hand, James suddenly felt invigorated by the scenario. Something about the nature of the blade and the desperation of the man in the chair stirred up deep-seated impulses, impulses which his rational mind had to keep consciously at bay. For a moment he felt like an actor in a dark play, filling a role that was as old as history. The stage was set, the shivering florescent lights of the elevator were ablaze, and here he was with blade in hand, prepared to do what was always there in the deepest, darkest nature of the protagonist, Man.

Fearful of himself, James threw the knife aside: a circuit interrupted. Before his desires could stop him, he rushed forward to remove the hood.

He looked himself in the eyes.

Beneath the hood was a perfect copy: his dark hair, the desperation in his eyes, even the cowlick tuft of hair that sprung up when the hood was removed. He noticed the red, swelling burns and the tears that ran down his would-be-victim doppelganger's face.

James removed the gag from James' mouth. His jittery movements made it hard to untie the knot at the back of the head. After a minute of fumbling, he pulled the gag from his jaw with jerky, shaking movements. The James in the chair spoke.

"*Please,*" he said, "please just . . . just make it quick."

James put his hands to his face and closed his eyes. " . . . I don't understand."

"You have to do it. You have to kill me. It's the only way." He paused for a moment, contemplative. "It seems to be the only way to change anything, maybe *escape.*" The last word the would-be victim hushed, fearful that something might overhear him. He made a motion with his chin toward the red floor indicator: brightly it read "-666."

James looked closely, the oddity of it reflecting in his expression.

The would-be victim continued: "What does it read to you?"

"Negative six hundred and sixty six," James said.

"Okay, that's what I thought. It reads negative six hundred and sixty five to me."

James looked back to make sure he hadn't misread. It still read the number of the beast.

"I still don't—"

"It read six hundred and sixty six before . . . " he closed his eyes, took a deep breath, and opened them again. "Before I did what I had to do."

A laugh from outside the elevator penetrated their conversation. Both winced, mirrored.

"I can't," James said.

"You can and you will. You almost did before you removed the hood. The knife helps somehow. Just give into the feeling. Put the gag and the hood back on. That will help, too." He closed his eyes and breathed deep again. "Don't bother with the wrists. We have to do this six hundred times. The neck, cut deep and all the way across."

James locked eyes with himself in the chair. He knelt down and fell backwards on his rear, his eyes burning with brimming tears. Sinking his head, he let go. The loud, desperate gasps of a grown man's sobbing echoed within the steel cage of the elevator car. Tears streaking down his face, snot dripping from his nostrils, James crawled away lifelessly. He wriggled himself into the far corner.

The man in the chair breathed deep, reveling in the last breaths he had allotted. It was the same thing James knew he would do if facing the same situation (and maybe he would be). What were the ramifications of the things the other him in the chair was saying? Would this mean that he was next in line to be murdered by another version of himself? And if so when would it end?

James looked up past the functionless elevator buttons for floors that had no relevance now. He focused on the red indicator above: "-666." How could he bring himself to do it once, let alone six hundred and sixty six times?

It might be the only way out, he thought, that's how.

James wiped the tears from his eyes. He stood and approached the chair in the same confident motion. The would-be victim drew a deep breath and exhaled at the footsteps. James tied the gag, replaced the hood, and retrieved the knife.

The scene resumed.

James placed his hand firmly on the victim's head. The victim tightened. In a swift, strong motion, James cut the line through the carotid arteries. Warm blood poured over his hands as he let out a yell of disgust.

His strength fleeing, James retreated. But the deed was done. His other self squirmed quietly in the chair, red coursing dark onto the speckled cream floor. James threw the knife aside again and backed against the wall, hitting it with force. He slunk down, the buttons of the elevator lighting up meaninglessly as he descended. James sat in a fetal position, hung his head, and closed his eyes to the sounds of his own final movements.

All went black.

***

James opened his eyes to more black. He felt for his arms and legs and found them bound to the chair. He called out only to himself gagged. It had come full circle. When the hood was removed, it was him looking at himself once again. The floor indicator read "-665."

James' head swirled with emotion. He could feel the beads of sweat caught in his eyebrows, hanging hesitantly over the gathering tears. He didn't know whether to feel relieved or fearful, happy or apologetic, excited or terrified in the face of himself. All he knew was that there was some progress in this: this repeated act of self-torture. Whatever entity he was trying to appease, whatever watched him (he could still feel its eyes even when it wasn't peeking through the elevator doors) seemed pleased by the spilling of his blood at his own hands.

His desperate eyes looked at the same desperate eyes, and when the gag was removed, James the victim explained the situation to James the victimizer as it was told to him. The script unfolded once again. The would-be victimizer crawled back into the corner as James had done before. Eyes closed, James remained silent as he sat in his sacrificial seat. He thought of what it would be like. He remembered how the victim squirmed as the blade ran into his neck and how he shook in the last moments of life. The previous version of himself didn't scream, though, which may have been a good sign; maybe it would be less painful than expected. When he finally heard the footsteps from the corner, he continued to keep his eyes closed. James breathed deep and tried hard to be brave so the victimizer would not waver. When he felt the hand on his shrouded head, he braced.

The pain made him want to jump out of his own restrained skin and tell himself to stop. Sharp and searing, it didn't recede like he'd hoped it might. He felt the warm blood flow from his neck and drench his clothes. Losing oxygen, he gasped for air but was met with the blood caught in his throat. He was only silent because he had no choice. He had no sound, no voice to use. Stars danced before his eyes as merciful death gradually took him. James eased off into a dulling of senses and waited for life.

***

James opened his eyes and took in his surroundings. He was in the fetal position in the far corner of the elevator once again. He'd woken up from his own death like it was a bad dream. Here he was again, looking at himself tied to the chair. This time, James the victim wasn't squirming. He sat still, knuckles clenched white, knowing how it would end this time. The victim knew how the victimizer would go about it. James looked up at the floor indicator: it read -664. That was proof enough. He walked briskly over to the chair, picked up the knife and made a quicker, deeper incision.

If there were some balance here, he didn't want to upset it. James returned to the corner he awoke from. From what he could gather, his struggles with death were less this time. He hoped it was due to the new confidence with which he made this cut. James laid his head between his knees and closed his eyes. He waited to be escorted to his death once again.

***

-650: James learned that it was better to go for the heart. It was more gruesome but much quicker.

***

-574: James' hands shook so bad he needed to pause the scene for many minutes to calm down. When the victim yelled at him to get it over with, James missed the heart on the first thrust and had to take another stab at it.

***

-501: Weak and overwhelmed by the road ahead,

James' movements became slow and labored. Still he pressed on. With desperate, muscular movements, he committed the act and continued the cycle.

***

-438: James was slipping. The foreboding sensation of his mind's decay was palpable. He felt something unraveling like a ball of yarn in his brain.

***

-374: James laughed as he took the knife to his chest.

***

-245: James lost control of his laughter in the grip of rising hysteria. His accuracy diminished in the wake of his incessant shaking.

***

-182: James stopped paying mind to anything but the act. He no longer knew what the floor indicator read.

***

-146: *It doesn't matter how I do it. It doesn't matter. I'll be there in a second. I don't care. It doesn't matter HAHAHA it doesn't matter!*

***

-47: Insanity, absurdity, bloodlust.

***

-15: The laughter from outside the elevator bellowed deep and vigorously. James laughed with it.

***

The security office finally got the video feed back. The static slowly faded, showing a blurry male figure standing in the middle of the elevator. There was a passenger aboard the stalled car after all. The figure moved erratically, seemingly panicked.

The clearing picture gradually revealed something more grisly.

***

B: The laughter had disappeared. James hadn't noticed. He drove the knife into his own chest, repeatedly, sloppily, until he crumpled to the floor.

***

What was left of the fabric of James' mind was puzzled. The pain was the same, but this wasn't like before. The other James had disappeared. There was just one James, alone with his blood. He felt a strange, exciting sensation, something his tattered thoughts seemed to have confused with freedom. He was ascending.

James looked up to the red floor indicator with enough time to see the cruel joke: He was on the ninth floor, approaching the tenth. He would be a little late to work, but was sure they would understand, given his condition. James tried to laugh, but what came out was a sorry gurgling noise. Blood rose up in his throat and began swallowing him from the inside. He made it to the tenth floor.

The jaws opened.

A man on the outside screamed. A woman vomited. All else stayed idle.

The jaws closed.

James knew no more.

***

Late that night, the janitors labored in the silent contemplation of men hard at work and hard at thought. Nights like this, when Henry and Tom were left alone to do their work in peace, they normally listened to the music of their heyday. Jimi Hendrix and Led Zeppelin would riff on down the empty corridors and halls of the hospital offices, quiet enough to keep from spreading down to patients' rooms, but loud enough for them to revel in it, playing to the pace of their work.

Tonight was not one of those nights. Tonight the weight of their thoughts would crush those delicate tunes into something sickening and grim. The pace of their work was much too slow to hold a beat. Too much was left unsaid.

The heaviness was something real, something that danced mockingly in the air between them. When the weight of it became too much, Henry's broom slowed, his concentration wavering. Tom looked up to find Henry's misty-eyed gaze: anguish crafted in the medium of face muscles. It was a moment Tom worked quickly to defuse.

"Hey, if you want the second floor tonight, I can take the third. I don't mind doing the shit work tonight . . . You look tired," Tom said over the rustle of emptying waste bins, "Just take this one easy."

"It's wrong," Henry mumbled. He swept slowly and unproductively, cleaning the same spots over and over as if it were a hopeless effort to ever make them clean again.

"Swear I don't mind . . . told you I'm feeling up to it."

"He was a good kid."

"*God damn it, Henry!*" Tom hissed. "He's dead. Can we stop this now? There's no use in it."

"That's it?" Henry said, gaining momentum, "We're just going to leave it at that? You haven't mentioned it once yet. It's like nothing happened."

"Don't." Tom pointed his finger at him. "I pushed a few numbers on an elevator. That's all I did. Now shut the fuck up," he spat.

"You didn't know him." Henry stared deeply at nothing in particular. "His eyes when the door closed . . . he had so much potential, so much life."

"That's enough. You know what we have to do. You know this is the only way we'll be able to keep . . . " His eyes drifted warily over to the elevator doors, not five feet away, " . . . keep *it* content."

Henry's gaze fell. His mind flashed dusty old memories: three drunken twenty-somethings laughing away in the basement after their shift. A circle of salt, candles, chalk inscriptions: a big joke. Incantations in the elevator, a ritual of floors and numbers. Three drunken twenty-somethings, in a world they should have never even dreamed of entering.

An unexpected result.

And a desperate solution.

"Mack had those eyes," Henry said.

"Damn it, Henry! It was so *long* ago. It was fair. We drew straws." He said it as though the God of Chance had already absolved his sins. "That's enough for me."

The pace with which he packed his cart and wheeled away said otherwise.

"I'll start on the third floor. You keep doing whatever it is you're doing," he condescended.

Tom had already rounded the corner and was out of sight when Henry resumed sweeping. It was the same distracted work of a man resigned to an engrossing thought. He swept and swept with no real reason to do so; the spot was clean half an hour ago. Yet he kept close to the elevator doors, as if something would happen, as if there were some chance he would be able to take it all back.

Henry kept picturing James' face, before the cruel

steel jaws of the elevator took him. The smile he wore was defiant and innocent, oblivious to what awaited him below. Who was he to give that wealth of life over to such merciless forces?

Tears began to blur Henry's vision until he could no longer pursue the menial tasks that usually distracted him from such thoughts. It did no good this time. His eyes fixed on the elevator doors. Something inside gave him the fleeting sense that they would open, that there would be some chance at a resolution to this, some merciful catharsis. But deep down Henry knew reality, and the dark forces that pulled its strings, to not be so forgiving.

Henry knelt to the ground before it and wept the ugly tears of an old man with a lifetime's worth of regrets. From the shaft below, he felt the muted vibrations of laughter, deep in the bowels of the Hell that surely awaited him.

Virtuoso

HAL BODNER

The **melodies from** the flute and oboe intertwined like two butterflies frolicking in a field of flowers. But the glorious notes from the violin were what held the audience enthralled. The woodwind players were mere hirelings for the evening, as was the harpsichordist, competent enough but not truly inspired players. But the violin! The violin was wielded with consummate skill by none other than Monsieur Alphonse DuTierre, Marquis de Paysnoir.

The instrument itself was a masterpiece of craftsmanship, obtained at an astounding cost. To DuTierre, it had been worth every *sou*—his most prized possession. A worthy vessel which gave voice to the beauty of his soul, he would gladly have paid ten times more than what its maker had asked. Given his other addictions, it was essential to his sanity, to his very health, that he have something to express holiness and purity or else, he was convinced, he would be damned for eternity.

The other diners listened with rapt attention to de

Paysnoir's recital. It was a rare treat; the noble was truly an inspired player. Even the constant preening, the jealous whispered critiques of fashion which passed for conversation amongst the women, and the blatant flashing of diamond encrusted buckles and cuffs which passed for sexual acumen amongst the men, gave way before the concert. The master had deigned to play; the guests would not want to miss a note so they could enthrall less advantaged members of society with the tale of how they adored DuTierre's performance and—Oh? But, *mon cher*, were you not there? *Je me regret* but I did not notice your absence.

Besides, all were aware that to offend the Marquis, especially in the matter of his music, could prove harmful to business and adverse to continued good health.

With part of his mind, DuTierre remained aware of the guests' adoration and of the élan he brought to Madam Roundevalle's gathering. He was, after all, suspected to be the richest noble in the province and, when one coupled the wealth with his strikingly handsome face and trim compact figure, also the most eligible bachelor. He saw from the corner of his eye the posturing, the struggle of the less socially advantaged to improve their status by physical proximity to their betters, the delight in the crafty hooded expression of men who overheard a scrap of information which might later prove financially beneficial, the mingled disdain and satisfaction of the gorgeously wigged matrons when they noticed the province's reigning young beauty was wearing a dress in which she had been publicly seen last season and their delight in the knowledge, coaxed from their husbands, that her family had suffered Louis' displeasure and had consequently fallen into hard times.

It was with only a small portion of his mind that DuTierre noticed these things. Most of him, most of the essence of DuTierre that was his very soul, was wrapped up in the violin, in the long sobbing notes he coaxed from the instrument and the soothing, comforting and almost religious quality of the music as he gracefully swept the bow across the rosined strings. Ah, what a Glorious Noise he was making! If only the angels could hear him, how jealous they would be. He smiled a secret and not entirely pleasant smile; even with his artistic genius, he doubted the angels would welcome him amongst them.

"Bravo!"

"*C'est bien fait!*"

"*Magnifique!*"

The accolades rang out across the salon when DuTierre finally relinquished his bow in favor of a bow. The usual rush to be near him, to clasp his hand with congratulations, followed. Though he normally would have breathed in the sycophancy like morning air, tonight he was impatient to be gone from this dreary dinner he shared with pompous men and extravagantly coiffed women. Tonight, DuTierre would find his own reward for a recital so well given.

He extricated himself quickly and bid his *adieux* to Roundevalle as hostess and to a few of the more influential men in attendance. It never hurt to be gracious; one never knew when one might need political assistance. Once ensconced in his carriage, a fur blanket comfortably arranged about his lap and legs, he banged thrice upon the interior roof with his stick—a prearranged direction to his coachmen to proceed directly back to DuTierre's estate this evening. Social etiquette demanded that he pay his respects to those titled lords and ladies of the King's Court whose homes were along his route. His presence, especially in the wake of the evening's triumph, was expected if he wished to curry favor. Tonight, however, DuTierre lacked the patience for such artifice; he had other needs to attend to.

There was a sharp jerk as the whip encouraged the horses to get going, followed by the familiar rocking back and forth of the carriage as the wooden wheels trundled over the ruts left by a recent storm. DuTierre hoped the rain would not return for several days; it would not do for his planned entertainment to be ruined. He sat, lost in anticipation of what the next few days might bring, until he began to smell the familiar scents of mown clover, wet hay and decaying manure which indicated they had reached a more rural area of the countryside. DuTierre lowered the shutter and looked out, recognizing the landscape as being far enough from his estates for his purposes. After two hard bangs of the walking stick on the carriage roof, it slowly rolled to a stop and he disembarked.

"Monsieur?" The coachman had been well-trained but he was a recent addition to the staff and had never taken this particular journey with DuTierre before.

"I shall walk a short distance. You will drive half a league down the road and await me there."

"But, monsieur . . . "

The dark eyes flashed, the handsome aristocratic face frowned at the coachman's protest. DuTierre did not brook insolence from his servants.

"I hope . . . ," DuTierre's voice was pleasant yet with an undertone of something not very nice. " . . . you do not question my commands. You *do* recall the penalty for disobeying the master on *my* estates, do you not?"

The coachman, a strapping young man who had on his first day of service found himself stripped to the waist and flogged with knotted rope for no other reason than to show him what the punishment would be should he ever transgress, swallowed convulsively.

"*Oui, monsieur.*" He dared not meet his master's eyes and feared to contradict him. But he had been born to service and could not stop himself from asking, "Would monsieur care to take the blanket with him? To keep off the rain should it decide to fall?"

"No, monsieur would not," DuTierre snapped. "Monsieur would, however, like to see the skin stripped from your back should you question me again—no matter how graciously disguised as concern for my welfare."

He snatched the violin from its case and, without sparing further thought for his servant, turned his back on the carriage and began moving off down the muddy road, idly drawing the bow back and forth across the strings, not playing anything in particular but merely to hear pleasant sounds. In moments, but for the instrument, he was alone. He walked for a bit, aware of nothing but the music until, as he passed a broken stile, something else intruded upon his consciousness. At the base of the rickety wood sat a peasant child, an urchin of about ten or eleven years old, amusing itself by tying bits of wood into a dirty length of string.

"Good evening," DuTierre called out.

The child looked up, its face so encrusted with dirt

that DuTierre was unable to tell whether it was male or female until it spoke.

"*Bonsoir, Monsieur*," it replied, eyes cast carefully down.

A boy then. Good.

"What brings you out into the night air on this cold evening?" DuTierre assumed an air of friendly curiosity, knowing it would throw the youngster off guard, and approached to squat next to him. "Have you no home?"

"*Oui, Monsieur*. I have a home. It is a good home with stout walls and a well-thatched roof. Two rooms!" He held up his fingers to indicate he knew how to count.

"I'm sure it is very fine. But why are you not in it?"

The child shook his head sadly. "Papa, he is not well. He has the devils in him, says Mama. Look . . . " A tiny hand pushed aside a long unwashed hank of hair to reveal a dark purple bruise on the right cheek. "It is better to be gone when Papa has the sickness on him."

"I understand." DuTierre commiserated. "*Mon dieu*, it is a cold night, do you not think? I have a house—a very fine house though . . . " He winked, knowing the child would get the joke. " . . . perhaps not as fine as *yours*. If you like, I could take you there to get warm. Perhaps there might be some sweet meats we could scavenge from the kitchen? And . . . " DuTierre paused as if an idea had suddenly struck him. "Tell me. Do you like music?"

DuTierre stood up and quickly drew the bow across the strings in a ditty which, while it was unworthy of the instrument, was calculated to appeal to the child.

Its eyes grew wide with wonder. DuTierre was well aware of the figure he cut and the effect he was having on the unfortunate creature before him. His wig was well powdered and made of the finest hair; his velvet coat bore a glittering border a full two inches thick, the tiny semi-precious jewels woven into the lace of his cuffs were the result of two years of peasants' labor and a single diamond chip was worth more francs than this boy's family would see in a lifetime.

"Oh yes! Please." The child stood and, in shy response to DuTierre's outstretched hand, intertwined its fingers with the Marquis's much larger ones. "You are a kind gentleman."

DuTierre threw back his head and laughed as he tucked the violin under his free arm.

"Kind?" he chortled. "*Au contraire, mon ami nouveau.* I am the most evil man in all of France."

"*Monsieur* makes a joke," came the protest.

"Perhaps. Perhaps. Now, would you like a ride in my fine carriage?"

DuTierre did not even give the boy time to nod before he ushered him down the muddy road to where the coachman sat waiting.

***

The rain had held off, fortunately, prolonging his ecstasy. From the deep darkness of the abandoned well the boy's sobs, though much weaker than they had been three nights before, could still be heard.

DuTierre, through long experience, suspected this night would probably be the child's last before surrendering to the arms of *le Bon Dieu.* In celebration, he'd decided to indulge in a particularly difficult piece to highlight his mastery of the instrument. Though his audience of one was incapable of appreciating the Marquis's art, it mattered not to DuTierre. He played for his own benefit, to revel in the glorious music; the sacrifice in the pit served only to inspire him. It was only in these last few hours, when the snuffing of an innocent life was imminent that DuTierre felt his creativity was truly freed.

From the first draw of the bow across the strings, long into the night, the Marquis played, absorbed in the music. He drew himself through a gamut of emotions from religious ecstasy to sexual bliss, all inspired by the notes spilling from the violin in brilliant waves of musical wonder and velvety sheaths of sublime richness. By the time dawn broke the horizon, DuTierre was exhausted, physically and emotionally, and the pleas and wails from the pit had ceased.

He walked back to the main house, dripping with sweat but sated. The music had revived his soul and would sustain him through a few more insipid court concerts and the other trivialities necessitated by his aristocracy before he would need to revitalize himself once more. He knew his acts were horrific. But he could not help himself and took solace that, in relieving the children of the misery their adult lives would undoubtedly have held, he had gifted them with something glorious to ease their journey home to God.

In the years to come, many more children would perish and, always, their deaths would be accompanied by the heavenly music. Eventually though, with the more strident chords of revolution pervading France, his oddities could no longer be overlooked. Other nobles charged him with all manner of foul crimes and offered him to the proletariat in sacrifice, hoping to save their own necks in the process. In his last seconds, with his chest pressed against the rough wood planking and his arms bound behind his back, he heard the creaking of the blade as it was winched into place and thought of the things he had done and the life he had led. An instant later, he passed from it with only a single regret—there would be no more music.

He was wrong.

***

Time passed—he wasn't sure how much—and when DuTierre realized he was trapped within the violin, his first emotion was one of joy. Though his essence might be caught in the instrument for eternity, the glory of its music would not be denied him. Doubtless, some higher being had thought to punish him for his crimes and, concentrating on the irony of DuTierre's particular incarceration, had overlooked the joy it would bring to his damned soul. So long as he had his music, what bliss it would bring to his spirit!

***

William Barnaby knew how to work a crowd—especially after a few tots of gin. In these hard times, Bill felt himself doubly lucky; he had a job *and* it was one he loved. Six nights a week, Bill and his fiddle packed the tables at the Cock and Oats Inn, although, he sometimes admitted to himself, the inexpensive gin and the free hand of the tavern-owner might also have influenced the crowd's density.

Most of Bill's repertoire was popular stuff—the kinds of tunes one could hear drifting out of any one of a dozen music halls along any one of a hundred of

London's streets. Occasionally though, when the night was very old and daybreak wasn't far off, Bill would indulge himself and begin the strains of a composition by one of the old masters—a Frenchie or an Iy-Talian. Weary heads would lift, eyelids swollen with drink would open and tired smiles would light even the faces of the drinkers who had passed out and remained collapsed over the trestle tables to "sleep it off."

It was in these times that Bill's talent shone. He would be lifted by the music, lost in it, inspired beyond the not insubstantial talent he had. It was as if some phantom hand guided his as he wielded the bow, coaxing more complex notes from the fiddle, notes that were almost heavenly in tone.

But there were other times as well. Times when the gin muddled his coordination so that he could barely put the bow to the strings. And those times grew more frequent as the years passed.

The patrons didn't seem to mind if Bill dropped the bow or hit a note that was jarring and sharp. Oh, they mocked and heckled to be sure, but it was all in good fun. Besides, there wasn't a real music lover among them; so long as the gin kept flowing, no one cared if a few notes went sour.

The only thing about his "off" nights which gave Bill pause was the tall, thin bloke who could invariably be found standing in a corner alone. If Bill flatted or sharped, or when the screech from the fiddle was truly discordant, the man would cover his ears and grimace as if in pain. Unlike the good-natured ribbing from Bill's mates, *this* bloke's antics were sincere and, to Bill, offensive. Yet, whenever he made up his mind to confront the man, to challenge him to prove *he* could play better after two pints of gin, Bill could never seem to find him.

The vanishing act puzzled him for quite a few years until the very last night he saw the stranger. When Bill collapsed after a particularly strident and off-key rendition of a popular ballad, and the gin finally took its toll, he seemed to see the strange man's face hovering over him before his vision went black. Oddly, as Bill died, the man's face seemed . . . relieved.

***

The violin case arced through the air and landed on the sofa. It slid to the floor unnoticed as the man and woman in the room pawed at the buttons on the young lady's blouse—him to open them, and her to keep them closed.

"Stop it, Rudy!" came the insincere protest. "I told you, I'm *not* that kind of girl!"

"Not until you've had a few more drinks anyway, eh?"

The speaker had not bothered to change into street clothes and still wore his nattily styled band uniform with the wide lapels. Rudy Montrose abandoned his onslaught on the bottle-blonde's clothing and crossed to the bar cart.

"What's yer poison, babe?"

"Scotch whisky. Neat." She pursed her cupid bow lips. "But don't you go getting any ideas about gettin' me bombed and takin' advantage of me, you hear?"

As if to belie her belief in her sobriety, she hiccoughed, belched daintily, and flopped onto the couch, her butt smacking into the violin case with a thump.

"Hey, hey, hey! Watch the fiddle, sweet cheeks.

Gotta earn the dough with it, dontcha know." He handed her the glass which she half-drained in a single swallow.

"Play something for me, Rudy," she whined.

"Now? I thought we had better things to play than that old thing." His grin was a veritable leer.

She tossed her head and the ringlet in the center of her forehead collapsed. "Play somethin' romantic and . . . we'll see."

Montrose shrugged and snapped open the case to reveal the violin, its lacquer finish now scuffed and with a few scars in the wood.

"You promise?"

"Maybe."

He grabbed the bow which could have used a good rosin and launched into the latest Benny Goodman hit. Though his technique wasn't half bad, Rudy sawed through the melody much too quickly and without a scintilla of feeling—as various conductors had told him over the years. Perhaps that was why he never managed to get the really good gigs; most of his jobs paid enough to cover the rent on his small apartment, get a new suit every year and to keep him supplied with booze decent enough to entice the dolls.

"Make ya hot, babe?"

"Ohhhhhh, buster!"

Rudy saw the liquor was finally having the desired effect. He tossed the instrument aside, not caring that it was gouged anew by the wooden arm of the sofa before it clattered to the floor. His concentration fixed on the buttons once again, he never saw the ghostly figure standing against the far wall wince as it removed its hands from its ears to shake its fists at him, nor its expression of angst when its eyes came to rest on the battered violin.

***

"*Nein, nein.* It is a G *minor!*"

Ernst Kettlemann corrected the position of Marjorie's fingers on the frets.

"Once more, *bitte.*"

As he listened to the screeches his newest student tortured from the violin, he silently longed for the old days when he played in the small chamber orchestra back in Dresden. But the War had relieved him of the job he so dearly loved, as well as almost relieving him of his very life and, in this great new city of New York, it seemed there were dozens of more accomplished refugee musicians, plying their talents for pennies. At least, he reflected whilst sending a silent thanks to God, he had been able to establish a small teaching clientele. If nothing else, their meager fees for lessons kept him fed and relatively warm.

Sadly, his inability to find employment as a violinist with even a mediocre orchestra had forced him to realize his secret had been revealed: Ever since he was a young man, his appreciation for the music had always far outstripped his skill. His career in Germany had thrived more due to luck than any talent.

Kettlemann still took out the battered violin sometimes late at night and sought to give substance to the talent he fervently hoped lurked inside him. But his ear was too good for him to fool himself. He could *hear* the music as it should be played; he simply couldn't produce it. Sometimes, he could almost feel invisible fingers trying to guide his own, a welling that seemed to come from the instrument itself, desperately urging him to somehow *get it right*. But, in spite of Herculean efforts, he was unable to meet its expectations.

The music was always flat, uninspired. He sometimes found himself blushing with shame in the solitude of his flat while trying to play—even though he was completely alone. It was as if some phantom audience cringed every time Ernst set bow to strings.

His attention was drawn back to the lesson as seventeen-year-old Marjorie produced a note which, in Ernst's opinion, God never intended to be heard by human ears. He re-positioned her fingers yet again, adjusted the angle with which she held the bow for the umpteenth time, gritted his teeth, smiled and encouraged her to try again.

He never saw the figure clutching its head, its features twisted in a silent scream of protest which hovered near the ceiling of Ernst's cold-water flat. He couldn't hear the curses, spat in outrage at his incompetence, nor see the agony in its eyes.

***

In excess of two and a quarter centuries, Alphonse DuTierre had endured. He had suffered the drunken sawing of that fat buffoon in the bar, the cavalier musical capering of that lecherous twit in the ridiculous uniform and the feeble attempts by that wretched old man.

Nor were they the only banes to what passed for DuTierre's existence; there had been many others. The woman in Austria who fancied herself a violinist when she wasn't sniffing white powder. The youth with the unwashed hair in the nineteen sixties who saw his attempts to make music as "innovative" when it was naught but pretense. The jewel-encrusted dowager who fancied herself a classical singer and who he was forced to accompany in the hands of a mediocre violinist. Perhaps worst of all, the collector in Louisiana who had merely acquired the beloved instrument, only to relegate it to a closet as a "curiosity" too beaten up to be worthy of display much less actual playing. These were his trials and, somehow, he had survived them all.

But this . . . this latest outrage, the pinnacle of two hundred-plus years of outrages, was undoubtedly the most vexing. The butchery was unspeakable. Each note sent ribbons of fire pulsing through him; each strident screech was as if red hot embers were piled about his soul and stoked. Even as he watched, helpless to intervene and halt the atrocities being perpetrated, the bow was being wielded as a makeshift pirate sword while the violin itself was used as a shield to fend off the attack.

The teacher relieved the little monsters of the instrument and delivered a strong lecture on the necessity of respecting one's tools. Then, to give lie to her admonitions, she demonstrated by playing it—or attempting to play it—herself. The result was so unskilled, so horrific, Alphonse would almost have seen his precious violin used in mock battle instead.

His days now were spent writhing in paroxysms of frustrated agony. He *knew* what wonders the instrument was capable of; he had played them himself. It was the worst torture to see it . . . to *hear* it . . . reduced to this. Only in the confines of the music room closet did he experience relief, but it was short lived. Daily, he was hauled out and subjected to the capering grotesqueries of the children of the Dolly Madison Elementary School's so-called Music Appreciation class, grade three.

In abject despair, DuTierre rode the waves of butchered notes produced when the children could be convinced to actually play his beloved instrument rather than using it as a toy. His wails of protest went unheard as the endless progression of flat scales wafted through the classroom, his soul was racked, the metaphorical winch turning tighter and tighter with each misguided effort of the teacher to produce *Claire de Lune.*

At night, in blessed silence, he was forced to ruminate on the irony of his fiendish imprisonment. It wasn't that he'd been condemned to this feeble existence inside the violin he treasured so dearly. No, it wasn't that at all. Instead, it was the mocking laughter of delighted children which provided a macabre counterpoint to DuTierre's memories of those sobs and pleas of so long ago. *This* was the true meaning of Hell.

He endured as best he could for a remarkably long time until, one day, he could stand no more. He felt his soul wrench, one final time, during a heinous attempt at a rendition of *Frère Jacques.* Down a long, long tunnel he seemed to fall and, at the bottom, he found himself surrounded by specters of what he first assumed were misbegotten notes. Yet, as their tenuous forms enveloped him, he saw the notes had faces, faces he dimly recalled from his past. Fresh-cheeked yet mournful faces, full of potential whose hopes had been quashed in vile suffering while DuTierre serenaded them, insensate to their agonies.

With each warped note from the classroom, the children grew stronger, rending his indestructible soul over and over, twisting it in an aural torture. His true Fate finally upon him, Alphonse DuTierre, formerly the Marquis de Paysnoir, began to scream, and his shrieks, like the notes . . . went on.

Chalk Face

RAVEN DANE

I remember it rained. The morning my wife washed away with cigarette butts, empty crisp packets, a few fallen leaves. Sluiced down a nearby drain with three teenagers and an elderly couple, their remains merging briefly in a swirl of grey sludge. At least she was not alone during her last moments above ground."

The man spoke as flames from a makeshift bonfire of burning rubbish flickered, illuminating a gathering of ragged figures. None listened, too wrapped up in their own misery and memories, but no one stopped him speaking. A local by his accent, the man was about thirty, always would be now. He wore what was once an expensive suit, designer, the sort successful business men still sported in the day lit world but his was worn and ripped, filthy from decades of dust and grime. He took a swig of boiled river water from an old coke can and continued:

"My name is Richard Craig. Another idiot to fall for the collective madness. I was safe that morning, sheltered by a gloomy underpass leading to the

Harlequin shopping centre. I stayed there until dark, staring first at the pile of white powder that had been Marielle. After the downpour I stared at the drain. Her grave."

He choked between a bitter laugh and a sob.

"Ok, maybe not a grave . . . eventual burial out to sea perhaps."

Someone coughed, struggling with a morsel of charred rat; a woman patted him hard on the back, an instinctive gesture of caring not lost in the process of change. The End of the World? Hardly, Craig mused, it had not been some great catastrophe of fire and brimstone, no comet hit the earth, none of the God bothering righteous beamed up to Heaven before Armageddon. The world had not come to an end, it was now less a few billion people, which many survivors thought a good thing for the planet. The same smug bastards that treated the last remaining Nighters with such contempt and persecution.

With no one bothering to stop him, Craig continued.

"I didn't take any notice at first. Bloody Internet was always swamped with lying crap. The Snopes site was busy debunking idiotic urban legends like a forthcoming night with "two moons" when Mars was closest to the Earth and some total old bollocks about a Babylonian goddess being the origin of the name Easter. Some people believed every word. The sheeple flock. Not my Marielle, my wife was too intelligent, too cynical to be so easily fooled.

So imagine my surprise when she started mithering on at me about a new pandemic spreading from the Far East or Africa. The Vanity Bug . . . The

Twilight Pandemic . . . of course it went viral like wild fire on the Internet, gave plenty of sensationalist fuel for the tabloids. A fast-spreading infection with no official name and enough strangeness to be a conspiracy theorist's wet dream. It had to be the result of deliberately released genetic engineering or sent by aliens, the revenge of Gaia, the work of Satan . . . or a gift from angels.

All I know is it was the first Pandemic to be welcomed with open arms. The first plague where people queued up to be infected. It made people healthy, cured all existing ailments including genetic diseases, terminal cancer and AIDS. For fuck's sake, it cured the common cold, even Man Flu. Why wouldn't people clamour to be infected? If that wasn't enough, scientists discovered it didn't just slow the aging process, it turned off the ticking biological clock all together. The world went batshit crazy after that announcement, the promise of a healthy immortality? No need even to become Undead and sleep in a coffin full of soil. No need to sparkle and mope around in permanent teenage angst. Unless you were a teenager at the time of infection . . . no cure for those tormented hormonal unfortunates. This amused us self-satisfied twenty pluses inordinately."

An old man huddled close to the campfire and snorted with a loud burst of laughter. Someone was actually listening. Craig turned to smile at him but was mistaken. The man was lost in his own thoughts like all the others, amused by some memory dredged up from his past. Craig wondered how old the man actually was . . . He looked well over eighty, add the forty years since the pandemic. Forever old. Was that such a good choice? Probably, many had done the same, life was life and never more precious than at its conclusion. Why wouldn't a man who had counted each year's survival as a triumph not crave the promise of more healthy decades of life?

"Marielle certainly did, I will never forget the excited, no . . . manic glow in her eyes as she devoured each report, each scientific document. For a few crazy weeks, it was all she could talk about, an obsession fuelled by my reservations and doubts. I could see the benefits of growing old, living and learning through a long, fulfilling life. But not Marielle, she wanted us to stay forever young, her English rose beauty preserved forever.

So I endured the indignity of having some sweaty, rotund accountant from her office bite me on the arm . . . hard. It had to be deep enough for the infected saliva to mix with my bloodstream, and there I was . . . as close to immortal as could be dreamt off in any vampire fantasy. The next few hours were something of an anti-climax. There was no dramatic reaction, my body accepted the changes without a fight. Maybe there would have been less of a clamour to be bitten if there had been pain, people doubling over, writhing in agony as their metabolism mutated forever. There was no cure for the infection, no turning back.

Instead, there was meek acceptance from our bodies with not even a headache or nausea. No drama at all, I had no craving for human blood, preferably that of a busty virgin, or the slightest desire to turn into a bat. At that moment all I wanted was a large latte and a cinnamon bun and to be out of that office and far away from my biter. Who actually wasn't sweaty, not since he had become bitten . . . he was no Adonis though which must have caused some considerable disappointment to him. The virus didn't change anyone into Robert Patterson, Snipes or Tom Cruise.

Months passed, societies around the world reeled with the changes, the religious riots, the social, financial, political and logistic problems caused by the Normals living alongside people who would never sicken and age. The lawsuits from people trying to prevent loved ones from getting infected, the counter suits from people trying to force their loved ones to get bitten. Chaos and insanity ruled."

Craig glanced across to the woman huddled away from the warmth and any scant comfort from the gathered Nighters. She hugged a beautiful child close to her, the woman's eyes fierce with protective love. One of the most tragic victims of the madness, the child with silver blonde hair and big, green eyes had been bitten while still little more than an infant. Preserved by some insane parent to be forever adorable, a living doll to dote over. The woman was not her mother, wrong ethnic group, but the child would not have lasted all these decades without her. Was that a blessing or a curse? Craig did not know. All he had left was his story, so he continued relating it to his oblivious, indifferent audience.

"All this turmoil passed me by. I gave up reading newspapers and watching the news on television. See one riot with people waving bibles or the Qur'an— whatever and you've seen them all. Marielle and I were fine; nothing had altered our little corner of the world. Until that Tuesday in February, at roughly 10 AM. I hated shopping with a vengeance, but Marielle switched on her ice queen mode, somehow my input into choosing a new leather sofa from the John Lewis store was of vital importance to her wellbeing. So, pasting on an "ok, no problem face," I drove her to Watford and its gleaming monument to consumerism, the Harlequin Centre. We parked in a friend's driveway . . . prearranged of course, to avoid paying parking charges in the mall underground car park. Have grief-fuelled regrets ever been based on anything so trivial? We walked the last half a mile to the town. I, the bloody fool who had begrudged paying the parking charges, had killed my wife . . . but I digress.

As we neared the short stretch of urine-stained underpass beneath the dual carriageway, the sun briefly appeared from behind a leaden pall of clouds, and it annoyed me. My skin felt prickly, my veins itched. Unable to bear it, I rushed the last few yards to join the pathetically inept busker in the tunnel as he attempted to play 'Baker Street' on a battered saxophone; busker in the tunnel; a man gifted only with immunity to the stench of piss. I turned back to see Marielle falter and stand still, her handbag falling to the ground, spraying a confetti arc of receipts, loose change, lipstick, her mobile phone and tissues . . .

Her eyes widened, her mouth dropped open. I think she was already dead, I hope she was. Marielle's face and eyes grew ghostly white then became textured, almost like a stone carving. A chalk face frozen in horror long enough for me to scream as it suffered some internal catastrophe and crumpled in on itself, her body collapsing into a pile of white powder partially hidden by her clothes and surrounded by the contents of her handbag.

If others were screaming, I did not hear them, my own screams were too loud. I found out later that every person bitten and exposed to sunlight turned to a chalk-like powder at the same time. The only survivors were those protected by night or artificial darkness, like me. So I have ended up a sort of vampire after all, though I still do not drink blood, sparkle or sleep in a coffin. I chose to live, even if only by night because it is still a life . . . I will not step out into the sun and join the many Nighter suicides. Not yet.

Perhaps the virus will have another shock in store for the survivors. No one knows . . . no one knows where it came from or how it works. Does it matter? It came; a wildfire spread around the planet fuelled by the dream of immortality and it has now gone.

I waited until dark, staring first at the pile of white powder that had been Marielle, then after the downpour, at the drain."

That was all he had left to say, but he would relate it all again on another night, around another fire with different victims of the vanity bug. Approaching footsteps snapped the group out of their apathy. The woman with the forever child bolted into the dark, the little girl held tightly under her arm. Others grabbed whatever weapons they had, uncertain whether to choose fight or flight. Craig remained by the fire, uncertain whether to join the woman and flee into the dubious safety of darkness. He stayed, the human instinct to remain with a tribe had never been stronger than among the refugees from sunlight. The footsteps grew louder, that of several individuals trampling through the scrub in silence.

The newcomers could be more Nighters seeking

company or a small band of compassionate volunteers among the Normals who brought them food and blankets. There used to be many such groups, usually those who had family or friends among the abandoned. Now the numbers of people prepared to help the discarded, unnatural ones had dwindled by the year. Soon there would be none and the passive life of the surviving bitten would have to change. Adapt or die.

Nighters dreaded the arrival of armed vigilantes, spurred on by religious zeal and/or sadism to wipe every virus victim off the face of the earth. The bitten were not immortal and made easy target practise, no laws protected them now, officially declared non-human by most countries around the world. The more sophisticated of their enemies used ultra violet torches to trigger the calcification process. They found that amusing, apparently. Once again, Craig's mind span with indecision . . . was turning into powder such a bad option? Not the quickest death but at least an end to this hated half-life as an outcast from all he had once enjoyed.

"They don't have dogs," someone cried out in relief. Their enemies usually brought fierce dogs to bait and maim the Nighters, an essential element in their idea of a good night out. Craig gave a brief sob at the reprieve; he did not need to make that decision, not tonight. A group of about a dozen men appeared, faces glowing demonic amber from the firelight. They carried boxes piled high with supplies and no weapons. The Nighter group relaxed. There was no fighting, no squabbling as the food was evenly distributed among them. The Nighters had too many enemies to turn against each other.

Chalk Face

The volunteers spent some time with the grateful exiles, passing on news from a world that had turned its back on them. Craig listened attentively, in case of any word of a potential cure, though he doubted any scientists would bother looking for one. The Nighters were an embarrassment, a living reminder of some rogue genetic meddling that had gone so horribly wrong. Yet the thought of an antidote kept Craig going, hope was a fragile, dying ember still smouldering, but there was nothing in the men's news that night to fan the flame. The volunteers went back to the city, leaving the outcasts bereft, alone again to face their banishment.

Even with the sky hidden by low cloud, the Nighters' awareness of the dark hours left to them was acute, a new instinct created and honed by survival. Craig packed up his new stuff into a battered rucksack, wool blankets and the gift parcel of bread, cheese and dried meats. His plastic canteen was also full of fresh, clean water thanks to the kindly visitors. He kept an old hand gun with no bullets close to hand in his jacket pocket. It was time to head for his latest refuge, a narrow wildlife tunnel built under the MI motorway, two hours walk from the camp. The same destination as other night dwellers, the badgers and foxes who used it to traverse in safety under the wide, fast road blighting their habitat. The nocturnal animals were on their way to their cosy underground dens. His home that day was a claustrophobic tube of rubbish strewn damp concrete.

Something moved towards him, attempting stealth but failing. Too big, too furtive yet purposeful to be anything but human. Dawn was a paling sky on the eastern horizon. Craig did not have long to secure his hiding place, there was nowhere else he could flee to in time. He pulled the hand gun from his pocket and prepared to bluff it out, hoping it was just another Nighter who followed him from the camp seeking shelter from the murderous sun. Plenty of room for another, who was he to object to company.

The dim, pre-twilight was of little help identifying the man who now broke cover and stood before him, but Craig remembered a shambling individual who had arrived among the volunteers. Someone who kept his hooded head down. Appearing uneasy in the company of the bitten in the Nighter camp, the man had still distributed food and supplies, though in unusual silence. The volunteers were always cheerful souls who meant well. This one's arrival at Craig's shelter screamed wrongness; this was not going to end well.

"You are a long way from the others. Why are you here?"

There was no answer, but the sight of Craig's gun stopped the intruder from approaching closer.

"You looked like you knew where you were going, mate. I'm new to the area, so I followed you. Seems I made the right decision; that tunnel will do nicely."

Craig raised the gun, not believing a word. The young man's coarse estuary accent was phoney, laughably so, his body language threatening. Craig knew sharing was the last thing on the newcomer's mind. The man pulled back his hood, his grin predatory, triumphant. Even in the dim pre-dawn light Craig could see that he was a Nighter, the washed out pallor of nocturnal living unmistakable. About seventeen, frozen by the virus into perma-youth, he wore old fashioned teen chav attire of rip off Nike trainers, matching grey baggy joggers and hoodie. Craig suspected the joggers were half-mast at the back, exposing well-worn Calvin Klein boxer shorts. An odd thought to intrude at this tense moment of danger.

"Actually, I have no intention of sharing your filthy hideout. I get to sleep out the daylight in a luxury hotel," the intruder boasted, "get anything I want. All I have to do is lead them to filthy vermin like you."

More approaching footsteps and breaking twigs shocked Craig into action. He saw the traitor reach into his pocket. Fearing an ultraviolet torch, he attacked using the useless gun as a bludgeon. The Nighter had perpetual youth on his side but Craig wanted to live, the sudden clarity of his need filling him with strength born of desperation. He pummelled his opponent with his fist and the heavy gun, but surprise had only delayed the youth's defences for a few seconds. He fought back, dirty and hard, easily overcoming Craig, leaving him pinned to the ground, helpless beneath his weight. The youth had been a seasoned brawler all his life. As an ex-office worker, Craig was no match for such practised violence.

"I am going to enjoy watching you turn to dust . . . slowly . . . " the youth sneered, pocketing Craig's gun, "very slowly. They know how to make it take a long time."

Craig heard voices, close enough to make out words. He forced himself upwards, enough to bite down hard on his enemy's wrist through layers of skin, sinew and muscle until his mouth filled with the youth's blood. Shrieking in pain and disgust, the lad leapt up, backing away from his still prone victim. He aimed a kick for Craig's head but missed, wildly, eyes widening in confusion.

Backing towards his only refuge, Craig watched horrified, fascinated as the youth began to change. His thin body thrashed, flexing with uncontrolled spasms, animated by some chaotic inner energy. The Nighter pallor blanching into the chalk face of the doomed yet he did not crumble to dust. His skin hardened, becoming a stone-like carapace enclosing the vulnerable flesh beneath. A process that rent the dying night with his agonised howls but the mutation did not kill him. Horrified, Craig backed deep into the tunnel, away from the monster, away from first sunbeams breaching the eastern horizon.

He heard the gang of vigilantes break through the undergrowth, heard their shocked, fear-angry shouts, their dying shrieks as the mutant Nighter ripped their bodies into shards of bone and torn flesh using his hands, his teeth. A creature immune to their bullets, their ultra violet lamps, to the sun. Terrified, Craig scrambled even deeper into the narrow concrete tube, weeping with fear at what he had created. The virus had indeed another cruel twist . . . twice bitten was far from shy.

Unable to sleep, shivering with shock and the tunnel's relentless damp, Craig wrapped himself with the new blankets, waited out the daylight hours, resigned to whatever fate threw at him. No one came looking for the missing vigilantes, and the transformed Nighter had gone, driven by some urgent, unfathomable motivation. Once safe from sunlight, he left the tunnel, fighting back nausea as he stepped through the reeking, flyblown flesh and bone wreckage of the mutant's victims.

For the first time in his prolonged life, Craig committed a crime. A man once too honest to take home office stationary or lie on tax returns, was now driven to hijack a passing car, steal the driver's wallet and clothes, leave him tied up and gagged in a dry, roadside ditch. Casting off his shabby Nighter garb, he changed into the driver's clothes; they were slightly too big but clean and new, less likely to raise suspicion. Using the stolen contactless debit card to buy food and fuel, Craig used mainly side roads and drove all night as far from the south and the monstrous being he had inadvertently created. With more than enough cash left in the stolen wallet to pay for a room in a cheap, anonymous travel lodge, Craig rested in comfort for the first time in many years. He broke down and wept at the forgotten sensations of a hot shower, clean skin, fresh bed sheets, television.

He could not stay at the motel for more than one day without raising suspicion, but there were other such places along the route, as far north as his luck, remaining cash and nerves could take him.

***

Shouldering a canvas bag laden with soil-encrusted root vegetables, Craig followed a winding, narrow path back through the cultivated fields, guided by the benign beam from an ordinary torch held by John Fallon, one of his new companions. The heavy sack dug into his skin, chafing and bruising but no matter. It would soon heal. Below him, lit only by candles was refuge, a secluded country house in a remote region of Northumberland.

He had no idea what led him to this place during his flight from Watford, luck, fate, or just another step towards a cruel twist in his fortunes. He was beyond caring, daring to be happy among the best organised exiles he'd encountered so far.

They lived on a large shooting estate, owned by a family of bitten old gentry and protected by loyal and loving Normal family members. A sanctuary functioning well, kept off the information super highway grid, designed to be self-sufficient and secretive. Craig accepted their hospitality in return for manual work, desperate for some security and peace. It could not last, but every daylight sleep without fear of discovery was precious. The tranquillity had so far lasted six months. Enough for Craig to let down his guard, to imagine life could go on being this sweet, this safe, enjoying the companionship of both Nighters and Normals in this hidden enclave.

A serenity shattered in a few moments of brutality and chaos. Explosions. Shock waves knocked Craig and Fallon onto their backs into dense bracken as smoke bombs detonated, designed to cause fear and confusion. Craig could see Nighters and Normals alike run from the house, only to be hit by beams from huge ultra-violet spotlights. How had such a coordinated, high tech raid got past their security? There was nothing they could do but run, their Nighter friends and family already turned to powder.

With nothing but a bag of muddy roots and a torch, Craig and the middle-aged man running at his side had little to survive on, nowhere to go. As they paused beside a stream, the older man fought for breath. With no containers, Craig cupped some spring water in his hands, offering it to his companion.

"What's the point of running," Fallon gasped, "I've had enough. I'm going back."

There was a time when Craig would have pleaded with him not to be such a fool, that life was still worth living. Now he was silent, too traumatised to argue. Craig listened for sounds of pursuit but the valley had fallen silent, all living things cowering in the darkness from the shock waves of violence. As his heart stopped racing, feeling calmer, images began to rationalise in his mind. This attack was not from a gang of hothead vigilantes but a well organised mission of extermination. Craig had caught the briefest of glimpses of the aggressors. They were clad in khaki uniforms; the British Army? Nighters were not dangerous beyond some petty crime in their battle for survival as outcasts. Why such a heavy handed and very final solution?

It had been many decades since he felt nausea, but a roiling sickness and dread churned in his guts now. The twice bitten Nighter was a horrific, powerful being. What if it had recruited more of its kind? That would make the most innocent of Nighters a potential monster. No wonder the Normals wanted all the bitten wiped out.

"I don't want to die," he muttered, mainly to himself, a statement of affirmation. He waited another few minutes as Fallon recovered before clambering back to his feet and continuing along the forest track. The older man did not follow.

Another night, another campfire. Any gathering of Nighters was dangerous, attracting either the growing legion of twice bitten or those determined to exterminate them at source before they were turned by the monster Craig had unwittingly created. These new entities were mindless, unable to function beyond following the malign control of their leader. Immune to sunlight, to bullets, to fire, if anything human remained beneath their stone-hard carapace, it was degraded down to the most basic of instincts—to survive and reproduce by biting. They were strong, fast, their numbers growing with the relentless drive of a virus, led by a creator driven by insanity and lust for destruction. Traits, Craig suspected had always been there when still a Normal. So maybe this was the End of the World at last, Craig hadn't only killed his wife, he'd broken humanity. A not inconsiderable feat for a humble pen pusher from Watford.

Craig looked up from his frugal meal of some wormy wind fall apples pilfered from an orchard, the badly plucked carcass of a road kill pheasant smouldered in the fire.

Despite devouring all the fruit, hunger clawed at his stomach, urging him to rip the bird apart and eat it still raw. Patience prevailed, far better to wait and savour delicious cooked meat. To pass the time, he gazed at his silent audience and began his story . . .

"I remember it rained. The morning my wife washed away with cigarette butts, empty crisp packets, a few fallen leaves. Sluiced down a nearby drain with three teenagers and an elderly couple, their remains merging briefly in a swirl of grey sludge. At least she was not alone during her last moments above ground."

The collection of rocks placed around the fire that night smiled back, their faces applied to the uneven surfaces with purple spray paint. Unlike the many gathered over the years to huddle for comfort around other camp fires, these companions listened, eyes wide open, attentive. Craig enjoyed such good company, he could tell his story as many times as he liked and they always appreciated it. Why else would they smile? Nor was he alone anymore, the new companions came with him wherever he went.

Like Disneyland

ROCKY ALEXANDER

Joshua Parker spent the night of May 18 alone in his bed, looking up at the ceiling of the second-floor bedroom of his mother's house, his mind whirling with visions and ponderings of his seventeen years of life in the Columbia Basin area of Washington State. He thought of his father, three years gone after the six-car pileup on I-5 just south of Tacoma, and how things were never really the same after that. His mother's depression: not quite as bad as it had been that first year, but still severe enough to keep her hidden away in bed, pills, and vodka more often than not. He wondered about his own lack of depression, and his guilt for allowing himself occasional feelings of happiness when his mom was clearly suffering. It wasn't as if she didn't want him to be happy, but he felt that expressing such an emotion in her presence seemed almost like a betrayal. It just didn't seem right that he had overcome his own despair when she was unable to do the same. Josh didn't know how long one was supposed to grieve over the loss of a loved one, but he felt he had done his time. He was seventeen now; he had to make room in his head for all the other things that normally come along with being a seventeen-year-old.

Things like Charlotte Salisbury, that super-fine redhead from school. Damn, was she amazing. Josh shared four classes with her, and it was miraculous he pulled off passing grades in any of them, given his fantasizing. She was a hottie, but not in a short-skirted cheerleader kind of way (although Josh was certain she would look absolutely delectable in a short skirt). She was an intellectual type, a sexy-as-all-hell in glasses sort of girl that dressed in a way that left a little something to the imagination. Not like that slut Allison Gordon, who must have been banged by half the guys in school. Nothing wrong with the Allison Gordons of the world, Josh figured. He had certainly jerked himself more than once while thinking of her, but that just wasn't the kind of girl he tended to chase. Mainly because he didn't think he had anything to offer a girl like that. Charlotte Salisbury on the other hand . . . well, she seemed like she just might be able to appreciate a nice guy like Josh.

He twisted himself over the edge of his bed and took a bottle of hand lotion and some tissues from the top drawer of his nightstand, and then he filled the space behind his eyes with imaginings of Charlotte Salisbury in action.

Ooooh yeah, baby. That's just how I like it.

***

The alarm clock on his nightstand buzzed at a quarter past six in the morning, and he reached over and switched it off without looking. He lay in bed for another fifteen minutes and then got up and went into the bathroom down the hall, cranked on the water, and stared at himself in the mirror until his reflection faded and disappeared behind a thick layer of condensation. He spent longer than usual in the shower, savoring the hot water on his skin and the images of Charlotte Salisbury still on his mind. Then he dressed in a hooded sweatshirt and black cargo pants and headed downstairs to the kitchen and poured himself a bowl of cereal. It wasn't long before his mother came in, as she did most school day mornings, to join him for breakfast.

"Good morning, my Joshy."

"Mornin', Mom."

She was wrapped in her usual pink bathrobe, and her furry house slippers scraped on the vinyl floor as she moved across the kitchen. Josh caught a faint scent of body odor as she stepped behind him to prep the coffee pot.

"Looks like it will be a beautiful day," she said. "I was thinking I might go for a little walk. Maybe take a nice stroll through the park and soak in some sunshine. It sure would feel good to get out."

Josh knew she didn't mean it. She might have liked the idea of doing something more than sitting on the couch all day and self-medicating her sadness away—might have actually *intended* to make an effort—but it was all bullshit. There was about as much chance of her going for a walk in the park as there was of Josh hooking up with the high school cheerleading captain.

Especially on *this* particular day.

"Yes, Mom. I think getting out of the house would be really good for you."

He finished his cereal and stared into the empty

bowl and struggled with his own pain as it tried to escape from that dark, oversized box deep inside of him into which he stuffed every bad memory, every hurtful thought.

Disneyland.

"Disneyland."

"Huh? What *about* Disneyland?" his mother asked as she took a seat at the table and stirred her coffee.

Josh continued to stare at his empty cereal bowl until his mom reached over and pushed it aside.

"What about Disneyland, Joshy?"

His eyes met hers for the briefest of moments and then his gaze fell upon the 2-slice chrome toaster on the countertop behind her. He was instantly reminded of an animated film he had seen as a child: *The Brave Little Toaster*. He smiled at the thought.

"Disneyland," he said. "Do you remember when we went? You, me, and Dad?"

His mother nodded. "I do remember, Josh. Like it was yesterday. Such a wonderful time, wasn't it? You were so young."

"Everything was good then. We were happy, the three of us."

His mom propped her chin on an upturned palm and closed her eyes, remembering. "Mmm-hmmm . . . yes. Yes we were. We had every reason to be happy. Your dad had just gotten a big promotion, and I was getting ready to open the bookstore–God, I miss that bookstore sometimes–and . . . *you* . . . " She smiled a big, genuine smile. "You were fascinated by just about everything. There was such wonder in your eyes. Little things we take for granted as adults were a really big deal to you at that age. Yes, everything was good then."

Her smile faded, and she ran her fingers through her tangled blonde hair.

"I wish things could be like that again," Josh said. He stood and carried his empty bowl to the sink and turned on the hot water. "I wish it could be like it was when we went to Disneyland."

"But it can never be, my Joshy. We've lost a huge part of what made that period of time so special, and we can't get that back."

Josh rinsed his bowl and left it in the sink, then stepped behind his mother and placed his hands on the chrome toaster. He unplugged the electric cord and ran his fingertips along the length of it. "I sure love you, Mom."

"Oh, I love you too, my Joshy," she said without looking up.

He wrapped his hands with the ends of the cord, and then he slipped the remaining length over his mother's head and pulled it tight across her throat. She fought hard, bucking and kicking and grasping at his arms. Her coffee mug shattered on the floor. Josh placed a knee against the back of her chair for leverage. Bad move. It put him off balance, and her thrashing caused him to stumble sideways, giving up enough tension on the cord to allow his mother to flop out of the chair. Now he was supporting all of her weight as she twisted and clawed and pounded the linoleum floor with her feet. His muscles burned and his hands felt as if their flesh were being torn away, but he held on.

He tried to avoid looking at her face, but he caught a glimpse nonetheless: her eyes bulging from their sockets, her swollen tongue protruding grotesquely from her gaping mouth. It was the most horrible thing Josh had ever witnessed, and it was enough to make him think he couldn't go through with it. How much longer until she died? It was always just a few seconds in the movies, but surely this had gone on for a full minute at least. That was a long time to die a violent death. A long time to feel the kind of terror and desperation and physical agony that his mother was surely feeling. Josh could end it. He could just let go and tell his mother how sorry he was and run away.

But he couldn't really do that, could he? No. You don't attempt to murder your mother with a toaster and just go on with your life. Besides, this is for her own good, isn't it? What she's feeling now will pale in comparison to the pain she will feel in the long run, if she were to continue living through what was soon to come. Josh loved her too much for that.

He pulled harder on the cord of the chrome toaster and clenched his teeth until his mouth filled with the taste of blood. He strained with such force he feared he might actually rip his mother's head off until, finally, she lay still. Josh gripped the cord for a few more seconds, then let her body slide down to the floor. Her head bounced slightly on the linoleum, and blood rushed from her mouth as if a dam had burst inside of her. Josh unwrapped the electrical cord from his hands and placed the toaster on the breakfast table, and then he headed upstairs to collect the duffle bag hidden beneath his bed.

With the bag slung across his aching back, Josh returned to the kitchen and took a corkscrew and a long carving knife from a drawer, then went through a door that opened into the adjacent garage. He gently placed the duffel bag into the backseat of his old Crown Victoria and climbed in and started the engine. The man in white was already waiting in the passenger seat. The man didn't speak. He only offered Josh an approving nod, laced his long, pale fingers together in his lap, and gazed out through the window.

***

They pulled into the high school parking lot a few minutes later. Josh parked close to the main hallway. He took his bag from the back seat, and another from the trunk, and then entered the hallway from the north end. Once inside, he knelt near the door and unzipped one of his duffel bags.

"Running a little late today, aren't you, Mr. Parker?"

It was Vice Principal Tanner, who seemed to have appeared out of nowhere. He was dressed in his usual pleated Haggar slacks and tan corduroy suit jacket with elbow patches, looking all vice principal-like. He removed a hand from his pocket and adjusted his wide-rimmed glasses and looked down at Josh scoldingly.

"I'm sorry," Josh answered. "My mother is sick."

"That's too bad. Nothing serious, I hope."

"Oh, I think she'll be okay now."

"Well, I understand that things happen, but we have rules at this school. You can't be in the halls during class without a pass. There are no exceptions, Mr. Parker."

Josh nodded. "No worries, Mr. Tanner. I have a pass."

"Oh? Well, good. I'll go ahead and have a look at that if you don't mind."

"No problem." Josh stood and reached behind him into his waistband and pulled out the carving knife he'd taken from his kitchen and thrust it into Tanner's Adam's apple.

For a moment, Tanner only stood there with wide eyes and mouth agape, and then Josh gripped the knife handle with both hands and brought the blade back out with a leftward slashing motion that caused Tanner's blood to spray across a wall of lockers. Tanner threw his hands up to his mangled throat and turned to run. He didn't get far, a few strides before he fell forward onto his face. He kicked around for a few seconds, tried to get back up, then fell over again and lay jerking on the polished tile floor as he drowned in his own blood.

Josh turned his attention back to his duffel bag. He reached inside and pulled out a length of chain, which he ran through the panic bars of the hallway's double doors and fastened with a heavy padlock. Then he hoisted both of his duffel bags and walked to the opposite end of the hallway and secured those doors, too. Now that the hallway's exits were sealed off, Josh removed a wine bottle from one of the bags and popped the cork. The smell of gasoline stung his nostrils. Halfway down the hallway, the man in white stood, smiling from ear to ear. His thick, furry rope of a tail danced and curled excitedly behind him.

Josh stepped to a red fire alarm box mounted on the wall and pulled the lever. It was only a few seconds before the classroom doors on either side of the hallway opened up, and dozens of students filed out along with their teachers. And it was only a few seconds after that before the fire alarm bell was nearly drowned out by the screams of those who discovered Vice Principal Tanner's body lying in a lake of blood. Some of the students broke into a run and headed in Josh's direction, until they saw Josh light the white cotton rag he had stuffed into the neck of the petrol-filled wine bottle. There was a twisting and contorting of their horrified faces as they turned to join the stampede toward the doors at the opposite end of the corridor. Some of them slipped in Tanner's blood and were trampled beneath a legion of panicked feet. Others bolted back into their classrooms, while those who remained in the hallway crushed each other in a mad attempt to exit through the chained doors. Josh threw the Molotov cocktail right into the middle of them.

Flame splashed across the floor, engulfing a handful of students who, in turn, flogged and flailed amidst the horde, igniting others around them. Josh stuffed a rag fuse into a second bottle of fuel, lit it, and hurled that one as well. It seemed like everyone was on fire. Burning bodies rolled and whirled and beat on themselves with charred hands. One student sat in a corner and shivered as if he were freezing as the fire consumed him. A teacher–Josh thought it was Mr. Southard, the music teacher–tried to save some of them by beating at the flames with a heavy jacket, but it didn't do much good. The corridor was filled with the screams of the dying.

Josh reached again into his duffel bag and brought out a pair of 9mm automatic pistols. He stuffed some spare magazines into the pockets of his hoodie and left the bags where they lay as he stepped slowly down the hallway and opened fire on anyone that moved. He emptied his first magazines quickly, putting more than thirty rounds into those who hadn't yet escaped the chaos in the hallway. Then he reloaded and went from classroom to classroom.

They cried and begged and tried to hide beneath their desks, but Josh cut them down one by one. Mr. Wilson, the math teacher, tried to be a hero. He lunged at Josh and stabbed him in the neck with a pocket knife, but the blade was short and didn't do much damage. Josh shot him right in his mustache, and Mr. Wilson dropped and didn't move again. Some of the students managed to escape through classroom windows. Josh shot a couple of them as they raced across the lawn. When Josh entered the room where Mr. Boggs taught history, he found several students in the midst of trying to break out the thick window glass with chair desks and other objects. They all fell away from the windows as Josh emptied his guns into them. Before he could reload, three students burst from a classroom storage closet and bolted into the hallway.

One of them was Charlotte Salisbury.

Josh slapped his last magazine into one of his handguns and stepped into the corridor and fired at the fleeing students. He aimed low, so as not to hit Charlotte in a vital organ. The three of them dropped and clutched their injured legs. One of them—it was Greg Mitchell, the first chair trombone player in the school band—got back to his feet despite the bullet hole in his right calf. Josh shot him twice in the back and he stayed down. Then Josh moved to the next one, Nancy Garrison, the principal's daughter. He put a round in her head as she pleaded for her life.

Then there was only Charlotte. She had been hit in

both legs and left a wide trail of blood as she tried to crawl away. She said something, but Josh couldn't make out the words through her crying. When Josh called her name, she stopped moving and looked up at his face and cocked her head, trying to find recognition. "J-Josh Parker?"

Josh was surprised she knew his name. They shared a few classes together, but there was a lot of students in those classes, and he wasn't the type who stood out in a crowd. *She* was that type; he was a nobody. Or rather he had been a nobody before today.

"Josh, why are you doing this?" She laced her fingers below her chin as if in prayer. "Listen, whatever happened that caused you to want to hurt all these people, it has nothing to do with me. Please . . . please don't kill me."

Josh looked down at her and thought she was the most beautiful thing he had ever seen. He thought he might collapse beneath the weight of his guilt and shame at having hurt her, at having put her here on the floor, crawling in her own blood as the stench of burned flesh fouled the air.

"I don't want to kill you," he said.

"You don't have to, Josh. You don't have to." There was hope in her voice now. "I'm a good person. I would never do or say anything that was hurtful to you. No, I would *never* do that. I wouldn't hurt a fly, Josh."

Josh knew it was true; she wasn't capable of hurting anyone. But it didn't really matter. It wasn't what this whole thing was about.

"Kill her." The voice flowed through Josh's mind like silk. It made him swoon. It gave him strength and made him weak at the same time. It was the voice of the man in white. "They are coming for you. Kill her now."

Josh heard the swell of sirens. It wouldn't be long now. The cops didn't waste time when it came to this kind of thing. "But I don't think I can do it."

The man in white moved closer. Josh could feel his hot breath on his neck. Charlotte was saying something. Josh saw her lips moving, but he was focused on the other voice in his head. The man in white never spoke with his mouth; he didn't have to. Josh could read his thoughts. At least those that the man in white wanted him to read. When the man in white spoke this time, his voice wasn't so silky. There was an impatient quality about it, along with a serpentine hiss. "Kill her, Joshua. She'sss jussst a girl."

Sirens.

Screaming, shouting.

In the distance, a man identified himself as a police officer.

Kill herrrr.

Josh raised his gun and shot Charlotte Salisbury between the eyes.

He put his back to a row of lockers and slid down into a sitting position on the floor. "It's done."

"Almost," said the man in white without speaking.

"Are you gonna take me to Heaven now?"

A smile stretched across the face of the man in white, a face that appeared as though it had been chiseled out of alabaster. His teeth seemed a little more cuspidate than they had previously. "*Heaven*? There will be no Heaven for you, Joshua Wayne Parker."

"What? What are you saying?" Josh rose and stood

on legs that felt as if they'd just carried him a thousand miles. "I did everything you told me to. You promised me that if I did everything you said, you would spare my mother and me from the coming apocalypse that will engulf the earth."

The man in white threw his head back and laughed, and now his mouth looked absolutely shark-like.

Josh's mind swirled. A voice on a loudspeaker ordered him to drop his weapons and exit the building with his hands raised. He looked down at Charlotte Salisbury's beautiful dead face, and then he threw up. *This can't be happening. This can't be happening. This can't be happening.* He turned to the man in white and said, "You told me you were sent by God."

The man in white clutched Josh's shoulders and slammed him against the lockers and spoke (this time with his mouth) in a voice that was juxtaposed with what might have been a billion screaming souls in Hell. "You *fool!*" The pearl irises of his eyes began to glow. "I ask you, what kind of *god* would send a devil like *me*?"

Josh found himself unable to move, not a muscle, he couldn't even breathe. To his horror, his hand began to move independently of his brain. Josh struggled against it, begged his own mind to regain control, but he was tired. So very tired. His hand tightened on the grip of the handgun and raised the weapon and stuck the barrel between his lips. The man in white stepped away, adjusted his ivory suit jacket, and said, "I'll see you soon."

And then Josh Parker blew his brains across the locker behind him.

***

Rocky Alexander

James Lowe cowered beneath the oak desk and prayed that the gunman wouldn't find him. He could hear the police outside, but there were still shots echoing through the building. The girl with the nasty stomach wound was crying in the back of the classroom, and James was terrified that the gunman would hear her and come back to finish the job. After a few minutes passed without gunfire, James began to wonder if the gunman had run out of ammo, or if perhaps the cops had gotten him. He was tempted to make a run for it, but then he heard the classroom door swing open and footsteps approach his hiding place. *Oh Jesus Christ I don't want to die. Oh please Oh please God save me.*

He saw a pair of flawless white dress shoes stop near the desk, and a moment later the desk slid away. James nearly pissed his pants in terror. He closed his eyes and waited for the gunshot that would end his life, but when it didn't come, he gathered enough courage to face the figure who stood above him. The man was dressed in an immaculate white suit, and his skin and hair were nearly as white as the suit fabric. Something dangled like a pendulum behind him, but James couldn't immediately tell what it was.

"Are you going to kill me?"

"No, James," said the man in white. His voice was loud and clear, even though James didn't see his lips move. "I'm not going to kill you. In fact, I'm here to save you."

It was then when James realized the thing that hung behind the man was a tail. A thick, white, furry tail. A lion's tail.

"Wh-who *are* you?"

The man leaned forward and smiled. His teeth

were perfectly set and beautifully white–the whitest teeth James had ever seen. "Who am I? Why, I'm your guardian angel."

Prime Cuts

GLEN JOHNSON

The heat was suffocating; he felt like he couldn't take a full breath. Jake Jefferson fidgeted on the wooden seat as the warm salty breeze off the ocean washed over him. Sweat beaded on his forehead, and he could taste salt as it ran from his top lip into his mouth, and it stuck his T-shirt to his back. His sunglasses rubbed his freckled nose, and between his toes hurt from wearing flip-flops.

He downed some luke-warm water. It did nothing to quench his thirst. He used to think of himself as healthy. Only twenty-two and he ran half-marathons once a month, mainly for charity. He played on the five-a-side football team every weekend for his workplace, which was an optical lab where he had worked since leaving school. However, his body was not used to the constant heat that drained every ounce of his strength. It wouldn't be so bad if it cooled down at night, but if anything, the nights were even muggier. His home country of England was in the grips of winter, and here he was sweating to death.

Glen Johnson

He looked down at the plate of meat. The juices covered his fingers. It was the best-tasting dish he had eaten since arriving in Thailand eight days ago. He wasn't a fan of pork, but he had to admit: It melted in his mouth like butter. In fact, it was probably the best thing he had ever eaten. The dish alone made all the discomfort worth it. Jake was on his second plate. He ignored the napkins as he covered his fingers and face in the sweet red BBQ sauce.

It was Jake's first time in the country, and to start with, everything was overwhelming and too in-the-face. It didn't help that his best friend Clark Middleton insisted they stay on the legendary Khaosan Road—a location known for its clubs and pubs, ladyboys and massage parlours with happy endings.

Jake was exhausted, psychically and mentally. And even though Clark looked similar—both were five foot eight, with light brown, short-cropped hair, and a muscular body—and had even been confused as his brother on more than one occasion, he didn't seem to feel the heat like Jake. In fact, he seemed to thrive on it.

Clark dragged him out to a different pub every night. Then after a beer tower, and multiple shots, they would head to the next bar. Thai girls would scream and dance and get you to buy them drinks, and promise you the best time of your life. They would gyrate against your leg and squirm on your lap, while filling your glass with another shot of some foul-smelling liquor, and spend your money like water. And if you decided to pay their bar 'bill' and take them back to your room, they were even livelier.

Jake and Clark would crawl out of bed at midday,

find somewhere that cooked something resembling an English breakfast, and down a Tiger beer to aid their recovery.

His kidneys were protesting.

He gulped some more warm water. He had ordered an ice-cold coke, but the small beach side restaurant was heaving, and the smiling waiter had yet to return. The special was the barbequed pork. It was always the BBQ pork—the only item on the menu. The small place was famous for it, and just like this evening, it was overflowing with customers. However, there was only so much meat slow cooked overnight, so it was first come first serve; he was lucky to get a second helping.

He noticed Clark had just ordered another bottle of Leo beer from the waiter.

After a week of late nights, loud music, party girls, expensive drinks, and ladyboys, he had put his foot down, stating there was more to Thailand than beer and long legs. Besides, he had blasted through his money, and they had not visited one temple or historical place, or even stepped foot off Khaosan Road.

After two days, Jake had convinced Clark to travel with him down to Krabi, in the South of Thailand. They would stay in a town called Ao Nang, which had an amazing beach, set on the Andaman Sea and more importantly, a small island called Phi Phi just off the coast, which was the location where the movie The Beach was filmed, and it had been on Jake's Bucket List for years—the movie was one of his favourites.

At first, Clark grumbled, until Jake pointed out all the semi-naked women who would be pacing the white sand and frolicking in the surf. Clark didn't need any more encouraging. Besides, he stated, his dick was itching from the last Go-Go girl he had taken back to his room, and he couldn't find his iPhone anywhere, and he was convinced the woman stole it.

It took a bus eighteen hours to get from Bangkok to Krabi. Clark complained all the way due to his hangover and the early start, until he realized two Spanish girls sat behind him. His composure changed, and he went into flirt mode. He explained there would be one each. Jake was assigned the flat-chested, goofy one, while Clark picked the buxom stunner.

They stopped in Krabi Town and caught a smaller minibus to Ao Nang. Clark made sure he sat next to the two girls. The bus was only three seats wide, and Jake had to sit behind, next to two grumpy German men who had flat-top haircuts he hadn't seen in over a decade, and muscle shirts. The problem with muscle shirts, he reasoned, is you need muscles. Theirs hung from their shoulders down their pigeon chests.

The minibus dropped them at a random corner. The driver shut the back tailgate, and without a word, climbed back in and drove off.

They had reached their destination.

Clark insisted on following the Spanish girls at a distance, and then made out it was a huge coincidence when they walked into the same hostel.

The two girls giggled and played dumb.

They were now a foursome, an unofficial group. The two girls shared the small round, paint chipped wooden table with them, as they all dug into the red sauce covered meat, and sipped their warm drinks.

The air was full of conversation, laughter, playful

arguing, and the music from the small hut where the meat was prepared.

Jake took another bite, as the meat slipped easily off the bone, and melted in his mouth. It was so sweet and juicy. He never realized pork could taste so good, or come in such large chunks.

Clark was flirting with both Spanish women. The grumpy, goofy one showed no interest in Jake. He wasn't bothered. There was more to life than sex. Besides, over the last week, he had had his fair share.

The funniest moment was three days ago when Clark burst into his room, stark naked, with his hands on his head, as if a realization was going to make his brain explode.

"She's a fucking bloke!" he stated, wide-eyed. "She got a cock bigger than mine!"

It took two days to live it down, and of course, Jake plastered the news all over Facebook. Clark was boycotting the social media site until he returned home to face the music.

Jake licked the sauce off his fingers. It was too good to wipe on a napkin. He tried to work out what part of the animal it was. Shoulder? Belly?

He checked his watch. It was 8:16 PM.

The surf boomed across the beach. The sky was darkening, turning a purple colour. The small BBQ café was right on the beach, with the tables nestled in the warm sand. Fairy lights twisted around wooden slats that surrounded one side next to the wooden decking leading out onto the sand. All the tables were painted a different colour. There was a large red sign with THE LONG PIGGY GRILL written in white letters. The waiter also had an apron with the name splashed across the front, next to his name badge—Son Chai.

Jake soaked it all in. It truly was paradise.

"They also want to see Phi Phi Island," Clark announced with his mouth full.

"Sorry?" Jake was pulled back from his relaxing thoughts.

"The girls want to join us tomorrow."

"Oh right." He was looking forward to the trip. It's not that he didn't enjoy the female company, but it felt like he was a spare wheel—it was obvious neither were interested in him.

"That's nice," he muttered.

"Right!"

"But Veronica and Alfreda don't have too much money to waste, so it will have to be a cheap trip."

The girls looked like their names. Veronica was slender with luscious jet black long curly hair, with a large shapely chest. While Alfreda looked more like a man, with a short boyish haircut and an awkward body with man sized hands. Veronica was wearing a swimsuit with a silky throw over her shoulders, while Alfreda wore thick shorts and an oversized T-shirt with the band Ramones on.

"I'm running a little low myself. We will find a cheap boat ride. No worries." Jake took the last bite. It fell away from the bone and dissolved in his mouth.

The waiter put down a coke and three tiger beers. Another man, who looked like this brother, cut up the large chunks of meat into servings.

"Could I have another plate full, please?" Jake asked.

"Sorry. No more. All gone for today." His accent

didn't sound Thai, but Jake didn't think too hard on it. What did he care where people came from?

"Come back tomorrow night. We are always here. Every night. Good food, yes?"

"Amazing!" And he meant it.

"I overheard you need a boat?"

It took a moment for Jake to get his brain in gear.

"Yeah sure. We want to go to Phi Phi Island."

"Yes, no problem. A friend of mine has cheap boat. He will take you."

"Really?"

Clark and the girls were also paying attention.

"Normal price, with boats, about one thousand baht each. My friend, only five hundred each. There and back. No problem. He wait for you."

"Really, wow," the one called Alfreda said.

They all looked at each other. A silent agreement circled the group.

"We're all in," Jake stated. "When and where?"

"Meet my friend, Ping there," he turned and pointed to the end of the beach by a large boulder, near where the monkeys hassled beach goers for food, right under the lip of a huge rocky outcrop. "8:00 AM sharp."

"Brilliant. Okay. We will see Ping at eight." He did wonder why they had to walk about half a mile down the beach. A boat could just as easily pick them up here.

"Ha-ha, Ping," Jake could hear Clark mutter to the girls. They giggled.

The man pretended he didn't hear. He cleared away their empty bottles and glasses, and two empty plates.

"You have fun tomorrow. Okay?" He stared at Clark a little too long. Only Jake noticed. "And I will see you again soon."

They all said they would.

It was dark by the time they finished at The Long Piggy Grill, because even though the food ran out, drinks were still available, and a guy started playing a guitar.

Jake sat with a Tiger beer in hand watching the surf roll in the distance, with the swishing sound over the sand. The soft guitar music drifted over from one side. Along with the darkness came a cooling breeze that ran over his body.

Life can't get much better than this, he decided. *Why couldn't we have come straight here, rather than spend it in a stuffy, loud city?*

He wiggled his bare feet in the warm sand. The condensation from the cold beer dribbled down his hand.

Ah, Paradise.

They had five days left. He decided he would spend every night here, eating the amazing food and just relaxing. He felt at home. He was completely at peace.

It is *paradise.*

Reluctantly, he downed the last mouthful. It was time to get some sleep; he had an item to tick off his Bucket List tomorrow.

***

Dawn arrived too early.

Jake had set the alarm on his phone, because he knew Clark wouldn't bother and would simply wait until Jake woke him up.

He waited outside his room for ten minutes for

Clark to sort himself out. He sat on a porch that looked over the small town right down to the beach. In the distance, he could see dozens of islands. He didn't know if one of them was Phi Phi.

Jake heard giggling from the room. It turned out Veronica spent the night. She ran out with a towel wrapped around her, and the clothes from the night before in her arms. She blushed.

Clark strode out with only his boxers on. His six-pack flexed as he stretched his arms. He smirked and slapped Jake's shoulder.

"One down, one to go," Clark stated.

"I'm surprised you didn't go for a threesome," Jake said.

"I'm trying to pace myself, you know?" He winked.

They waited another ten minutes for the girls. Once they arrived, they jogged along the beach in order to get there by eight o'clock. As they ran down the beach, kicking at the surf like children, they could see a Thai boat in the distance. It was long and thin and colourful, with a metal pole hanging from the back of a motor that must have been fifteen feet long with a propeller on the end.

The boat was grounded up the sand. There was a man on the beach who gave a friendly wave. He was thin and middle-aged, with lanky sparse black hair and a lazy eye, with tattoos covering his skinny arms and shoulders—Ping.

"Yakuza!" Clark muttered.

"That's the Japanese Triad, ya idiot. And if he was, I think he would've changed his name from Ping."

The man stood with his hand out. Jake handed over the two thousand baht.

Glen Johnson

The man counted the money twice, nodded once, and then motioned to the boat.

The girls jumped aboard giggling, while the boys helped push the boat back out into the surf.

Before long, they were bouncing over the waves, with the warm wind blowing over them and the sun beat down.

The boat was made of thick wood. The planks used for seating were worn down from use. A little warm water slopped around in the bottom from the mist raining off the prow as it cut through the water.

"How long will it take?" Jake shouted over the sound of the outboard motor, while the land started to dwindle into the distance.

The man simply smiled and nodded.

Jake noticed both his front teeth were missing.

The man pointed at a cooler wedged down between two seats. Inside were some beers packed in ice.

It was too early for beer, but it was so hot. They sat sipping from a cold Chang bottle each, enjoying the view.

The motor roared, and the mist of water sprayed over the cover above their heads, which was keeping the sun from beating down upon them. The girls chuckled at things Clark said, while Jake watched the islands in the distance.

Last night, Jake looked Phi Phi up on his laptop. The Internet connection was rubbish, but eventually he managed to get online. Phi Phi was, in fact, an archipelago—a series of small islands that sat roughly between Phuket and Krabi. It stated the distance from Ao Nang Beach was about twenty miles. He had no idea how long that would take in the small boat.

However, he was concerned. The island was right out to sea, and so far they had kept close to the coastline.

Jake turned to try and talk to the man, to see why they weren't heading out into deeper water. His vision blurred. His head felt strange. He slumped in the seat, sliding down into the warm water in the bottom of the boat, he could see Alfreda was slumped against Clark's shoulder. Clark and Veronica looked like they were slipping under, as well. Confusion was registered on both their faces.

Just before he blanked out, Jake noticed the thin, tattooed man talking on a handheld radio. He was also smiling as he watched Jake fall unconscious.

***

Jake had the worst hangover ever. His head throbbed like nothing he had even experienced before. He also felt like throwing up; it was so bad. His mind was blank. Then realization dawned. He had been drugged.

He went to sit up. He needed to get some answers and see where Clark was. When he tried to move he realized he was strapped down. He noted he was also naked.

What the fuck?

His arms and legs were held down by leather straps. He pulled as hard as he could. No good, they were too strong.

What the fuck is happening?

Then the smell hit him, like a bloated chicken left to float in rancid water.

He gagged.

His head wasn't strapped down. He looked around.

He was in some kind of large metal shed, the walls and roof rippled corrugated iron. The shed was sectioned off, and it was uncomfortably hot, as if the shed sat out in the baking sun. He could just make out a large slab of wood to his left.

Fuck!

Alfreda was lying on it, naked. Her short hair was plastered to her face with sweat. Her breasts were so small she looked like a boy.

There was another wooden block next to her. He could just see Veronica. Her larger breasts sagged to the sides, with her black hair cascading down over her face and the side of the block.

He twisted his head. Right next to him, maybe five feet away, was Clark. He was naked and strapped down.

"Clark! Clark! Wake the fuck up, man!" Jake quickly looked around to see if anyone had heard him. His throat was parched. What he wouldn't give for a glass of cold water. He wondered how long he was unconscious for.

Clark was motionless.

Shit! Shit! Shit!

He pulled at the straps again. He was about to hyperventilate. He strained against the straps so hard he almost passed back out. He lay still, catching his breath. His head pounded so hard it felt like his skull was going to split. He licked his parched tongue over his hot teeth.

Why is this happening? What does the man want? Were they now kidnap victims?

He realized he could hear something, a motor of some kind. It was getting louder. A vehicle pulled up outside. He heard two doors thud shut one after the other. There were people talking, but he couldn't understand them. It could be Thai; he wasn't sure.

Shit!

The sound of a chain rattling then a large door swung open. It was dark outside.

Two men entered. One was the boat driver. The other looked similar, also covered in tattoos. As one passed Veronica, he gripped one of her breasts and gave it a hard squeeze. Both men laughed.

Jake had his head back down and to the side, pretending to be unconscious while looking through the slits of his eyes. Then he heard groaning. Alfreda was waking up. She started groaning louder. Then the groans turned into screams when she realized she was tied down.

He wanted to shout at her, tell her to lie still, to shut up. Don't aggravate them.

One man causally headed toward her, while carrying on with his conversation with the other man. He waved a cigarette in the air as he chatted. As he neared Alfreda, he reached below the large wooden block she rested on, and without breaking stride or interrupting the conversation he pulled out a cleaver and swung it in an arc and cut straight down through her neck. He left the cleaver half-buried in her throat.

Alfreda's body jerked and spasmed with blood spurting from the lethal wound as her eyes stretched wide-open in pain.

Jake almost threw up. Instead, he had to pretend to be asleep.

Oh God no! Please God, let this not be happening! FUCK!

He lay as still as he could, with tears running down his face. He had to listen to Alfreda gurgle and thrash, and slap her arms and legs around on the wooden block. The sound was the worst thing he had ever heard in his life. Hot piss ran down his leg and dripped off the block.

Alfreda became weak. Her blood flowed onto the floor, as she made horrendous wet throaty sounds. All the while, the two men had a conversation in the background. With a couple more grunts and a cough, Alfreda went silent.

Jake could hear something drip onto the concrete floor. He didn't know if it was her blood or his urine.

Then the voice got closer again. He tried not to move. His chest was rising and falling fast. He tried to steady his nerves.

The two men continued to chat as they started to chop up Alfreda's warm body. The sound of the large heavy cleaver crunching through her muscles and bones was sickening. He could hear them slap parts of her body down onto a large metal sheet, while they chatted and laughed. The bits they didn't want were tossed into a large blue tote bin. As one tossed her head in, both cheered as if scoring a basket.

Jake's body was shaking with fear. He shit himself. Not that anyone would notice over the stink hanging in the air.

He could hear the last of Alfreda's body get de-boned and cut down into manageable hunks of meat. Jake risked a look. What was left of her didn't look human. Blood and bruise coloured intestines covered the block, along with other body fluids. It ran down the block, pooling on the dirty floor.

Another motor approached. A door slammed. The large shed door opened. Another man walked in. He looked different. He conversed with the two men. They laughed some more.

Jake could hear flip-flops slap the concrete. He felt the man's presence over him.

Jake knew the man knew he was awake. He was covered in shit and piss, and tears streaked his face. He didn't want to open his eyes.

Let the cleaver drop. I just hope it's a clean, quick chop. Please God, don't let me suffer like Alfreda.

He could hear the man breathing.

Slowly, Jake opened his eyes.

First, he saw the two men behind smearing some kind of red liquid, like a thick sauce over the remains of Alfreda, slapping it down into the meat.

What the fuck?

He looked up at the man staring down at him. All the while, Jake was twisting and pulling at the straps holding him down.

It was the waiter from the café. He even had the same apron on, with The Long Piggy Grill written across the front, along with his nametag. Just as Jake registered that, the man said, "Ah, you have caught us, no?"

"Y-y-you are f-fucking crazy," Jake stuttered, while spittle dribbled from the corner of his mouth and tears flowed down his face.

"No. No crazy. We use only the best, prime cuts, well fed European, and American meat." He smiled, thinking his joke was funny. The man used the large cleaver in his hand and brushed it against Jake's face.

The two other men were cutting up Veronica. The sound of the bones snapping echoed around the metal hut.

"You fucking loud-mouthed Americans. Always so happy and looking down on everyone else."

"I'm fucking British." Jake managed to say just as the strap snapped on his right wrist. He snatched the cleaver out of the man's hand, and with one swing sliced it across the waiter's throat before the man even knew what was happening. He tumbled backwards, clutching at the spurting wound. Jake swung the cleaver and cut the strap to his left wrist, then each leg.

The other two men rushed over. One man went to his bleeding companion's aid, while the other rushed at Jake.

Jake dropped to the floor just as a heavy blade thumped down into the wooden block. He scrambled to his feet, slipping in his piss. He managed to gain his footing, while wildly swinging the cleaver. By pure luck, it caught the man's arm as it missed a swing at Jake's head. It severed a main artery; blood shot high into the air. The man roared in pain.

Jake raced across the concrete floor to the other side of the room. He slammed into a sliding door, and ripped two fingernails off as he fumbled to slide the door open. The door jerked aside, and Jake fell forward onto his knees.

Jake was shocked at the sight inside. A dozen naked bodies were suspended from the metal rafters on thick hooks. They were gutted with the heads and hands and feet missing. They looked like deformed sides of beef. To one side was a pile of boxes, with the Long Piggy Grill logo stamped on the side.

Jake was dumbstruck. He wasted precious seconds.

"You fucking pig," a voice spat behind him. A foot

stood on his hand holding the cleaver, crushing his fingers. The cleaver was kicked away. A punch landed against Jake's kidneys, an elbow caught him in the spine, and finally a blow to the side of the head. A hand gripped his hair and pulled his head back.

Jake looked up into the eyes of the waiter. Blood ran down the man's throat, but the cut wasn't deep.

The waiter's eyes were wide with anger. Spittle flecked from his lips. "I think you have been tenderized enough," he said as he raised the blade.

"I hope you fucking choke on me, you bastar—"

The Lake Is Life

RICHARD CHIZMAR

Police officer: When did you realize something was wrong?

Witness: When I saw the blood.

Police officer: Where was the blood?

Witness: Everywhere.

***

My parents decided to separate the summer I turned fourteen.

It was a bad time. Not a lot of screaming or yelling or fighting. Just long, awkward silences and the occasional sniffle or dirty look exchanged between Mom and Dad.

June passed in a blur of family counseling sessions and solo shopping dates with Mom and dinners with Dad. When I wasn't being dragged to one place or the other, I hid away in my old tree house rereading *Harry Potter* or listening to my iPod.

By the time July rolled around, Dad was drinking again and I was living with Mom in a second floor condo near my school and going alone to counseling twice a week. I had finished all the *Harry Potters* and moved on to my mom's old Sidney Sheldon paperbacks. A little racy, but I was growing up fast by then.

On the Fourth of July, Mom and I went to dinner at Harrisons and watched the fireworks from the pier with about a billion other people. On the way home, she broke the news to me. In a week, I was heading to Grandma's house at the lake. I was going to spend the rest of my summer there, while she "sorted out some things."

I could tell Mom thought I might be disappointed with the news. Maybe even angry. But I wasn't.

I loved the lake with its quiet coves and peaceful woods. And I adored my grandma. She was the one who taught me how to fish and pick berries and mark a trail. She was the one who gave me my love of books and astrology.

I felt bad thinking it, but when Mom told me, I was actually relieved.

I was tired of my counselor's voice and the way my friends all looked at me. I hated the condo, it smelled funny, and my dad was starting to scare me.

The lake sounded wonderful.

It felt a little like running away from home.

***

"My gosh, Becca, look at you. So tall!"

I rolled my eyes, but I was smiling as I lifted my suitcase out of the trunk of Mom's car. "Grandma Maggie, you just saw me a month ago."

"I know I did, and if you haven't grown another inch, I'm Raquel Welch."

I hugged her in the driveway and she hugged me back twice as hard. It felt good, like what I remembered happy to feel like.

"Don't break her, Ma."

Grandma laughed at that and hugged my mom next. "Don't break me either."

Then we were all laughing. A boat buzzed by and I could hear muffled laughter on the evening breeze.

"It's so beautiful," I said, mostly to myself.

In my peripheral, I saw the two of them exchange a look that said: *We did good bringing her here.*

"You know what your Grandfather always said . . . "

Grandpa had died of a heart attack when I was seven, but I remembered him well. I smiled. "The lake is life."

"Yes, indeed." She laid a wrinkled hand on my shoulder, and I touched it with my own. "The lake is life. So let's get on living it."

We headed inside the house.

***

I saw the boat again three days later.

I was sitting on the pier with my toes in the water, writing in my journal and soaking up the sun, when I heard the whir of a small outboard. I looked up just in time to see a dinghy round the point and come into view. There was only one person in the boat, and as they drew closer, I could see it was a boy. Probably not much older than I was.

I felt exposed sitting there, so I pulled my feet out of the water and propped my legs up under my chin.

The boy was shirtless and wearing a red baseball hat. Even from fifty yards away I could see he was tanned from the sun and had muscles. I guessed then that he was older. Maybe even old enough to drive.

He waved as he passed me, and after a moment's hesitation—born of equal parts sheer panic and excitement—I casually waved back and then looked down at my journal again.

I counted to ten. Slowly. And then I looked up again.

The boat and the boy were gone.

***

With one exception, my first week at the lake passed in a kind of drowsy haze, as time there usually does, and I was happy to settle into a daily routine.

Each morning I would wake early and eat breakfast with Grandma Maggie out on the deck overlooking the lake. After we did the dishes together, we would walk the winding dirt path to the point and back. Grandma was in pretty good shape for a woman her age, but she was finally slowing down, so I never pushed her to go farther. I saved those longer hikes for the afternoon and did them solo.

In the evenings, we cooked dinner together and often left our dirty dishes on the table to sneak away and fish for crappie or sunnies or bass before the sun went down. Other times, we cleaned up our mess and sat in rockers on the porch and read or talked. She had a television in the den, but we rarely watched it before bedtime.

We hardly talked about Mom and Dad and what was going on at home. Sometimes she would tell me stories about Mom when she was my age or when she was in high school. I had mostly heard them all before, but I still liked listening. And I know it made Grandma happy to tell them.

Grandma never mentioned it, but I'm sure Mom had told her all about my mini-breakdown and the resulting appointments with my counselor. I was certain it would come up in time, but for now I was grateful it hadn't.

Mom called to say goodnight every evening around nine, but I didn't ask many questions and she didn't offer much in the way of news. It was still good to hear her voice. My dad hadn't called yet. I had tried to call him a couple times, but it always went straight to voice mail. I didn't mention this to Mom, and she didn't ask.

It was a good first week.

***

The exception happened as I was getting ready for bed one night.

Grandma was already asleep in her room, and I had just come upstairs after watching a late movie by myself. I was certain my bedroom window was shut because I remembered pausing to close the curtains right before I took my shower.

But when I came out of the bathroom fifteen minutes later, freshly clean and wrapped in a towel, I saw the thin curtains fluttering in the night breeze.

I stood there in the bathroom doorway, staring at the window. Momentarily frozen with fear. Holding my breath.

Then, as if waking from a dream, I quickly glanced around the room, searching for an intruder. I found nothing out of place and realized there were only two places someone could hide: under the bed and inside the closet.

I considered yelling for Grandma Maggie or making a mad dash for her room, but the longer I stood there, the more foolish I felt. I had just watched a stupid horror film. My imagination was probably running wild. *What did I expect?*

Richard Chizmar

I took a deep breath and, before I could change my mind, dropped to a knee on the floor and checked under the bed. Nothing but dust bunnies.

Emboldened, I walked over to the closet and flung open the door. Nothing inside except my summer clothes.

I walked over to the window and pushed it closed.

Just as I was turning around, I saw a flash of movement in the yard. A shadow shifting within a larger, darker shadow.

I stared outside for a long time, and then I locked the window and went to bed.

***

Police officer: What were you doing in the woods again?

Witness: I told you, we were playing a stupid game.

Police officer: (checks notebook) Hide and Seek?

Witness: (nods) Yes.

Police officer: Aren't you all a little old to be playing a kids' game?

Witness: I said the same thing to Benjamin.

Police officer: And what did Benjamin say?

Witness: He said they played it all the time. They liked to scare each other.

***

Two things happened on the Monday of my second week at the lake:

Grandma Maggie brought up the "D" word for the first time and I met the boy from the boat.

We were on the way home from our morning walk and Grandma had been extra quiet, so I wasn't at all surprised when she finally asked, "What would you think, Becca, if your parents got a divorce?"

I think she expected me to stop walking or start crying or something equally dramatic, but I didn't have it in me. "Why? Did Mom say something to you?"

Her eyes widened and she shook her head. "No, no. Nothing like that. I was just wondering if now that you're feeling better . . . if you had thought about the future."

I shrugged my shoulders. "I don't think it really matters what I think, do you?"

"Of course, it matters, honey."

"Not really." I helped her over a fallen log. "I'll be okay with whatever happens. I have to be."

She took my hand in hers, and that's how we walked the rest of the way home.

***

"Hey, you're Rebecca, right?"

Startled, I looked up from the shallow stream bed, and there he was: the boy from the boat.

And standing next to him, a very tall and very pretty blonde girl. Wearing very short cut-off jeans.

"Sorry, didn't mean to scare you."

He was shirtless again, and barefoot, and wearing the same red baseball hat.

"I'm Benjamin."

I stood up. "You didn't scare me. I was . . . I was just looking for crayfish."

He stepped forward and smiled, and it lit up the entire forest. "Not many crayfish round here, but if you follow it back a ways, you'll find a deep pool crawling with 'em. Just watch out for snakes."

And then that smile again.

"How did you know my name?"

"My ma knows your grandmother. Told me you were staying the summer here."

I waited for the inevitable "sorry about your folks" but it didn't come. The blonde girl shuffled her feet and made a noise in her throat.

"Oh yeah, this is Kelsey."

I started to step forward to shake her hand, but stopped. *Don't be stupid.* "Hi. I'm Becca."

The girl looked away, disinterested. "I know."

I looked down at my feet, embarrassed.

Benjamin flashed the girl a dirty look I wasn't supposed to see and said, "We're running over to the north side to see some friends. You wanna come?"

I hoped my face didn't show how surprised I was by the invitation. "Thanks, but I can't. I have to help my grandma with dinner."

Kelsey grabbed his arm, held it in both of her hands. "Can we *please* go now?"

I started walking. "I have to get back anyway."

"Hey, we're thinking about having a bonfire tomorrow night," Benjamin said. "You should come."

I stopped walking. I could feel my face flush. "Maybe."

"I'll clear it with your grandma and pick you up."

I heard Kelsey hiss something under her breath.

And then they were gone.

***

By the time I got back to Grandma Maggie's house, it was dusk and a light rain was falling. I was twenty minutes late for dinner and in a daze, wondering if I had imagined the whole thing.

***

Police officer: How long were you up in the tree?

Witness: A long time. My legs started to hurt.

Police officer: Give me an estimate . . . ten minutes?

Witness: Longer. Maybe a half-hour.

Police officer: You say you didn't see anyone?

Witness: (shakes head) No.

Police officer: Did you hear anything?

Witness: Just what I told you before. Footsteps in the leaves. Some branches breaking. And then a scream.

***

But I hadn't imagined it.

At breakfast the next morning, I told Grandma about meeting Benjamin and the girl in the woods, and she told me all about Benny. She had known him since he was a baby and that's what she had always called him—and his mother, too. Benjamin's father had died in a logging accident when Benjamin was only five, and Grandma and his mom had grown close over the years. Just a couple of lonely widows, she joked, without a smile.

"I'm glad you ran into Benny," she told me, munching on a piece of dry toast. "They're good people."

"So it would be okay . . . if I went with him to the bonfire?"

"Do you want to go?"

I tried to play it cool. "I'm thinking about it."

Grandma saw right through me, as she often did. "Uh huh, I can see that," she smirked. "You just keep on thinking about it and let me know when you come to a decision, okay?"

I flipped a hand at her and didn't even try to hide my smile. "You hush, Grandma."

***

"Your chariot awaits," he said with a dramatic bow, as the boat settled alongside the pier.

He was wearing a T-shirt this time. Faded jeans and tennis shoes. And no hat. He looked beautiful.

He reached out a hand and helped me onto the boat.

I was wearing a sleeveless sundress, the only one I had brought with me, and although I felt overdressed, I didn't care. I never wanted to let go of his hand.

I sat down at the front of the boat, facing him.

He pushed off from the pier and cranked the throttle on the outboard and we were off, Grandma's house growing smaller behind us.

I waved goodbye because I knew she was watching from somewhere inside the house, and then my eyes went right back to Benjamin.

His curly brown hair danced in the breeze and the muscles of his arm flexed as he maneuvered the outboard. He smiled at me and raised his voice above the motor. "You look nice."

I felt my face get hot. "Thank you."

"Ever been out to Soloman's Island?"

I shook my head. "The old prison?"

He put a hand up next to his ear: *can't hear you.*

Louder this time: "Is that where the old prison was?"

"Yeah," he nodded. "From the Civil War. Nothing left of it now except some crumbling sections of wall and part of the old watchtower."

"That's where you have your bonfires?"

"Usually, yeah. Sometimes we even camp overnight."

"My grandma said I had to be back by ten o'clock."

He laughed. "I'll have you back in time."

I silently scolded myself for sounding like a dumb kid.

"So, do you have a boyfriend back home?"

I shook my head and wanted to ask if Kelsey was his girlfriend, but I didn't dare.

"Why the heck not? You're gorgeous."

I blushed again and then I was smiling, and I didn't remember a single thing either of us said after that until we reached the island.

***

The island was gross.

That was my first and lasting impression. I think I expected a secluded and tranquil paradise, and instead what I found was a rock strewn chunk of land littered with beer cans and cigarette butts and used condoms. There weren't even that many trees.

It was an ugly place, but I understood why they all liked it. The island belonged to them.

When we beached the dinghy and jumped ashore, the bonfire was already raging, and I could see maybe a dozen or so kids clustered around it. Drinking and smoking and dancing to a boom box.

I recognized one of the dancing girls as Kelsey, and

when she saw us, she made a beeline to a couple of other girls and then they had their heads together, whispering and scowling.

I started to think I should've stayed home, and it was as if Benjamin read my mind.

"C'mon, it'll be okay," he said. "You'll have fun."

I looked at him doubtfully and he just had time to take one more step before he was tackled off his feet by one of the largest kids I've ever seen.

"Benny boyyy!"

Benjamin and the human boulder crashed to the ground and rolled to a stop a full five yards away from where they had started. Somehow, Benjamin ended up on top and was holding the much larger boy down by the arms.

"Jesus, Mark. You *gotta* stop doing that."

Benjamin released his grip and got to his feet, brushing dirt from his jeans and T-shirt. He reached down and helped Mark to his feet. I stood there staring at them both, unsure of what I had just seen.

"Mark, this is Rebecca. Rebecca, Mark Andrews. All Conference linebacker on the football team. All Conference *retard* everywhere else."

I couldn't help it. I started to laugh.

"Rebecca, my dear, I am charmed." Then he actually took my hand and leaned down and kissed it.

I looked at Benjamin, speechless. and then we all cracked up laughing, and I thought: *Maybe he's right; maybe this will be fun.*

***

It was like a scene from one of my books.

A bunch of teenagers huddled together in the dark

around a campfire. Telling scary stories. Except it was real, and I was actually living it.

I sat on a blanket on the ground between Benjamin and Mark. Kelsey was with her friends right next to us, and every once in a while, I caught her whispering or staring at me. I always looked away first.

When it was Benjamin's turn, he surprised me by telling the story of the Soloman's Island slasher. According to legend, there was once a drifter who had gone crazy and started kidnapping local girls and bringing them here to the island. Once he had them trapped, he would let them go and then hunt them down in a sadistic game of cat and mouse, ultimately capturing them and slicing them to pieces with a hunting knife. Eventually the townspeople discovered what was happening and they tracked the drifter to the island, where they caught and executed him with the same hunting knife he used to kill his victims.

But the story didn't end there.

For the grand finale, Benjamin got to his feet and walked closer to the bonfire. Turned around and faced us. "According to the legend, the drifter's evil spirit still inhabits this island. And on very special nights, when the wind and moon are just right, you can still hear him taunting his victims, calling out to them as they cower in terror."

He lowered his voice for this last part: "But, most frightening of all . . . it is said that the drifter's *spirit* remains here . . . waiting . . . waiting for someone else to come to this island so he can possess them. Someone with dark thoughts and even darker potential. Someone to carry on his evil legacy and—"

"DIEEEE!!!"

The bushes exploded and there was the flash of a knife blade in the firelight, followed by a fleeting dark shadow, and I screamed and scuttled backward on my feet and elbows like a sand crab.

I screamed until my throat was sore, and I realized everyone else was rolling on the ground—laughing.

I looked up at the shadow standing above me and watched as Kelsey pulled the hood of her black sweatshirt down and dropped the knife to the ground.

Benjamin brushed past her and snatched up the knife. "That was a shitty thing to do and you know it."

"God, I was only joking," she said with a victorious smile.

And then Benjamin was helping me to my feet. "Are you okay, Rebecca?"

"I . . . I just want to go home. Now."

He took my arm and guided me away from Kelsey and the others. "She didn't hurt you, did she?"

But I couldn't answer. Tears were spilling down my cheeks and it was all I could do not to burst out in sobs.

"Hey, it's okay," he said, wiping my cheek with his hand. "It was just a stupid prank. I never would have let her do it if I had known."

He helped me into the boat and dropped the knife at his feet before cranking the motor. He held my hand the entire way back to Grandma Maggie's, and by the time he walked me to the front door and said goodnight, I had almost forgotten about Kelsey and her dirty trick.

Almost.

***

I was eating cereal on the deck the next morning when I heard the sound of tires on gravel in the driveway. I looked up and saw Mom parking next to Grandma's truck.

"Mom?" I left my bowl on the table and jogged down to the driveway.

She got out of the car and smiled at me, looking better than she had in months. She pulled me into a long, tight hug. "God, I missed you, baby."

"What are you doing here? Why didn't you tell me you were coming?"

She laughed. "Whatever happened to 'I missed you, too, Mom?'"

"I did miss you. I *do* miss you! So much. I'm just surprised."

From behind me: "That was the point, kiddo."

I turned around to find a beaming Grandma Maggie standing there with her hands on her hips. "We wanted to surprise you."

"Well, it worked." I hugged my mom again. "I'm so happy you're here."

"I have a present for you, too." She walked to the car and pulled a plastic bag from the back seat and handed it to me.

I opened the bag and pulled out a stack of new Stephen King paperbacks. I squealed with delight. "Thank you! Thank you! Thank you!"

"There's also a new journal in there, so you can write if you feel like it."

I gave her a look. "Is that my counselor talking or you?"

"It's from *me*, you little smart aleck." She looked at Grandma. "Now am I too late for breakfast? I've been driving all morning and I'm starving."

"Let's see what I can whip up," Grandma said, and

I watched them walk into the house arm in arm like schoolgirls.

It was the happiest I had felt in weeks.

***

After breakfast, Mom and I went for a long walk in the woods. Just the two of us.

We hiked past the point and into the valley beyond where the lake had eaten into the land, forming what Grandma always called Tranquility Cove. It was my favorite part of the shoreline and we spent a lazy hour there, skipping stones on the glassy surface of the lake and looking for driftwood.

And Mom talked a lot. Of course. I could tell she was worried about me.

"I'm fine, Mom, I promise."

"And you've been taking your pills?"

"Like clockwork."

"No more episodes?"

"I told you, I'm fine."

She sighed. "You always say that."

I tossed another stone and counted. Four skips. Not bad.

"I heard you met a boy."

I nodded. "He's just a friend."

Another stretch of silence, then:

"You know what the counselor said. You can't keep it all inside you. You'll explode again. It has to have a release."

I looked up at her. "*This* is my release," I said, gesturing to the lake and the trees and the sky around us. "This is where I come to feel better."

She looked around, *really* looked, and I could tell I had said the right thing.

"You promise you're still taking your meds?"
I crossed my toes inside my right boot.
"I promise."

***

Police officer: Did you recognize the voice of the person screaming?

Witness: (shakes head) No. Just that it was a girl.

Police officer: Then what happened?

Witness: The screaming stopped.

Police officer: And then?

Witness: I heard more footsteps. Running away.

Police officer: What did you do next?

Witness: I waited. For what felt like a long time. Then I climbed down out of my hiding place.

***

I said goodbye to Mom the next morning after breakfast. She had to work that evening and wanted to get back in time to shower and change clothes. I thanked her again for coming and for the books and watched her drive away until her car disappeared around the bend.

Grandma was feeling tired—probably because her and Mom had stayed up late talking in the den—so we skipped our morning hike, and instead I walked down to the pier to read.

The sun was already hot, so I rolled up the sleeves of my T-shirt and dropped my feet into the water. I turned the page and for the next couple hours, I found myself lost in a small Maine town infested with vampires.

I was just getting ready to take a break and check on Grandma Maggie when I heard the buzz of Benjamin's outboard. I looked up and there he was: typical Benjamin. No shirt. Dirty red hat. Big beautiful smile.

He cut the motor, drifted the final twenty feet to the pier, tied off the bowline, and plopped down right next to me. I could smell his sweat.

"What ya readin?"

I showed him the cover.

"*Salem's Lot*. Any good?"

"Better than good. It's amazing."

Neither of us said anything for a time. Both of us just staring out at the lake. Then, he moved a little closer, and I could feel the warmth of his leg against mine.

"Sorry again about Kelsey. She can be a bitch sometimes."

"I won't argue with that."

He laughed. "She's not always like that. She can be sweet, too. I guess she's just jealous."

"Jealous? Of what?"

He leaned forward so he could get a better look at me. "Of *you*, silly."

"Well, she obviously has nothing to be jealous about. I'm . . . me. And she's . . . *Kelsey*. All legs and boobs and blondeness."

He laughed again. "She *is* a big deal around here. But you're . . . *different*. And she knows it."

"Different," I repeated.

He splashed the water with his foot. "And she knows I like you."

I didn't say anything. I couldn't.

I felt the pressure on my leg increase, and before I realized what was happening, he was leaning in again, this time so close I could feel his breath on my cheek and then *oh, my God*, we were about to kiss . . .

"Howdy, kids." Right behind us. "Beautiful morning, isn't it?"

I jumped and he pulled back, and it was over. Just like that.

Benjamin stood up first. "Morning, Mrs. Maggie. How are you?"

"I'm right as rain. And you?"

"I'm good. Was heading home and saw Rebecca on the pier. Thought I'd say hello." He glanced at his boat. "I should probably be going now."

"No need to rush off on my account."

"Thanks, but I'm already late and you know how my ma gets."

Grandma Maggie smiled, and I saw the beautiful young woman she once was. "Your ma is a saint, boy, and don't you forget it. You say hi to her for me."

"Yes, ma'am. I sure will."

He hopped down into the boat with practiced ease. "I'll see you later, Rebecca. Thanks for telling me about your book."

"Bye, Benjamin."

He cranked the engine and pushed off.

Grandma Maggie walked up next to me, watching him motor across the lake.

"Thanks for telling me about your book? Uh huh."

"Hush, Grandma."

She giggled like a little girl and headed back to the house.

I turned to follow and my good mood vanished

when I saw a flicker of color in the woods along the far shoreline.

I stopped and stared and saw it again, just a flash of yellow shirt, and then it was gone.

Someone had been watching us.

***

I was watching a *The Big Bang Theory* rerun in the den when the phone starting ringing.

"Got it," Grandma called from the kitchen.

I glanced at the clock: *Early for Mom.*

Grandma Maggie came in holding the phone against her chest, a strange look on her face. "It's your father," she whispered.

I took the phone and stared at it for a moment before lifting it to my ear.

"Hello."

"Hi, baby, it's Dad."

I didn't say anything.

"I'm so sorry, Becca. Let me explain."

"Let you explain why you haven't called me or returned my calls for three weeks?"

"I understand you're angry. I really do. But if you hear me out, you'll—"

"I'm not angry, Dad. I'm confused. I was worried."

"I'm at a place getting help, Becca."

"What kind of place?"

"A *good* place. The kind that helps people with their addictions."

"You're in rehab?"

He laughed. "Well, yes, honey, I'm in rehab."

"How is it?"

"It's going really, really well, baby. I wish I had done this sooner."

"How come you didn't tell me?"

"Today's the first day I was allowed to call anyone. I only have another minute and then I need to call your mother."

"You're gonna call Mom?"

"I am. Hopefully, she'll listen and maybe even come to visit me."

A flood of emotions washed over me. I didn't know what to think or say.

"Honey, I have to go now, but I'll call again next week. I promise."

"Okay."

"I love you, Becca. It's gonna be okay."

"I love you, too, Dad."

We said goodbye and hung up.

And then I started crying.

***

Police officer: When did you realize something was wrong?

Witness: When I saw the blood.

Police officer: Where was the blood?

Witness: Everywhere.

***

I sat on the sofa and rested my head on Grandma Maggie's shoulder until the tears stopped. She stroked my hair with her fingers, comforting me like a little girl.

"Just when I had convinced myself everything would be okay one way, it changes and now the other way is a possibility again."

She nodded. "I understand how confusing it all must feel."

"Confusing and scary and—"

Before I could finish, the doorbell rang.

"Now who could that be," Grandma said, getting up to answer it.

I heard voices in the foyer and then she walked back in the den with Benjamin trailing behind her.

"You have company, Becca."

I sat up straight. "Hey, what are you—"

"You ever play flashlight tag before?"

"What in the world are you talking about?"

He smiled and came closer. "Flashlight tag? Hide and seek?"

"Umm, yeah, when I was like ten."

He pretended to be insulted. "Well, unlike you fancy city folks, us dumb country bumpkins have to make our own fun around here." He reached out a hand. "C'mon, let's go."

I took his hand and let him help me up. "Go where?"

"I told you. To go play games in the dark. Your grandma said it's okay."

I looked at Grandma Maggie. "You sure?"

She smiled and nodded. "Might be good for you, honey."

***

Twenty minutes later, I was standing in the dark woods just past the point with Benjamin and Mark and Kelsey and a half dozen other kids I had met earlier on the island. Several of them were passing around a bottle of wine and a joint. I turned both down when they were offered and did my best to stay clear of the smoke.

"Jimmy, you're it first," Benjamin said, gesturing to a tall kid dressed all in black.

Then he looked at me. "We get to the count of a hundred to hide and then he comes looking for us. He can use the flashlight to find us, but has to tag us with his hand to win."

He pointed at a cluster of large rocks. "Get back to base without him touching you, and you're safe."

"We don't get flashlights?" I asked, feeling a little foolish.

"Only the hunter gets the flashlight."

"Why? You scared of the dark?" Kelsey asked, smirking.

"Just making sure I know the rules," I snapped. I was actually proud of myself for standing up to her.

Jimmy turned on the flashlight and shined it on his face. "I'm coming to get youuu, Barbaraaa!"

Everyone laughed and starting spreading out in anticipation of the game starting.

Benjamin came up close to me, lowered his voice. "You gonna be okay?"

"I'll be fine. It's just a game."

"If you need me, call out and I'll come find you."

Jimmy started counting in a booming voice. "One, two, three . . . "

"Thanks, I'll be fine."

He looked at me, making sure.

"Go!" I said and pushed him playfully away. He flashed me a grin and took off into the woods.

" . . . nine, ten, eleven . . . "

I looked around. Only Kelsey and I remained in the clearing. She had been watching us the whole time. She glared at me, and then without a word, spun on her heels and disappeared into the shadows.

" . . . fifteen, sixteen, seventeen . . . "

I took off running.

***

I *was* scared.

I had been hiking in these woods dozens of times but never at night. Never alone in the dark.

There was a sliver of moon high in the August sky but not enough to do anything but cast more shadows. I felt like I was lost in a haunted house.

I stopped running after a few minutes and caught my breath. I looked around for a place to hide, deciding it would probably be better if I stayed close to base.

I worked my way toward the shoreline, looking for a stand of thick enough bushes to hide under. The night was sticky and hot and I could feel mosquitos buzzing my arms and neck. The idea of crawling under a bush or a fallen log didn't seem so appealing.

Instead, I looked for a tree to climb and found the perfect specimen only a few yards away from the lake. It was an ancient weeping willow, gnarled and bent over, like a tired old man waiting at a bus stop.

I scuttled up a thick branch and found a natural nesting ledge where two other limbs branched off. It was perfect.

I sat there in silence and waited for something to happen.

I didn't have to wait long.

Maybe five minutes passed before I heard the crash of heavy footsteps in the woods below. Leaves crunching. Branches breaking. Whoever it was wasn't being very cautious or quiet.

And then I saw the stab of a flashlight beam on the ground below and understood why. It was Jimmy. No need for him to be as stealth as the rest of us.

I held my breath, a chill of nervous delight spreading through me, and remained perfectly still.

He paused for a second, fanned the light out over the water, and then continued on his way.

I let out my breath and relaxed.

If Jimmy was heading down the shoreline, away from base, shouldn't I make a break for it? Or was it a trick and he was down there hiding, waiting for someone to make a move?

I thought about it some more and had just made up my mind to climb down and sprint for base when I heard more footsteps, and then whispering:

"You're being silly, babe."

"Don't you dare tell me that. I heard what you said to her."

I chanced a peek—it was Benjamin and Kelsey.

"*If you needdd me, call out and I'll come find youuu,*" she mocked.

"I was just being nice, babe."

"You were flirting."

"She's a kid, Kels. I told you what my ma said about her folks and her having a nervous breakdown."

"I don't care if she's some kind of mental case."

"She's not a mental case. She's just a dumb kid. My ma's making me be nice to her."

"I don't care what your mom says. I don't like it."

"Babe—"

"Let someone else be nice to her. You've done your charity work for the summer."

I don't remember anything else after that.

My brain shut off then . . . and everything went black.

And then it went red.

Richard Chizmar

***

Police officer: It's okay to tell the truth now, Rebecca. We found the knife.

Witness: (starting to cry) I *am* telling the truth.

Police officer: We found Benjamin, too.

Witness: Benjamin?

Police officer: His body. Floating in the lake, Rebecca. Covered with the same knife wounds we found all over Kelsey.

Witness: (crying; unintelligible)

Police officer: We know, Rebecca. We know what you did.

Witness: (crying) No. I was hiding in my treehouse.

Police officer: We know you killed Benjamin and put him in the lake, and then you ambushed Kelsey in the woods.

Witness: (crying) No. The lake . . . is life.

Police officer: Just help us understand why.

Witness: I was in my treehouse.

Police officer: Your grandmother is downstairs and your mother is on the way.

Witness: The lake is life. The lake is life. The lake is . . .

Police officer: (to Officer #2) I think we're done for now. She's already been photographed, but we need to get her clothes logged in evidence.

Police officer #2: Yes, sir.

Police officer: Be careful. She's covered in their blood.

Witness: The lake is life . . .

Damned if You Do

JACK KETCHUM

I don't know where to go with this anymore," Brewer said.

The clock on the wall above and behind his newest patient told Sullivan they were just under forty minutes into their fifty-minute hour.

Sullivan watched the folded arms and the tightly crossed legs come apart all at once like a man trying to unravel whatever knot lay inside him, saw the head droop slightly. He had noted this body language before with Brewer and knew it to be a sham—a dumb show of submission to the fates—and knew it was only temporary. Brewer was tougher than that.

"I don't know what to do with her."

He shook his head. Clasped his hands.

The pause lengthened.

"Are you waiting for me to tell you, John?"

"Yes. No. Oh hell, I don't know. I don't know what I'm waiting for."

"You realize that's not my job."

"Of course I do."

"My job is to help you draw your own conclusions. Make your own decisions."

"I know that. But I've come to this total impasse. Jennie doesn't listen anymore. It's as though I'm not there. Not even in the room."

"Why do you think that's happened?"

The arms and legs snapped into place again. Privates hidden. Chest hidden. His maleness trapped once again from the outside in. He sat back rigid in his chair.

"Why now?"

"Maybe it's the work."

"The work?"

"Maybe she doesn't respect my work anymore."

That was an evasion.

"Why would that be? You're a carpenter. You make furniture. And from what you've told me about your prices you must be pretty good at it."

"Yeah, but I'm not selling the way I did. It's this damn economy. This is a tourist town for godsake. Leaf-season wasn't half what it ought to be."

"You're not poor, John. You can afford me."

That drew a smile.

"No, I'm not poor. She gets everything she needs. So maybe it's not the work or the money. I dunno. But I'm an old-fashioned guy, Doc. My word used to be law around that house. The way I was brought up that's how it's supposed to be. But now . . . "

He sighed.

"Have you talked about it?"

"No."

"Why not?"

"I told you. I've tried. She doesn't listen!"

Sullivan watched his eyes scan the room—the simple office furniture, the painted landscapes, the open window behind his desk—as though they'd taken on a sudden interest. When in fact he'd been seeing them once a week for over two months now.

"So you feel you've got to do something, that some action on your part might change things. Is that it?"

"I've got to do *something*. End it maybe, just get her the hell out of my life. When I really don't *want* her out of my life. At least part of me doesn't. I feel like, you know, damned if you do and damned if you don't. Know what I mean?"

"You ever consider the problem might be hers to solve? Not your own?"

"Huh?"

"That maybe it's simply something *she's* going through. That maybe she should be in therapy, too. It's possible."

He laughed. "She'll never be in therapy, believe me."

"Why's that?"

"She just won't."

He heard that familiar brick wall vocal tone. Knew it was prudent to back away. Leave it be for now, he thought. Try another tack.

"You have any dreams for me today, John?"

Sullivan was a firm believer in dreams as metaphors for problems left untended to, each with its own symbolic language. Anything from a reminder to pay that overdue gas bill to resolving the guilt over a loved-one's death. That by penetrating the meaning of these metaphors the truth of what was foremost in the mind clarified, its emotional resonance understood for what it was. A dream was a nudge in the ribs reminding you what still needed doing.

Brewer smiled. "You and your dreams. Yeah, as a matter of fact I do. Night before last. I wrote it down, like you said."

He took a folded yellow post-it note out of his pocket.

"I'm just a kid, nine or ten maybe. I'm with a younger boy, probably six or seven I guess, and we're out in my yard and I have an axe. So I start hacking away with this axe at a tree-stump on the lawn while this other kid stands back watching, and the stump becomes my dog Tiger's head."

He looked up. "I really had this dog Tiger, this brown-and-white mutt, when I was about that age. Weird, huh?"

"Do you hit the dog with the axe?"

"Once. Like he turns from stump into dog mid-stroke. Like by then I'm committed to the downswing, you know? And this single drop of blood trickles down off his head and off his eye."

"That's all? One drop?"

"Yeah, like a tear. But the thing is, he *bears* it. He doesn't die or anything, or run away howling like a normal dog would. He just sits there looking at me. The axe is still in his head. And then I wake up."

Sullivan wished now he'd gotten round to asking him about dreams earlier. They were nearly out of time. They'd need to go into it further next session. But he'd ask the three basic questions, anyway. He had the time for that.

"What was your day like, day before yesterday?"

He shrugged. "Nothing out of the ordinary. I was

building the cabinet for the Sebald woman most of the day, took a break for lunch over at Duras' Deli, went back to work, knocked off about four-thirty, five."

"Was it going well?"

"It's a standard model. I could build it with my eyes closed by now."

"How are you at chopping wood?"

"Same thing."

"How did you *feel* in the dream? Do you recall?"

"Well, at first I guess I was having fun. Kind of showing off for this other kid, know what I mean? Then with Tiger . . . I'm not sure. Scared? Shocked?"

"Anything else?"

Like *guilt* for instance?

"No. Not that I can remember."

"Okay. What does Tiger represent for you?'

"A dog. A dog I had as a kid."

"And what does a dog represent?"

"I dunno. You trust a dog. He looks up to you. He goes where you go."

"Unconditional love?"

"That too I guess. Yeah."

"Sound like anybody you know? Or *thought* you knew?"

He grinned. "Jesus. Yeah. Sounds a little like Jennie, doesn't it?"

He let that sink in for a moment.

"And I hit her in the head with an axe."

"That's right."

He had time for one last line of questioning.

"What did you say Tiger did when you hit him?"

"Nothing. He didn't do anything. Just looked at me."

"Did you get any kind of feeling from him? Read anything in his expression, maybe?"

"Nothing. Just a dog thing, you know? Those big sad eyes looking at you. Still sort of expectant I guess is the word. Like what's next? Like whatever you do, it's okay by me."

He's looking for forgiveness, Sullivan thought.

The dog will forgive him anything.

Jennie will forgive him anything.

Only not anymore.

They'd get deeper into this next time.

He stood up from behind the desk.

"I don't normally give advice, John. You're aware of that. But this once I'm going to break my rule and ask you not to do anything over the coming week you might regret later. I'm not talking about inaction. You go ahead and do what you have to do. Only think about it very hard beforehand. Okay?"

"Okay."

And after the man left, Sullivan wondered why he'd said that. It wasn't like him. A patient learned by his mistakes as much as by anything else. But despite his disclaimer about going ahead and doing what you have to do he'd essentially told Brewer to hang in there for a week, and wondered why.

He thought it possibly had to do with the single part of the dream they hadn't touched upon yet—the watchful boy in the background. Somehow the boy disquieted him.

His next patient was due in five minutes. He'd think it over this evening. Maybe talk to the wife.

Ella was a good listener.

***

Damned if you do and damned if you don't.

Never mind that everything Sullivan had said made sense to him—that even the dream made sense to him now to a degree—it all came back to that. Damned if you do and damned if you don't. He could be screwing himself as easily by holding onto her as by dumping Jennie once and for all. He couldn't get a handle on it either way.

Think very hard, Sullivan had said. Well, he could do that.

He walked up the steps to the sturdy wooden porch he'd added on for them in happier days and used his key in the lock. He could remember a time when nobody on this quiet little street even bothered to lock their doors, when everyone felt safe.

He walked through the living room past the empty kitchen to his right and down the short narrow corridor to their bedroom and opened the door . . . and there she lay.

He could almost hear her breathing—that was how peaceful she looked. How she could look so peaceful and be so bloated by now that it was impossible even to see the length of baling wire around her neck was a mystery to him.

He spoke to her. Tender endearments like in the old days.

She didn't answer. He hadn't expected her to.

She didn't listen.

He felt the rage rise again and fall.

He took a moment to admire the craftsmanship of the knotty pine box he had made for her which exactly fit the length of the bed from headboard to baseboard, and thought suddenly for a moment of the boy—the younger boy—watching in his dream. He realized that he had never seen or could not remember the face of the boy. He doubted it mattered.

Dump her? Or leave her be?

It was possible he could wait until his next session with Sullivan, but he didn't know. He wasn't sure.

She was really beginning to stink.

The First Header

EDWARD LEE

Ten minutes was all it took for the young and eagle-eyed Micky-Mack to bag several squirrels, and a few minutes after that, those squirrels were promptly skinned and gutted via Helton's big buck knife. Now the tasty rodents roasted slowly on stake-skewers over the roaring campfire outside the truck. The smell was delectable, and it was unfortunate that one of the family's favorite meals would be tainted by the specter of death, sin, and secrets that hovered over many backwoods folks. They all sat on logs, keeping warm the way men were meant to. Dumar and Micky-Mack looked expectantly to their elder.

"Well, Paw?" Dumar asked.

"We'se waitin'," Micky-Mack added, antsy by the mystery of what it was that so pained Helton to relate.

"The time'a reckonin' is upon us, boys," Helton began, eyes reflecting fire-light and something like dark wonder. "We done got our chops busted by this evil man Paulie, and now's we'se out fer our revenge. It's been the law of the land since time began. Someone do you wrong when you ain't deserved it, then ya got no choice but to do him wrong even worse. Says so in the Bible"—he pronounced "Bible" as *bob-ul.* "Says *'a eye fer an eye.'*" Helton sipped some soda yet scarcely tasted it. "What I got ta tell ya both tonight hurts me right in my heart—"

"It hurt me in *my* heart, Paw," Dumar raised his voice, "seein' my boy kilt so awful!"

"Simmer down," Helton ordered. "And listen. In these parts, for *years and years*, folks been feudin' over this'n that. It's part'a man's nature, I s'pose. But sometimes folks can be so blammed *evil* that they'll do ya a wrong that's so ever-livin' bad it seems there ain't *nothin'* you can do back to get yer proper revenge. This happened to *our* family way back in a war they calt the *Civil War* when the Yankee Army come through here'n started burnin' our ancestors' houses down for nothin' more than retrievin' the *nails* out the ashes, which they'd melt down to make more bullets so's ta kill more decent Southern folk. But that ain't all they did, see?"

Micky-Mack was so intrigued he sat on the edge of his log. "What else they do, Unc?"

Helton's voice lowered to a grim rattle. "They round up all the gals in all the nearby towns, even li'l girls nine, ten years old, and they made 'em all live fer a month in what they called a *Sibley Camp* on account that's what the tents they put up was called—*Sibley* tents, and what they turned this camp into . . . was a *fuckin'* camp."

"A *what,* Paw?" Dumar asked.

"It were a *camp,* son, where Yankees from all over could come and git thereselfs a piece'a ass. A blammed *rape* camp's what is was! The Yankee general was a black-hearted cad the name'a Hildreth—it's him was the one who order this big camp put up, and by the hunnerts, the Yankee soldiers'd come to git their willies up in our gals and fill 'em with their evil Yankee peckersnot, and General Hildreth, what he done is he charged each soldier a five-cent piece fer each nut they git in the camp, making *profit* on his crimes against our gals!" Helton's rancor echoed through the woods. He recomposed himself.

"And, see, bein' that the gals was forced ta live in this camp fer over a month, they'se all wound up *pregnant,* and General Hildreth, he like that a whole lot, he did, 'cos even after his Yankees left, these poor gals'd pop out kids they'd have to raise, just bringin' more'n more hardship on 'em. And worser than that even was that whiles the gals was in the camp, they weren't givin' nothin' to eat, so's one'a the gals— name'a Constance McKinney, it was—she were kind'a the speaker fer all the poor gals. What she do is she say to General Hildreth, 'Please, general, ya gots to give my gals some food ever so often, else we all *starve to death!*' So ya know what General Hildreth did? He give each gal a tin cup and then he laugh back ta Constance'n said, 'Each time one of my men gets his nut up your dirty Rebel pussies, you just stand up and put this cup between your legs and let my men's jism dribble in the cup . . . 'cos that's all you're *ever* gonna get ta eat while you're here! Ain't no way I'm wasting a *single morsel of food* on Rebel bitches!'"

"God dang, Unc Helton!" Micky-Mack wailed. He and Dumar were clearly unsettled. "Shorely only the most evilest'a men'd make gals live on *cum!*"

The shadow of Helton's nodding head loomed huge

in the forest behind them. "Oh, they was evil, all right, boy, evil as if they was the sons'a Lucifer hisself. Our poor gals got fucked or sodder-mized probably a *thousand times each* by those dag-blasted Yanks. Eventually, though, they moved on, leavin' our towns burnt and dester-toot. See, the Yanks et all the livestock theirselfs, but what was left they kilt'n left ta rot so's no one else could have it, and they burnt all the fields, too. That blammed Hildreth even sent his men inta the *woods* to kill *every animal they could see;* he didn't want *nothin'* left for the folks here to eat. And, a'course, all them poor gals was knocked up and their bellies full'a Yankee bastards . . . "

Dumar and Micky-Mack shivered, not from the chill air but from the macabre suspense being conveyed by the fire.

"Weren't long after, the War ended, and the town's men that didn't get kilt or die in Yankee prison camps, they come back home, but imagine their horror when they did. Town in ashes, fields destroyed, folks livin' on roots'n head-lice'n tree bark'n worms, their wives rack-skinny'n traumer-tized'n with a Yankee baby on their tit. It's said that a good many'a our boys hanged theirselves in despair when they seed that." Helton eyed the two young men. "But there were a pair'a Rebel soldiers who come back, and they *didn't* kill theirselfs, no sir! They decided to *do* somethin' 'bout it!"

"What, Paw? What?" Dumar pleaded.

"They hunt down them evil Yankees'n kill 'em, Unc?"

Helton raised a silencing finger. "Listen ta me now, 'cos this is important. These two men I'm speakin' of? One was a fella named Clyde *Martin—*"

"Hey!" Micky-Mack exclaimed. "That's *my* last name!"

"Dang straight it is, boy, 'cos this soldier, Clyde Martin, is yer *direct ancestor,* and the other fella, he was Lemuel *Tuckton—*"

"So, Paw," Dumar calculated, "You'n me, we'se related to him?"

"Yes, we is. He's my great, great grandfather, son. It's the blood'a these two men—these *heroes*—that all of us gots runnin' in our veins. When they seed what General Hildreth did to the town, they got all in a *swivet,* they did. And they decided to go *after* him."

"Please, Paw! Tell us they kilt Hildreth in a bad way!"

Did Helton smile in the crackling firelight? "After the War, Hildreth, he go back to someplace calt Filler-delfia, became mayor. Lived in a big mansion with pillars out front, had a beautiful wife and couple'a children, and his two best officers from the War, he hired 'em ta run his estate. See, Hildreth, he were *pig-shit rich* from all'a his war crimes over the years. So what Clyde Martin and Lemuel Tuckton do one night is after ridin' on horseback all the way to Filler-delfia, they snatch them two'a Hildreth's officers . . . "

Micky-Mack and Dumar stared.

"Their bodies was found the next day, both dead as dead could be. Had their heads busted open, they did . . . but it weren't no *ordinary* head wound, no. Hildreth ain't never seen nothin' like it, so's he called the family doctor to inspect the bodies. Both the tops'a their skulls was busted open—a ballpeen hammer, probably, the doc said—and ya could see their raw brains still sittin' inside'a their skulls. But the doc look *close* at them brains with a magnifyin' glass, and ya know what he saw?"

"What, Unc Helton! What?"

Helton nodded. "He seed what look like a single *knife-slit* in *each brain,* then he took a *whiff* a them brains—"

"He smelt the dead fellas' *brains?*" Micky-Mack questioned in utter puzzlement.

"He smelt 'em, all right," Helton assured, and it appeared by his demeanor that something joyous deep inside was just itching to get out. "And he *rekka*-nized the smell, and then he stick his finger inta each slit and felt somethin' *slimy,* like *snot . . . "*

Dumar's brow furrowed. "Paw, ain't no way *snot* could wind up in a fella's *brain.*"

"It *weren't* snot, son. It was *cum*—"

"Cum!" Mick-Mack yelled.

"Dick-loogie, Paw? *Pecker*snot? *That* what you'se talkin' 'bout?"

"It shore is, Dumar! Man-batter! Joy juice! Cock-hock!" Helton affirmed, rising to his feet as the frenzy of the tale he told began to unwind like a spring. "What Clyde Martin'n Lem Tuckton did is they cracked them two officers hard on the top'a their skulls, picked out the pieces'a bone, and stuck a knife in each brain ta make a *slit* fer their dicks, and then—then, " Helton began to *shake.* "and then they *fucked their brains!*"

Micky-Mack almost fell off the log. "They fucked their *brains,* Unc Helton?"

"Holy sheeeeeeeee-IT, Paw!"

"They *fucked* their evil Yankee brains, and I'se mean they fucked 'em *hard,* and they each got theirself a *nut,* boys!" Helton was reeling. "Then they done the same to all'a Hildreth's housemaids and servants, snatchin' 'em two at a time and humpin' their heads!"—the frenzy rose, veins bulging in Helton's forehead, eyes wide and gleaming in vengeful delirium—"then they snatched Hildreth's children—his *children!*—and they fucked *their* heads, and then they done the same to his *wife!* And then, then, they snatched Hildreth himself and they fucked his head ta kingdom come! They fucked that head *three times apiece,* boys, comin' each time'n blowin' their load right inta the middle'a Hildreth's twisted brain, they did, till his head was full *up* with their cum, and *that,* boys"—Helton stomped the ground—"*that . . .* is what'cha call a *header!*"

Love Amongst the
Redback Spiders

AARON DRIES

ONE

They say nothing in life is free, except for maybe happiness. Well, I call bullshit. When you lose something important, something that makes you who you are, expect a whole basket of goodies you didn't bargain for in lieu. And I'm not talking about the casseroles and sympathy cards, all the shit that comes flowing in from folks you don't even know once the casket's in the pit.

No, the goodies I'm talking about arrive later.

Something gets taken from you, something slips in. That's the deal.

But of course, they don't tell you about this because they don't know. And you can't blame them for that. Like children sticking their fingers into pots of scalding water, they're learning too. Some things aren't parented.

You live, you learn. If you're lucky enough.

People die, and sometimes it's your fault, and once they're gone and those sympathy cards stop coming in and you're forced to give back all those empty crockpots, the vultures sweep in. Your torture is the carrion upon which they feed, and man-oh-man, do they know how to eat. Their feeding fills the space she left behind, and given time, you learn to love the brushing of their wings.

***

By the dry and dusty winter of 1951 in Australia, there had been the Viet Minh offensive against Hanoi, the Walt Disney Company had released their version of *Alice in Wonderland* in oh-so glorious Technicolor, and I'd celebrated two years of successful deceit. And although it may come as a surprise to you, I took no joy in any three of these landmark occasions. After all, I was a shitty pacifist, I never was really one for toons, and as for lying, well—there's not much to celebrate about 'second nature.' That's why it's always the runner-up in the game. No, my stray pleasures were limited to the smell of struck kitchen matchsticks, the hot burn before the cigarette caught. That smell, that sound—hell, it was maybe better than the drag itself.

My wife, as hot-tempered as she could be, didn't smoke.

"You ought to dress with more color, more flair," she would say, icy. "A new coat or hat would do you wonders. You're drab."

Loneliness palsied my fashion, apparently, jaundiced the skin, made it hard to keep down the meals she cooked up. And then she would go off and compensate for my lack of hue—the palette she needed to see in order to feel content—by layering her own face with makeup. A china dolly propped in a storefront window at Christmastime. Damn.

Love Amongst the Redback Spiders

"I love you." This I would say, despite the ugliness I drove her to.

Her name was Patricia.

I only knew her as something tangible, something I could taste, and love, and try to make love to. She was real, selfless. All she had to do was kiss me back. But no, she gave me everything. And I *liked* her everything, needed it. So when she died, when she sat in our bathroom without her makeup on and swallowed my sleeping pills, all the shit that kept me alive went with her. Now, all that I've got is the three-storey house by the Hawkesbury River in Long Swamp Bay. That, and a handful of memories. Man, she loved this place. We'd sit in the parlour and listen to the radio, the two of us sipping sloe gin fizzes, me smoking my Lucky Strikes. I've since moved the radio upstairs, which is where I live now almost without exception. And all I get on the old tune-box is static.

The house is almost empty.

Look around and you won't find any photos or the half-read book she'd left on the bedside table with the feather still wedged between the pages. I still remember the title, *A Woman Called Fancy*. Not my literary cup of tea. You won't find any of this stuff because I trashed it all. Emotional landmines. Sure, I could've kept them around, substituting them for the rungs on the ladder people use to climb themselves out of their grief, only no. Didn't seem right.

So this is all I've got: the house by the river and the scars in my brain where the doctor drove his icepicks.

"I've a steady hand," he'd said.

Unlike myself, he'd spoken the truth.

There are empty picture hooks around the upstairs

rooms, little upturned fingers beckoning to me. There's the wall-to-wall carpet. It's pink.

Carpet.

I'll get to that. But I've got a lot to get through before I die. Such as the alleyway in Sydney, dark and stinking of piss and wet dog. And the man there who changed everything with a whistle from the public restroom.

He wore a thin moustache. Hummingbird eyes, flittering here and there, up and down. This man, in his yellow raincoat and battered fedora, took me by the hand and led me into one of the stalls. Fluorescents threw sporadic light, electric crackles. There were families of redback spiders all over the walls, but they only moved when the room went dark. Webs quivered in a draft as the man closed the door behind me. Behind us.

He slipped the lock into the latch and put his lips to mine. Fear: it tastes like alcohol, only sweeter.

"So you're from Long Swamp?" he said. "What brings you to the city?"

"I come to watch the greyhounds race."

"Did you pick a winner?"

"Not this time." My throat was dry. "You ever done this before?"

"Yeah, mate. I guess I have."

Shaking as he held me in his hand. Stubble sharp against my skin. And through the panting, the inevitable gasp, those redback spiders watched. Our writhing reflected in their eyes. I was grateful they were too dumb to judge because just one bite would've been enough to end it all.

At the time, I thought it was a risk worth taking.

Love Amongst the Redback Spiders

Looking back, I'm not so confident. Perhaps I should have offered my wrist and let them scurry from their webs to seek out my veins. A direct hit. Poison pumping into my body.

Maybe. Maybe not.

Afterwards, the man took me to a bar. He bought the first round, sloe gin fizzes—watered down but heavy on the guilt. Before we left, I went to the men's room, relieved myself for what felt like forever, washed my hands in the adjoining basin. I saw a splash of dried cum on my trousers and cried a little.

We went to his place, a shoebox he rented on George Street. There, I noticed the handmade quilt over the bed, something he'd brought with him, debris from another domesticity. The stitching. Patchwork beauty. It struck me as feminine.

"Tell me your name," I said.

"Nope. No names."

"Well, tell me *a* name. Any name."

"You'se can call me Raymond. That name's as good as any." His voice was wax, dripping, burning, moulding me into something I didn't want to recognize. Something that looked and sounded like him. "We're safe here. Ain't nobody gonna come burstin' in, screamin' queer, screamin' Commie, and drag us off to the fruitcake factory. There's just you and me. 'A Lovely Way to Spend an Evening,' as ole Blue Eyes sometimes sings."

Only it wasn't an evening; it was many. Memories stacked back to back, wedged between then and now. It went by fast, days tick-tocking closer to the moment when there's tick-tocking no more. Looking back, it feels like I haven't lived, just watched my life flash past.

In that blur I thought I learned a lesson: that nothing, not even happiness is free. There are hidden costs. A bitch of a bargain, I know. But nobody said this carnival came without its fair share of evil clowns, which dance and laugh because they know what we don't: that the clock runs at you, not you at it, and this is the secret behind their painted smiles.

TWO

Raymond and I had but a single ally: the sheets, just as they had been for the past year-and-a-half. He reanimated me, despite the agony that followed when he left. I cried my weight more than once, hating every part of me that he found attractive. When Raymond wasn't around, and Patricia was at her brother's place upstate as she was that weekend, I drank too much. Cussing, punching myself until I bruised.

It was a nasty lot. That sickness.

The week before he was due to visit my place in Long Swamp Bay for the last time (our Sydney rendezvous dictated by the ebb and flow of my primary excuse to leave, the greyhound season), I wrote out my confession with a ballpoint pen. Coming clean stripped me bare, left me weak and empty, no less afraid. My secrets spelled out on the page did nothing to alleviate the disease. All it did was confirm two things: firstly, that nothing was going to change, and secondly, my spelling ain't worth a dime.

Burning the confession wasn't enough. I tore it to shreds. Ate the pieces.

Raymond and I were in the bed, sweating sin, when Patricia and her brother came home. We didn't hear the car pull into the drive, or the front door, those creaking steps. Her brother slugged me across the face. Patricia screamed.

We were undone.

Raymond left no forwarding address at his apartment. The city laughed at me with its honking horns, the sound of shattering glass. Times like that I missed living in Long Swamp. I had moved out and was renting my own shoebox on Elizabeth Street. It was above a butcher's shop and stank of blood and sweat. Patricia had the house to herself. Nothing was on paper regarding the property yet, but I figured it would be soon. On nights when I missed her and the river at the end of the drive, I sometimes went back to that bar, ordered a sloe gin fizz and didn't bother to ask the poison dealer if he'd seen a tall fella in a big yellow overcoat and a battered fedora come by.

"Has a funny moustache," I never said.

Hummingbird eyes.

Sometimes there was only the dark throat of the alleyway where we'd met, and the public restroom at the end of it. Other fellas lurked there now. Sleeves rolled up to the shoulder, exposing tattoos that seemed to bleed into the graffiti-covered brick around them.

Nicotine kisses, shared cigarettes. All of those redback spiders.

'A Lovely Way to Spend an Evening.'

The police came a-knocking at my door a week later. They told me Patricia was dead, that she'd phoned for an ambulance, but it arrived too late. She'd been found on the upstairs bedroom floor, a trail of pills leading back to the ensuite where she'd shattered the mirror. Facedown in a pool of candy-colored vomit.

THREE

"Will it hurt?"

"You won't feel a thing, sir. You'll be out like a light. Unconscious."

"And then? What happens when I'm in the dark?"

"You'll be attached to this electro-convulsive shock machine." The doctor gestured to the suitcase-sized box on a gurney at my side. A chill ran through me. It looked like a face sitting there, watching me. Two dials for eyes. Its nose an energy meter display, like a rainbow of char-blacked numbers caught behind glass. An unlit, emotionless mouth of bulbs. "Electricity will flow through your body until you are in a deep state. Enforced sleep, if you will. During that window of time, which will total, say seven or eight minutes give-or-take, I'll conduct the surgery."

"How dangerous is it? You've got to break it down for me, doc."

"Trans-orbital lobotomy is invasive, and success varies. There are some who walk away from it cured of the homosexual ailment."

"Only some?"

"Well, to be frank, there are those who don't walk away at all. There are risks with every procedure, sir. This is no different."

"Goddamn."

"It all comes down to a matter of priority. And choice. See, you've got to ask yourself: Where do your loyalties lie? Man has little choice over the hand he's dealt, the diseases the Lord bestows on him. But in some cases, like the one we're facing now, man does have the choice to risk curing it. I'm sure someone like you understands the value of a gamble."

"Only greyhounds, doc. Look, I just don't know about this—"

"I've a steady hand, sir, and I'm not in the business of malpractice. It's not popular. The same cannot be said to all surgeons on these streets, believe you me. It's nothing short of providence that's brought you here."

"So how does it work? No spin,"

"I will use what you would commonly refer to as an icepick, no different to the one you would find in your own home. Comforting, eh? A nurse will then lay a towel over your face, even though there isn't a great deal of . . . spillage. Your eyelids will be peeled back, the icepick inserted into the socket, and with a hammer, I'll drive the point through the skull and into the brain, thus severing the frontal lobe. Only that which is not needed will be excised. I'll steel away your homosexual impulse. It shouldn't take longer than three to four minutes. Less time than it takes to hard-boil an egg!"

"Jesus."

"And then you walk right out of here. I'll dress you up in a pretty lookin' pair of black sunglasses to hide the bruising, and off you go. Easy as pie, that's what my wife's always saying."

"Your wife, she uhh, approves of your line of work then?"

"Approve, sir? Why, she's the nurse."

***

I remember the black and white chequered floor of the surgery room, like something I'd seen in a photograph of a Yankee diner. Only the kind of things they dished up in this place you'd have to be mad to order. And yet I did. I hated myself that much.

It occurred to me that I may die there, and I regretted not letting the redback spiders come at me way back when. All those fangs, all that mercy. And perhaps Patricia would still be alive, too. I'm just glad that the concept of Hell didn't cross my mind as the doctor strapped me down; otherwise I might have backed out when I saw the mouth of the machine begin to glow, bulb by bulb.

Hell.

I never was really one for hot climates. The cool breeze off the Hawkesbury suited me just fine.

My heartbeat rose and each thrust of blood made the world grow larger around me. Chug-chug. Chug-chug—my pulse like a locomotive carrying me to nowhere. The doctor and his pretty wife soon towered over me, sliding into silhouette from the ceiling light.

Chug-chug.

I felt the size of a needle's eye.

Chug-chug.

It wouldn't be the last time.

Chug-chug.

FOUR

It began with pens.

I don't know how and I don't know why. I only knew that they had to go, and that pens wouldn't be the last inanimate objects I would come to fear.

This happened almost a month to the day after my surgery, which had been, as the doctor said it would be, a success. The proof was in the pudding. So yessir, he did have a steady hand indeed. To prove it to myself, I tried to think of Raymond. His stubble against my cheek.

Nothing. Where he'd walked in my mind there was now an empty space.

Though of course, that wasn't enough. I bought one of those Queer funny-pages. I brought it back to the old house in Long Swamp, which I had moved back in to now that Patricia was gone, and studied the drawings. Muscled men pushed their chests together, oversized phalluses intertwined—imagery that only months before would have brought a flush to my face and set my hand wandering.

Now? Nada.

By day, I told myself I was free. By night, I knew it was a case of too little, too goddamned late.

***

I woke that morning, swimming through my usual pre-coffee cloud and settled again into a life without my wife in the house we'd once called ours. She was never my "Honey Bunch" or "Sugar Dumpling," or any of those other diabetic love-a-boos, just plain, simple, Babe. It suited her. I'm old fashioned like that, and maybe that was why she loved me. For a while.

I sat and chewed my cereal, surrounded by the bare walls and the smell of my own unwashed skin. Then I saw it, glimmering in the morning light.

It.

Your average ballpoint pen is just under six inches long. Inside, viscous ink waits. There is the tungsten carbide sphere, the pen point. It peered at me just like Patricia used to do when I smoked in her presence.

Aaron Dries

Her eyes above the nimbus, the rest hidden by black waters.

It terrified me.

Real fear starts in your loins; so cruel that other pleasure in life should spring from the same place. It starts with a tickle and then grows into a full-blown cramp. Fear hurts. It's an old friend.

I woke that October morning terrified of ballpoint pens.

I couldn't bring myself to touch them with my bare hands so I used a pair of yellow cleaning gloves. Once the pens—all eleven of them that I could find—had been thrown into a plastic drawstring bag, my fingers smelled of chlorine and rubber. I sat the bag on the Formica kitchen counter. They writhed. Mewled.

I could only manage to throw the bag into the drive beside my old LaSalle Coupe, which was all covered in bird shit. A ballpoint speared the plastic, spitting an orgasmic stream of blue ink onto the tarmac.

I felt dizzy, and had nibbled my fingernails down to the quick. I spat out the remains, not caring where the clippings landed.

I felt like dying, but would settle for a drink instead. Pacing. My steps echoed through the empty upper floor.

I tried to impose rationality upon the irrational (I may have been dumb enough to let a carrion-cook jab an icepick in my brain, but I ain't no Silly Sally) asking myself, over and over: Why the hell did I find pens, of all things, so goddamned scary? Was I worried that I'd trip and land on the pointed tip? That was a stretch to say the least. So maybe it was the ink. When it smudged on my fingertips was there a risk that poison would be absorbed into my skin?

No, none of these reasons. I didn't know how I knew it, but I did.

It was just fear. And once the source of fear had been removed, like the homosexual disease that had destroyed my life, there was nothing but dread left. I went to the window overlooking the water—so far down below—until I calmed. My breath fogged the plate glass. I had a mean case of the shivers.

The following days were a haze of unanswered phone calls and white noise from the broken radio. Nothing felt solid, as though I were a ghost, my hands passing through coffee cups, unable to flick light switches. I couldn't eat, became drained. There was daylight and moonlight—heat and cold. I slipped in and out of sleep, but there were no dreams, only the sensation of shifting from one kind of silence into another.

FIVE

Linen.

It wrapped around my limbs, strangling me. Sucking at my skin. Breathless, I threw off the sheets. A thudding ache in my jaw from grinding my teeth in my sleep. Nearly choked when I attempted to swallow. A headache bloomed behind my eyes, in the places where the icepicks had been hammered. All this agony—and agony was what it was—funnelled down into those two little holes in my skull. It was colossal. I fought the urge to throw up.

I snaked to the end of the bed, hands clutching the

bare mattress. Peered over the edge. The linen looked like a coil of entrails, stinking and putrid in the semi-dark. I didn't know what to do, or how to digest this new anxiety. Morning had never seemed so far away. I backed up and drew my knees against my chest. I must have drifted off at some point because I remember bolting awake, thinking to myself, *what's that sound?*

A delicate scratching.

***

I pulled the gloves back on, their smell my saviour, and left the sheets in the driveway.

In the bathroom I stared at the mirrored stranger. The same logic—which implied that pens were harmless, that linen didn't want to strangle me—told me that the sick man in the mirror couldn't be me. No, the reflection was the instigator of lies; he was *They*. And I knew this because they cry crocodile tears. Watch as their tongues slither out to lick the salt.

Slu-uuuurrrp.

I smoked my last Lucky Strike. It had no taste.

SIX

Next came clothing.

I didn't want to pull my shirt up over my face, just in case the fabric scratched at my eyes, so I slit the shirt off my chest with a pair of scissors, too frightened to think about nicks and cuts. Their eventual stings were small compared to the headache, which I had, with resignation, come to think would be with me forever.

Naked and kneeling on the floor. Screamed into a pillow.

Love Amongst the Redback Spiders

There was no reason to fear my clothes, and yet I did. It seemed so simple, really. Fear can make logic out of anything.

I ran to the bathroom and cut the shirt into ribbons. Fed the shreds into the toilet. The water rose to the lip of the bowl when I flushed, a single matted sleeve waving at me. I duct-taped the lid shut; the clothes banged against it.

Slammed the door. Backed away. I didn't know what to do, so I crossed the room and plugged in the radio. The soft hum of electricity reached my ears and I broke out in a sweat. All I could find was static.

***

At first, I thought propping a chair against the door handle of my wardrobe would be enough to trap my attire inside. I laughed.

A goddamned chair? Who was I kidding?

I could hear Patricia's voice telling me to wise up, that a job half done is a job undone. She was always like that, with her little sayings masquerading as big disciplines. It used to make me mad enough to spit— but now, looking back, all I can hear are the wonderful things she told me to do that I never did, all the advice I never took. Yeah, that's happiness for you.

The chair just wouldn't do. No way.

I taped the handles together and stuffed rolled-up tissue paper under the door. The clothes were trapped.

I ended up pissing in cups, shitting into toilet paper. I was too afraid to go outside. Sometimes I heard the telephone ringing downstairs. I no longer went below. Not anymore. My boss at the mill must've thought I was dead.

Cold came with the night. The venetian blinds

shivered in the breeze, as did I. Something scurried in the dark, louder now than ever before.

SEVEN

My breath was ragged, the fever strong. The only heat in the room radiated off my flesh in waves. It was sometime after midnight. The scratching had woken me again.

I felt the crust of sleep in my eyes when I blinked. There didn't seem to be any water in me anymore. Icy blue moonlight caught flakes of skin peeling from my arms as I climbed to my feet and reached for the cabinet beside the dead radio. That's where the scratching sound was coming from.

Sudden rapping at the window. I spun on my heels, almost in tears, and saw the glimmer of small eyes and a shiny beak through the glass. The moon highlighted the bird's charcoal-black wings. It was a crow, lost in the night, not a vulture, which had been my first thought. Strangely, that didn't make its presence any less hair-raising. I had to turn away, focussing instead on the cabinet again.

On the scratching coming from within.

A hand that couldn't be my hand grasped the handle. It couldn't be *my* hand because *my* hands, as I remembered them, were not so skeletal, so yellow, with the fingernails almost completely bitten off and scabbed over.

My stomach rolled. Bile climbed my throat.

The cabinet door swung open and the scratching stopped.

There was only one thing on the shelf and it was

covered in a thin layer of dust: a three-inch cylindrical vial. As soon as I saw it I had a sense of having put it there, but couldn't remember when. Time no longer existed in the apartment. Knuckles crunched as my hand—

(yes, *my* hand)

—gripped the little glass to see what it kept. I pursed my lips together and blew. A thin whistling sound. Dust coiled.

The milky liquid within the vial settled and I saw the chunk of brain. It was bobbing, maybe even pulsating with blood-filled vessels and thoughts. My little souvenir.

This sickness of mine.

The sound of a thousand icepicks thundering through bone—shattering skull, piercing sinew. Disease bubbling out like blood, clots and all. Everything went white, and then black. I thought someone was in the room with me, flicking the ceiling lights on and off. But no. The strobe was in my head. And the flashes were only growing brighter, just as the darkness was getting deeper. I could feel myself being torn between the two, jolted back and forth, until something in me ripped.

The vial slipped from between my fingers and hit the carpet, the lid bouncing free A cold splash across my toes. I stumbled back a few steps and my calf muscles pressed against the bed—my safe place. I allowed myself to fall, arcing down, down, onto the mattress, just as my mouth filled with coppery heat and those thousand icepicks withdrew all at once. The sound of wings on the other side, fading.

***

I woke to daylight. A moment passed. I took a couple of deep breaths and studied the ceiling. Delicate tree shadows.

The memory of her fingers, tickling my arms. His tongue in my mouth.

I have nothing.

Babe.

A word I'd shared between two people, and which now belonged to nobody.

I swung off the mattress and my feet touched the floor. The pink carpet slipped between my toes.

Burning coals.

My yell echoed across the almost empty room. Knees gave out. A forest of synthetic fibres and wool piles rushed at me. My outstretched hands landed first, followed by my knees, my balls. Bolts of white-hot pain—like the electricity that had flowed through the face of the shock machine once they'd put the leather strap between my teeth and attached electrodes to either side of my head. I squeezed my eyes shut as my face hit the carpet. I inhaled dirt. Coughed once, twice. And then nothing.

***

The room was gone.

If I concentrated hard enough I could distinguish the ceiling, but looking for it was like stargazing in the mid-afternoon. Thick pillars of material swayed around me: the great stalks of carpet yarns. Pickled nylon binding and winding strands of hair underfoot. Some were mine, some belonged to her. I don't know if Raymond's hair had fallen here, too. It probably had.

I dropped to my knees, muffling a scream. "Help me!"

Love Amongst the Redback Spiders

There came the beating of wings. Stilled. Crows perched in the tall piles. They had ballpoint pen talons.

I ran, passing keg-sized dust balls. It was humid; the dirt turned to sludge beneath me. I wove through the piles, experiencing what I imagine is the pure fear a newborn feels: the unconsented terror of being forced into a new world.

I told myself that this wasn't real, that it was a dream. I knew better. I almost always did. The doc had taken away my sickness, not the part of my brain that made me lie to myself. No, that part of my brain still worked fine.

Things that had once belonged to my wife, objects I had thrown away when I moved back in, towered over me. Her copy of *A Woman Called Fancy* was the size of an upended above ground swimming pool. A gigantic makeup case.

These were tokens of her independence from me, her betrayals—only amplified, as everything now was. They frightened me as they had frightened me then.

"Babe!"

My voice woke something in the dark beyond my vision. Something big.

It had been sleeping, and like most things born to eat and drink and breed, it woke knowing only one thing. Hunger. I could hear it scurrying.

***

The creature in the dark must have smelled my stink. It drew closer, stampeding, snapping the woollen spires. The patchwork crows took flight. Their inkblot scat landed on my shoulders. Burned.

I ran. My tiny strides nothing compared to those of the monster. And hold no delusion—that's what it was.

A monster. It had my scent and I knew it would never give up.

My screams vibrated through my body. I felt pain. Real pain.

I slammed against a dripping wall of meat, cursing myself for not looking at where I was going. I bounced backwards and watched the great mass rear up on gigantic segments. From the gnarled knots of its hair, eight black legs stretched and cracked to life. It turned, the great abdomen swinging past, a red hourglass etched across its hide. It rose up, the head towering half the height of the piles. A slit opened along its girth, revealing pinched teeth.

It bellowed radio static.

I dove beneath it as it arched its back, escaping. There were other rows of carpet on the other side, and somewhere there was light.

Running.

The spider bleated behind me as the first, still unseen monster, intercepted it. I glanced over my shoulder. Another redback scurried on a series of unstable legs, as one joint buckled and the next carried the weight. Its face was ornamented with many eyes.

The giant spiders fought, territorial and defensive, before the smaller of the two rolled onto its stomach and curled into a ball. Clouds of dust through the twilight.

My pursuer pointed its head skyward, revealing a soupy, wet mouth and long incisors. It continued its march. I lurched through the forest, passing more remains of my former life. More magnified landmines.

I crawled over hills of grime and purple crumbs. Despite the unreal landscape around me, it was these random objects from our past that disturbed me the most.

I tripped, my ankle flaming with pain. Sweat dripped into my eyes. Blood hung thick in the air—my blood. The wound was deep; bone through the cut. My heart skipped a beat when I saw what I'd tripped over.

A crescent moon. Or at least that was what I thought at first. Curved as a scythe, it gave off the rich stench of spoiled cheese.

A giant fingernail.

I ignored the bleeding gash and limped on. There was brightness ahead. Warmth through semaphore flashes of dark-white-dark-white.

(A broken fluorescent. Flickering. Dead. Alive. Dead. Alive.)

Sunlight, strong and warm and kind against my face.

I fell again, landing hard. Winded. Carpet rot, salts and dank liquid splashed into my mouth, making my stomach lurch. I spun my head so quick the bones in my neck cracked. The spider scurried behind me, so close. It stopped short, its stench, like shit and dishwater, crashing down on me.

It reared up on its hindquarters again, only this time convulsed, exposing its flexing abdomen. I knew that what I was seeing was impossible, insane—yet no more insane than living in a world without Patricia.

The veins in my arms pushed up through my skin as though my blood were offering itself as sacrifice to the monster. *Don't give up. You haven't come this far to give up now.*

The spider's mouth parted and belched, splattering me with a scorching film of bile. Its many legs twitched, playing with its own filth and past meals, some fresher than others.

Steaming gastric juices. Ticking chewed-up clocks. Human flesh.

A broken head—still spilling brains—rolled in my direction, thumpedy-thumpedy-thump, and landed face up between my legs. The beaten-in features dripped acidic green; its boiled eyes were pierced by twin icepicks.

"I've a steady hand," the doctor gurgled through a wet, red smile.

I pushed away, gagging. I wiped the spider vomit from my face as my legs carried me off.

The creature roared behind me, but no longer chased. I dared a glance over my shoulder and saw it watching me, as the spiders had always watched, cold and neutral and without a trace of judgement. It lowered its head, as though in reverence.

EIGHT

A loud crashing sound. Bursting glass. I don't think there was any pain; it's hard to tell. The light took it all away. It was so bright. It illuminated the shadowed cabinet and the contents of my keepsake, the empty apartment, the doctor's office, the public restroom where the spiders spun their webs and truths were told for the first time.

All burned away.

Now there is just the tinkering sound of broken window shards, the rushing wind as I fall.

***

Silhouetted against the brightness is a shape, like a

flick of charcoal on empty canvas. It's Patricia, or at least I hope it's her. Unlike happiness, there comes a time when the cost of hoping is free. Now with the tick-tocking over and done with, I figure this moment of gratis is well earned, if nothing else.

I never thought it was possible to miss someone who hated you so much.

And then she—it—is gone.

Grief for what is lost fills me like venom. It dizzies. The haunt of a taste on my tongue.

Sloe gin fizz.

The End?

Not at all.

Have you read *Tales from The Lake Vol.1*—Remember those dark and scary nights spent telling ghost stories and other campfire stories? With the *Tales from The Lake* horror anthologies, you can relive some of those memories by reading the best Dark Fiction stories around. Includes Dark Fiction stories and poems by horror greats such as Graham Masterton, Bev Vincent, Tim Curran, Tim Waggoner, Elizabeth Massie, and many more. Be sure to check out our website for future *Tales from The Lake* volumes.

If you enjoyed this book, I'm sure you'll also like the following titles:

Fear the Reaper anthology—Did you know Death was a girl? Ever wondered if it was possible to cheat death? To kill Death? Or that it's possible to escape and even become death? Includes Grim Reapers stories by legends like Rick Hautala, Gary A. Braunbeck, Joe McKinney, Richard Thomas, Jeremy C Shipp, Jeff Strand, and many more.

Flowers in a Dumpster by Mark Allan Gunnells—The world is full of beauty and mystery. In these 17 tales, Gunnells will take you on a journey through landscapes of light and darkness, rapture and agony, hope and fear. Let Gunnells guide you through these landscapes where magnificence and decay co-exist side by side. Come pick a bouquet from these Flowers in a Dumpster.

Children of the Grave—Choose your own demise in this interactive shared-world zombie anthology. Welcome to Purgatory, an arid plain of existence where zombies are the least of your problems. It's a post-mortem Hunger Games, and Blaze, a newcomer to Purgatory, needs your help to learn the rules of this world and choose the best course of action.

Samurai and Other Stories by William Meikle—No one can handle Scottish folklore with elements of the darkest horror, science fiction and fantasy, suspense and adventure like William Meikle.

Stuck On You and Other Prime Cuts by Jasper Bark—A word of caution gentle reader, these tales will take you places you've never been before and may never dare revisit. They'll whisper truths so twisted you can only face them in the darkest hours of the night. They'll unlock desires so decadent you'll never wash their taint from your flesh.

Wind Chill by Patrick Rutigliano—What if you were held captive by your own family? Emma Rawlins has spent the last year a prisoner. The months following her mother's death dragged her father into a paranoid spiral of conspiracy theories and doomsday premonitions. But there is a force far colder than the freezing drifts. Ancient, ravenous, it knows no mercy. And it's already had a taste . . .

Eidolon Avenue: The First Feast by Jonathan Winn—where the secretly guilty go to die. All thrown into their own private hell as every cruel choice, every deadly mistake, every drop of spilled blood is remembered, resurrected and relived to feed the ancient evil that lives on Eidolon Avenue.

The Dark at the End of the Tunnel by Taylor Grant— Offered for the first time in a collected format, this selection features ten gripping and darkly imaginative stories by Taylor Grant, a Bram Stoker Award ® nominated author and rising star in the suspense and horror genres. Grant exposes the terrors that hide beneath the surface of our ordinary world, behind people's masks of normalcy, and lurking in the shadows at the farthest reaches of the universe.

Little Dead Red by Mercedes M. Yardley—The Wolf is roaming the city, and he must be stopped. In this modern day retelling of Little Red Riding Hood, the wolf takes to the city streets to capture his prey, but the hunter is close behind him. With Grim Marie on the prowl, the hunter becomes the hunted.

The Outsiders Lovecraftian shared-world anthology—They'll do anything to protect their way of life. Anything. Welcome to Priory, a small gated community in the UK, where the only thing worse than an ancient monster is the group worshipping it. Is that which slithers below true evil, or does evil reside in the people of Priory? Includes stories by Stephen Bacon, James Everington, Rosanne Rabinowitz, V.H. Leslie, and Gary Fry.

Through a Mirror, Darkly by Kevin Lucia—Are there truths within the books we read? What if the book delves into the lives of the very town you live in? People you know? Or thought you knew. These are the questions a bookstore owner face when a mysterious book shows up.

If you ever thought of becoming an author, I'd also like to recommend these non-fiction titles:

Horror 101: The Way Forward—a comprehensive overview of the Horror fiction genre and career opportunities available to established and aspiring authors, including Jack Ketchum, Graham Masterton, Edward Lee, Lisa Morton, Ellen Datlow, Ramsey Campbell, and many more.

Horror 201: The Silver Scream Vol.1 and *Vol.2*—A must read for anyone interested in the horror film industry. Includes interviews and essays by Wes Craven, John Carpenter, George A. Romero, Mick Garris, and dozens more. Now available in paperback, as well.

Modern Mythmakers: 35 interviews with Horror and Science Fiction Writers and Filmmakers by Michael McCarty—Ever wanted to hang out with legends like Ray Bradbury, Richard Matheson, and Dean Koontz? *Modern Mythmakers* is your chance to hear fun anecdotes and career advice from authors and filmmakers like Forrest J. Ackerman, Ray Bradbury, Ramsey Campbell, John Carpenter, Dan

Curtis, Elvira, Neil Gaiman, Mick Garris, Laurell K. Hamilton, Jack Ketchum, Dean Koontz, Graham Masterton, Richard Matheson, John Russo, William F. Nolan, John Saul, Peter Straub, and many more.

Writers On Writing: An Author's Guide—Your favorite authors share their secrets in the ultimate guide to becoming and being and author. With your support, *Writers On Writing* will become an ongoing eBook series with original 'On Writing' essays by writing professionals. A new edition will be launched every few months, featuring four or five essays per edition, so be sure to check out the webpage regularly for updates.

Or check out other Crystal Lake Publishing books for your Dark Fiction, Horror, Suspense, and Thriller needs.

Biographies

Rocky Alexander is the author of the internationally best-selling apocalyptic horror novel, "Rag Men," published by Severed Press. His horror short stories, novelettes, and articles have been published in several anthologies and magazines.

He is also an editor whose projects include the acclaimed Bizarro Pulp Press anthology, *Bizarro Bizarro*. http://bizarropulppress.com/

In addition to being a writer and editor, Rocky is an accomplished musician, animal behaviorist, and boxing coach. He lives with his wife in central North Carolina.

He is an Active Member of the Horror Writers Association.

Contact him at rr.alexander@yahoo.com, connect with him on Facebook

http://www.facebook.com/rocky.alexander.56, or visit his blog at

http://rockyalexander.wordpress.com/

Emma Audsley has been a horror fan from an early age. A two-time Bram Stoker Award nominee for her non-fiction editing, Emma also edits fiction, hosts a (currently undergoing reconstruction) review site at The Horrifically Horrifying Horror Blog and mentors new and upcoming writers.

A member of the British Fantasy Society and the Horror Writers Association, Emma is also an author in her own right, and has a number of projects, both fiction and non-fiction, upcoming in the near future.

From Detroit, Michigan, **Vincenzo Bilof** has been called "The Metallica of Poetry" and "The Shakespeare of Gore." With a body of work that includes gritty, apocalyptic horror (The Zombie Ascension Series), surrealist prose (*The Horror Show*), and visceral genre satire (*Vampire Strippers from Saturn*), Bilof's fiction remains as divisive and controversial as it is original. He likes to think Ezra Pound, T.S. Eliot, and Charles Baudelaire would be proud of his work. More likely, Ed Wood would have been his biggest fan.

During the day, Bilof repairs arcade machines in semi-operational billiards clubs, or he chases his children around the house in between episodes of *Teenage Mutant Ninja Turtles*.

You can check out his blog here: http://vincenzobilof.blogspot.com/

Hal Bodner is a Bram Stoker Award nominated author, best known for his best-selling gay vampire novel, *Bite Club* and the lupine sequel, *The Trouble with Hairy*. He tells people he was born in East Philadelphia because so few people know where Cherry Hill, New Jersey is located. The first person he saw ever saw was the doctor who delivered him, C. Everett Koop, the future US Surgeon General. Thus, from birth Hal was ironically destined to become a heavy smoker—a habit he greatly misses. He moved to West Hollywood in the 1980s and has rarely left the city limits since. In fact, he is so WeHo-centric that he cannot find his way around Beverly Hills—the next town over. In a burst of over optimism, he bought a six bedroom mansion in Highland Park, a supposedly up-and-coming area of East Los Angeles. After three years of watching the street gangs doing drug deals in his back yard, he fled back to WeHo.

During his sojourn in East L.A., he was protected from the harm because of his habit of chasing his escaped pet peacock down Figueroa Boulevard at night, dressed in his fluffy bathrobe and fuzzy Cthulu slippers while yelling "Apollo! Apollo! Come back!" None of the gang members would shoot him; they were laughing too hard.

His various professions have included stints as an entertainment lawyer, a scheduler for a 976 sex telephone line, a theater reviewer and the personal assistant to a television star. For several years, he owned Heavy Petting, a pet boutique where movie stars bought gold-plated water dishes and designer wardrobes for their Chihuahuas and Pomeranians.

In the erotic paranormal romance genre—which he refers to as "supernatural smut"—he is best known for having written *In Flesh and Stone* and *For Love of the Dead*. His comic gay super hero trilogy will hopefully debut shortly with *Fabulous in Tights* to be followed by *A Study in Spandex*. He has recently agreed to write a series of mystery novellas featuring a gay detective and his Watsonian sidekick, who is the madam of a bordello.

Hal married a man roughly half his age who had no idea that Liza Minnelli and Judy Garland were related. In consequence, he has discovered that the use of hair dye is rarely an adequate substitute for Viagra.

The *Oxford Companion to English Literature* describes **Ramsey Campbell** as "Britain's most respected living horror writer." He has been given more awards than any other writer in the field, including the Grand Master Award of the World Horror Convention, the Lifetime Achievement Award of the Horror Writers Association, the Living Legend Award of the International Horror Guild and the World Fantasy Lifetime Achievement Award. In 2015 he was made an Honorary Fellow of Liverpool John Moores University for outstanding services to literature. Among his novels are *The Face That Must Die, Incarnate, Midnight Sun, The Count of Eleven, Silent Children, The Darkest Part of the Woods, The Overnight, Secret Story, The Grin of the Dark, Thieving Fear, Creatures of the Pool, The Seven Days of Cain, Ghosts Know, The Kind Folk, Think Yourself Lucky* and *Thirteen Days by Sunset Beach*. He is presently working on a trilogy, *The Three Births of Daoloth. Needing Ghosts, The Last Revelation of Gla'aki, The Pretence* and *The Booking* are novellas. His collections include *Waking Nightmares, Alone with the Horrors, Ghosts and Grisly Things, Told by the Dead, Just Behind You* and *Holes for Faces*, and his non-fiction is collected as *Ramsey Campbell, Probably*. His novels *The Nameless* and *Pact of the Fathers* have been filmed in Spain. His regular columns appear in *Dead Reckonings* and *Video Watchdog*. He is the President of the Society of Fantastic Films.

Ramsey Campbell lives on Merseyside with his wife Jenny. His pleasures include classical music, good food and wine, and whatever's in that pipe. His web site is at www.ramseycampbell.com.

R.J. Cavender is an Active member of the Horror Writers Association and the thrice Bram Stoker Award® nominated editor of the +*Horror Library*+ anthology series and co-editor of the Bram Stoker Award finalist *Horror For Good: A Charitable Anthology*, all from Cutting Block Press.

He is the managing editor of horror at Dark Regions Press, the co-founder/editor emeritus at Cutting Block Books, and co-chair and pitch sessions coordinator for StokerCon2016. He is also the host of The Stanley Hotel Writers Retreat, Tucson Festival of Books Writers Retreat, and Winchester Mystery House Writers Retreat.

R.J. lives in Tucson, Arizona. His favorite book is *The Shining*.

Richard Chizmar is the founder/publisher of *Cemetery Dance* magazine and the Cemetery Dance Publications book imprint. He has edited more than 30 anthologies and his fiction has appeared in dozens of publications, including *Ellery Queen's Mystery Magazine* and *The Year's 25 Finest Crime and Mystery Stories*. He has won two World Fantasy awards, four International Horror Guild awards, and the HWA's Board of Trustee's award.

Chizmar (in collaboration with Johnathon Schaech) has also written screenplays and teleplays for United Artists, Sony Screen Gems, Lions Gate, Showtime, NBC, and many other companies.

Chizmar is the creator/writer of *Stephen King Revisited*, and his third short story collection, *A Long December*, is due in 2016 from Subterranean Press.

Chizmar's work has been translated into many

languages throughout the world, and he has appeared at numerous conferences as a writing instructor, guest speaker, panelist, and guest of honor.

You can follow Richard Chizmar on both Facebook and Twitter.

Raven Dane is an award winning fantasy author based in the UK. Her published works include the highly acclaimed *Legacy of the Dark Kind* series; Dark Fantasy/Sci-Fi crossover novels: *Blood Tears*, *Blood Lament*and *Blood Alliance*. However, Raven's skills in fiction don't end there. Comedy fantasy—a scurrilous spoof of High Fantasy clichés—*The Unwise Woman of Fuggis Mire* was published by Endaxi Press in 2009. In more recent years Raven has met with critical acclaim for her Steampunk/Occult adventures: *Cyrus Darian and the Technomicron* and the sequel, *Cyrus Darian and the Ghastly Horde. Cyrus Darian and the Technomicron* was the winner of best novel at the inaugural international Victorian Steampunk Society awards in 2012.

Raven has had many short stories published in anthologies including in *Full Fathom Forty*, a celebration of forty years of the British Fantasy Society. She also has stories in four horror anthologies published by Western Legends Press. Raven had a story accepted for Fright Mare—Women Write Horror, an international anthology edited by Billie Sue Mossiman, published February 2016.

Raven was the first author to be signed with Telos Moonrise, a new fiction imprint for Telos Press. They published her collection of spooky and macabre Victorian and Steampunk short stories, *Absinthe and*

Arsenic in 2013. In 2015, Telos published her alternative history/supernatural novel *Death's Dark Wings*.

She is currently working on her third and fourth Cyrus Darian novel and more short story commissions.

Author, illustrator, and filmmaker **Aaron Dries** was born and raised in New South Wales, Australia. When asked why he writes horror, his standard reply is that when it comes to scaring people, writing pays slightly better than jumping out from behind doors. He is the author of the award-winning novel House of Sighs, and his subsequent books, The Fallen Boys and A Place for Sinners are just as—if not more—twisted than his debut. ChiZine Publications, Samhain Horror, Crystal Lake Publishing, Scarlet Galleon Press, and a number of international magazines and online venues have published his fiction and art over the years. As a filmmaker, Dries' short films have garnered awards in Australia, the UK, and the USA, and he is currently at work on multiple feature screenplays. Feel free to drop him a line at aarondries.com or contact him through Twitter and Facebook. He won't bite. Much.

Ben Eads lives within the semi-tropical suburbs of Central Florida. A true horror writer by heart, he wrote his first story at the tender age of ten. The look on the teacher's face when she read it was priceless. However, his classmates loved it! Ben has had short stories published in various magazines and anthologies. When he isn't writing, he dabbles in martial arts, philosophy and specializes in I.T. security. He's always looking to find new ways to infect reader's imaginations. Ben blames Arthur Machen, H.P. Lovecraft, Jorge Luis Borges, J.G. Ballard, Philip K. Dick, and Stephen King for his addiction, and his need to push the envelope of fiction. His horror novella, *Cracked Sky* was published by Omnium Gatherum, January 2015.

Jan Edwards is a British author. She was born near Horsham, Sussex but now lives in Staffordshire with her husband Peter Coleborn and the obligatory three cats—between the Peaks National Park and the Potteries district. She has a life-long passion for folklore and the supernatural and draws on this for her fiction. She has had numerous stories published in anthologies such as the *Mammoth Book of Dracula, Mammoth Book of the Adventures of Moriarty* and *Terror Tales of the Ocean.* Much of her published short fiction is reprinted in her collections *Leinster Gardens and Other Subtleties* and *Fables and Fabrications.* Jan has won a Winchester Slim Volume prize and was short-listed for a BFS Award for Best Short Story. She edits anthologies for the award winning Alchemy Press and also for Fox Spirit Books. In a previous existence she was a Chairperson for the British Fantasy Society. Also by Jan Edwards: *Leinster Gardens and Other Subtleties, Sussex Tales, Fables and Fabrications, Winter Downs* Penkhull Press (expected 2016) Anthologies edited by Jan Edwards and Jenny Barber: *The Alchemy Book of Ancient Wonders, The Alchemy Press Book of Urban Mythic, The Alchemy Press Book of Urban Mythic:2, Wicked Women.*

Her story 'Bone Wary' takes place in the Potteries—

which was once the home of the world's ceramics industry.

For more details on Jan and her fiction visit: http://janedwardsblog.wordpress.com/

Jim Goforth is a horror author currently based in Holbrook, Australia. Happily married with two kids and a cat, he has been writing tales of horror since the early nineties. After years of detouring into working with the worldwide extreme metal community and writing reviews for hundreds of bands across the globe with Black Belle Music he returned to his biggest writing love with first book Plebs published by J. Ellington Ashton Press. Along with Plebs, he is the author of a collection of short stories/novellas *With Tooth and Claw*, extreme metal undead opus *Undead Fleshcrave: The Zombie Trigger*, co-author of collaborative novel *Feral Hearts* and editor for the *Rejected For Content* anthology series (taking over the reins after volume one Splattergore. He also has stories in both *Splattergore* and *Volume 2: Aberrant Menagerie*).

He has also appeared in *Axes of Evil, Terror Train, Autumn Burning: Dreadtime Stories For the Wicked Soul, Floppy Shoes Apocalypse, Teeming Terrors, Ghosts: An Anthology of Horror From the Beyond, Suburban Secrets: A Neighborhood of Nightmares, Doorway To Death: An Anthology From the Other Side* and edited volumes 2 and 3 of RFC (*Aberrant Menagerie* and *Vicious Vengeance*). Coming next from Jim will be appearances in *Drowning in Gore, Full Moon Slaughter, MvF, Trashed*, another collab novel *Lycanthroship* as well as follow-up books to

Plebs and *Rejected For Content 4: Highway To Hell* (editor).

He is currently working on two new novels with plans to wrap them up before beginning further installments of both the Plebs saga and *The Zombie Trigger*.

Glen Johnson was born in England in 1973. He used to live in Devon, just a stone's throw away from the English Riviera, but in August 2014, he gave away all his belongings and bought a backpack, and he has been traveling around Asia ever since. He is the author of 54 fiction and non-fiction books. While he travels he is also helping charitable organizations, writing and releasing books about their foundations, leaving them with all the royalties. So far, he has released two charity books. The first is called *Soi Dog: The Story Behind Asia's Largest Animal Welfare Shelter*, and the second is called *BEES Elephants Sanctuary: A Haven for Old and Retired Elephants*. He has also started to release a collection of books about his travel adventures as they unfold, and *Living the Dream: Part One—Khaosan Road, Thailand* is available from all good eBook retailers. He is also on the development team for a new computer game called *The Seed*, from the creators of the award-winning *S.T.A.L.K.E.R Misery Mod*. He loves to travel and has already visited thirty-six different countries, and lived in Mexico City, Mexico for far too long for a pale skinned European. He has also been married twice—and still refuses to say where he buried them.

Why not add Glen Johnson as a friend on Facebook.

www.facebook.com/GlenJohnsonAuthor

Jack Ketchum is the pseudonym for a former actor, singer, teacher, literary agent, lumber salesman, and soda jerk–a former flower child and baby boomer who figures that in 1956 Elvis, dinosaurs and horror probably saved his life. His first novel, *Off Season*, prompted the *Village Voice* to publicly scold its publisher in print for publishing violent pornography. He personally disagrees but is perfectly happy to let you decide for yourself. His short story *The Box* won a 1994 Bram Stoker Award from the HWA, his story *Gone* won again in 2000—and in 2003 he won Stokers for both best collection for *Peaceable Kingdom* and best long fiction for *Closing Time*. He has written over twenty novels and novellas, the latest of which are *The Woman* and *I'm Not Sam,* both written with director Lucky McKee. Five of his books have been filmed to date—*The Girl Next Door, The Lost, Red, Offspring* and *The Woman,* the last of which won him and McKee the Best Screenplay Award at the prestigious Sitges Film Festival in Spain. His stories are collected in *The Exit At Toledo Blade Boulevard, Broken on the Wheel of Sex, Sleep Disorder* (with Edward Lee), *Peaceable Kingdom* and *Closing Time and Other Stories.* His novella *The Crossings* was cited by Stephen King in his speech at the 2003 National Book Awards. In 2011 he was elected Grand Master by the World Horror Convention.

Tim Lebbon is a New York Times-bestselling writer from South Wales. He's had over thirty novels published to date, as well as hundreds of novellas and short stories. His latest novel is the thriller *The Hunt,* and other recent releases include *The Silence* and

Alien: Out of the Shadows. He has won four British Fantasy Awards, a Bram Stoker Award, and a Scribe Award, and has been a finalist for World Fantasy, International Horror Guild and Shirley Jackson Awards. Future books include *The Rage War* (an Alien/Predator trilogy), and the *Relics* trilogy from Titan.

The movie of his story *Pay the Ghost*, starring Nicolas Cage, was released Hallowe'en 2015, and other projects in development include *Playtime* (an original script with Stephen Volk), *My Haunted House* with Gravy Media, *The Hunt, Exorcising Angels* (based on a novella with Simon Clark), and a TV Series proposal of *The Silence*.

Find out more about Tim at his website www.timlebbon.net

Edward Lee is an American novelist specializing in the field of horror who has written 40 books, more than half of which have been published by mass-market New York paperback companies such as Leisure/Dorchester, Berkley, and Zebra/Kensington. He is a Bram Stoker award nominee for his story "Mr. Torso," and his short stories have appeared in over a dozen mass-market anthologies, including the award-winning 999. Several of his novels have sold translation rights to Germany, Greece, Romania, and Poland. He also publishes quite actively in the small-press/limited-edition hardcover market; many of his books in this category have become collector's items.

Rena Mason is the Bram Stoker Award® winning author of *The Evolutionist* and *East End Girls*, as well as a 2014 Stage 32 / The Blood List presents: The Search for New Blood Screenwriting Contest Finalist. A longtime fan of horror, sci-fi, science, history, historical fiction, mysteries, and thrillers, she began writing to mash up those genres in stories revolving around everyday life.

She is a member of the Horror Writers Association, Mystery Writers of America, International Thriller Writers, The International Screenwriters' Association, and Stage 32. She writes the "Recently Born of Horrific Minds" column for the HWA Monthly Newsletter, as well as occasional articles. An active volunteer and event planner, she's Event Co-Chair for StokerCon2016® at the Flamingo hotel in Las Vegas.

An R.N. and avid scuba diver, she has traveled the world and incorporates the experiences into her stories. She currently resides in Reno, Nevada with her family.

Lisa Morton is a screenwriter, author of non-fiction books, award-winning prose writer, and Halloween expert whose work was described by the American Library Association's *Readers' Advisory Guide to Horror* as "consistently dark, unsettling, and frightening." Her most recent releases include *Ghosts: A Haunted History* and the short story collection *Cemetery Dance Select: Lisa Morton*. She currently serves as President of the Horror Writers Association, and can be found online at
http://www.lisamorton.com.

Joe Mynhardt is a two time Bram Stoker nominated South African publisher, editor, and teacher.

Joe is the owner of Crystal Lake Publishing

(Publisher of the Year in the 2013 This Is Horror Awards), which he started in August, 2012. Since then he's published and edited short stories, novellas, interviews and essays by the likes of Neil Gaiman, Clive Barker, Ramsey Campbell, Jack Ketchum, Graham Masterton, Adam Nevill, Lisa Morton, Elizabeth Massie, Joe McKinney, Edward Lee, Wes Craven, John Carpenter, George A. Romero, Mick Garris, and hundreds more.

Just like Crystal Lake Publishing, Joe believes in reaching out to all authors, new and experienced, and being a beacon of friendship and guidance in the Dark Fiction field.

Joe's influences stretch from Poe, Doyle and Lovecraft to King, Connolly and Gaiman. You can read more about Joe and Crystal Lake Publishing at www.crystallakepub.com or find him on Facebook.

Mark West was born in Northamptonshire in 1969 and now lives there with his wife Alison and their young son Matthew. Since discovering the small press in 1998 he has published over seventy short stories, two novels (*In The Rain With The Dead* and *Conjure*), a novelette (*The Mill*), a chapbook (*What Gets Left Behind*), a collection (*Strange Tales*) and two novellas (*Drive*, which was nominated for a British Fantasy Award and *The Lost Film*). He has more short stories and novellas forthcoming and he is currently working on a novel.

Away from writing, he enjoys reading, walking, cycling, watching films and playing Dudeball with his son.

He can be contacted through his website at

www.markwest.org.uk and is also on Twitter as @MarkEWest

John Whalen: The horror genre is my passion. In literature, film, music, and about any other medium you can think of, I have found myself drawn to the macabre for as long as I can remember. Though I am no stranger to writing horror, Tales from The Lake Vol. 2 marks my first step into the publishing world. I have always been proud of my writing in an individual sense, but modest about its reception. I'm lucky to have gotten past that step in my writing career and submitted to the Tales from The Lake Horror Writing Competition.

My story "Descending" is greatly inspired by my years as a Psychiatric Technician working the graveyard shift on a Behavioral Health Unit. Hospitals are creepy enough at night. Throw an old, rickety, malfunctioning elevator into the mix, and you've got the groundwork for a horror story. The doors of the elevator on the second floor would slide open like a beast, brandishing its teeth. Sometimes they hesitated menacingly like hungry, quivering jowls. It was certainly enough to get the creativity flowing.

My story also draws inspiration from the "The Elevator Game," an urban legend I was first introduced to in elementary school. It was one of those tall tales that used to be shared while huddled around a lunch table or in whispers on a playground. Legend had it that if you pressed certain elevator buttons in a particular pattern and acted in a very specific manner you could find yourself stepping off into another dimension. As an adult doing research on the story's origins I was led to the true and chilling tragedy of Elisa Lam. In 2013 Ms. Lam was filmed acting quite strange on a security camera of an elevator in a Los Angeles hotel. After walking on she presses a bunch of buttons in a seemingly deliberate pattern and begins exhibiting other bizarre behaviors. Sounds like a dare between a few young people that have nothing better to do, right? Well here's the catch: that's the last known footage of Ms. Lam. Two weeks later her body was found in a water tank on the hotel's roof. So many factors in Elisa Lam's disappearance and subsequent death simply didn't add up, and even to this day her death remains a mystery. Her tragic tale was certainly another influence while writing "Descending."

After being awarded first place in the Tales from The Lake Horror Writing Competition, I have challenged myself like I have never before. Since that time I have written more and improved my skills, writing more confidently than I ever have. I have since written numerous short stories, novellas and a full-length novel which I completed recently. In October, I will be attending The Stanley Hotel Writer's Retreat, continuing my dream of writing horror. I owe it to Crystal Lake for rekindling my fierce passion for the genre. I hope you enjoy my story, and hey, keep a lookout for my name in publications to come!

Jonathan Winn is a screenwriter as well as the author of *Eidolon Avenue: The First Feast* (Crystal Lake Publishing), the full-length novels *Martuk . . . the Holy* (A Highlight of the Year, 2012 Papyrus Independent Fiction Awards), *Martuk . . . the Holy:*

Proseuche (Top Twenty Horror Novels of 2014, Preditors & Editors Readers Poll), the upcoming *Martuk . . . the Holy: Shayateen* and *The Martuk Series*, an ongoing collection of short fiction inspired by *Martuk . . .*

His work can also be found in *Horror 201: The Silver Scream* and *Writers on Writing Vol. 2*, both from Crystal Lake Publishing.

Connect with Crystal Lake Publishing:

Website:
www.crystallakepub.com
Facebook:
www.facebook.com/Crystallakepublishing
Twitter:
https://twitter.com/crystallakepub

With unmatched success since 2012, Crystal Lake Publishing has quickly become one of the world's leading indie publishers of Mystery, Thriller, and Suspense books with a Dark Fiction edge.
Crystal Lake Publishing puts integrity, honor and respect at the forefront of our operations.
We strive for each book and outreach program that's launched to not only entertain and touch or comment on issues that affect our readers, but also to strengthen and support the Dark Fiction field and its authors.
Not only do we publish authors who are legends in the field and as hardworking as us, but we look for men and women who care about their readers and fellow human beings. We only publish the very best Dark Fiction, and look forward to launching many new careers.

We strive to know each and every one of our readers, while building personal relationships with our authors, reviewers, bloggers, pod-casters, bookstores and libraries.

Crystal Lake Publishing is and will always be a beacon of what passion and dedication, combined with overwhelming teamwork and respect, can accomplish: Unique fiction you can't find anywhere else.

We do not just publish books, we present you worlds within your world, doors within your mind, from talented authors who sacrifice so much for a moment of your time.

This is what we believe in. What we stand for. This will be our legacy.

Welcome to Crystal Lake Publishing.

We hope you enjoyed this title. If so, we'd be grateful if you could leave a review on your blog or any of the other websites and outlets open to book reviews. Reviews are like gold to writers and publishers, since word-of-mouth is and will always be the best way to market a great book. And remember to keep an eye out for more of our books.

THANK YOU FOR PURCHASING THIS BOOK